WHEN CICADAS CRY

WHEN CICADAS CRY

CAROLINE CLEVELAND

**UNION
SQUARE
& CO.**

NEW YORK

UNION SQUARE & CO. and the distinctive Union Square & Co.
logo are trademarks of Sterling Publishing Co., Inc.

Union Square & Co., LLC, is a subsidiary of Sterling Publishing Co., Inc.

Text © 2024 Caroline Cleveland

ISBN 978-1-4549-5231-2
ISBN 978-1-4549-5232-9 (e-book)

Library of Congress Control Number: 2023051926
Library of Congress Cataloging-in-Publication Data is available upon request.

For information about custom editions, special sales, and premium purchases,
please contact specialsales@unionsquareandco.com.

Printed in Canada

2 4 6 8 10 9 7 5 3

unionsquareandco.com

Cover design by Elizabeth Lindy
Cover art by Shutterstock.com: Atomazul (cemetery), Phyllis Peterson (tree),
Martins Vanags (abstract light)
Interior design by Kevin Ullrich

For my husband, David.

Summoned by some ancient call only they can hear, *Magicicadas*—a genus of cicadas—appear only once every seventeen years. The red-eyed creatures swarm like locusts, their incessant whirr dominating the summer air for weeks before they disappear as mysteriously as they came. In dormant years, their larvae lie deep in the ground. But they are not hibernating. They are burrowing. Becoming. Destined to reemerge.

They were last seen in South Carolina in 2017.

That same year, a brutal murder took place in a rural church nestled deep in the brooding shadows of the South Carolina Lowcountry. Like so many evils, its seed had been sown years before where it had since lay burrowing. Becoming. Destined to reemerge.

CHAPTER 1

2017

I NEVER MEANT TO KILL THE FIRST ONE. SHE WAS AN ACCIDENT—her own fault, for the most part. And that second one? She was a casualty of necessity. Wrong place, wrong time. But this one . . . this one was different. I crouched in the dampness of the night air, watching her through the leaded window of the old church. She seemed to glow under the soft light shining down from the rafters, and I couldn't help but marvel. She had that unforced beauty some women are born with. The kind that turns heads . . . and clouds judgment. Killing this one would be painful for both of us. But she hadn't left me a choice, had she? My thoughts faded into the papery rustle of wind through the thick palmetto fronds.

She paused in her work for a moment, the cloth in her hand resting along the rough-hewn wood of the ancient altar. Her head turned slightly. Not so much that I could see her eyes, but enough to see it—a quickening. It was as though she could feel me there. A week ago, I would have believed that was possible—believed our connection was that strong. That's what she wanted me to believe. But not now. Now I knew better—knew what had to be done. That's the thing with a secret this old. You're not keeping it anymore. It keeps you.

I eased up the steps to the door, pocketing my gloved hands and careful not to make even the smallest sound. Something old and dark within me began to uncoil, to make ready. Even so, my stomach quivered as I thought about what I would have to do inside—how hard it would be to raise my hand and kill this creature I had so adored. Would she know as soon as I walked in? Would it show on my face? Or would she not understand until it was too late?

Then again, it was already too late.

CHAPTER 2

THE CLOCK READ 4:23 A.M. WHEN THE CELL PHONE BUZZED. ZACH didn't recognize the number, but it was likely a client in some kind of trouble. Again.

"This better be bad," Zach warned the caller, shaking off sleep.

"We're way past bad. . . . This Zach Stander?" The deep voice was familiar, but Zach couldn't quite place it.

"Who wants to know?"

"Eli—Elijah Jenkins. From over near Walterboro," the voice added when Zach didn't respond right away, and then the memory clicked into place. Zach practiced in Charleston, South Carolina, but he had held a one-day free legal clinic over in rural Colleton County—giving advice to anyone who wanted to attend about low-level criminal matters. Things like speeding tickets or driving under the influence. Mostly small-time stuff, but, miraculously, it had led him to a few clients with bigger problems. Sounded like Mr. Jenkins might have found himself in that unfortunate category. Zach recalled him as an older Black man—probably in his early seventies—with noticeably little to say. Like maybe he had more than his share of stories to tell but knew better.

"You still there?" Mr. Jenkins asked. Behind him, Zach heard Addie stirring, and he eased up and toward the door. The woman had many fine qualities, but being gracious when roused from sleep was not among them.

"I'm here," Zach said, closing the bedroom door and padding down the dark hall of the too-small apartment toward the kitchen where a white stream of light from the streetlamp spilled in and puddled across the floor and countertops. "Odd hour for a social call—you in some trouble?"

"Yeah, only it's not me. It's my grandson, Samuel Jenkins. Sam's in big trouble and we need a lawyer—a good one."

Zach winced at the last comment and inwardly questioned what Eli Jenkins would think if he knew Zach had been required to offer that pro bono clinic as penance for misdeeds of his own. "Is Sam a minor?" he asked instead, staying on task.

"No, sir—he's twenty-four. Anyway, I got a call last night from a cousin who works with EMS. Said they'd been dispatched to the New Hope Baptist Church out on Cicada Road—a man called in and said he needed an ambulance. Gave them the address, said something about blood everywhere, then hung up. Didn't give his name, but they got equipment tells 'em who a number's registered to most times. It was Sam. Cousin told me he'd let me know more once he got there. Said I shouldn't go over to the church—"

"But of course, you—"

"—jumped in my truck and drove over there. You gonna tell this, or you want to listen up?"

"I'm listening. You went to the church." Zach ran his free hand through his dark, sleep-tousled hair, then dropped it back to his hip.

"Yeah. Took me about fifteen minutes from the farm."

"And?"

"Man, it looked like a war zone. Red lights, blue lights, yellow lights, headlights. I haven't seen so much chaos since Nam. I parked the truck out of the way and ran for the door, but a couple of cops— big fellows—stopped me and wouldn't let me near the place. Said it was a crime scene but wouldn't say more. Couldn't get a soul to tell me what was going on. Seemed like days, but it probably wasn't more than an hour before they brought Sam out. His head was hung low, and he was walking all wrong—like his legs might give out. They'd parked some cruisers with the headlights pointed toward the door, so I could see him clear even from way back there—could see it all over him."

"See what?"

"Blood." The old man's voice caught in his throat, and he paused like he might be choking back something too big to risk losing control of.

"I broke free and ran toward the EMS truck to meet him there. Only they didn't take him to EMS. They walked him the other direction—that's when I noticed he was in cuffs. Next thing I knew, they were putting Sam in the back of a cruiser—hauling him to the sheriff's office. I called over there looking for him, but they said they done took him to the detention center."

"That was fast. It probably means he wouldn't talk to them— that's good. Have they charged him?" Zach asked, afraid he already knew the answer. The vestiges of sleep were long gone now, and adrenaline coursed through his system like an electric current.

"Murder, Mr. Stander." The older man's voice caught again. "I know in my bones he didn't do this, but I've been around long enough to know being guilty and being found guilty are two different things, especially for a young Black man."

"I take it they found a body in that church. Someone Sam knew?"

"A white woman named Jessica Gadsden—apparently went by Jessie. I didn't know her, and, far as I know, Sam didn't either. At least he never mentioned her to me. I met her daddy a time or two over the years—Buford Gadsden. His family's been in these parts for generations. Not someone I'd expect Sam to have a lot in common with—has a Confederate flag sticker on the bumper of his truck, and he hangs out at a hunting lodge with a tight-knit group."

Zach leaned against the counter and let out a slow breath as it sunk in. The Lowcountry was already teeming with racial tension. Two years ago, in 2015, a local cop, Michael Slager, had gone rogue during a routine stop for a missing taillight and shot Walter Scott, a Black unarmed suspect, in the back five times. Months later, Dylann Roof, a young man from the Upstate with stark white supremacist views, had ruthlessly massacred nine Black parishioners attending Bible study at Mother Emanuel African Methodist Episcopal (AME) Church, an historic church with ties to slavery abolitionists. Roof had been sentenced to death six months ago, in December 2016. That same month, Slager's first trial had ended with a hung jury, but the dauntless female solicitor had charged back for a second round, and that second trial was anticipated to take place later this year.

Now, amid that mayhem and social unrest, Zach was being asked to represent a Black man accused of murdering a white woman—from a family with deep roots in the community—and in a church of all places. In a small southern town like Walterboro, this wasn't a murder case—it was a powder keg rolling through a wall of fire. Having gone down in flames himself in the past, Zach couldn't help but hear a little voice inside urging him to turn and run.

"Did they let you talk to Sam?" Zach asked, though he knew the likely answer.

"No. I hung around for hours, but they wouldn't let me see him. Said only his lawyer could see him for now and asked if he had one. I said yes but didn't say who. Just said they'd be getting a call."

Glancing at the blue glow of the digital clock on the microwave, Zach did the math. If he left Charleston now, it would be 6:00 a.m. before he could get to the jail. The Colleton County Detention Center was located in the county seat of Walterboro.

"Mr. Jenkins—"

"Call me Eli."

"Okay, Eli. I'll call the detention center now and let them know I'm his lawyer and confirm they can't talk to him until I get there. I'll arrange to see him at seven, if not before."

"Will they let me come with you?"

"No, and you couldn't anyway—my conversations with Sam are only privileged if they take place with no one else present. You understand what that means?"

"I think so."

"Stay away for now. I'll call you after I've spoken with Sam, and we can meet and talk about where we go from there. Can you do that for me?"

"Sam's all the family I have left. I'll do whatever you need me to do."

"Okay, then. I'll talk to you later this morning."

"'K, then. And Mr. Stander?"

"Call me Zach."

"Zach?"

"Yeah?"

"Thank you."

The phone went dead, and Zach laid it on the counter. He flipped on the small light over the sink and reached for the coffeemaker. As he stood in the soft shadows of the room listening to the hiss of the water heating, he replayed the conversation in his mind until it hit him. Unlike most callers in trouble, Elijah Jenkins hadn't bothered asking if everything would be all right. That old man knew better.

CHAPTER 3

"I'D LIKE TO SEE MY CLIENT, PLEASE," HE SAID AGAIN, THOUGH HE knew damn well the civilian at the front desk of the Colleton County Detention Center had heard him the first time. She tucked an imaginary strand of hair behind her ear and took her sweet time looking up.

"Of course, Mr.—"

"Stander. Zach Stander." But she knew that. He busied his hands straightening his tie and fought to push the impatience out of his voice.

"And which inmate is your client, Mr. Stander?" she asked, though she had, he was certain, heard that the first time too.

"Samuel Jenkins—same as two minutes ago."

"Fellow who killed Buford Gadsden's daughter?" Her eyes narrowed accusingly.

"*Allegedly.*" He was no longer trying to mask his irritation.

"You made an appointment?"

"Seven o'clock," he said as her eyes followed his to the clock on the wall: 7:02. She shrugged and reached for the phone. Zach couldn't hear what was said, but he got the impression that at least someone now knew he was here.

"Take a seat," she said, gesturing dismissively toward the waiting area behind him. "Someone will be with you in a moment." She was still trying to appear disinterested, but the angry red stain spreading a path up her neck betrayed her.

Zach sat in one of the plastic chairs lined up against the institutional gray concrete block wall. These seats would be full in an hour or two, but for now he was alone. His leg bounced up and down on the ball of his foot with restless energy as he mulled over what little information he'd had time to find on the Internet about Jessie Gadsden. She had been good with computers and something of an entrepreneur with her own growing enterprise called IT.Girl. She had a splashy website advertising a variety of IT services to small businesses, such as designing websites, creating online presence, setting up paperless filing systems, and a host of other things. According to her website, she'd graduated from the University of South Carolina. The photo showed a strikingly attractive young woman with arresting pale eyes and heavy blond hair pinned up with a pencil, long strands spooling out. She was seated at a computer with a phone in her left hand as though scheduling services for a client. There was no wedding ring.

"Well, damn if it isn't Zach Stander. The law business must be busy—I see you still haven't had time for that haircut."

Zach looked up to find Deputy Frank Parsons grinning down at him. They had met when Parsons testified in a DUI case Zach was handling and had forged a working relationship that was at least cordial. An older guy who likely couldn't engage in a foot chase if his life depended on it, Parsons had that man-pregnant thing going on—thin, but with a round belly that made it appear his belt was holding his belly up. Hell, maybe it was. With what was left of a frosted Pop-Tart in his left hand and the door wedged open with his shoe, Parsons strained forward and held out his right hand.

"Thanks," Zach said, accepting the firm handshake and entering the door Parsons held open. "What brings you to the jail this morning?"

"I dropped off a guy we hauled in after a domestic violence call," Parsons answered. "The bigger question is, what are you doing here?"

"Here to see an inmate—Sam Jenkins."

"Guy who killed Jessie Gadsden?"

"Accused of."

"You got appointed to represent this guy?" Parsons asked with thinly masked pity.

"No—the family asked me to take the case."

"And you said yes?" Parsons seemed genuinely surprised.

"Why wouldn't I?"

"Are you serious? Jenkins was found kneeling over her body, blood all over him, fresh scratches on his arm. No one else in sight. Seems pretty cut-and-dry. Besides, Buford Gadsden is going to do his best to make things hard on anybody defending the guy who killed his daughter."

"Accused of. You have a murder weapon?"

"That's one of many things that aren't going to play well, Zach. She was hit multiple times in the head and face with a cross—a heavy brass one like sits on a church altar. This one actually did sit on a church altar. What kind of sick fuck kills someone with a cross?" He shook his head. "Don't know if she died from the blows or blood loss. Guess they won't know for sure until an autopsy comes back."

"Prints?"

"I'm not part of that unit, so I wouldn't know."

"And you wouldn't tell me if you did," Zach countered.

"Should probably stay in my lane either way."

"Speaking of staying in your lane, I trust no one in this fine establishment has violated my instructions and spoken with my client before I got here."

"No need to worry about that with this one. EMS was on scene before we were. According to them, he had so much blood on him, they asked if he was hurt too. He shook his head and said 'just her' and backed over to a front-row pew and sat down. Wouldn't say anything at all to our guys other than yes when they asked if he understood his rights. Hasn't uttered so much as a single syllable since. Doesn't even make eye contact. Done more than his share of crying, though."

"Crying? He get roughed up?" Zach asked sharply.

"Nope—but that wouldn't have been the case if her daddy had gotten to him first. You sure you don't want to change your mind and leave right now without complicating things by meeting with Jenkins?" Parsons asked. "Like I said, Buford Gadsden is going to do his best to make this hurt, and the court can appoint someone from the PD's office to try to negotiate a plea." Parsons shifted and hitched up the belt straining under his belly.

"Why are you so convinced he's guilty?"

"Have you heard a word I've said?" Parsons threw his hands up and his voice raised an octave.

"Yeah, but Jenkins is the one who called for help. If he had murdered her, he could have walked out and left however he came with no one the wiser. Why make that call?"

"Maybe so his smart-ass lawyer could stand here and ask that question? Or, more to the point, so you can stand in front of a jury and ask it. Because it's looking like that might be all you'll have to work with." Another belt hitch. From around the corner came a detention officer looking harried and already breaking a sweat at seven in the morning.

"Sorry for the wait—we're short-staffed this morning," the officer said. "Again."

"Last chance," Parsons said.

"I'm ready when you are, officer. See you later, Parsons," he added as Parsons shrugged and left.

Zach followed the *click-click* of the officer's standard issue shoes against the vinyl floor as he led him down a hallway and stopped in front of a meeting room.

"You know the drill," the officer said. "There's a buzzer inside. When you're done, someone will escort you out."

Zach nodded and braced to meet his newest client.

Samuel Jenkins stared blankly at his hands in the lap of his orange jumpsuit, as though he couldn't quite make sense of the cuffs that bound them. He didn't look up when Zach entered and the door closed behind him.

"Mr. Jenkins, I'm Zach Stander—your lawyer."

No response.

Zach eased into the chair on the other side of the table and put his briefcase on the floor as he studied the young man in front of him. Zach knew it was dangerous to judge a book by its cover. He also knew jurors entered a courtroom with their own prejudices and preconceived notions—many of which were spawned by cliché movie scenes—and he was looking for markers that might trigger those biases. There were no visible tattoos or scars. Any earrings or studs would have been confiscated during booking, but Zach saw no evidence of piercings. Jenkins's hair was cut short, and his face was clean-shaven except for a slight shadow of new growth. He was tall, but average size for his height. Nothing about him looked threatening.

"Sam—can I call you Sam? It's okay to talk with me. I'm your lawyer and anything we say is privileged."

Jenkins showed no sign of noticing anyone else was in the room, though it would have been impossible not to in those close quarters.

"Did they feed you anything?" Zach asked, trying a new tactic.

More silence. Zach huffed out an exaggerated sigh and settled back in the chair, resting his head on the wall behind it. He laced his fingers and tapped out the seconds with his thumbs, hoping Jenkins would come around if he gave him a little space. That hope began to evaporate as minutes ticked by and the insistent buzz of the fluorescent light overtook the quiet of the room. The longer this went on, the harder it would be to establish any kind of rapport.

"Fine," Zach said, finally. "It's your ass on the line, not mine." He made as much noise as he could shuffling his briefcase and standing, but he kept his eyes trained on Samuel Jenkins. "I'll let Eli know you don't want his help or mine." At the mention of his grandfather, Sam's head shot up. He still didn't speak, but he held Zach's gaze with bloodshot eyes teeming with desperation.

Zach jumped at the meager opening. In one fluid movement, he dropped the briefcase and braced his hands on the table to lean down to Sam's eye level.

"Look, I know you're scared. Hell, I'm scared for you. But I can't help you if won't let me." Zach sat back down and pulled his chair closer. "Talk to me, man."

"Yeah," Jenkins finally croaked out in a voice hoarse from crying.

"Yeah?"

"Yeah, you can call me Sam. You really talked to Lija—my grandfather?"

"I did."

"How do I know that's true?"

"He told me his cousin was EMS—that's how he knew to come to the church." Zach watched the subtle easing of the young man's expression. "You call him Lija?" Zach asked.

"He was never keen on being called Grandpa, and when I was little, I couldn't say Elijah. It always came out Lija, and I guess it took." Then, after a pause, "What is it you want to know?" Sam sat up slightly straighter and leaned forward.

"Let's start with easy stuff," Zach said, steering clear of the obvious question. If Zach asked Sam if he did it and Sam said yes, that would limit Zach's options for a defense. "Did you know Jessie Gadsden?" he asked instead.

"Only through work."

"Work?"

"Yeah. I work for a local accounting firm—helping small businesses with their bookkeeping and tax things. She owns a business, and I work her account."

"Ever see her outside of work?" Zach asked, not missing Sam's use of the present tense—as though she were still alive.

"It's a small town—I've probably run into her on the street same as anybody else."

"Nothing other than that?" Sam slowly shook his head after what felt like a beat too long.

"Do you know what her connection was to that church?"

"I know it was on her client list from preparing her books."

"So, she was there working?"

"That'd be my guess."

"Okay." Zach ignored the evasiveness of the answer. "So, what were *you* doing at the church?"

"She called me at the office earlier that evening. I was working late on something that had a deadline. She asked if I could come by the church and pick up some records for her accounting."

Zach's bullshit radar went off. "Why in the hell would she need you to pick up records—why not send them in an email or set up a drop box?"

"Said her scanner wasn't working and it was a lot of stuff in odd sizes. Receipts and things."

"Why couldn't she bring the records in herself?"

"She said she was crazy busy—with a tough week coming up. Said it would help her out if I could save her the trip." Sam shrugged, and his eyes drifted to the wall and stayed glued there, as though he were expecting some revelation to magically appear.

"And you said . . . what? 'Sure thing, Ms. Gadsden, I'll drive all the way out to Cicada Road at night and pick up your records to save you a trip'? Really? That's what you want me to ask a jury to believe?"

Sam's gaze jerked back at the word *jury*. "Look, Walterboro is a small town with old-fashioned ways. People still expect personal service. Besides, there aren't a lot of opportunities for a newbie accountant who doesn't have his own clients. I landed a decent job and was trying to work my way up. Jessie's business is growing, and her family knows everybody in this Podunk town. Having her tell friends I went out of my way for her could help me build my own book of business. So, yeah, Mr. Stander, I said '*sure thing, Ms. Gadsden.*'"

Zach was unconvinced, but let it go for the time being.

"Okay, so you went to the church. And . . . ?"

"And." Sam slumped as a ragged exhale deflated his body. He closed his eyes as if watching the scene play out again. "When I pulled up, her car was out front and—"

"Wait, how do you know what she drives?"

"Her company logo was plastered all over it."

"Okay. Any other cars around?"

"No. Only hers. It looked empty, and lights were on inside the church. As I got closer, I noticed the door was cracked open, but not enough to see inside. I pushed it open and called out, but she didn't answer. I didn't see her at first, but then I looked down." His voice faltered and tears began to course down his face.

Zach waited without interrupting, not wanting to influence where Sam might go with this.

"First thing I saw was her feet—up near the altar. They were sticking out beyond the pews to my left, and one of her shoes was off. I called her name again and started to walk toward the front of the church." He was sobbing openly now, and his breath was hitched. "It's a sm-small church, so it only took a few steps for me to see. There was bl—there was blood. Lots of it. Oh, God. Oh, God, I'm not sure I would have recognized her if I hadn't known who she was. It was so awful—I've never seen anything like it. She'd been hit in the head and the face so many times by something heavy or sharp or both. What was left of her face was covered with blood. Then I saw . . . a brass cross. On the floor by her—by her head, and it was bloody too." Sam raised an elbow and wiped first his eyes on his sleeve and then his nose before dropping his arm back. He struggled to settle his breathing.

"A *cross!*" he said, looking up at Zach like he wanted an explanation that would make it all make sense. Zach didn't have one.

"I froze for a second—my mind not quite believing my eyes— but then I got it together enough to think to call for help. My phone was in my pocket. I dialed 9-1-1 and told the dispatcher I needed an ambulance and where I was. I remember telling her there was a lot of blood, but before I could say more, I saw it and hung up."

"Saw what?"

"Saw her chest move—she was breathing. Up till then, I thought she was dead."

"What did you do after you hung up?" Zach asked.

"What any decent human being would have done." Sam lurched forward and put his forearms on the table, the cuffs clattering against it. "I knelt down to help."

Zach eyed the fresh scratches on Sam's arm but didn't say anything.

"I remember putting my hands on her shoulders and saying her name to see if she could hear me. She must have thought whoever did that to her was back for more because she struggled—kind of clawed at me," he added, following Zach's gaze to his forearm. "Then her eyes—one of them anyway—fluttered open and she looked at me, or at least toward me—who knows if she could even see with what had been done to her. I'm not sure whether she knew who I was or whether she finally realized I wasn't who she'd been afraid I was. She was gasping for a moment, but then she went still. And then she stopped."

"Stopped what?"

"Everything. Just . . . stopped. I never took a CPR class, but I tried to do what I've seen on TV. It didn't work."

"Then what?"

"Then EMS got there, and you already know the rest." Sam fell back against his chair, spent, and Zach knew he wouldn't get much more out of him this morning.

"Did you give your phone to the cops?" Zach asked. If they could talk about something other than the murder scene for a minute, Sam might hold out a little longer.

"They took it. Will they give it back to you?"

"Eventually, but they'll search it first."

"It had a password on it."

"They'll get around that. Why—is there something on that phone that doesn't line up with what you just told me? If there is, you need to tell me now."

"No," Sam answered, but, again, a beat too late. "What about my Tacoma? Will they give that back?"

"It's not like you're going to be driving anytime soon . . ."

"I know, but Lija's truck is a piece of shit—breaks down more days than it doesn't. He could be using mine. And how long do I have to stay in here anyway?"

"I can get the Tacoma. They'll search it first, but when they're done, they'll let me take it to Eli, maybe in a day or two."

"You didn't answer me about how long I have to stay here."

"Because I don't know."

"Don't like the sound of that."

"I know, but I expect you to tell me the truth, and I'll do the same for you. There will be a bond hearing shortly. Colleton County holds bond hearings at eight in the morning and four in the afternoon. By law, they have to be within twenty-four hours of your arrest, so you'll likely go at four. The magistrate we'll have is Judge Strickland. For a lesser offense we'd ask him to set bail, but for murder the magistrate will say we have to wait and petition the general sessions court."

"You mean I have to stay here? Can't you say something to convince the magistrate?"

"No—by law the magistrate doesn't have the authority to set bail for someone charged with murder, even if he wanted to."

"So that's it? I'm stuck here with no recourse?"

"No. There's a process to move your case up to the higher court, and we can ask for bail there."

"Okay," Sam answered, though he didn't sound comforted. "But get my Tacoma and give it to Lija, okay? I know this has him worried, and I hate that. I don't want him having to deal with a broken-down truck too. You won't forget?" He seemed anxious about the vehicle, but Zach knew he was probably anxious about everything right about now. Feeling like he was taking control over one small thing might help Sam hold it together.

"I'm on it. I'll ask about it on my way out." Zach reached for his briefcase and pulled out documents Sam needed to sign. Sam listened quietly as Zach explained what each provision meant, then he signed them without questions. Zach put the papers away and stood.

"I have to leave now, and they'll come and take you back to the holding cell. Once I'm gone, keep your mouth shut and don't talk to anybody. Anybody. Understand?"

Sam nodded.

"Before I go, is there anything else you need to tell me?"

Zach had expected a dismissive "no," but what he got was an uncomfortable silence. Sam might as well have sent up a flare, and Zach pounced.

"Sam, is there anything else that you remember from the church? Anything at all?"

Sam stared at him wide-eyed and wary, but still silent. Zach wasn't giving up.

"Are you sure Ms. Gadsden didn't say anything in that instant she seemed conscious?"

"I never said that," Sam said, slowly.

"What the fu—? Well, you sure as hell didn't tell me she did."

"I said she was gasping."

"And?"

"It seemed like she was trying to tell me something. But it was hard to tell what she was trying to say. Her lips were moving, but it was mostly air coming out. It sounded like two words, and then she repeated the same words a couple times, but maybe I misunderstood because it didn't make sense to me."

"What did the two words sound like?" Zach was trying to appear calm, but every cell in his body lit up as Sam looked around as though for listening ears and leaned forward.

"*My father*," he whispered.

CHAPTER 4

ADDIE—ONLY HER MOTHER STILL CALLED HER ADELAIDE— propped her bare feet in a chair at the little breakfast table and shifted to avoid the glare of the morning sun that filled the kitchen. She lifted her coffee mug and stared at the cryptic text: *Gone to Walterboro. New client—murder suspect. Could be big. Back for dinner.*

"Please let this be the case that puts him back on track." She spoke quietly to the room as though there might be someone nearby to hear and grant her wish. Zach had been riding high when he first hired her as a private investigator to help with one of his cases. She'd served as a sheriff's deputy before she had her fill of bureaucratic red tape and quit to open her own shop. Her training and insatiable curiosity made her a natural at sniffing out information, and Zach had a gift for incorporating that information into a compelling trial strategy. Their collaboration on that first case had turned into a regular gig, and one thing had led to another as their relationship evolved from working together to living together. She'd kept this small downtown apartment, but they'd spent most of their time at Zach's much nicer place on Daniel Island. The one with high ceilings and big windows and a water view. They had been talking about making it official when *The Trouble* hit.

A teal dragonfly droned outside the window as she exhumed the memories for the millionth time. It had been easy for Zach to find clients who needed a lawyer. It took more traction and name recognition to attract clients who could pay a reasonable fee. Zach had finally made a splashy name for himself, and it paid off with a steady stream of paying clients. Clients like Robbie "Gator" Crosby. Paying fees had never been a problem for Gator. He was always in some kind of low-level trouble; smoking weed, DUI, and the like. But his brother over in Georgia owned a car wash with gaming booths you could play at while your truck was getting spruced up after a good go in the mud—sold lottery tickets and beer too. A cash cow. Gator was big and dumb, but likable, and the brother was always willing to pay legal fees or fines or bail—whatever. Gator became a frequent flyer with Zach, and he even referred friends. Gator would get busted for some small-time shit, Zach would clean it up, and brother would pay. What more could a lawyer want in a client?

Two years ago, Gator had been busted for pot—simple possession, nothing alarming. That had quickly morphed into federal charges when a post-arrest search of Gator's apartment yielded cocaine and black market oxy in quantities that supported charges for intent to distribute. Gator swore he was being set up, and his brother put up a whopping retainer fee—in cash. These were serious charges, and the fee was big even for a thriving law practice. It was too good to resist, and Zach ignored the voice in his head warning him something was off—nobody paid that kind of fee in cash.

Turned out, the only thing real about Gator was his size. The dumb-but-lovable act was nothing more than a con. Gator operated on the fringes of a lucrative drug trafficking ring, and his "brother's" car wash was a thinly veiled money laundering scheme. By the time Zach admitted to himself what he'd suspected deep down all along, the feds were swarming all over him too, making noise about his being an accomplice to the money laundering because of the source of the fees.

Zach cooperated every way he could without breaching privilege and gave the feds access to his financial records. They identified—and confiscated—the funds in his account. Zach ended up broke and in trouble with the bar. A bit of luck had helped him avoid criminal charges, and the South Carolina Supreme Court stopped short of suspending Zach's license on the condition he provide some pro bono legal services, including offering free legal seminars to underserved rural areas. Addie knew Zach was lucky to keep his license and avoid criminal charges, but it had been a hard road after the dust settled. The name recognition he'd worked so hard to build had cut both ways, and he was big gossip all over the street. Who wants to hire a criminal defense lawyer who couldn't even keep himself out of trouble? He'd had to sell the nice house with the water view. He gave up the prestigious downtown office and settled for a dingy space in a dilapidated strip mall where careers go to die. Now he spent his days haggling over fees for traffic tickets and child support arrears. Addie wanted to help, but he was adamant about doing it himself, so all she could do was keep this apartment for them.

Draining her coffee cup, Addie wondered about this new case. She'd found some posts about a murder in Walterboro—in a church of all places—but it had just happened, so there wasn't much detail. One of her three brothers was a local cop, but he would be falling into bed after the night shift right about now, so she knew better than to call him, and her best source at the Charleston County sheriff's office was in specialized training this morning. She would have to be patient for now.

I'm sick to death of being patient, she thought. She'd grown up locally in a big family with three brothers, two parents, a host of dogs and cats, and lots of love. She wanted to build a family like that with Zach. He claimed he wanted that too, but he was adamant that he needed his momentum back before they talked more about marriage. Addie understood that, or at least she was trying to, but she didn't believe his career was the only problem.

She emptied the coffeepot down the sink and put her cup in the dishwasher before she went to get dressed. Pulling the soft summer blouse over her strawberry blond hair, Addie thought again about the absentee father she suspected had something to do with Zach's hesitance to get married and start a family of his own.

Zach didn't talk much about his father—all she knew was he had disappeared from Zach's life when he was a child. But she didn't need to know the details to know Zach dealt with the loss by closing off a part of his heart, and until he was ready to open that to her, it would stand in the way of their future. But when would he be ready? And how long was she willing to wait?

CHAPTER 5

IT WAS BARELY 10:30 A.M., BUT ALREADY THE ASPHALT RADIATED heat and Zach welcomed the cooler air as he stepped through the door and took in the room. The smells of bacon and country ham were as familiar as childhood. This was no gentrified retro diner with gleaming Formica tables and trendy posters. This was the real deal, with a concrete floor and Naugahyde-covered booths worn thin and torn in places from decades of locals sliding in for a bellyful of the Lowcountry's famous comfort food and an earful of gossip. Second helpings were always available for both. It was late for breakfast and early for lunch, so the place was deserted. Eli was easy to spot.

He would have been easy to spot anywhere. White hair gave away his age, but he was wiry and lean, and his leathered face hinted at a toughness forged by the weight of harsh years trailing behind him. But what stood out this morning was not his looks so much as the air of anguish that hung like a shroud around him. His eyes locked on Zach instantly and held steady.

The waitress made it to the table as quickly as Zach did and was turning over the cup to pour coffee as he sat down.

"Something to eat?" she asked, steam rising from the dark liquid.

"No, thanks. Coffee's good." Eli had a plate of eggs and grits that was untouched, though it had been there a while, judging by the congealed look of the grits.

"How is he?" Eli asked after the waitress left the table. There was an edginess to his voice that warned how hard the older man had worked to hold it together while he waited for news.

"Physically, he's okay, but he's scared shitless."

"That makes two of us. What did he say? What the hell happened last night?"

"I can tell you some of it," Zach answered, stepping carefully. "He gave me permission to talk to you, but I need you to understand that Sam is the client, and there may be some things I can't discuss."

"As long as you're doing whatever you're doing to protect Sam, I'm good with it. What can you tell me?"

Zach started with Sam's explanation of how he knew Jessie and why he was at the church.

"What the—? Kids that age don't drive records to town nowadays. Why wouldn't she send them on the computer or the phone like they do everything else?" Eli's reaction reinforced Zach's concern. If a man from Eli's generation didn't think it made sense to drive records to town in the age of the Internet, jurors would balk at the story too.

"She told him her scanner wasn't working. According to Sam, he was willing to go out of his way to help her because she and her family know so many people and he is trying to win over new clients."

Eli sat back in his seat and his gaze wandered upward for a second before he leveled it back at Zach. "That last bit rings true at least," he said. "Been working his ass off at that job. He respects the owner, George Holden, and sounds like the feeling's mutual. George is mid-sixties, wants to retire in a few years. Both his kids moved away to take fancy jobs in big cities with no plans to come back to this place, so he'll be looking to sell the business. Sam has it in his head he might be the one to buy it—make his place in the world. He's been putting in every hour and kissing every ass he can to make that happen. No denying the Gadsdens know everybody who's anybody round these parts. Having them put in a good word might help and having them talking bad if she wasn't

pleased would hurt plenty." Zach's confidence lifted ever so slightly
at this news.

"But that only explains why he was there, which is a far cry from
explaining a dead white woman in a church," Eli went on. "Tell me
you got more. Was she dead when he got there?"

Zach walked him through Sam's account of finding Jessie and
calling for help. He kept the bombshell last words out. Only he and
Sam knew that and, for now, it needed to stay that way.

"He said there was a lot of blood. Was she shot? Stabbed? What?"
Eli asked. "And do they have a murder weapon?"

Zach lowered his head, searching for the right words to explain
something so ugly. "She was bludgeoned to death," he said, raising
his eyes to meet Eli's. "Based on what they found at the scene, it
looks like someone beat her in the head and face with a heavy metal
altar cross."

"With a cro—? No. *No!*" The look of total disbelief slowly gave
way to one of horror as the realization came to the old man.

"Eli," Zach started gently. "Sam had her blood all over him."

"Because he knelt down and gave her CPR, you said he told you
that's what he did," Eli argued.

"So he says. But that doesn't explain the fresh scratch marks on
his arm."

"So what—that could've been from cuffs when he was arrested."

"Did he seem to be resisting when you saw him come out of
the church?"

"No," Eli admitted reluctantly, "but that don't mean it went that
way inside where I couldn't see. Could be they were something less
than gentle. At least you could argue that, couldn't you?"

"And when they find his skin under her nails? Because I think
they will."

Eli didn't offer an answer to that.

"Sam said he saw no sign of anyone else being in the church—"

"You mean other than the dead white woman he didn't kill?" Eli cut in.

"—or any other car parked outside. If it wasn't Sam, Eli, who was it?"

"Seems to me that's your job—finding out who did this so we can prove Sam didn't."

"I'm sure going to try, but I need you to have a firm grasp on how bad this looks right now. Need you to be prepared."

"Prepared for what? To watch my grandson convicted and locked away like an animal for something I know in my soul he didn't do? No. There've been too many young Black men to meet that fate as it is. I need to know you're the one who will fight to keep my Sam from becoming another one of those numbers." Eli's eyes were hard now, and his nostrils flared. "Because that can't happen."

"I know, I know." Zach held his hands out palms down, signaling they needed to keep it down.

"So how do I help?" Eli asked, lowering his voice again.

"You can start by educating me about Buford Gadsden. You said you knew him?"

"Some. Know of him is more what it is. His family's been in these parts for a long time. Own a lot of land in Colleton County, including some farms and shrimp boats. Buford was already working the boats when he was younger than my Sam is now."

"You said he had a Confederate flag sticker on the bumper of his truck?"

"He does."

"Would you describe him as prejudiced?"

"Reckon we all are to varying degrees," was the old man's measured answer. He did not so much as blink and Zach could almost hear the unspoken dare: *Go ahead, white boy—tell me you see a man sitting here and not a Black man.*

"You're saying there's some racist in you? That you might see a person differently because of the color of his skin?"

"Has it really not occurred to you yet that yours was the number I called in the dark of night because you are white? Get over yourself, Zach Stander. I know enough about you to know about the trouble you were in, and I know enough to know you had a lot more wins than losses before that. Sam needs a good lawyer, but not nearly so much as he needs a good white lawyer. So, yeah, I guess you could say I see color too."

"Is being tuned in to someone's color the same thing as being racist?" Zach asked, feeling more stung by the old man's words than he hoped showed on his face.

"You tell me."

"So, the Confederate flag on his bumper doesn't say anything to you?

"There's another bumper sticker on that same truck that says '*Heritage, Not Hate.*'"

"And you believe it?"

"So far, Buford Gadsden hasn't given me a solid reason not to believe it. Let's just say there are other people who don't leave any room for doubt—like that buddy of his that goes by JB. Those are the ones that give hate a bad name."

"So, Gadsden's not racist?"

"I said no such thing. For all I know, he could have a white hood in his closet. I'm simply making room for the possibility that not every white man with a Confederate flag on his truck is a bigot."

Their voices were still quiet, but harsh now, and Zach paused, searching for the right thing to say to ease things back down.

"What?" Eli taunted when Zach didn't respond. "Does it upset your notion of who I'm supposed to be if I argue your side of it?"

"How do you know who I think you're supposed to be, and why do we have to have presumed sides? And why do we have to argue about *this* now when we need to be working on Sam's case?"

"Because *this* is what Sam's trial is gonna be about. It won't be about an ambitious young professional wrongly accused of killing a woman he drove out of his way to help and called EMS for and tried to give CPR to. It will be about a Black man found with a dead white woman. And I need to know you understand *this* is real, and that you can talk about and argue about *this*—from both sides—and can find a way to reach the people on that jury who can't see past color. 'Cause if you can't do that, you can't help me save Sam—white or not."

The expression on the old man's face was open and raw, and Zach tried to imagine what it must have felt like growing up Black in the rural south in the 1950s and '60s. It didn't take long to admit to himself he probably couldn't even imagine it. As though he could read Zach's thoughts, Eli answered them.

"I hear a lot of talk about how things have changed, and since I'm old enough to remember how it used to be, I can admit some of that's true. Sam's got a job I couldn't have hoped for in this part of the world at his age. He earned a business degree at Carolina, and he's got a future using his brain and not his back—at least he did until last night. But there are still things that haven't changed, and I'm not going to stand by and let his life be ripped away for something he did not do. Not if I can help it." Eli folded his arms and sat back with a clenched jaw that said he was done for now.

"Then help me," Zach said, trying to steer the conversation back to facts he might be able to use. It took a minute, but Eli relaxed and leaned forward, putting his forearms on the table between them and nodding consent.

"You said Buford worked on the shrimp boats when he was young."

"He did," Eli said, nodding again.

"Sounds like hard work."

"It is. Got himself in a bit of trouble back in the eighties for trying to make it pay better."

"Come again?"

"He figured out the same boat that hauled shrimp to the dock could haul in bales of pot for a lot more money. Sold some weed to the wrong kid and got caught. Did a little time, but not long. Far as I know, he's been clear of trouble with the law since then."

"The eighties were a long time ago. How do you know all this?"

"That might be a longer story than you want this morning."

"Give me the skinny version for now," Zach said, reaching for his coffee.

Eli sighed as he looked out the window and feigned interest in a lizard on the outside sill soaking up the sun. "Well, the story starts long before the eighties. Not a lot of opportunity for any poor kid in the rural south when I was coming up, even less for a poor Black kid. Then came Vietnam." Eli's eyes were still glued on the lizard, its red throat expanding and contracting like a balloon.

"After December '69, most of the local boys were waiting around with the draft hanging like a sword on a string over their heads. Me? Hell, I figured at least it was a way out. I enlisted in the army and was bound for the jungle. Turned out, years of hunting squirrels and rabbits had given me a skill set they needed. I outshot everyone in basic training and that got me some notice and some special training. I was a sniper—could shoot the hind end off a grasshopper from a mile away. That gained me some respect, which was a new experience for me. Funny what comes to matter to the folks around you in a world where every single day is about shoot or be shot.

"I guess I got used to that respect—a little level of pride, you know? But boy, did I get a rude awakening and a kick in the ass when I got home. You're too young to remember, but do you know what they called us? Baby killers! They would wait for us at the airport with signs they made with their little poster board and crayons and stand there with flowers in their stringy hair and yell shit at us. It wasn't like I was expecting a damn ticker-tape parade or nothing, but they spit on us. *Spit* on us."

The lizard roused and sprung to the branch of a sago palm and disappeared, and Eli turned his face back to Zach's. Zach had expected to read pain in his expression, but it was something far beyond that. A stillness that said there were few things that could cause him pain now.

"One disappointment led to another," Eli went on, "and I guess you could say my life kind of spiraled to a low point. I did some things I'm not proud of, including becoming one of Buford's more frequent . . . customers."

"Pot? Did he turn you in when he got caught?"

"No reason for him to even have known my name. My connection was through a cousin who knew Buford's brother, Edward. But no, Buford never gave up Edward's or my cousin's or any other names far as I know. Did his time quietly and moved on." Eli picked up a fork and listlessly poked at the grits that now peeled up on the edges like rubber. The fork dropped back to the plate with a *plink*. "I got myself together by and by, and it looked like Buford did too. He married a girl from his high school class, and they had a few kids. I think the girl who was killed last night was the only daughter."

The clinking of dishes and glasses from the kitchen signaled that the early lunch crowd would be along any minute and, right on cue, the door opened and three men in blue work uniforms entered and sat down at what Zach guessed was their usual table. They were followed by others, and it didn't take long for Zach to pick up on a buzz in the room that Eli's expression said he'd already sensed. Comments made in hushed voices and open stares from other tables. Rumors were already flying.

"We'd best be leaving," Eli said as he glanced at the check on the table beside him. He slipped double the amount of the tab under the edge of his plate of untouched food and nodded to the waitress, who seemed relieved to watch them go as Zach followed Eli out to the parking lot.

The two men paused behind Zach's car. "I know this is a hard time and I hate to bring this up—" Zach started.

"—but you need to talk about getting paid," Eli finished for him. "Just tell me how bad it is."

"I'm going to need $35,000 to start," Zach said. Eli didn't flinch, though Zach suspected that had hurt. Zach also knew that, while it was low for a murder case, it was the biggest fee he'd scored in a while.

"I've got some savings and I own the farm free and clear. None of it means anything without Sam anyway."

"I'll need more if we have to go to trial," Zach added.

"I'll find a way to take care of it. You take care of Sam. How soon can he get bail—I see on all those lawyer commercials that he's supposed to get a hearing for bail within twenty-four hours? Is that true?"

"Unfortunately, Eli, what you hear in commercials isn't quite accurate. Yes, you get a bond hearing within twenty-four hours. Sam's will be at four this afternoon, but that hearing is before a magistrate judge—Judge Strickland—and a magistrate can't set bail for murder charges. That has to be done by the circuit judge in general sessions court."

"So, what good is requiring a bond hearing to be within twenty-four hours if it's impossible to get bail from the magistrate hearing it? How does that even make sense?"

"I'm not sure I can make an argument for it making sense, but that's how it works. Sam will get a second hearing, though, in front of a general sessions court judge, and that judge can set bail."

"When will that be?"

"That's harder to say. It depends on the timing and availability in the courts."

"And my grandson has to sit and wait who knows how long to be heard on that? Whatever happened to innocent until proven guilty?" Eli looked dangerously close to losing it.

"It's complicated."

"So why bother with the bond hearing today?"

"It has other purposes, too. The magistrate will use the hearing to give Sam notice of all charges against him and his right to a preliminary hearing. That preliminary hearing has to be requested within ten days, or it's waived."

"And we can request bail at the preliminary hearing?"

"Well, no, the preliminary hearing will be before the magistrate as well and—"

"And a magistrate can't set bail on a murder. So, a preliminary hearing doesn't get us anything either?"

"The preliminary hearing doesn't get us bail, but it does get us something. We get to hear at least the nuts and bolts of the state's grounds for the charges."

"Don't we know that already?"

"Yeah, but we will likely get a little more and a chance to size up at least one of their witnesses and maybe to examine some of their evidence."

"Okay. When we finally do get to a judge who can set bail, do you know how much bail will be for Sam?"

"Look, Eli"—Zach shifted his weight uncomfortably—"courts rarely deny bail outright, but you and Sam need to be prepared for the possibility that bail will be set so high that it isn't practical or maybe even possible to pay it."

"Couldn't we use a bondsman?"

"You could, but that may not work the way you think it does. See, you have to pay up to 10 percent of the bail amount to the bondsman to post a bond."

"But when Sam shows up for trial, I get my money back?"

"No. He gets to keep your money either way. If bail is set low enough, maybe that hit doesn't hurt too bad. But if it's high . . ."

"So, if a judge sets bail at a million dollars, I would have to come out of pocket a hundred grand that we wouldn't get back? Hell, that would put us in the position of having to choose between bail and a lawyer."

Zach nodded apologetically.

"But he didn't do it," Eli argued, his voice heavy with frustration and lack of sleep.

"I know you don't want to hear this, but that's what they all say. And the judge doesn't know Sam like you do. Try to imagine that Sam had been found dead with someone kneeling over him, covered in his blood, scratches on their arm, and no explanation for what happened other than what Sam has now. Now imagine you're the judge. Would you feel comfortable setting that person loose on bail? Or facing another family if someone else ended up dead? It's an issue with no easy answer."

The old man's struggle with the anger inside him played out on his face, but eventually, he came to some sort of acceptance. "Got it," he said, though his stony expression said more. "Can I at least be there for this thing today?"

"Sure, it's a public courtroom. There will likely be other lawyers and clients there, for either their own bond hearings or other things. Some of the matters may involve witnesses who will be there, or family members like you. Four o'clock—I'll meet you there. You won't be able to talk to Sam," Zach warned, "but you'll be able to see him, and your support will mean a lot to him. Like I said—he's scared."

"Like I said—me too." Eli had had enough, and he turned and headed toward a 1999 Ford F-150 that looked like it might have been some shade of red before weathering nearly two decades of hard time on a small farm. It was parked at the far end of the lot, under the cooling shade of the only tree. The gun rack was empty, and the windows were down as though there were nothing inside worth stealing. The truck fit the man to a T. Watching Eli walk toward his battered old truck reminded Zach about Sam's. "Oh, hey, hang on a minute. Sam wants you to get his Tacoma. I still need to get the all-clear from the cops, but you can have it as soon as they've searched it. Said it would probably be late this afternoon or tomorrow. I'd count on tomorrow."

"No problem. I'll take it back to the farm and store it in the barn for him," Eli answered, shielding his face from the sun with a palm.

"I think he meant for you to be using it."

"Why?"

"Said yours is less than reliable," Zach said, instantly regretting a remark that likely embarrassed Eli. Eli gave him an unreadable look and shrugged.

"Sure thing. Let me know when." He climbed into his truck and started the engine. It sounded rough, but it started the first time.

The parking lot was filling up and there was no mistaking the looks in their direction. News was spreading fast, and this was only the beginning. When the details started filling in, it would get a lot worse. Zach pulled his car next to Eli's truck. He leaned out toward the open truck window but instantly jerked back as a large dog leapt up from the seat beside Eli and lunged toward him.

"Down, Buck," Eli commanded. The dog backed away, but his hackles were still up, and he stared at Zach with an intensity that matched his master's.

"Look, Eli," Zach said, recovering quickly, "I heard what you said about giving Buford Gadsden the benefit of the doubt. But, prejudices aside, a man who believes your grandson murdered his daughter—well, that kind of grief can change a man. Make him do things he might not have thought he could do. Be careful."

"Don't worry about me. Old Buck here makes sure nobody gets close without my knowing. And if anybody does come looking for trouble, I can fend for myself."

Zach watched him pull away. *Let's hope it doesn't come to that.*

CHAPTER 6

THE WARM TANGY SMELL OF MARINARA SAUCE ENGULFED ZACH AS he opened the door a few minutes after six o'clock, and the watering in his mouth reminded him he'd not eaten anything since leaving that morning. He'd briefly considered stopping off at the office on the way back after Sam's 4:00 p.m. bond hearing, but the thought of that dismal place was more than he could handle right now. Besides, his cell phone and his office phone were one and the same, and he could check whatever unpromising messages had come in just as easily from the car. The no-frills, used Camry with over ninety thousand miles on it. A perfectly respectable car and generally reliable, but definitely not the sporty new BMW M4 he'd had to sell when things went to hell in a handbasket. Now, closing the apartment door behind him, he was sure he'd made the right call by coming straight home.

From the kitchen, he could hear Kid Rock's raspy voice singing "All Summer Long" with Addie chiming in, slightly off-key, but right on target with the heart and soul. Leaning against the door, Zach paused, marveling again at the many facets of this crazy, beautiful, fierce, and scary-smart woman. She was the one bright spot left in his wretched life. Addie could handle herself with the toughest of criminals, come home and cook a meal that would put those television chefs to shame, and then party as hard as she worked. Better yet, she seemed incapable of giving up on him. He couldn't wait to tell her about his day because he had come to feel like nothing ever really happened—good or bad—until they had shared it.

Because she was employed by him to work on his cases, he could share privileged information with her. He already knew that by now she would have put her investigator skills to work and would tell him things he did not yet know about his new case, but that was part of what made it all so amazing.

"You going to drag your ass in here and eat this dinner or what?" she called from the kitchen.

"On my way." He smiled and tossed his briefcase on the floor beside the hall table.

She had one hand on the knob of the cooktop, adjusting the flame, while the other stirred the thick sauce. She lifted her face for a kiss as he slipped one arm around her slender waist and gave it his best effort.

"Nice," she said. "Now wash your hands and set out some plates. This stuff is ready." She gestured with her head toward the table where salads and warm bread waited.

"Yes ma'am." Moments later, they had steaming plates in front of them.

"So, tell me already," she said, winding a fork through her pasta. "How did things go today? I'm assuming you had a four o'clock bond hearing—and the magistrate couldn't grant bail."

"That's right. We'll ask for bail once we get to general sessions court, but I'm not optimistic about what the bond amount might be." Zach shrugged. "I've already filed a request for a preliminary hearing," he added, reaching for the bread. "The worst of it, though, was Buford Gadsden and his wife showing up for the bond hearing. Buford is a big guy. His size alone is intimidating, but the look on his face was the thing. He didn't look angry or sad or any of the things I was expecting. It was like his face was made of stone with no clue about the extent of the storm behind it. That was unnerving, like being in the dark and hearing a noise—it's scarier when you can't see what's there. His eyes never left Sam, and I thought Sam would come unglued for sure."

"What about the mother?" Addie asked.

"Complete opposite. Petite and made of anything but stone. I don't think she stopped crying the whole time we were there. My job is to defend Sam, but her grieving was heartbreaking to watch. After the hearing, when I was walking to the car, I saw them getting in a truck to leave. Buford gave me that same stare he'd been giving Sam. If he meant it to shake me up, it had the intended effect."

Zach took another bite of his pasta and then went on to fill her in on his meetings with Sam and Eli, but he left out Jessie's last words. He wanted to hear Addie's first impression of the other facts before throwing that in. By the time he had finished, their meal was almost done.

"That's some case you landed there," she said, pushing her plate away. "I know it's early yet, but I can tell your first impression is Sam didn't do it. What I can't tell is why. They have damning evidence against him, and that lame excuse about going to get business records from an old church in the dark of night screams *I'm lying*. I'll admit the call to EMS helps some, but he's an educated guy—he could have been thinking that when he made the call."

"You're right—he's definitely hiding something and that bothers me. A lot. But maybe whatever he's hiding is something that isn't material?

"Such as?" One eyebrow lifted over a silvery green eye.

"Remember the Brightwell case from a few months back?" Zach reached for the last piece of bread.

"DUI?"

"Yes—he kept hedging on where he had been earlier that day. What he was really hiding," he said, punctuating the *really* with a stab of the bread into the air, "was that he was gay, which had absolutely nothing to do with the charges against him. But it was something important to him—something personal—that he wanted to keep private." The last bite of bread disappeared into his mouth.

"You think Sam Jenkins is gay?"

"Hm-mm." He signaled as he shook his head and swallowed the bread. "No. I mean, I don't know one way or the other, but his hiding something doesn't convince me he's a murderer. Besides, he said something telling. When he finally started talking about Jessie, he talked about her in the present tense—like she was still alive."

"Well, she had been a few hours earlier," Addie said, as she poured more Chianti into their glasses.

"But think about how she died—the ugly, brutal violence of it—and how physical it would have been for the killer." Zach paused to let that sink in. "There is no way the person who bludgeoned that girl to death still thinks of her as being alive after that."

"Okay, I'll give you that one. But you can't use that at trial."

"No, but there's something else."

"Isn't there always?" she asked, leaning in for whatever he'd been holding back.

"The gasping Sam heard—he thinks Jessie was trying to tell him something. Said it sounded like she repeated the same two words several times: *my father*."

"'My father'?" Addie's wineglass went down with a plunk. "What does he think she meant?" Her green eyes were wide now.

"He doesn't know, and I've been racking my brain about it all day."

"God—you don't think it's possible her father could have done this."

"Anything is possible, but that seems farfetched. And there are so many other things it could mean—"

"She could have been asking him to go get her father," Addie interrupted.

"Or trying to tell him her father would know who did it, or maybe even that someone came after her because of her father. For that matter, she was dying at a church altar. Could she have been praying?"

"Whatever it meant, can you even get it in? Isn't that hearsay?"

"Maybe as a dying declaration—that's one exception to the hearsay rule," Zach explained.

"We need to look at what we know about Buford Gadsden. Try to put it in a context that might support a defense theory— something a jury can run with."

"Eli was able to fill me in a little," Zach said. "Buford's family has deep roots here. Eli also told me Buford did some time in the eighties for dealing pot off a family shrimp boat—in an interesting twist, Eli was one of his customers back in the day."

"Buford did do time, but not much," Addie said as she reached over to touch the screen of the notebook that was never far away. "I was able to get some history from my law enforcement sources while I was waiting for you to get home. Seems they found traces of marijuana on the boat, but, by that time, there was no evidence as to how much of the stuff he'd had. Word has it his father was tight with the prosecutor, and they negotiated a plea that let Buford do under a year for a misdemeanor.

"And what Eli told you about the family having deep roots in the Lowcountry is an understatement," she added. "They trace back to the family of Christopher Gadsden—a radical during the American Revolution credited with designing the DON'T TREAD ON ME flag with the rattlesnake."

"Buford's family is wealthy?"

"According to public records, they own a lot of land in these parts. Doesn't necessarily mean they have a lot of cash lying around. The house Buford and his wife live in looks modest according to the photo on Zillow and the vehicles registered to their names are decent, but nothing flashy."

"Still, having the influence to get his charges reduced to a misdemeanor is a big deal," he remarked.

"A particularly big deal in that family—if he'd been convicted of a felony, he wouldn't be able to lawfully own a gun. Not much worse to a family of men who live for hunting."

"Yeah, while I was waiting for the hearing this afternoon, I found a clip about Buford being an NRA member. That didn't seem to fit with what Eli told me about the bust and the jail time."

"Yeah, well, there's your answer. Apparently, Buford did his time quietly and went home. No trouble since," she said.

"Nothing?"

"Not so much as a parking ticket that I could find. Now, Jessie, on the other hand—"

"The victim has a record?" Zach's attention dialed up another notch. A criminal record might help identify enemies with a motive to harm her.

"Nothing serious," Addie answered, "but she had a string of lesser offenses her first year in college. Mostly related to underage drinking or public disturbance. Seems Jessie went on a wild streak her first time away from home."

"Odd that a family that could keep Buford from a felony charge couldn't shelter Jessie from underage drinking charges. I would have guessed the cops would leave her to the mercy of her parents."

"Buford Gadsden has local pull, but it wouldn't have mattered to cops in Columbia. Besides, given his past, maybe Buford decided it might do her good to learn a lesson before it progressed to anything else."

"And did she?" Zach asked.

"As far as I can tell, she did. Graduated, stayed out of trouble, started her own business, and was doing great. Well, at least until last night."

"Eli says Buford has a Confederate flag sticker on his truck. Given the race issues, that's an optic that is likely to play into things. Did you find anything that might shed light on whether he's into heritage or hate?" Zach drained the last of his wine.

"No, whatever his stand is, he seems to keep it to himself other than a couple of decals on his truck. But my sources say he has a tight group of friends, and some of the fellows he hangs with are a different story."

"What do you have?"

"Well, the most notable is a guy with the last name of Beaman—James Beaman," she said as she scrolled through the notebook.

"Tell me they don't call him Jim Beam."

"Close, but not quite—he goes by JB," she answered with a grin.

"So, what does JB bring to the picture?"

"For starters, he's been front and center at several local rallies. You know the drill: BLM—Black Lives Matter—shows up to protest what they see as racist treatment of Blacks, and the local guys show up to counter-protest that their civil rights matter too. Some of it centers on Civil War monuments. It's mostly both sides hollering with nobody listening, but it sounds like it would be fair to say JB's voice rises above the rest, and his rhetoric gets heated. He's prone to violence, too—been hauled out of some bars for fights sparked by racially-tinged arguments." She'd been scrolling through the screens and, as she spoke, Addie held up the tablet to show a mug shot.

"Well, he certainly looks the part," Zach said, noting the almost-mullet and the thick muscular neck.

"Hey! That's as unfair as looking at a picture of a Black guy with dreads and saying he's a gangster. I had friends—and dates for that matter—who *looked the part*, as you put it, who were not racists. A Lynyrd Skynyrd T-shirt does not a racist make." There was a little flash in her eyes now.

"Well, there's a strong percentage of openly racist guys sporting that look."

"Same could be said for a *strong percentage* of thugs wearing the waist of their pants down around their thighs and having a front grill of gold teeth. But a *strong percentage* is not exactly a definitive test. You of all people should know the dangers of judging a book by its cover."

"Ouch, that was cold."

"Sorry," she said, meaning it.

"God, Addie, how did the whole world get so divided? I've never seen it so bad." Zach rubbed his temples. That second glass of wine had settled in, and the long day was finally starting to wear on him.

"Me either. It doesn't help that CNN and Fox News are both hell-bent on keeping it that way. No stoop too low for ratings, huh?"

"Some of what both networks broadcast sounds like actual news, but they've both crossed the lines of news reporting and turned into editorial pulpits for deeply opposed sides. Which group you choose to believe depends on what flavor of Kool-Aid you prefer to drink."

"Do you think the national groups will take an interest?" she asked.

"You mean like BLM? I don't know—they've mostly focused on police and government behavior, like the Slager trial. And incidents like the one at Mother Emanuel with Black victims—not Black suspects."

"A lot of people think that last part shows that racists come in all colors."

"I can see both sides on that," Zach said.

"And there it is," she declared with a triumphant slap of her hand on the table. "That's what I've been waiting for since this conversation started." She was smiling that high-wattage smile he could never get enough of.

"There what is?"

"You aren't just saying that—you *do* see both sides, Zach, you always have," she said, placing her palm against the side of his face. "And that's what makes you perfect for this case. We're living in a world where everybody's talking about race and nobody's listening, and when people are talked *at*, they shut down. You see both sides because you are listening, and I believe that will give you a fighting chance to get through to a jury and make them see past color. It has to—Sam's case depends on it."

He wrapped his fingers around her wrist and turned his face to kiss her palm. "No, Adds," he said. "Sam's *life* depends on it. What if I'm not up to it?"

"You're not considering turning down this case, are you?"

"Sam signed the contract, but I haven't accepted a fee yet. I could still back out."

"Why would you do that?"

"Adds, the whole state, maybe the whole nation, will be watching this one. If it doesn't go well—even if it's not my fault—I'll crash and burn in front of a big audience."

"Baby, you already did a crash-and-burn in front of an audience. Do you want to spend the rest of your life scratching out a living with the small-time stuff because you're afraid to put yourself back out there?"

"Wow, that was brutal," Zach said, recoiling and taking her hand from his face.

"No, baby, that was honest. And so is this: you have something special that lets you wade through the bullshit to get to the truth and convince the rest of us. That's what Samuel Jenkins needs right now—like you said, his life depends on it. And maybe . . . just maybe . . . while you're saving his life, you can save your own." She paused a moment before going on.

"Tell me when you were working this case today that you didn't feel like you were finally doing something that mattered again. Tell me you don't believe your path has crossed Sam Jenkins's for a reason."

Zach turned his head away, but she reached out and gently pulled it back so he had to meet her gaze. "I believe in you. And it sounds like Eli and Sam believe in you. But that isn't going to fix you. And until you fix you, I don't know how we move forward with us. You're going to have to learn to believe in yourself again, and maybe that starts with this case."

"And if I fail?"

"The only way you fail is by not trying."

"What did I ever do to deserve you?"

"Who the hell said you deserve me?"

CHAPTER 7

I WENT TO THE MAGISTRATE'S BOND HEARING AT FOUR O'CLOCK this afternoon. Walked right in and sat down, and no one gave it a second thought. And why would they? Hiding in plain sight, I believe is the worn-out expression. After the hearing, I drove out here and I've been sitting under this oak tree ever since, replaying it over and over in my head. Not sure exactly how long I've been here, but I know it's been hours. When I first sat down, the cicadas were whirring themselves into a frenzy and then winding down like old clocks, but they quieted around dusk. After that, the darkening sky began to fill with the urgent trilling of needful, hungry night things. And still I sat here.

There were only two inmates on the roster. The first was a young woman who made the regrettable decision to drive home shit-faced. Luckily, the only casualty was the front end of her car when she hit a utility pole. The magistrate read her charges, explained her rights, and released her with a Form 1 on her own recognizance.

Then came the main attraction: Samuel Jenkins. He was the reason something as routine as a bond hearing had suddenly become a hotbed of prurient interest. Family members were usually at these hearings, of course, but today the room also held a host of the curious, including most of the criminal bar, all of whom likely had been speculating about who might be defending Jenkins before they finished their first cup of coffee this morning. There were a few media members, but they hadn't gone full scale yet. That would change by the time of the preliminary hearing. All eyes were glued on Jenkins,

and everyone in the room was wondering whether and how he could
have done what he was accused of. Well, all but two of us. Two
people in that courtroom knew for sure Samuel Jenkins hadn't killed
Jessie Gadsden. But only one of us knew who had.

Zach Stander from Charleston was there as Jenkins's attorney.
Interesting choice. He'd had a thriving practice at one time, but I'd
heard he'd fallen on hard times after he got in that bit of trouble.

The magistrate—Judge Strickland—read the charges and asked if
Jenkins understood what he was being charged with. Sam responded
with a yes, but I wondered how much he really understood at that
moment about how his life was about to change. Judge Strickland
reminded him of his Miranda rights, and Stander signed the notice of
his client's right to a preliminary hearing and the ten-day deadline for
requesting one. I watched Samuel Jenkins's head drop as Strickland
explained that he wasn't authorized to set bail and Jenkins would
have to wait in jail until the general sessions court could hear the
issue. What must that feel like, for a crime you didn't commit?

While everyone else was watching Sam Jenkins, my gaze strayed
to Buford Gadsden. I was sitting only two rows back, almost close
enough to touch him. I could see the subtle contraction of that little
facial muscle in front of his ear as he clenched his jaw. His wife was
huddled under his arm and seemed to crumple with each breath.
With every sob that escaped her, that muscle by Buford's jaw strained
harder to hold that stony expression. His arm rested along the top
of the bench behind his wife, and his knuckles were white from the
grip. I could almost feel the hate radiating off him as he stared at
Sam, surrounded by law enforcement, so close yet untouchable. I
suspected Buford would kill Sam with his bare hands if he could get
to him. And there I sat within arm's reach.

After the hearing, both lawyers took advantage of the media
presence to unload their positions on bail. Stander worked in all the

expected points: his client was a white-collar professional with no criminal record. He had grown up here and had ties to the community, including the grandfather who raised him. Blah, blah, blah. Not to be outdone, the solicitor put on his best show too. He railed on about the stark brutality of Jessie Gadsden's death and the power of the threat of a murder conviction to make a defendant consider desperate measures. I couldn't argue with any of that, but I had a hard time keeping my opinion off my face when he launched into the part about what a "lovely person" she was. She was lovely to look at, all right—but that's where it ended. There's a reason for the cliché *no fool like an old fool*, and I should have been suspicious of such a beautiful young woman feigning attraction to me. Jessie was not what she had seemed to be. Unfortunately for her, neither was I. She should never have played me for a fool.

No one had any reason to suspect me. But would that last? And how could I keep tabs on things so I would know for sure? It would be easy enough to blend in at public hearings, but that wouldn't tell me much about what was going on behind the scenes.

I needed a way to get inside information on an ongoing basis. That was going to take some doing, but I had some ideas.

CHAPTER 8

Titus Strickland had been a county magistrate for twenty years, and in five months—on his sixty-fifth birthday—he would qualify for full retirement benefits. He stopped pacing long enough to look out his office window at the lawn. The reporters and lawyers who'd been blustering out there after the four o'clock bond hearing were gone now, but they would be back. His face was pinched with a mixture of disgust and aggravation.

Strickland was coasting these last months with no intention of suddenly developing a work ethic, and he was none too pleased with the idea of living under the microscope that was applied to a high-profile case. There was no scenario under which any magistrate could be a hero for anything relating to this case, and plenty of chances to screw something up or be made a scapegoat if someone else did. He wanted the Jenkins case and the unwelcome attention that came with it out of magistrate's court and bound up to general sessions sooner rather than later. Let the circuit court judges worry about it.

Sitting down at his computer, he scrolled through the court schedule and found what he was looking for—an empty time slot. He picked up the phone.

"Mary, I need you to schedule a preliminary hearing for me in the Jenkins case," he said, and waited while she pulled up the calendar screen before telling her the date he wanted.

"Yes, I do know that's only five days from now. I can count, thank you. Please put it on the schedule and let Jake Barton and Zach

Stander know immediately." He listened to her blather on for another minute before he thanked her and ended the call.

Five days was fast for a prelim, but no one would be complaining. Strickland already knew through backchannels what the evidence was, and it was far more than enough for the meager showing needed for probable cause, so the solicitor would be fine with it. As for Stander, he'd be thrilled to get in so quickly. All Strickland had to do was get through the hearing and, in five days, this mess would be somebody else's problem.

He powered down his computer, done for the day. Before leaving, he took a red pen and put another "x" on the little calendar he kept in his top drawer. One hundred and forty-two days to go.

CHAPTER 9

To Zach's astonishment, Sam's preliminary hearing was set for five days later. Zach could have waived the hearing—there was no question what Sam was being accused of and why—but he didn't want to miss his chance to get a first glimpse at the arresting officers and hear how their testimony lined up with what Sam and Eli told him about that night.

Zach had left Charleston two hours before the hearing, and it was a good thing he had. He'd gotten stuck behind a slow-moving tractor trailer on the long portion of the Jacksonboro highway where it was hard to pass. By the time he got to Walterboro, there was already a crowd at the courthouse. Sitting for a moment in the quiet of his car, he took it all in. Local CBS Live Five, NBC's Channel Two, and ABC's Channel Four were on scene. The national stations didn't have trucks on-site that he could see but there were a few reporters holding equipment with their logos. He recognized Haley Walker, a reporter from Charleston's *Post and Courier*, and there would, no doubt, be someone from the local weekly, the *Press and Standard*, as well. Police incident reports were public information, but this was the first opportunity to hear live testimony from the arresting officers. The media had played up the grisly story the last few days. No specific mention of race, but they couldn't resist plastering photos of the attractive, fair-skinned blond on the screen beside Sam's mug shot. Nothing more needed to be said.

Watching the commotion, Zach made the mistake of imagining the same crowd turning on him if this went badly, and for a moment, his confidence wavered again. But, after a lot of soul-searching and a hefty push from Addie, he was committed to fighting for Samuel Jenkins. Whether Sam walked free or went down in flames taking Zach with him, there would be no turning back and no regrets.

Inside, the solicitor, Jake Barton, was already at his table, wearing a custom-tailored suit and a starched white shirt that seemed impervious to humidity. Zach paused to shake his hand and offer a perfunctory hello. Then he made his way to the defense table, though he continued to watch Barton from the corner of his eye. Barton's family was affluent, with strong ties to the community, including politicians and successful lawyers in the civil and criminal bar. Love him or hate him, there was no getting around the fact that Barton had a lot of social pull and political power backing him, and that was bound to influence jurors. Zach was feeling outgunned right now.

Eli sat on a bench directly behind the defense table. His gaze was on Barton, too, and his dark eyes were full of worry as he watched Buford Gadsden approach Barton and give him a "man-hug," arm around the shoulder and a pat on the back. There was a relationship there, and Gadsden glared over at the defense table to be sure it was noticed. Zach wondered briefly if that relationship and Gadsden's own pull in the community would play into whether Barton asked for the death penalty. Eli and Zach exchanged troubled glances but didn't have time to do more than say hello before the court was called to order and the magistrate, Titus Strickland, took the bench. The room was packed and hotter than usual, and Judge Strickland's brow was already damp with sweat. He nodded to a bailiff and a deputy led Sam and another prisoner in. Still in his orange jumpsuit, Sam had the fugitive look of a rabbit under a sky full of hawks. The deputy hovered nearby, as though there were any possibility Sam would try to skitter away.

A soft buzz had risen in the room as Sam was led in, and Judge Strickland wasted no time addressing that. "Ladies and gentlemen, we have a small room and a large crowd this morning. We will not be here long for our purposes, but I will not tolerate any disruption." Strickland didn't exactly strike fear in the hearts of anyone, but nobody wanted to miss this, so the room went quiet. Although the murmuring had stopped, the searing stares from the Gadsden family had not. Buford's gaze was locked on Sam, and that stony expression had been replaced by one that suggested he would sell his soul for ten minutes alone with him. Zach could sense Sam's fear from where he sat.

Judge Strickland acknowledged both lawyers, and Zach stood and waived reading of the charges.

"Very well, Mr. Stander, thank you," Judge Strickland said. "We'll turn to the matter of probable cause then," he added as he turned to the solicitor. "Mr. Barton, the burden is yours, and I am ready when you are."

"Thank you, Your Honor," Barton said, buttoning his suit jacket with a swift, practiced move as he rose from his seat. "The State calls Captain Harold Chambers to the stand." Chambers was barrel-chested with a full head of prematurely gray hair. He swore his oath with a clear, calm voice. Zach noted his solid demeanor and air of credibility. Chambers would present well at trial.

"Captain Chambers, how long have you been in law enforcement?" Barton asked.

"Twenty-four years."

"All of them here?"

"No sir, the first two were with a federal DEA unit. The rest have been here."

"And were you on duty the night of July 11, 2017?"

"I was not scheduled, but I was called in."

"And did you respond to a scene at New Hope Baptist Church on Cicada Road?"

"I did, along with other officers."

"Do you recall the time?"

"According to the dispatch recordings, I reported arriving on scene at 23:03."

"Were you the first law enforcement officer on scene?"

"No, but I was the senior officer once I arrived. The first officers arrived at 22:53. We were asked to wait outside briefly and secure the building while EMS attempted to render aid to a victim on scene."

"And were you then the first officer to enter the church?"

"I was."

"Can you please describe for the court what you witnessed?"

"Yes, sir," Chambers answered, turning toward the magistrate. "The victim was on the floor with trauma wounds to the head and face. There were no vital signs and EMS had been unsuccessful in attempts to resuscitate."

"That victim was Jessica Gadsden?"

"Yes."

"Was there anyone else present other than the victim and first responders?"

"Yes, sir." Chambers turned toward the defense table. "Samuel Jenkins was present."

"Was anyone else present at the church?"

"Not other than Mr. Jenkins, the first responders, and, of course, the victim."

"How do you know that?"

"My officers searched the building and found no other persons present and no evidence that anyone else had been present recently. We also searched the grounds around the church, including a utility shed behind the church as well as some of the wooded land nearby and, again, found no persons present nor evidence of anyone else on the property. I have since spoken with a Church official who confirmed there were no services scheduled that would have placed anyone there that evening other than the victim who, according to that witness, came periodically to clean the sanctuary."

"Objection, hearsay." Zach was on his feet.

"Your Honor, this is a preliminary hearing, intended only for the prosecution to present probable cause. Hearsay is permitted at the discretion of the court," Barton replied in a voice laced with camera-ready confidence and without so much as a second's pause.

Zach had known that but wanted to see how the solicitor and the witness handled a distraction.

"I'll allow it. Overruled, Mr. Stander. Continue with your witness, Mr. Barton."

"Did you find vehicles on the property?" Barton asked, clearly undisturbed by the interruption, and Chambers stayed equally focused, to Zach's disappointment.

"Yes, sir. We observed a gray Tacoma which we confirmed was registered to Mr. Jenkins, and a white Honda Element registered to Ms. Gadsden."

"And no other vehicles present on the property?"

"None other than those of first responders."

"And what condition was Mr. Jenkins in when you first saw him?"

"He was covered in blood. It was observable on his hands and clothes, and even his face."

"Did he appear to be injured?"

"He had some open scratch wounds on his left forearm, but nothing that would suggest the amount of blood on him could have been his."

"If the scratches weren't serious, what made you notice them?"

"Based on my experience, they were consistent with defensive wounds—meaning the victim could have inflicted them during an attack. That is something officers are trained to look for."

"Did you find a murder weapon?"

"The victim appeared to have been bludgeoned to death with an altar cross—heavy, made of brass. It was found beside her on the floor, with blood and clumps of hair on it."

Barton paused his questioning to enter a photograph of an altar cross as State's Exhibit 1. The image flashed, larger than life on a screen at the front of the room. Although information about the cross had been published in the media, the gruesome display still had the expected effect. The cross was brass and partially covered with a dark-colored substance and clumps of something.

"And is this State's Exhibit 1 an image of the altar cross in question?" Barton asked, pausing for the witness to turn and look at the screen.

"It is," Chambers confirmed, turning back to face the jury.

"Was the cross tested for fingerprints, Captain Chambers?"

"It was," Chambers replied, "but no prints whatsoever were found."

"And the dark substance and debris on the cross—were they identified?"

"Yes, sir. It was confirmed to be human blood and hair, matching the DNA of the victim."

"And did you obtain a statement from Mr. Jenkins?"

"We attempted to do so, but Mr. Jenkins would not respond to any questions, either on scene or at any time thereafter."

"Do you know if he provided information to EMS about what happened?"

"EMS reported that he confirmed he was uninjured but said nothing more."

"And what happened next?"

"Based on our observations at the scene, we arrested Mr. Jenkins. We initially took him to the Sheriff's office for questioning. When he declined to talk, he was transported to the detention center."

"And the charges?"

"He was charged with the murder of Jessica Gadsden."

"Thank you, Captain Chambers. Please remain seated until the court dismisses you." Chambers nodded curtly, acknowledging the instruction and looking to Zach every bit like the kind of leader men were willing to march behind. *Hooah.*

Damn if this guy wouldn't play well at trial.

Barton took his seat, unbuttoning his jacket using the same polished flourish with which he had buttoned it.

"Your witness, Mr. Stander," Judge Strickland announced dryly. "And I remind you that your questioning for the purposes of this preliminary hearing is limited to the issue of probable cause."

"Thank you, Your Honor." As Zach rose from his chair, he self-consciously smoothed the front of his own shirt, rumpled from spending an hour and a half strapped under a seat belt.

"Captain Chambers, I believe you testified earlier that you observed Mr. Jenkins on the scene, and that you observed his person closely enough that you were able to see blood on his hands and clothes, and scratches on his arm?"

"I did."

"Was Mr. Jenkins wearing gloves when you observed his hands?"

"No, he was not."

"Did you find any gloves on Mr. Jenkins's person or anywhere at the scene?

"No."

"Captain, did you have an opportunity to handle the cross at any point?"

"Sure, once it had been processed for prints and touch DNA and placed in Evidence, I was able to hold and examine it."

"Can you tell us how heavy it was?"

Chambers cocked his head. "I didn't weigh it, but I'd estimate it to be more than ten pounds, less than fifteen."

"And you mentioned touch DNA. Was there any DNA recovered from the cross other than that of the victim?"

"No, sir."

"Thank you, Captain Chambers. Your Honor, the Defense has no further questions at this time."

"Solicitor Barton—do you have another witness?"

"No, Your Honor."

"Very well, then. Mr. Stander, would you like to offer argument?"

There was no credible argument that the evidence didn't meet the low hurdle required for probable cause, but Zach managed a straight-faced attempt, which Judge Strickland heard patiently before ruling.

"I find that the solicitor has met his burden of providing substantial evidence of probable cause of the charges against Mr. Jenkins. A recording has been made of this hearing and will be provided to the parties for transcribing. Any transcripts made will be reviewed and certified by the court. This ends this court's jurisdiction over this case, and it will now be bound over to the general sessions docket. If there's nothing else, gentlemen . . . ?"

"Nothing, Your Honor," the two attorneys responded in unison.

"This hearing is adjourned," Strickland announced with a rap of his gavel, and he quickly rose and exited the room, looking every bit the part of a man just released from indenture.

The room hummed with the rustle of people rising from seats and moving toward exits, most of them straining to get a last look at Sam.

Zach knew the officer would take Sam away in seconds, so he moved quickly, producing a paper from seemingly nowhere. "We don't have much time here, Sam," he whispered to avoid prying ears. "I need you to sign this release—it will let the cell phone provider produce your cell phone records so that I can get an idea of what the police are looking at on your phone."

"Zach, I'll sign whatever you need, but I don't see how that's going to help you—it isn't my phone," Sam whispered back.

"The phone you used to call for help—the one they took from you—it's not yours? And you're just now telling me this?"

"Well, it is, and it isn't," Sam added. "It belongs to the company I work for, but it was assigned to me, and I was allowed to use it for personal calls, too. Nobody else used it but me, and I carried it everywhere."

"Sorry, Mr. Stander, but you know the rules. I need to take the prisoner back immediately." The officer spoke politely, but his tone made clear that he was not in the mood to play nice for very long.

"Of course, Officer." Zach stood and helped Sam slide his chair back. As he rose, Sam turned and looked at Eli. The old man had been sitting behind them, and he stood so close that Zach was worried he would forget his instructions not to touch Sam.

"Lija, I'm so sorry," Sam said with tears in his eyes.

"You've got nothing to be sorry for, son. You keep your head about you, and me and Mr. Stander will find a way to fix this," Eli answered. Before either of them could say more, the officer led Sam from the courtroom.

"We will find a way, won't we, Zach?" the old man asked as the door closed behind Sam.

"I'm trying, Eli—"

"And maybe I can help with that," a booming voice interrupted, and Zach turned to find a bear of a man with an outstretched paw.

"Colleton Burns," he said as Zach took the offered handshake, and Zach recognized the name immediately. Burns had been a successful and respected criminal lawyer back in the day, and his family was as prominent in this and the surrounding counties as the solicitor's. Everyone knew he'd been out of the criminal law game for many years now, but murder was an old sin, and Zach suspected he still knew a lot of people and a few tricks that might come in handy.

"I'd like to hear more about exactly what it is you're offering," Zach said.

"And I'd like to tell you, but this is not the place," Colleton answered with a knowing look, alluding to the curious stares they were already getting from the crowd filing out of the room, especially Buford Gadsden, who was watching their exchange with narrowed eyes. "How 'bout y'all come back to my place for some lunch, and we'll talk more."

"Sounds like a plan. What's the address?"

"Afraid a GPS isn't going to get you there, buddy, you'd better follow me. Or you can follow Eli—he knows where it is," Colleton said with a wink and a nod to Eli before making for the door.

"So, you going to tell me where it is we're headed?" Zach asked Eli as he closed his briefcase and joined him in following Colleton out of the room.

"What would be the fun in that?" Eli chuckled lightly, and Zach realized that was the first time he'd seen him smile.

CHAPTER 10

THEY HAD BEEN DRIVING FOR OVER TWENTY MINUTES OUT INTO the country before Colleton's black Tahoe turned onto a ragged dirt road, followed by yet another and finally a third that was barely more than a path before the Tahoe stopped and Colleton climbed out, opened a padlocked gate, and waved them through. The trail made a hard turn to the left, and Zach found himself staring down a grand avenue of massive live oaks trailing dusty veils of Spanish moss, like one might expect to see leading up to an old home. Only there was no home at the end, and what was there had Zach shaking his head in astonishment as he got out of the car and tossed his jacket onto the car seat, where it joined the tie he'd already escaped.

On the left side of the avenue, what looked to be a nineties-era Airstream Safari was nestled under the shade of one of the large live oaks, the gleam of its iconic silver-colored metal surface defying its age. Across the lane under the opposing tree stood a primitive wooden structure with raisable shuttered sides—currently raised to expose what was left of an old formal dining table and a host of mismatched chairs. Beyond that was a brick BBQ pit with an open flame grill, and scattered about were more mismatched chairs with overturned wooden crates and buckets as side tables. It was one massive man cave, or man camp as it were, and Zach was beyond impressed. As he walked past Eli's truck while admiring the setup, the truck door opened, and Eli climbed down.

"Eli, why the hell are you driving that old bucket of bolts? Didn't you get Sam's Tacoma?" Zach asked as he rolled up his sleeves.

"I did, I did."

"So why aren't you driving it?"

"Old Buck says he don't much care for that new car smell. Says it messes with his mojo." As soon as Buck heard his name, the dog came bounding out and barreled toward Zach who—quite sensibly—froze in his tracks.

"Buck!" Eli growled, and the dog stopped on a dime, though he was clearly disappointed.

"What is with that dog?"

"I don't reckon he sees too many white fellows, Zach," Eli answered with a wry chuckle.

"A racist dog?"

"You two cut it out." Colleton was chuckling too, as he pulled cold cuts and cheese out of an oversized cooler. "Old Buck ain't racist—he just doesn't take too quickly to strangers. Here, Buck," he called, tossing out a scrap of meat the dog caught and devoured in a single snap before settling into the bare dirt under the shade of a tree.

"Not much seems to have changed around here in the decade or so since I saw it last," Eli said, plucking a cold Pluff Mud beer from a Yeti chest and easing cautiously into a wobbly wooden chair.

"And that is exactly how I like it," Colleton added.

"Wait, Eli, if you haven't been out here in a decade, how is it that Buck—who apparently isn't too keen on strangers—seems so familiar with Colleton?"

"That's an easy one," Colleton said. "Traveling by roads our places are a good hike apart, but if you're not scared of gators or snakes and you don't mind wading across a creek and then battling through thick woods full of briars and a bit of swampland only to find yourself in that old family graveyard"—he paused, nodding at the timeworn markers—"this land backs up to Eli's farm. Buck here isn't scared of much of anything, and he's a steady customer when Eli lets him out to run and I've got the grill going."

"What is this place, anyway?" Zach asked.

"It was a plantation—belonged to a distant relative of my mother's. His name was Andrew Colleton, which is where my name came from. According to my mother, Andrew was some relation to Sir John Colleton, one of the eight Lords Proprietors granted Carolina by the king. Anyway, most people know Sherman spared Charleston during his scorched-earth campaign, but that didn't stop his men from pillaging and burning some of the homes in our area. The plantation that stood here was one of them.

"Some of those old places were rebuilt after the war, but I guess Andrew Colleton didn't have the heart for that. He came back briefly and found most of the former slaves, freedmen by then, still on the property, planting the soil. He kept this small parcel because of the family graveyard, but he deeded the rest of his land—and there was a lot of it—to the former slaves. He returned to Virginia where he had a second homestead that had been spared and lived out the rest of his days there. This small parcel we're sitting on passed from father to son for generations till they ran out of sons and it passed to my mother in the sixties. I bought it from her with the fee from the last criminal trial I handled. It always stuck in her craw that her only son spent his life representing *all those criminals*, as she so fondly referred to them, and I think she was only too happy to see me end that part of my career and move out here."

"She might also have been a little raw about your unwavering bachelor status and notorious weakness for younger women," Eli threw in.

"Leading to my abysmal failure to provide grandchildren," Colleton added as he put the finishing touches on the lunch he'd been preparing as they talked. "Whatever her reasons, she offered no argument, and I've been living out here ever since."

"In that?" Zach asked, eyeing the aging Airstream.

"That there's Betty," Colleton said, gesturing as though he were making a formal introduction, "and she's as fine a shelter as I've ever known."

Zach nodded toward Betty, acknowledging the introduction. "So, now that you've given up your criminal practice, what are you doing when you're not grilling and drinking beer?"

"You know, it's funny how life can take a turn you didn't expect, and that's what happened for me here. I didn't have to fire up the grill too many times before neighbors started showing up, some with fish or venison, and before long we were having potluck suppers."

"Speaking of eating with neighbors," Eli prompted as he popped open another beer and eyed the spread Colleton had before him.

"Your subtlety never ceases to amaze," Colleton said as he handed them plates with overstuffed sandwiches before getting back to his story.

"Most of my neighbors are descendants of the freed slaves that Andrew Colleton gave the land to. Their families have been living on this land and paying the taxes for a century and a half, and it's the only home they've ever known. Now some are in danger of losing it because it's heirs' property."

"Heirs' property? Never heard of it."

"You're not alone, Zach, but it's a big problem in the South— especially in the Black community where, for reasons relating to our harsh history, there is still a lot of mistrust in the legal system. That leads to people not leaving wills or wills not being probated. When land is left in intestacy, it's not always clear whose it is. Families living on the land for generations can suddenly find their ownership in question. This can make it impossible to get loans to improve the property or, worse yet, they can lose their homes.

"With Charleston and the beaches getting more and more crowded, developers started moving outward. It didn't take long for someone to set their sights on the land out here and position themselves to take advantage of the title weaknesses. A couple of locals showed up on my doorstep one day asking if I could help. The more I learned, the madder I got. It's bad for the whole area—not only the Black community—because it pushes segments out and erases the cultural aspects that made this part of the South and our quieter way of life special.

"Once we got past the deal that was threatening, we started the process of protecting the other properties. It's tedious work, interviewing family members, finding long lost relatives, and tracing the tangled lines of inheritance back to the last solid deed—sometimes all the way back to that original deed from Andrew Colleton. I'd like to think the man whose name I share would approve."

"And that takes up your time now?" Zach asked.

"It did at first, but now we have a few nonprofits in the Lowcountry providing resources that didn't exist before. Bottom line is, it doesn't take as much of my time as it once did. Here, lately, in the quiet of the evenings when it's just me and those infernal no-see-ums, I've found myself hankering for a new project to sink my old teeth in. When I heard about this powder keg of a case of yours, I thought maybe I'd found it. I'd like to help, if you'll have me. You'd be first chair, of course, Zach—I'm only here to help."

"We could sure use some help," Zach started, "but—"

"Hey, look—I know I'm not the young buck I used to be, and my courtroom chops may be a little rusty. But I know a lot of people in the criminal court system, not to mention the local law enforcement—and a few of them still owe me a favor or two. Plus, my roots are strong in this community and my familiar mug sitting at counsel table could help Sam with a jury."

"It's not your age, and heaven knows you'd be an asset to us. But—" Zach exchanged an uncomfortable look with Eli.

"What Zach's trying to get to," Eli interrupted, putting his empty beer can down and leaning forward with his elbows on his knees, "is what's this going to cost me?"

"Well, I was thinking a flat fee, plus maybe reimbursement of whatever minor expenses I might incur."

"What kind of flat fee we talking about, Colleton?" Eli asked.

"I was figuring on one dollar."

"A dollar?" A startled Zach clawed at the air in a futile attempt to catch his plate before it was knocked from his lap to the ground. Fortunately, it was empty. "That's a generous offer, Colleton. Are you sure?"

"Oh, I'm sure, all right. I know the optics were bad for Sam on that scene, but I of all people should know he didn't do it."

"And why is that?" Zach asked.

"Um . . . because of my work with Eli—his farm was one I helped clear the title on," Colleton answered after a moment, an uncomfortable look crossing his face as he realized he'd said something he shouldn't have. "Sorry, Eli—didn't mean to be disclosing your legal issues," he added, recovering quickly as he glanced over at Eli. Eli nodded his approval to continue, and Colleton turned back to Zach. "While I was working on Eli's title, I got to hear him talk about Sam and how hard Sam worked to get through school and college and make a better life for himself. Hard to reconcile that young man with one who would do what somebody did to Jessie Gadsden. You know?"

"I do know, and you're hired," Eli answered before Zach could, and held out a single dollar bill.

"Ah, beloved filthy lucre," Colleton said, sliding the bill into his wallet with a theatrical flourish.

"Seriously, though"—Colleton's voice took a lower tone—"we have our work cut out for us. Jake Barton is a pretentious little shit, but he's a razor-sharp lawyer, and one we shouldn't underestimate. And his power over a jury is amplified by his family's stature here, not to mention his own connections."

"So let's get to work," Zach said.

"Damn straight. Where do we start?" Eli asked, scarfing down most of what was left of his sandwich and handing the last morsel to Buck, who had been at his feet eyeing the plate from the moment Colleton had handed it to him.

"We start with Zach here getting me up to speed on all the facts. I know what's on the street and what I heard in that hearing, but I need to know what things look like from the inside. Then we need to brainstorm about what a trial strategy might look like."

"Sounds like you're up, Zach." Eli pushed to the edge of his seat, eager to get started. This time it was Zach and Colleton who exchanged uneasy glances.

"Eli, Colleton and I can have privileged conversations now that he's co-counsel, but—"

"Not that privilege shit again. Dammit, Sam means more to me than anything in this world, and I fucking hate that I can't help other than to pay you two to take care of a grandson I should be able to take care of myself." Eli was up and pacing now.

"There will be plenty of chances for you to help," Colleton said.

"Oh yeah? When does that start?"

"How about now?" Zach asked.

"I thought you said I can't stay for this conversation."

"You can't, but there's something else that needs to be done, and you may be the only one who can do it."

"I don't need you to pacify me with busywork."

"I swear I'm not. At the hearing, when I asked Sam about his cell phone records, he said the phone doesn't belong to him—it belongs to his employer."

"That's true. If I'd known that was important, I could have told you. Why does it matter?"

"The police took the phone, which means the solicitor will soon have it, if he doesn't already. They'll be able to see his calls and texts immediately—and we won't."

"Don't they have to share what they find?" Eli asked.

"Yes, some of it, but sometimes they get a little busy and it gets put off for a while, if you catch my drift," Colleton interjected.

"Who do you think you're talking to?" Eli reminded him before turning back to Zach. "Can't you send a subpoena or something? Seems like that's what they do in the movies."

"Yes, I could send a subpoena to the cellular service, but that takes time—time Sam can't afford," Zach said. "That's why I wanted Sam to sign a release—if the phone's owner requests it, the phone provider will hand over records immediately. And unlike the bills they send you every month, some of the records show when and to what number texts or voice messages were sent. Won't give you the content of the texts, but at least you can see who he was texting with—and see it now. Only, it turns out Sam's not the owner."

"Could George Holden—Sam's boss—help us?"

"He could, but he wouldn't know me from Adam, so I'm not sure he will."

"But he knows me." Eli was finally catching on.

"So you mentioned. You know him well enough to ask?"

"I wouldn't call us close friends, but we're friendly when we meet, and he never misses a chance to tell me how much he thinks of Sam. I'm willing to try if it will help. I guess the worst that can happen is he can say no."

"Well, don't just stand there, you old mule," Colleton said. "Get your ass moving."

"I'm on it. But I still fucking hate how that privilege shit applies to me too. And I'm taking this for the road," he added, grabbing another beer can from the cooler as he turned and marched back to the truck with Buck close on his heels.

"This ain't no convenience store," Colleton yelled after him. "I'm adding that beer to my list of expenses."

Eli didn't bother to turn around, just raised his hand high above his head and gave a one-fingered salute as he followed Buck into the battered old truck.

"He might regret that bird if his rattletrap doesn't start and he has to ask for a ride home," Colleton said.

Eli's truck started the first time, and he eased it down the long dirt drive with Buck hanging out the passenger side and an ominous mix of dust and exhaust trailing behind.

"What kind of dog is Buck?" Zach asked, watching them roll away.

"Safe to say diversity isn't new to Buck—he's some of everything. Now," Colleton said, not wasting any time, "from what I've heard so far, the strongest thing Sam has going for him is there doesn't seem to be any connection that would give him a motive to kill that girl. But you know as well as I do, that can change, and every tick of the clock gives the other side more time to come up with something—anything—that might look to a jury like a motive. Or to find something on that phone or somewhere else that doesn't line up perfectly with Sam's story. We have to work faster and smarter, so tell me what you know so far."

A lazy summer wind ushered in the calls of wild birds and cicadas trilling in the distance. And there, with only the ghosts lingering in an ancient graveyard to hear, Zach leaned in and told the older lawyer everything.

CHAPTER II

Z<small>ACH FROZE AT THE SIGHT OF PACKED SUITCASES AND CARDBOARD</small> boxes crammed into the entryway of the apartment. She couldn't be moving out on him—it was her apartment. Then it dawned on him; the suitcases were his. Well, shit. What now? He knew she was frustrated with his practice on the skids and the wedding on hold, but he sure as hell hadn't seen this coming.

"Zach?" Addie called from the bedroom. When he didn't answer she stepped out into the hallway. She had piled her strawberry-blond waves on top of her head, but random strands had fallen down around the shoulders of her Darius Rucker T-shirt, and she had a smudge of something dark down one cheek. She couldn't have looked more gorgeous.

"Surprise."

"Well, I'll give you that one," Zach answered cautiously. "Am I moving?"

"We both are, silly."

That sounded better. "May I ask to where and why?" Zach slowly released the briefcase he'd been clutching to his chest like a shield.

"Walterboro," she announced triumphantly. "Isn't it fantastic? It's only temporary, until you can get through this trial, but this will make your life so much easier, right?"

"Um, well, yeah, I'm sure it would, but don't you think this is something we should have talked about first?" He felt a brick forming in his stomach as the excitement melted from her face, revealing disappointment. She had expected a different reaction.

"Baby, I don't see what there is to talk about—and, frankly, I thought you'd be thrilled. Sam needs your very best, and you can't be that if you have to keep driving over an hour each way, and who knows how long that Camry will be able to keep that up."

Zach winced at the mention of the car.

"Besides, you know how important it is from an investigation standpoint to be there where things happened. Trying to investigate from here gives the prosecution an advantage—another one—Sam can't afford."

"Addie." He was struggling to keep his voice low and calm. "I could not agree more that being local would be the best thing all around. But, honey, in case you haven't noticed, I'm not exactly loaded with extra cash at the moment. As great as your idea is and as much as I adore you for trying, I don't think I can afford to rent a house right now. Eli gave me a retainer, but we're going to have expenses in the case. I don't think I can swing a house too."

"But that's the best part," she jumped in. "It won't cost you a dime."

"Oh, hell no, uh-uh." Zach was no longer trying to sound calm. "It's bad enough that I'm sponging off you to live in this apartment. There is no way in hell I'm going to have you renting a second place so I don't have a commute to work. Believe it or not, I still have a scrap of pride left—bruised and battered though it might be."

"Oh, for crying out loud." She blew an irritated stream of air at a strand of hair falling over her eyes. "You are not sponging off me. We're supposed to be a team, and it pisses me off when you act like I'm not capable of helping. And what about when you still had the house on Daniel Island? You were paying for that without any help from me."

"That was different."

"Because you're the man and I'm only a woman? This is 2017, not 1917."

"Stop it, you know I don't think that. But I'm the one who made this mess, and I need to be the one to clean it up if I'm ever going to put it behind me." The last thing he needed tonight was to hash this out again, but the flares firing off in her eyes made it clear she wasn't backing down.

Zach stepped over a box and sank wearily onto the couch. He propped his elbows on his knees and rubbed at his forehead. From the hallway, Addie's footsteps retreated to the kitchen, and he heard the soft suck of the refrigerator door opening and the clink of glass as she came back and lowered herself to the seat beside him, tucking a leg beneath her.

"Here," she muttered over the unmistakable hiss of a bottle opening.

"Thanks." Zach sat up and tipped up the beer before settling back against the cushion behind him. Addie opened the second beer and turned to face him.

"Why are you being so hardheaded about this?" she asked.

"I know you're ready to take things to the next level for us, and I'm trying to get there, girl, I really am."

"Are you sure it's only finances that are in the way?"

"What else would it be?"

"Maybe it has something to do with your father leaving you all those years ago?"

Oh God, not this again. "No. He's nothing to me."

"If that's true, then why is it you can't talk to me about it?"

"What is it you want me to say?" Zach threw his empty hand up in exasperation. "The bum said he was going to get milk, walked out the door, and never came back. He took the rent money with him and left my mother stranded with a toddler, a broken heart, and a stack of bills she couldn't pay. As far as I know, she never heard from him again, and I don't have a clue where he is. Hell, I wouldn't know him if he passed me on the street. And for the record, that's fine by me." He had never told Addie those details, but if they shocked her, she was doing a good job of not letting it show. Her eyes never left his, and Zach went on.

"You know my mom died young, but what you don't know is she worked herself to death trying to clean up the mess he left behind. She never talked about him, but I could see what he'd done to her. I promised myself that I would never do that to anyone. So, yes. It is the money that's holding me back. I'm not going to saddle you with cleaning up my mess." Zach could feel a sting behind his eyes as tears tried to form, and he stopped while he still had things under control, raising the beer bottle to his mouth as cover.

"Well—for the record, as you put it—I'm not sure I'm buying that you're as *fine* with it as you claim to be, but we don't have to go there tonight. And I certainly don't agree that letting me carry some of the financial load in our situation would make you anything like him. But, if that's really all that's bothering you—we can still take the house in Walterboro because I won't be paying for it either. This house is free."

"Free? Addie, don't be ridiculous. There's no such thing as a free house."

"Well, there is this time—if only for a while. The guy who owns it is a friend of one of my brothers—"

"Which brother?"

"Steve, and why does that matter?"

"I guess it doesn't, but I'm trying to wrap my head around this."

"Well, if you had let me finish earlier instead of jumping all over me, I could have explained. The owner's working in another state for a few months training for some new job. He needed someone to house-sit. He had to leave day before yesterday, so he wants to get someone in there fast. I drove over to see it this morning, and it's perfect for us. It isn't fancy, but it's less than a mile from the court-house, and it even has a second bedroom that he has set up as an office. It's furnished, so we only need to take the personal things we'll need. We will pay the electric and water bill, but we'll be saving on that here, so it's a wash. Baby, it's a perfect setup—and a win-win at that because it helps him too."

"That doesn't make any sense. Why wouldn't he charge us rent? Not to doubt you, but are you sure you understood it right? I mean, you know what they say, if something sounds too good to be true, and all."

"Yes, I'm sure I understood it right—and thanks for questioning my common sense, by the way. It's perfectly free. We'll have to move out when he comes back, but, hey, a lot can happen in a few months."

"And all we have to do is keep an eye on things and take care of the utilities?"

"That's right." She smiled. "Well, that and the cat." She cocked her head to the side and twisted a lock of hair around her finger.

"The ca—Wait, what cat?"

"Well, the owner has a house cat. He couldn't take it with him, and the cat obviously can't stay alone for that long."

"So, what—he locked the cat in the house and hoped it would survive until he found someone?"

"Now who's being ridiculous? A neighbor agreed to feed it in the short-term, until he could find someone to move in. The owner called Steve when he heard about your taking the case in Walter-boro, and the rest you know. Besides, cats are easy to take care of. You put out food and water and change the litter box."

"Litter box?" Zach wrinkled his nose.

"Relax, I'll take care of that. It's not a big deal."

"There's no denying this will make my life a hell of a lot easier while this case is pending." Zach felt himself relenting. "And it will free up a lot of drive time that I can put into working Sam's case."

"You think? Gosh, don't overwhelm me with gratitude here." Her eyes were sparkling again.

"Sorry," he said. "What I meant to say is, this is a game changer, and you're a goddess for making it happen."

"Attaboy," she said as she leaned over to kiss him. "Way to rally enough to begrudgingly accept a small miracle."

"I'm sorry, Adds. I know all you were doing was trying to help, and I was being a jerk. This case is important for Sam, but it's important for me—for us—too. If I can get a good result for him, it could be a big step toward rebuilding my credibility, and my practice. Thank you."

"Don't mention it—it comes with being a goddess. So how did it go at the preliminary hearing today?"

"Actually, I had a small miracle of my own. Colleton Burns has volunteered to help with Sam's case—and pro bono at that."

"For free? Are you sure you understood it right? Did you confirm there's not a cat involved?"

"Very funny. Seriously, this is a big deal."

"Fabulous—I can't wait to hear about it. Change your clothes and you can fill me in while we're packing."

"Do we have to do it tonight? I'm beat."

"Sorry—I promised the neighbor we'd be moving in tomorrow," she said as she headed back into the bedroom.

"Of course you did," Zach said to himself with a grin.

CHAPTER 12

THE HOUSE IN WALTERBORO WAS CONSIDERABLY QUIETER THAN the apartment in downtown Charleston, and Zach had slept later than usual. In the few days they'd been here, they had come to feel at home. Zach loved Charleston, but he had to admit the charm of small-town life had its own appeal. The day they moved in, Karen, the neighbor from next door, had walked over with a casserole to welcome them, although Zach suspected that might have been motivated less by neighborly love and more by her relief at no longer being responsible for the cat. The smell of coffee and breakfast coming from the kitchen let Zach know that Addie had been up for a while, but he was not alone in the bed. He rolled over to confront the big black cat staring at him as if he were an aquarium full of fish.

"Careful, Elvis. If Addie catches you up here shedding black hair all over her white quilt, she's not likely to be very understanding," Zach warned. Elvis didn't show any sign of relinquishing his cushy perch. "Okay, play the tough guy if you like, but I've seen her pissed off, and she scares the shit out of me." Zach rubbed the morning stubble on his chin, rolled out of bed, and pulled on a T-shirt and shorts. Sensing a change of venue, Elvis indulged in a luxurious stretch before he leapt down and moved fluidly through the bedroom door, radiating an aura more panther than housecat.

"Perfect timing," Addie said when Zach made his way into the sunny kitchen as the toaster popped up. There were eggs and fruit on the table.

"Thanks." He took the mug of coffee from her hand as he leaned down for a quick kiss. Addie put toast and jam on the table and slid onto the bench window seat as Zach settled into the chair across from her and helped himself to eggs.

"So, what's on the agenda for today?" she asked as she spread strawberry preserves on her toast, then shamelessly licked her spoon.

"Going to the detention center to review phone records with Sam. I want to make sure everything is consistent with what he said about his working relationship with Jessie."

"Are you worried it won't be?"

"Not really, but the solicitor will be looking for anything that doesn't quite fit, and I don't want any nasty surprises at trial."

"And?"

"And I still can't shake this nagging sense that there's something Sam's not telling me," Zach admitted, cupping his hands around the warm mug. "I don't want to go into a murder trial not knowing everything that might come into play." Zach tried to shut out a mental visual of Jake Barton in the courtroom smoothly pulling the proverbial rabbit out of a hat.

"It sounds like we have to find a way to get Sam to come clean," Addie said. "What time do we leave?"

"Um, well, actually, Colleton is going with me. He's supposed to be picking me up in about an hour."

"Colleton?" A tiny dark cloud passed briefly over Addie's face. "Oh, sure. Of course," she added as she gathered some of the dishes and silently carried them to the sink behind him. He couldn't see her face now, but he didn't need to see it to know this was not sitting well.

"You know, now that I think about it, that will probably work out better," she added, a little too brightly. "While y'all are meeting with Sam, I'll pay a visit to Sam's boss. George Holden, wasn't it?

Maybe I can convince him to give me some invoices or report dates from work Sam did for Jessie's company. Then we can meet back up here afterward to compare whatever I can get from the boss to the phone records you're meeting with Sam about. If we can show that the dates of the work Sam did for Jessie correlate to the dates of any calls between them, that would help support Sam's testimony that their only interaction was about work. Right?"

"Yeah, well, I guess great minds think alike."

"You were thinking the same thing, then? Great—it's a plan." Her voice was taking a slightly warmer tone.

"No, well, yes. What I meant was, Colleton paid George a visit yesterday afternoon and he's bringing all of that with him so we can compare notes with Sam today when we see him."

"Oh. I see." She was quiet for a moment. "Well, that Colleton is worth his weight in gold, isn't he?" Dishes in the sink were clanking with a bit more force now, and Zach held his breath, half expecting one of those dishes to find itself propelled across the room at the back of his head. From the corner of his eye, he saw Elvis slink out from under the table and dart out of the room. Coward.

"Here, let me help," he offered weakly as he pushed back his chair and reached for his plate.

"Leave it. I'll take care of it."

"I can help."

"No. I said I've got it."

"You're sure?" He slipped up behind her and leaned in for a kiss. She leaned away. He got the message.

"Of course I'm sure. Go shave and change so you're ready when Colleton gets here. Wouldn't want him to have to wait."

"If you really don't mind . . ."

"Go."

Seizing the opportunity, Zach cut and ran. Closing the bedroom door behind him, he spotted Elvis hunkered beneath a chair. "I see you're not on the bed now, tough guy. I told you she was scary." The cat's luminous gold eyes blinked as if to say, *I have no idea what you're talking about.*

"I'm gone, Addie," Zach called in the general direction of the running shower as he bolted for the door at the first sign of Colleton's Tahoe.

"Hit it," Zach urged as he jumped in, slamming the door behind him. Colleton responded immediately and without question—like a man accustomed to hasty getaways—and the Tahoe lurched onto Wichman Street, upsetting the gravel beneath them.

"In a little hot water with the missus, are we?" Colleton glanced at the rearview mirror as though someone might be giving chase. His expression was nonchalant, but there was more than a hint of amusement in his tone.

"You don't want to know," Zach answered. "Wait—the detention center is that way," he added as Colleton turned left on Jefferies Boulevard.

"I know where the detention center is, thank you, Mr. Stander, but now that I've been made an accomplice in your cowardly escape, you aren't getting out of this truck until I hear the sordid details of your transgressions."

"Truck? Does an SUV count as a truck? It's more like an overgrown station wagon."

"This coming from the guy in the Camry. Now give it up."

"Wait—you're riding around with an empty beer can from last night?" Zach stared at the console.

"No, idiot, that's an empty beer can left from this morning, and stop stalling."

Zach sighed and leaned back against the leather headrest. "Seriously?"

"Seriously. Your ass is stuck here until you spill it. What'd you do?"

"It's nothing. Just, for some reason, I think maybe she's a little jealous."

"Jealous? Really? Damn—no offense, buddy, but I didn't exactly take you for a horndog."

"Only you could manage to make that sound like an insult," Zach said, shaking his head.

"Who's she jealous of? And why?"

"You, apparently," Zach answered, bracing himself for what he knew would come next. Colleton did not disappoint. The big man slapped the steering wheel and convulsed with laughter that shook the vehicle and turned his face red.

"And the why?" Colleton choked out between fits of laughter.

"Addie's a private investigator—one of the best I've ever seen. That's how we met, and we've been a team ever since. She's smart and tenacious and has a knack for finding information. She works with me on all my cases—not that there have been very many lately. I think she thought she'd be the one coming along this morning."

"Oh, for the love of God, Zach, how does a guy so smart about the law get to be so clueless about women?"

"Dunno. It's a gift, I guess. Not sure I'm that smart about the law, for that matter . . ."

"Hold on a minute," Colleton said, sobering instantly. "If you're talking about that business with Gator Crosby, I know all about it, and you shouldn't be too unforgiving on yourself, especially since you took your lumps for it. I was a criminal defense lawyer for decades, and the reality is that some of our clients really are incorrigible criminals, and they got as far as they did because they were masters at looking like something else. It's a fine line we walk when we try to represent them without getting caught up in whatever shit they were into. What happened to you is an occupational hazard, and there but for the grace of God go all of us who are brave—or maybe foolish—enough to shoulder this line of work."

"Thanks for saying that."

"I'm not just saying it—it's true," Colleton insisted. "Now, your current problem with Addie, on the other hand, that's entirely on you, you loser." The laughing returned, though now Zach found himself joining in.

"You've got the solution, do you, Mr. Burns? Maybe some secret weapon?"

"Oh, hell yeah. Eli wasn't kidding when he was prattling on about my admiration of younger women, and the attraction is mutual. They love me—with a few unfortunate exceptions."

"Now I understand why you need the big vehicle—have to put that ego somewhere, I guess. And, thanks, but I'm not thinking your offering to hit on my fiancée is helping."

"I would never! But young women are one of the world's most underestimated groups. Me? I knew from the beginning they were smarter than me, and usually harder working. Like any creature—man or beast—they're drawn to those of us who appreciate them. Look, I'm tagging along to be extra help, not to replace the crackerjack help you already have. We'll go see Addie after we leave the jail and patch things up."

"Somehow I'm not convinced it will be quite that easy."

"It will be, trust me. But there is something else that won't be easy, and we need to talk about it before we get to the jail."

"Oh, shit—you found something in Sam's phone records?"

"No . . . at least not yet, but it's something we can't afford to ignore. Walterboro is a small town—in my day it was even smaller."

Colleton turned on to Main Street. The street sign read *Washington Street*, but all the locals called it Main Street because, well, it was. Zach took in the tree-lined street with colorful awnings shading quaint antique shops and watering holes that were slowly replacing the old five-and-dime and work-boot stores. Pedestrians stopped to chat or waved at one another from across the street. A twenty-first-century Mayberry.

"Some folks have this fantasy that small-town life is somehow idyllic—a throwback to simpler, easier times," Colleton went on. "And to be fair, in many ways it is. I grew up in a world where my friends and I could ride our bikes everywhere and the biggest threat to our safety was that someone who knew our moms would see us and rat us out for whatever we were up to. I can't imagine a different kind of childhood. Everybody here knows everybody else and sometimes that familiarity can be reassuring, feel safe." Colleton turned right and stopped one block later at the intersection with Hampton Street, where the Methodist and Baptist churches loomed on opposite corners, entrenched in a perpetual contest for salvation of the most lost souls. "But, on the other hand, in this microcosm of society, sometimes prejudices and stereotypes can be . . . magnified."

"You're talking about the race issue with a Black defendant and a white victim."

"Of course I am. The Slager and Mother Emanuel tragedies cut a raw swath through the Lowcountry, and I guess you heard that last week the US District Court in Ferguson approved a big settlement in a civil suit over what happened there."

"I did." Zach nodded. "But we knew all along that Sam's trial would get a lot of publicity, and people will have strong opinions."

"Unfortunately, it sounds like there's going to be more to it than that, and it isn't waiting for the trial to start. Some of the locals have whipped themselves into a frenzy—on both sides of the fence—and they've applied for public demonstration permits. I made a few calls and confirmed one of the permits is for outside the jail this morning."

"Why this morning? There's no hearing set anytime soon, and they couldn't know we'd be coming."

"Questioning why implies reason, Zach. I sincerely doubt there was any reasoning involved. Word on the grapevine is there's a crowd clamoring that Jessie Gadsden deserves justice—swift and hard. The crowd on the other side insists that version of swift justice is shorthand for railroading a Black man without a solid investigation or a fair trial. Both sides seem convinced they're on the right side of the angels. That's likely to get painful for anyone caught between the two."

"Do you think Sam is in danger inside?"

"He's probably safer in there than out here, but I'm not sure how much that's saying."

"And Eli? Do you think they'll go after him because Sam is his grandson?"

"Eli's a tough old bird and far from defenseless, but one man is no match for a mob."

"You can't possibly think there's an actual mob at the jail this morning."

"Today? Nah. Probably not more than a handful of scraggly rabble-rousers. But give 'em time and they'll gain steam. Same way a small storm system can turn into a hurricane, a small group of folks hell-bent on hate can turn into a rabid mob without a lot of warning. And, Zach?"

"Yeah?"

"In case you're missing my point, I think you need to face the fact that a lot of people see you as protecting the man who bludgeoned Buford Gadsden's daughter to death with an altar cross."

"Are you suggesting I'm in danger? Here in Mayberry?" Zach asked, looking out the window.

"All I'm saying is, it wouldn't hurt you and Addie to be careful."

"Addie? Colleton, before she opened her own shop, Addie was a law enforcement officer. She's trained in self-defense and has a working knowledge of the kinds of situations that lead to trouble. Not to mention she shoots better than most."

"Does she carry?"

"Not routinely because we're in and out of courthouses and public buildings, but she has a concealed weapons permit, so she has that option when she thinks there's a need." Zach was trying to sound confident, but he felt like he'd been punched in the gut. How had it not occurred to him that moving here might not be safe for her? After being the subject of stage-whispered comments and brazen stares for the past year, he hardly cared if anyone disapproved of him, but the thought that anyone might harm Addie because of him was not something he was prepared for. The concern must have shown on his face because Colleton's voice softened.

"Sorry. I'm not trying to scare you, but be careful. Okay?"

"Okay, okay. We'll be careful. Now let's get to the jail and get some work done." Zach made a weak attempt at a grin. "Damn, for a man who had beer for breakfast, you sure are a buzzkill."

CHAPTER 13

COLLETON'S INFO ABOUT THE DEMONSTRATORS TURNED OUT TO BE spot-on. Despite the sweltering summer heat, the two groups had lined up on opposite sides of the sidewalk outside the jail. Two deputies standing nearby were watching to make sure they didn't crowd the entrance or block the sidewalk. The group to the right of the entrance—all white—had signs with slogans like JUSTICE FOR JESSIE and YOUR RIGHTS END WHERE MINE BEGIN. Someone had made T-shirts with photos of a brightly smiling Jessie on the front, but Zach saw a few shirts bearing Confederate battle flags too. The group to the left—mostly Black—had slogans like JUSTICE = FAIR TRIAL FOR SAM and WHAT INVESTIGATION? One had a drawing of a train headed for a stick figure with the word *Railroaded* at the bottom. Most of the T-shirts on that side had BLM logos. Colleton put the Tahoe in park, and they sat for a moment surveying the scene. There weren't more than eight or ten people on either side, but even that was troubling for a day with no court appearance this early in the game.

"That's Buford Gadsden," Zach said, spotting the big man towering over most of the others.

"Mm-hmm. The younger guy behind him is one of Jessie's brothers—don't recall his name."

"I don't see Jessie's mother, though."

"From what I'm hearing on the street, she hasn't left the house since the funeral."

"Say, is that JB Beaman?" Zach pointed to a scowling man sporting what roughly resembled a mullet and brandishing a JUSTICE FOR JESSIE sign with a little more zeal than most.

"It is, unfortunately. That one is nothing but trouble. How did you know about JB?"

"Addie dug up some information about him when Eli first asked me to take Sam's case. Eli mentioned him too but didn't go into detail other than to say JB didn't leave any room for doubt as to where he stood on race issues. I think his exact words were that he was one of the sort that give hate a bad name."

"That sounds like Eli," Colleton said with a weak chuckle that was tinged more with timeworn sadness than with laughter. "I've known Eli Jenkins a long time. He came up hard and got knocked back down almost every time he tried to make his place in life better. He has more reason than most to be bitter, yet he's one of the most fair-minded people I've ever met. He's not wearing any rose-colored glasses, mind you, but somehow, he's willing to give the benefit of the doubt to whoever leaves a little room for it. Like he said, though, JB doesn't leave any room for doubt. Make no mistake—he's one of those I was warning you about."

"Eli says JB and Buford are close friends."

"They are," Colleton agreed, "have been most of their lives."

"You think they're cut from the same cloth?"

"For what it's worth, my impression is no," Colleton answered after taking a moment to consider the question. "Back when we were all kids, I might've said differently. Buford got in a bit of a scrape with the law back in the eighties."

"But according to Eli, Buford did his time quietly and came home and settled down."

"Eli has his own reasons for being able to look past that."

"Yeah, Eli was one of his customers for a while after Vietnam," Zach added, drumming his fingers on the console between them. "Wow, that must have been one hell of a conversation you and Eli had." Colleton's expression gave away that he hadn't expected as much, and he shifted in his seat, turning toward Zach. "Eli isn't one to wear his heart on his sleeve or put his business out on the street, and Sam is the single most important thing in his life. For him to trust you with his past and his future, Eli must have a lot of confidence in you, my friend. In my book, that's saying something."

"What if it's saying he's finally lost his mind? Maybe it's crazy to think that an old Black farmer and a young white lawyer who's stuck in what might politely be called a prolonged slump are enough to save Sam from this shitstorm."

"Not that you need us, but you're not alone. I'm here to help and—far better—so is your Addie. If anybody can do this, we can."

"*If* anybody can do this . . . ," Zach trailed off. "What if it can't be done?"

"We won't find out sitting in this truck. Let's get our asses in there and get to work."

The crowd's enthusiasm had dialed back as the morning temperature surged, but when Zach and Colleton slammed the Tahoe's doors and the opposing groups realized they had a new audience, things picked up. Seconds later, when someone recognized who the new audience was, things escalated again. Posters and voices rose simultaneously with one side demanding "Justice for Jessie" and the other side demanding "Fair Trial for Sam." The irony that both sides wanted justice seemed lost on all of them.

As Zach made his way through the crowd, what struck him hardest was the unvarnished anger and hate on many of the faces— on both sides. Jessie Gadsden's horrific death and Sam Jenkins's presumed guilt may have been the catalyst for this confrontation, but it was not the only source of all that anger and hate. This was about something older and deeper, and if Zach hadn't fully appreciated the magnitude of what he would have to overcome to save Sam, he felt its full force now.

"How do you sleep at night, Stander, you bastard?" Buford Gadsden's voice rose above the others, and the din quieted as the crowd gave him the floor. "Your piece of shit client killed my daughter"—the big man's voice cracked—"and you're trying to get him off. What the hell is wrong with you?" Zach knew better than to answer, and he turned to the deputy instead, who stepped up and held the door as he and Colleton approached.

"Thank you," Zach said. Glancing back once more, Zach found himself caught not in Buford's sights, but in JB's. The man's earlier scowl had been eclipsed by the hard-eyed focus of a predator zeroing in on its prey, and Zach felt a chill slither down his spine despite the stifling summer heat.

The staff inside were tense and in no mood to socialize, and Zach and Colleton were escorted briskly to a room where Sam was waiting. The reassuring smile Zach had forced onto his face disappeared the second he laid eyes on Sam.

"What the hell happened to your face?"

"An accident—wasn't watching where I was going, I guess," Sam answered, making only brief eye contact, and then turning his face away to hide the bruise along his cheekbone.

"And you what—accidentally punched a wall with the side of your face? Turn back around here so I can get a look." Zach's tone did not invite argument, and Sam did as he said, but with a roll of his eyes.

"Really, Zach, it's nothing," Sam said.

"Nothing my ass! Tell me what happened."

"I told you. I had an accident."

"That's bullshit, and we both know it. If you let them get away with it, they'll keep coming."

"No, if I rat them out, it will get worse. Let it go, Zach." Then: "Please," he added more gently. "I didn't know what to expect before—it's not like I've ever been in jail. But I'm figuring out how to take care of myself now, and the best thing you can do for me is to leave this alone for now and focus on getting me out of here."

"I don't like it."

"That makes two of us," Sam said.

Zach huffed out an exaggerated sigh, and Colleton gently nudged his arm.

"Listen to Sam, Zach. We need to play this his way for now."

"Hi, Mr. Burns." Sam jumped at the chance to change the subject. "Wow—how many years has it been? I was just a kid the last time I saw you."

"I think you can call me Colleton now."

"Okay, then. Eli told me you'd volunteered to help us. Can't tell you how much we appreciate it."

"Don't mention it. Eli and I go way back."

"So," Sam said, motioning to the file in Zach's hand, "we all know this isn't a social call. Please—tell me you've got something there that will get me out of this shithole."

"No, but it's a start," Zach said as he opened the file and spread a set of documents on the table. "These are the call records from the company phone you were using. We got them from George Holden."

"Do I still have a job?"

"We didn't put him on the spot about that, but I can tell you he's cooperating with us, so that has to mean something," Colleton said. "He even gave us some invoices for Jessie's business so we could compare the dates you were doing work on her account with the dates of any calls."

"They should match pretty closely—there may be some dates that I worked on the account that Jessie and I didn't talk, but the phone calls should be centered around work dates."

"Here." Zach slid a page closer to Sam. "I've highlighted the calls between your phone and the phone number Jessie had on her company web page. Do you know if she had any other numbers?"

"If she did, I don't know anything about them—the number from the company was a cell phone she carried. It's the only one I would have called."

"What about calls *from* her—any of them from another number?"

"I don't think so, but I'm not sure I would have noticed," Sam answered. "Does that matter?"

"Right now, we have to assume everything matters."

"Zach, I still don't understand how the phone records can prove I'm innocent."

"They don't. But the manner in which she was killed indicates the killer had deep-seated feelings about her. You say you barely knew her, and any evidence we can offer to show you're telling the truth has the potential to create reasonable doubt for the jury."

"That doesn't sound like much . . ."

"Here, let's just see what we have," Colleton said, adding the invoices to the documents on the table. The three began to compare them to the phone records, working their way forward from the oldest records to the most recent. There were only a handful of calls and all the call dates correlated to invoices for work on Jessie's account. Sam turned over the last page and traced his finger down to the only highlighted call.

"This is it." There was a tremor in his voice. "This is her calling me asking me to come that night."

"Hang on," Zach said, turning the page around so that he could look more closely. "This call was received at 8:38 that night."

"Yeah, so?"

"You told me earlier that you found her as soon as you walked in the church and the first thing you did was call for help."

"That's true." Sam's eyes were wet now.

"So, the next call on this list from that night was you making that 9-1-1 call—at 10:41. How the hell do you explain that it took you over two hours to get there?"

"I told you that first day—I was working late on something that had to be electronically filed that day. I told Jessie that when she called. Told her it might be a couple hours. She said no problem. Claimed she was just then pulling up at the church and it would take her at least that long to finish. Then she said something like *just get here when you can.*"

"I don't get it," Zach said. "Why not go pick up her documents before it got late and then come back and finish what you were doing?"

The tremble began with the young man's mouth and spread across his face before it flooded the rest of him in a storm of silent heaving. "God help me, I ask myself that same question every day. Maybe if I had done that one simple thing, she'd still be alive, and I would still have my life too." Sam buried his face in his hands.

Watching Sam battle with his choices, Zach could relate. How many times had he thought that he could have avoided the mess with Gator if he'd listened to the warning voice in his head instead of the siren song of all that cash? He would still be living his old life instead of scratching and clawing to get it back. Zach could not have been more grateful when Colleton interrupted his thoughts.

"Sam, we can't change what happened that night. All we can do is focus on getting you out of here. But we need to cover as much ground now as we can. Can you hold it together a while longer so we can go over a few more things? The more you tell us, the more we have to work with."

Sam slowly slid his hands from his face and wiped them on the legs of his jumpsuit. "What else do you want to know?" He took a deep ragged breath.

"Well, one thing that's had me puzzled is the State's witness, Captain Chambers, testified at the preliminary hearing that Jessie was there cleaning the church. Her business specialized in IT work—not cleaning work. That didn't make sense to me. Why would she be there cleaning?" Colleton asked.

"I asked her the same thing when I took over her account," Sam responded, "thinking I might get a few points if I gave her some business advice to improve revenues. It probably won't surprise you to know a country church like that isn't exactly rolling in money. They couldn't afford to pay someone to work full-time doing administrative things. So they hired Jessie to scan and computerize some of their records. That way, members could volunteer to do those things from home. She also helped them set up a basic social media presence, a way to spread information about events and communicate with members who were homebound.

"While Jessie was working on those things, the lady who'd been cleaning the church quit. Given she was almost ninety, nobody was surprised, but for what she was charging they didn't think they'd be able to find anyone to replace her. Nothing about Jessie Gadsden struck me as a bleeding heart, but something about that old church got to her—touched her. When I asked her why she was spending her time cleaning there instead of taking on more lucrative jobs, she said it was a special place and being there made her feel peaceful and safe. Based on her accounting records, she went every few weeks.

Sort of adds to the ugliness of it all that it happened in a place so special to her."

"I guess that makes sense," Colleton said.

"What else do you need to know?" Sam asked.

It was clear Sam was running out of steam, so Colleton moved on to his last set of questions quickly.

"The police have searched your apartment by now. A warrant allows them to go in and take anything they find that's covered by the warrant, but they have to leave us a list of everything they take. The list will be somewhere like on a counter or right inside the door, but we need to get in to find out what they took."

"No problem. Eli has a key."

"It would help us if we knew what they might find. I'm guessing you have a computer or laptop there?"

"I do. Or I did, anyway. I guess it may be gone now."

"Count on that. Will they find anything on it we should know about?"

"No. I'm a pretty boring guy. Searching my browser history won't give them more than some sports stats and a few accounting newsletter services. Some solitaire and maybe checking tides or weather or something like that."

"Photos?"

"A few."

"Any that could hurt us at trial?"

"Not unless you think a jury would be offended by Lija and Buck or the occasional fish hanging from a line. I've never been into selfies."

"Anything pornographic?"

"Maybe Buck licking his own ass? Sorry—couldn't resist that," Sam added in response to Colleton's frown.

"What about email?" Colleton asked.

"Email?" Sam managed a weak laugh. "Colleton, you're showing your age. People my age use email for work or school, but anything personal or private is going to be on something like WhatsApp or texts."

"Hmm. Maybe we should go back to Mr. Burns, after all. Okay, here's a big one: if you were going to the church to pick up documents from Jessie, where are the documents?"

Sam looked like a deer caught in headlights. "Honestly, I haven't given that any thought," he said after a long, empty pause. "I mean, I guess they could have been somewhere in the church. I didn't notice them, but I wasn't looking at anything but her. If you didn't find them in the church, maybe they were still in her car? Or maybe the cops have them? I—I don't know."

"Did she give you any idea how many documents? Are we talking about an envelope, an expandable, a bankers box—what?"

"She didn't say."

Colleton nodded and flipped through the pages of his yellow legal pad, checking to see that he had covered what he wanted to ask about.

"Anything else you need to know?" Sam asked after a few moments.

"Actually, my next question was going to be exactly that." Zach swept the last of the phone records and invoices into a pile and leaned his elbows on the table, leveling his gaze at Sam.

"Huh?"

"Is there anything else we need to know?"

"Like what?"

"I don't know, Sam, that's why I'm asking. Right or wrong, my gut tells me you didn't murder that girl, and most of the time I can trust the old gut. Trouble is, that same fairly reliable gut is also telling me that there's something else—something you aren't telling me. And if the solicitor finds it before I do, he could use it to destroy your credibility and get a guilty verdict."

Sam shook his head and shrugged, then took an intense interest in his hands folded in his lap.

"Okay, then." Zach and Colleton exchanged a long look. "If that's all, I'll let them know we're ready to go." Still nothing from Sam. Zach hit the buzzer, and a detention officer came and unlocked the door.

"Ready, then?" she asked. All three men nodded.

"See you next time, I guess," Sam said, rising.

"Sure—and try not to punch any more walls with your face, would you," Zach said, taking more than a little satisfaction in the discomfort that flashed across the officer's face.

"I'll be back to escort you two out in a minute," the officer said as she led Sam out.

"Hiding something?" Zach asked Colleton after the door closed.

"Definitely hiding something. Question is, how do we get it out of him?"

"That, my friend, is only one of way too many questions that I don't have the answers to."

CHAPTER 14

THE NOON SUN HAD DRIVEN THE DEMONSTRATORS AWAY FOR THE day, and only the heat roiling up from the pavement greeted Zach and Colleton as they left the jail. Walking toward the Tahoe, Colleton suddenly stopped and bellowed at a familiar figure.

"Fishburn, you old fart! How the hell are you?"

The sergeant was clutching a fast-food bag, and his jowly face glowered in Colleton's direction. Clearly, he didn't share Colleton's glee at this chance reunion.

"Play along," Colleton said under his breath, making a beeline for his target. "Waylon Fishburn—damn, it is you—I can't believe it." Colleton slapped the increasingly dour Sergeant Fishburn on the shoulder as he drew close. "How long has it been? Five years? Ten? I swear I don't think I've laid eyes on you since that night I hustled your ass out the back of BJ's bar so your third wife didn't catch you with the—er—company you were keeping. Or, no, maybe it was the night I smuggled you out of the Pink Pig in a fortuitously commandeered beer truck when we heard your fourth wife was out in the parking lot screaming obscenities and slashing your tires. How long ago was that?"

"Lower your voice, you insufferable prick."

"Perhaps we'd have more privacy in your office?" Colleton cocked his head toward the sheriff's office on the other side of the parking lot. "Wouldn't want to make a scene out here."

"You wouldn't dare." Fishburn's eyes narrowed.

"You know better. Come on, let's sit and have a friendly talk for old times' sake," Colleton insisted. "Oh, wait, where are my manners? Let me introduce my colleague . . ."

"No need, I know who he is." Fishburn jerked his chin in Zach's direction. "You're that lawyer defending the guy who killed Buford Gadsden's daughter."

"Accused of," Zach replied dryly. "Pleasure."

"Hmph," Fishburn grunted.

"Your pal here is a brilliant conversationalist, Colleton."

"What do you say, Fishburn? Shall we go in and have a visit?"

Sergeant Fishburn hesitated, weighing his options until he realized he didn't have any when Colleton inquired as to the well-being and current whereabouts of the fifth Mrs. Waylon Fishburn.

"Oh, fuck it. By all means, gentlemen"—he gestured with a mock bow—"please, join me in my office."

A few minutes later, Zach and Colleton were sitting in Sergeant Fishburn's cramped office. He tossed the fast-food bag next to a tottering pile of papers that was anchored by an ancient paperweight that read SUPPORT YOUR LOCAL JAYCEES and looked like it might have been used as a hammer at some point. Fishburn glared across the desk at them. "So, what is it you want, Colleton?"

"What makes you think I want something?" Colleton feigned insult.

"Past experience. What is it?"

"Nothing complicated, just a little information."

"What kind of information?"

"A little birdie told me you were working on Sam Jenkins's case . . ."

"Oh, hell no, there is no way I'm compromising the most high-profile case we've had in years, no matter what you threaten me with."

"Calm down, already. I wouldn't ask you to compromise any investigation, and you know it. I only want you to confirm something I heard."

"Confirm what?" Fishburn eyed him suspiciously.

"I heard you got Jessie Gadsden's phone records, and they show a boatload of calls and texts with a number that isn't the number Jenkins called EMS from that night. I also heard that mystery number isn't registered to Jenkins."

"How did you find out about that?" Fishburn's bushy eyebrows lurched halfway up his forehead.

"Doesn't matter. Just confirm the intel is good."

"I'm not giving you copies of her phone records if that's where this is headed."

"Not asking you to. Tell me if what I heard is true."

"And I'm not telling you the number, either."

"Not asking you to."

Fishburn looked furtively from Colleton to Zach and back again, then gazed longingly at the bag of food that sat on his desk with a grease stain slowly spreading across its surface.

"Yeah," he muttered finally. "It's true. Right up through that last day." Fishburn winced, realizing immediately that he'd given Colleton more than he'd asked for.

"Have you turned the records over to the solicitor's office yet?"

"Of course. What kind of idiot do you take me for?"

Colleton let the softball drift past him. "Who's the assistant solicitor on the case?"

"You know damn well Jake Barton is handling this one himself—no way he's going to let someone else have a case that will get this much press."

"Yeah, and I also know that egomaniac isn't doing his own grunt work. Who is?"

"One of his baby lawyers. Name's Serena. Serena Davenport."

"Great. Make it easy on me—what's her direct number?"

"Why should I care about making anything easy on you?"

"I thought we covered that outside."

Fishburn's face scrunched. "I'll give you her number if you'll tell me how you found out Jessie Gadsden had a ton of calls with that other number."

"Fishburn, you know I'd never give up a source. That's the reason you caved as fast as you did—your name's as safe as theirs. Now, we both know all the solicitors' office numbers are the same except for the last three digits. Tell me hers or I'll call another mutual acquaintance of ours. It's been forever since I saw your lovely wife number five."

"It's one-five-seven. Now get your ass out of my office and take your friend here with you. This little party is over." Fishburn was already tearing into the fast-food bag.

"Fair enough," Colleton said, opening the office door and motioning Zach through. As he followed behind him, Colleton stuck his head back inside the office and spoke quietly as though he didn't want Zach to hear.

"Still want to know who leaked the information about the mystery phone number?"

Fishburn nodded, wide-eyed, his mouth full of chili cheese dog.

"You just did." Colleton managed to slam the door shut seconds before he heard the thud of the paperweight against it, followed closely by the crash of papers to the floor and Fishburn's miserable howl.

As Colleton jacked up the Tahoe's air conditioner to full throttle, Zach was punching Serena Davenport's number into his cell phone. "That was masterful," he whispered to Colleton as it rang.

"Serena Davenport," she answered. Zach could hear the tapping of a keyboard in the background. Apparently, she was a multitasker.

"Good afternoon, Ms. Davenport. My name is Zach Stander. I'm—"

"I know who you are." The tapping stopped. "How can I help you?"

"I'd like to get a copy of Jessie Gadsden's phone records. I understand your office has them?"

"Well, Mr. Stander, assuming your *understanding* is correct, I don't recall receiving any discovery requests from you. Did I miss something?"

"No, ma'am, though I'm sure we'll be sending those over shortly."

"Wonderful, then," she said. "I look forward to receiving them, and, assuming you include a request that would cover any phone records we might have, I'll get those right to you. Now, if there's nothing else . . . ?"

"Not so fast, there. I don't think I need to send discovery requests for those. I do believe you're required to give them to me even without a request."

"Interesting. My copy of the *Rules of Criminal Procedure* looks to be the 2017 version, and Rule 5 indicates that only the defendant can elect to start the reciprocal discovery process. Does your copy say something different?"

"This isn't about discovery. This falls under *Brady*. You've heard of it—that pesky Supreme Court case that says you are required to hand over any evidence that would tend to show my client is not guilty."

"Oh yes, I've heard of that one. But how, pray tell, would the victim's phone records tend to show your client is not guilty?"

"For starters, my sources say there are numerous calls and texts between Ms. Gadsden and a phone that isn't registered to my client—right up through the date of the crime."

"What sources?"

"Sorry, ma'am, that's attorney work product. Privileged and all."

"So, Jessie Gadsden had calls with a friend," Serena said, not giving him the satisfaction of rising to the bait. "You've heard of friends, right?"

"A very close friend, it would appear."

"And?"

"And my client barely knew her."

"Is that so?"

"Does the way she was killed strike you as something that even a murderer would do to a mere casual acquaintance?"

"My mental impressions about the case would be attorney work product. You know, privileged and all."

"Ah, yes. Well, you still have to hand those over."

"I'm not sure I agree with your assessment," she huffed, "but there is one thing I am sure of. I'm not about to let my good reputation and professional conduct come into question over something as inconsequential as phone records you'll eventually get during discovery anyway. I'll drop them in the mail to you today."

"No need to waste a stamp. Let me give you my email address."

"How convenient. Fine, I'm ready—what's the address?"

Zach could hear her tapping on the keyboard as he spelled out the email address. Ms. Davenport was an aggressive typist.

"It is on its way now. Anything else I can help you with, Mr. Stander?"

"Actually, there is. You could call me Zach. It looks like we're going to be working together for a while." He heard a weary sigh on the other end.

"Of course. Please call me Serena."

"Thank you, Serena."

"Oh—and one more thing."

"What's that?"

"Those records show a call the evening of the murder with your client, too," she said.

"To borrow your phrase, so what?"

"There may have been multiple people she spoke with that night, but your client was the only one found kneeling over her covered in blood."

Zach heard the phone drop into its cradle and the call ended.

"How come she gets the pithy one-liner at the end?" Zach asked as he watched Serena's email pop up on his phone.

"I told you already—they're smarter than us," Colleton said as he turned onto Wichman Street. "Now let's go see Addie."

CHAPTER 15

ADDIE'S JEEP WASN'T IN THE DRIVE. "SORRY, NO IDEA WHERE SHE went or when she'll be back," Zach said with a shrug, but what he was wondering was *if* she was coming back. What if she'd gone back to the apartment?

"I'd say we're about to find out." Colleton's eyes were on the rearview mirror, and Zach turned in his seat to see Addie pulling in behind them. The door opened and a shapely pair of legs swung out onto the ground. Addie reached back behind the seat and retrieved a twelve-pack of beer and a backpack, and pushed the door closed with her hip. The gold and copper highlights in her hair lit up like sparklers in the midday sun.

"You realize you're out of your league with her, right?" Colleton asked and then he was out of the truck.

"You have no idea," Zach assured the empty seat beside him.

"Let me help with those," Colleton said, taking Addie's things before she could protest.

"I take it you're Colleton Burns." She brushed away a stray piece of hair and folded her arms in front of her, looking less than pleased to see them.

"At your service," Colleton answered. Zach was out of the Tahoe now and close enough to hear the conversation. "And you must be Addie. I've heard a lot about you."

"What a coincidence," Addie drawled, exuding all the empathy of a fox with her jaw around the neck of a chicken. Zach winced inwardly at the too familiar tone, but Colleton laughed openly and flashed an easy smile that left no doubt he was comfortable having beautiful women point out his many shortcomings.

"So I hear," he said. "I've spent the better part of the morning trying to help our friend Zach here extricate his feet from his mouth."

"And now you're here to sweet-talk me and save the day, is that the plan?"

"Oh, hell no, ma'am," he said, putting two syllables in *hell*. "I came for a front-row seat to watch him replace those feet with the crow he's likely to be eating for lunch."

Now it was Addie's turn to laugh. "We'd best get inside, then. Don't want to give the neighbors too much more to talk about." She led the way up the stairs. She still hadn't spoken to or even acknowledged Zach, but the mischievous sparkle in her eyes suggested the tide was turning.

"You can put my backpack on the kitchen table, Mr. Burns."

"Colleton, please. You want this twelve-pack in the fridge?"

"Sure, but pull out two for us, why don't you, Colleton." Addie slid into the window bench behind the table.

"Sounds good, could you make that three, Colleton?" Zach added.

"Not up to me. Her beer, her call," Colleton said, locking eyes with Addie. He pulled open the end of the box and set two beers on the counter beside him. Then he stood there with one hand on the refrigerator door, giving Addie a questioning look. "Well? Moment of truth here."

"I'm not sure. What do you think?"

"Seems to me he ate his blue plate special of crow without too much of a fuss. Perhaps you could show a little mercy and give him something to wash that shit down with."

The little tug upward that had been forming at the corners of her mouth finally won the battle and exploded into that smile that always brought Zach to his knees. "Okay, okay. You two win. The prodigal can come back into the fold. But don't go thinking there's another get out of jail free card left in the till," she said, looking at Zach.

Zach felt something inside him settle.

"Don't stand there letting all the cold out of the icebox. There's a bottle opener in that first drawer. Bring the beer and come sit down so we can compare notes from this morning."

"So, what were you up to this morning?" Zach asked as he pecked a quick *I'm sorry* kiss on her cheek and sat down across from her at the table.

"Thanks," she said, taking a beer from Colleton. "First I went to see George Holden—yeah, I know, I know," she said, seeing the looks on their faces. "You told me he'd already given you the phone records and some invoices, and that was good information to get. Kudos and all that. But"—she paused to take a drink—"it occurred to me that you were overlooking some things that might have a more significant impact on Sam's defense."

"Like what?" Colleton asked.

"Let's think about what we know—or at least what Sam has told us. First, he's working late and at the office when Jessie calls him sometime that evening asking him to come to the church."

"We now know it was 8:38 when she called," Colleton said, "and we have the phone record to prove she made the call."

"But that was hours before Sam says he got to the church, found her, and called for help. If you were a juror, wouldn't you want to know what took him so long?"

"He has an explanation," Colleton said. "Says he had to finish something and file it that night. Once he did, he swears he went straight to the church."

"Yes, but do we have any *proof* that part of his story is true?"

"Not yet, but something tells me you're about to change that." Zach loved watching her in action.

"That's what George and I worked on this morning. George confirmed that the computer program they use requires the user to log in and log out. Sam had been logged in all day. He was still logged in at 8:38 p.m. when Jessie called, and he didn't log out until 10:14 p.m."

"That doesn't prove he was there, does it? Could someone else have logged in or out for him?" Colleton was playing devil's advocate with Addie's theory.

"That someone else would have had to know his password to log in as him."

"But what about logging out? Most computer programs don't require you to enter a password to log out—only to log in. He could have left his computer on and left the building earlier—been at the church long before he made that emergency call. A coworker could have come along, noticed his computer on, and powered it down for him."

"That was my thought too. I might have figured it out earlier if I'd known he filed something electronically because there has to be a record of it, right? But it finally occurred to me that he might have sent some email or something, so George looked through Sam's email, and he identified an email confirming that he submitted something to LLR—the State's Department of Labor, Licensing and Regulation—for one of his clients at 10:12 p.m."

"May it please the court, Jake Barton for the prosecution," Colleton said, imitating Barton's Charleston brogue and mimicking his slick coat-buttoning move. "Ms. Stone has offered evidence that Mr. Jenkins sent an email at 10:12 the night of the crime. To which the prosecution responds *big fucking deal*. Maybe someone else was using his computer, or maybe he can access his email from his laptop at home or, better yet, he used his cell phone—while parked in front of the church where Ms. Gadsden was so brutally murdered by him moments later. The defense still hasn't proved that Sam was physically in the office as he claims."

Colleton was right, of course, but Zach still wasn't betting against her—Addie had something else in her back pocket.

"Ah, but I can, Mr. Barton," Addie shot back. "Because right after he filed the document and logged off of his computer, Sam Jenkins walked out the door to the parking lot and entered the security code to lock the door at exactly 10:16 p.m."

"And still so what? You've proven that *someone* locked the door, but you haven't given this jury one shred of evidence that it was, in fact, Samuel Jenkins."

"Not so fast. The office doesn't have any security cameras, but it's across the street from a fast-food place with a drive-through window. I drove through and bought a Coke to check it out. Sure enough, they have a camera aimed at that window and another pointing out the drive—probably intended to read license plates. I think there's a chance that one might have a view of some part of George's office parking lot. If it does, that could prove exactly what time Sam left the office."

"Impressive work." He was back in Colleton Burns mode now and raised his bottle in a salute before turning it up.

"Thanks," Addie said, beaming.

"That is good, Addie." Zach had been quiet as Addie and Colleton sparred over the new evidence. "It shows that Sam is telling the truth about those details, which gives him more credibility on the things we can't prove, but it certainly doesn't prove he didn't kill Jessie Gadsden."

"I think it does more than support his credibility. Doesn't it create sort of an alibi?"

"An alibi? Addie, Sam was with Jessie when she died—he saw her take her last breath. There's zero argument that he was somewhere else."

"Sam admits he was in the church at the time of death. That doesn't mean he was there when she was attacked."

"But we don't know what time that happened."

"Hear me out," she said. "The phone records show Jessie made a call to Sam at 8:38 p.m., and she was fine then. We know that Sam was at the church and called EMS asking for help at 10:41 p.m. and Jessie had already been attacked by that time. We also know Sam was at the office between 8:38 p.m. and 10:16 p.m., when he left."

"Yeah, but there are twenty-five minutes that are unaccounted for between 10:16 when he punched the security code and 10:41 when he called EMS. A lot could happen in twenty-five minutes."

"That's the thing—there aren't twenty-five unaccounted-for minutes. The church is all the way out on Cicada Road. How long would it take for Sam to drive there, and would that give him enough time to be the attacker? I'm guessing it would be more than twenty minutes—even at that time of day. Think about what someone did to that poor girl. There's no way that happened in an instant like a gunshot could. Granted, it's far from an airtight alibi, but it does create a real question as to whether it was physically possible for Sam to get to the church in time to attack her like that before making the call to EMS at 10:41. All I need to do is find out who's in charge at the fast-food place and convince them to let me look at the footage."

"Hold that thought." Colleton was already punching numbers on his cell phone.

"Bobby!" Colleton boomed. "No," he laughed, "I am not calling about that money you owe me—even if I did win that bet fair and square." It sounded as though there was some trash talk coming from the other end.

"Tell you what," Colleton said. "I need a favor and then we'll call it even. I'm working with Zach Stander on the Sam Jenkins trial." There was a pause.

"Yes, of course you already heard that on the street." Colleton rolled his eyes. "Look, I can't go into details, but we're thinking it's possible that some of your security cam footage caught something that night that we're trying to track down. Would you mind letting us take a look?"

Another pause.

"That's great, yeah. I'm not sure we can get there today, but can you download everything for a twenty-four-hour period going back from midnight the night it happened—July eleventh? Perfect . . . yeah, thanks, buddy, downloading to a thumb drive would be excellent. I'll pick it up sometime in the next day or so. And could you keep this between us for now? Great. Thanks again, man."

"Mission accomplished." Colleton hung up and put his phone away.

"Good job," Addie said, brushing aside the bruised feeling that she'd been upstaged again by Colleton and all his connections. "If we can prove it was Sam who set that alarm at 10:16, we can create a question as to whether it would even be possible for him to have killed that girl."

"A question, maybe." Zach nodded. "But what it keeps coming back to is that Sam was there. Without any evidence of anyone else around, I'm not sure Sam's credibility on where he was earlier or the travel-time thing is enough to persuade a jury to make that big of a leap."

"Yeah, well, there is that." Addie let out a huff of exasperation as she leaned her head back and closed her eyes. The room went silent as they contemplated the realities of Sam's plight.

Zach drummed his fingers on the table, looking glumly out the window behind her. The sunny afternoon sky had seamlessly shifted to dark and heavy. "Looks like we're going to get the usual Lowcountry afternoon thunderstorm."

"Mm-hmm." Colleton nodded. He was meticulously peeling up the edges of the label on the beer bottle in front of him when he broke the reverie. "Oh, shit—I got so caught up in Addie's news that I forgot all about Jessie's phone records. We haven't even looked at them yet."

"Looked at them? How in the hell did you get Jessie's phone records?" Addie asked.

"Perhaps I should plead the Fifth on that."

"No way—she's going to want to hear this," Zach said. "Addie, it turns out our newfound friend here is something of a con artist."

"Do tell," Addie said, looking at Colleton with a bit more interest.

"We were leaving the jail this morning, and Colleton spotted an old friend. Turns out he wasn't quite as thrilled as Colleton was by the encounter." Zach went to the refrigerator and opened three more beers, which he brought back to the table as he regaled Addie with the tale of Colleton's intel caper. Then Colleton followed suit with an only slightly embellished version of Zach using the information from Fishburn to get the phone records from the assistant solicitor.

"Y'all, this is great news. Where are they?"

"Serena emailed them to me," Zach said, pulling out his cell phone, "but this phone screen is probably too small for us to read them."

"Forward them to me," Addie said, reaching for the backpack on the table and pulling out her laptop. As the laptop came to life, they heard the small *ping* of Zach's email coming through and Addie clicked to open it and then turned the screen so that they could all see. "It looks like the bills go from the most recent to the oldest," she said, scrolling quickly. "This first one includes the night of the murder. Do we know what mystery number we're looking for?"

"No," Zach said, looking at the screen. "And the process of elimination may take longer than I was hoping—looks like this girl spent a lot of time on the phone."

"Some of those are landlines," Colleton said. "The 843 area code numbers that start with 5-3-8 and 5-4-9 for sure. They'll be easy to identify. But I don't know how to identify the cell numbers unless we can find them in her contacts list."

"This is her wireless bill, Colleton. The only way to access her contacts list would be to have her phone itself."

"Sorry—afraid I'm not too tech savvy."

"Don't worry, I've got this. This is one of those times when a private investigator comes in handy."

"One of many, it would appear," Colleton said.

"I can identify the cell owners by looking them up in a service to see who the number is registered to. I have to search them one by one, but I can probably cut down on the time by making a short list of the numbers that come up most frequently. Hopefully that gives us some leads." She was already jotting down numbers as she spoke.

Moments later, Colleton was once again torturing the label on his beer bottle when his stomach rumbled as though he'd not eaten in a week.

"Me too," Addie said, without looking up. "This is going to take a little while. Maybe you two could go get some takeout for a late lunch while I try to put together a list?"

"Sure. What do you want?"

"I hate to admit it," Zach said, "but that bag of grease Fishburn had earlier was smelling pretty good to me."

"Ah, that was no ordinary fast food. That was a chili cheese dog from Walterboro's own Dairy-Land. Place is legendary around here. If we go now, we might be able to beat this storm."

"Make mine a cheeseburger and fries," Addie said, still immersed in her laptop screen. By now, she was lost in what Zach called "the zone."

"We're on it," Zach said, and the door closed quietly behind them with Addie hardly noticing they were gone.

Addie was startled out of her work as a clap of thunder punished the ground and shook the house. Not wanting to tempt fate, she slipped the power cord out of its socket and switched to battery. According to the time at the bottom of the computer screen, she'd been at it for about forty-five minutes. Were they still not back with lunch? As if on cue, the front door opened, and Colleton and Zach hustled in, the sky breaking open only seconds behind them. With the same overwhelming velocity as the rain pummeling down outside, the heady perfume of junk food filled the room.

"Oh, sweet Jesus, that smells good," she said, closing her eyes and breathing in. She pushed the laptop aside to make room, and Zach replaced it with the coveted white sack as he and Colleton took their seats and paper bags were unceremoniously ripped open to claim the prizes inside.

Barely fifteen minutes later, the food had magically disappeared.

"Did you make any headway with the phone records?" Colleton asked as he gathered the wreckage and tossed it into the trash can.

"Some," Addie said, reaching for the laptop. "There were a lot of numbers she called sporadically—mostly clients. She called only two numbers on any regular basis. The one she called the least of those two turned out to be registered to her mother, and I'm thinking that is not who we're looking for."

"Agreed. And the other?"

"That one she called a *lot*. I was about to run a search on it when you two walked in and ruined me for anything but lunch."

"Ready to get back to it?" Zach asked.

"Way ahead of you," she said as she clicked on the link. "That's odd," Addie said, looking at the screen and twisting a lock of hair around her finger.

"What?"

"Give me a sec," she said, clicking through a series of options. "Same thing." She went through the process several times. "Well, I'll be damned."

"What? *What?*" Colleton's voice was laced with impatience.

"It looks like our mystery number is registered to Cricket," Addie said.

"Who the hell is Cricket?"

"Not who—what," she said. "Cricket is one of those companies that makes burner phones."

"Like the bad guys use in the movies so no one knows who they are?"

"Exactly like that."

"But those things have been around for a while now. Surely technology has come up with a way to trace them."

"Well, sure," she said, "but you have to have an idea of who it is and access to some of their information."

"Like what would we need?"

"Well, if the person who bought it used a credit card for the purchase, or later used a credit card to pay for additional minutes, it would show up on their credit card records, but we'd need to know whose credit card records to subpoena."

"Which we don't."

"Which we don't. And besides, a smart user can get around the added minutes thing by using cash to buy one of those prepaid credit cards at a convenience store."

"Could you trace the computer's IP address to find out where the extra minutes were purchased from?"

"Maybe, but again, a smart user can get around that by using a public computer—like one at the local library."

"Anything else?"

"Not without a lot more information about who we're looking for or where the phone was purchased and when."

"Which we don't."

"Which we don't."

"What about law enforcement? Wouldn't they have some way to get it? Then we could get it from them through discovery."

"Without something more, I don't think they can get to it any more than we can."

"But that seems impossible. This number has calls to and from Jessie almost every day—sometimes late at night. We really can't trace it with all those calls?"

"Well, we can tell that the caller is local."

"How?"

"The log of calls shows the tower location. They're all in this area."

"Why can't we go to those addresses?"

"It's not that simple. A single tower covers a pretty big area, not a specific address."

"That sucks."

"Maybe, maybe not." Zach had joined them at the table. "Maybe a mystery is more valuable to Sam."

"Come again?"

"If we *could* identify the caller, for all we know it would turn out to be her grandma or something else benign."

"But?"

"But this way, our caller is a mystery—could be anybody. Better yet, our mystery caller is local and—oh man," he said, leaning closer and pointing. "Take a look at this entry. Our caller called several times on the date of the murder, including after Jessie called Sam. And do you see what else?"

"What?" Colleton asked, peering at the screen.

"There are no calls from that number after she died—even though it wasn't until the next day that her identity was made public. It appears our mystery caller had some immediate way of knowing she wouldn't be answering anymore."

"Whoa, that could be huge."

"Even better," Zach said, sitting back in his chair with a wide grin. "That could be reasonable doubt."

It was late—after midnight—but Zach couldn't sleep. He turned and draped an arm across a lightly snoring Addie as he sorted through the day in his mind: the phone records and invoices that supported Sam's story, Addie's driving time alibi theory, and, best of all, the mystery caller who gave him a spotlight to shine on something other than Sam at trial. Abracadabra—reasonable doubt. For the first time since Eli's call in the wee hours after Sam's arrest, Zach felt a glimmer of hope.

Could it really be this easy?

CHAPTER 16

NOTHING IS EVER EASY. ADDIE GRIMACED AS SHE TURNED THE wrench a final time and sighed gratefully as the pipes under the sink finally pulled tight. She lingered for a moment to be sure the drip was gone and then crawled out from under the counter. Now came the fun part—putting everything back.

When the last of it was put away, Addie rummaged through the fridge for a Diet Coke. She bent back the tab and let the satisfying bubble and fizz trickle down her throat as she sat back at the table where she'd been working before the *drip, drip, drip* of the leak had interrupted her. She had spent hours scouring every article, blog, and chat room she could find in case there might be some new software or technical breakthrough that would give her a way to trace the mystery number. Zach might be right that the caller was more valuable to them unidentified, but that meant she needed to be sure the solicitor couldn't identify the caller either. She had phoned her brother to ask if law enforcement had come up with some new way of tracing burners. In the end, all she'd accomplished was to confirm that still wasn't possible, at least not with the limited information they had to work with so far. Their mystery caller, whoever it was, had been extremely careful. Why?

Draining the last of the soft drink, she tossed the empty can across the room for a perfect drop into the trash can. She propped her elbow on the table and rested her chin against the palm of her hand, searching for some new angle to try. What her thoughts kept wandering back to instead was what Zach had told her last night about the demonstrators at the jail yesterday. They had known this case would get a lot of unwanted attention—especially from the media hounds they knew would materialize for all the public hearings. Still, neither of them had anticipated demonstrators showing up at the jail on random days this early in the case. Zach had tried not to let it show, but she could tell he was shaken by Colleton's sense that they might be in harm's way.

Curious, she trolled through social media pages looking for photos of the crowd from the jail. Sure enough, someone had posted them. Several were of Buford Gadsden. Only now, the stony expression Zach had described from the bond hearing had been replaced by one that suggested a strong desire to hit something—or someone. Addie clicked on another photo that had captured JB. She dragged the edges of the image with her thumb and forefinger to enlarge it. She could only see the side of his face from this angle, but there was enough detail for her to translate the unveiled threat. Somehow, JB looked like more of a danger than even Jessie's father. Colleton might be overreacting a little, but she had seen enough now to convince her there was no harm in being a bit more careful.

Brain-dead from sitting in front of the computer most of the day, Addie yawned and stretched before she leaned her head back against the cushion behind her. She could hear the faint murmur of Zach's voice on the telephone—probably with Colleton—in the little office down the hall, and the steady tick of the vintage Coca-Cola wall clock. She let her mind drift.

"Addie?"

She opened her eyes to find Zach standing in front of her.

"You okay?"

"Sure—tired is all."

"It's Colleton," Zach said, gesturing at the phone. "He wants to know if we want to go to the camp for a cookout this evening. Eli will be there too. Feel like going?"

"Sure—sounds great," she said, suddenly wide awake.

"Colleton?" Zach raised the phone. "Count us in. What time?" He paused, listening. "Okay—see you in a bit."

He turned his attention back to Addie. "You sure you feel like going out, Adds? If you're too tired, I can call him back."

"Are you kidding? After all your raving about this outdoor man cave? No way am I missing this."

"He said to come on as soon as we're ready."

"Give me a few minutes to change and brush my teeth and we're out of here."

"Hey," she called a few minutes later as she spit toothpaste into the sink. "Didn't you tell me the roads to Colleton's place are dirt?"

"Yeah—the worst. Potholes the size of a VW Beetle."

"Want to take the Jeep?" she asked. "With all the rain we had yesterday, it might be messy, and the Jeep has a higher clearance."

"Yeah, that would be great if you don't mind," Zach answered from the living room.

Addie pulled on a pair of jeans and an Aerosmith T-shirt with her favorite knock-around boots and walked out of the bedroom.

"Jesus, you're beautiful."

"Flattery will get you anywhere with me."

"Counting on it." Zach turned to pull the door behind them.

"Hang on a sec."

"What's wrong?"

"Nothing," she said, as she reached back in and flipped the switch to leave the porch light on. "Can't be too careful," she added.

"Colleton would be so proud."

"Here," Addie said, tossing him the keys. "I don't know where we're going."

"You're going to let me drive your Jeep?"

"Yeah, but don't ride the clutch like you usually do."

"I get no respect . . ."

The evening had been the stuff the Lowcountry is legendary for. Colleton had conjured a pot of Frogmore stew full of sausage, sweet corn on the cob, shrimp, potatoes, and a combination of secret spices he refused to reveal despite intensive questioning. Perched near the edge of the grill—cooking slow—was a cast-iron pan of corn bread. After dinner, they had lingered to talk about the mystery caller, and Eli seemed comforted a bit by this latest news. Buck, who had been off romping through the woods, came back tired, wet, and wagging. He scarfed down the scraps Colleton had saved him and was soon snoring at Eli's feet.

There had been just enough afternoon cloud cover to keep the heat down and make for a spectacular sunset as the afternoon sounds of songbirds and cicadas gave way to the low *ooo-OOO-ooo* cooing of mourning doves. By the time they'd said their goodnights and promised again to be careful, the stars were out and a full moon hung low and heavy beyond the trees. "Watch out for deer—they're everywhere this time of year," Colleton had warned, and Addie had to stop the Jeep twice as white tails sprinted across the dirt roads.

Back at home, Addie turned into the drive and killed the engine. "Glove compartment," she said, handing him the key. "We need to take the Beretta inside. Careful—safety's on, but it's loaded."

"Anything else I can do for you, ma'am?" Zach asked, handing her the gun and closing the compartment door.

"There might be—want to come in for a nightcap?" She smiled provocatively.

"I was hoping you'd ask." Zach leaned over for a long, wet kiss.

On the porch, Addie held the screen door while Zach fumbled for the house key.

"What's wrong with this picture?" she asked.

"Absolutely nothing as far as I'm concerned," Zach said. Then he followed her gaze to the porch light. "Odd, I could have sworn you turned that on before we left."

"I did." Addie reached up and gave the lightbulb a quick twist to the right, and a bright light shone across the porch and out into the yard.

"That bulb didn't unscrew itself," she whispered as she instinctively removed the safety on the gun in her hand. Her thoughts jumped to JB's threatening scowl and Colleton's warning.

"How do you want to play this?" Zach asked. "We can leave now and go ask for some help."

"And tell them what—our porch light was out? Don't be lame. But, if there is anybody hanging around, they know we're here, and we don't know where they are. Let's get our asses inside."

Zach opened the door and bolted it closed behind them once they were in. Addie switched on a table lamp and sighed as light flooded the empty room. The house was quiet, and nothing looked out of place. She put the gun on the coffee table.

"Maybe we're a little on edge from listening to Colleton harp about danger. It looks like everything is fine," Zach said.

"Yeah, I'm sure that's all it is."

The crash from the direction of the kitchen shut them both up. It was followed by a muffled bumping sound. "Does it sound to you like someone is trying to get in the back door?" Zach picked up the Beretta and questioned her with his eyes. She nodded and followed him toward the kitchen.

The bumping noise again, but it was nowhere near the door. The window over the sink, maybe? Addie moved closer to the noise and peered out the window. "Nothing out there." Another bump. "It sounds like it's right here." She opened a cabinet and let out a startled scream as something shot past her, barely missing her face. They both turned to see Elvis tear a stunning black streak out of the kitchen.

Addie dropped to the kitchen floor, laughing uncontrollably. "There you have it, Clue fans. It was Professor Elvis in the kitchen with the wrench."

"How would he even get in there?"

"I guess he crawled in after I finished fixing that leak under the sink." She closed her eyes, feeling the cool of the floor against her back.

"About that nightcap you were teasing me with earlier . . ." Zach sat beside her, admiring the way her hair spilled all around her on the floor. He held out one of the two bottles he'd taken from the refrigerator. "Join me?"

"Don't mind if I do." She propped up on one forearm, took a long pull, and let out the first easy breath she'd had since they'd first noticed the porch light.

"The porch light," Zach said, remembering it at the same time. "Elvis couldn't have done that."

"You're right about that."

"Maybe we scared off whoever it was with the headlights or when you tightened the bulb and flooded the yard with light. For that matter, it could have been some neighborhood kids playing a prank. Whoever it was, there doesn't seem to be anybody around now."

"No, thank goodness—we've certainly had enough excitement for one night."

"Hmm. I'm not so sure about that." Zach eased down beside her and nuzzled her neck, his lips moving to her mouth. Addie slid her arms around his neck and returned his kiss, at first soft, then hungry. Zach's weight shifted as he gently moved on top of her, and her body melded into his as his hand slipped underneath the hem of her shirt and moved upward. All was right with the world.

Right up until the brick shattered the window, raining shards of glass all around them.

CHAPTER 17

ZACH SWEPT THE LAST OF THE GLASS SHARDS INTO THE TRASH AS the morning sun filtered through the windowpanes—at least the ones that weren't covered with plastic and duct tape. The officers had been nearby and were there within seconds after the call last night. They searched the surrounding yards but found nothing. Both officers had been sympathetic, but there wasn't much they could do after the fact, especially since he and Addie hadn't seen anything that might help identify who'd done this. Officer Mixon had explained that it usually wasn't possible to lift fingerprints from a brick because of the rough, porous surface, but Zach and Addie already knew that. Some of the bloodred paint that had been used to scrawl *N-LOVR* along one side of the brick had smudges, but they didn't look like prints. Unless they identified a suspect who happened to have the same red paint in his garage, Officer Mixon said that wasn't likely to be helpful either.

When Mixon had asked if they had any idea who might have done it, Zach mentioned JB Beaman having been with demonstrators at the jail. "If that dirtbag is involved, he'll have an alibi in the form of a half dozen buddies who'll swear they were together all night," had been Mixon's immediate reply. The officers had offered their cards, but little hope that they'd be able to give them any answers.

"Want to walk next door with me to ask if Karen or Mark saw anything?" Zach put the broom away and turned to Addie, who was contemplating something within the seemingly infinite depths of her coffee cup. She was trying to act like this was just another day at the office, but he could tell she was shaken. She'd tossed and turned all night, and this morning she was quiet. Addie Stone was rarely quiet.

"Couldn't hurt," she finally answered, rubbing her eyes. "I've been meaning to get over there anyway—I still have Karen's casserole dish. Give me a minute to put on some shoes."

Karen answered their knock, wiping her hands on a kitchen towel, a fine mist of sweat already on her forehead. "Sorry, I was finishing up the breakfast dishes. You two okay? I mean—after last night?" she asked.

"I take it you heard about our excitement?" Zach said.

"Tiffany Sanders's husband is a cop—works night shift. She called her sister, Janet Monroe, this morning to tell her all about it. Janet and I do volunteer work together over at the Victory House senior center—you know, the one for veterans—and so Janet called me right after."

"Well, that was fast and efficient," Addie remarked.

"Hard to keep a secret in a small town." Karen smiled. "Were either of you hurt?"

"A few little cuts and scrapes from the glass, but we're fine," Addie said, shaking her head.

"At least that's good."

"Addie and I were wondering if maybe you and Mark saw anything or heard anything that might help identify who did this. Even if it seems small, it might help," Zach said.

"We were home, but that movie *Forsaken* finally came on TV. You know, the one with Kiefer and Donald Sutherland? Kiefer is a gunfighter who goes home to make peace with his father and finds more trouble instead. Mark's been wanting to see it. Says it's because both of the Sutherlands are in it together, but I suspect it had more to do with Demi Moore," she added. "Anyway, we were glued to the screen and wouldn't have heard anything over the gunfighting scenes. I'm afraid we didn't even realize anything had happened until the phone started ringing this morning. I take it you two didn't see whoever it was? No car or anything?"

"No. We could hear them running away from the house, but they were running back toward the houses behind us, like they were going through to Hampton Street. If there was a vehicle, they left it on that street so we wouldn't see it."

"They? You think it was more than one person?" Karen looked pale. She was twisting the dish towel in her hand.

"Definitely more than one set of feet running after the brick came through the window. Maybe two or three, but we're not sure."

"Good lord, that's awful. I hate to think we have one person running around doing something like this—much less two or three." She paused a minute before adding, "I heard there was something nasty painted on the brick. Something like N-LOVR. That true?"

"It is." Zach paused, not able to think of anything useful to say about that and letting the subject drop. "Are you sure you didn't see or hear anything?"

"I'm so sorry, I wish we could help. We hate that this happened," she said, and her voice trailed off as she looked at each of them. Then her eyes fell on the dish in Addie's hand.

"Oh, my casserole dish," she said with a smile. "How nice of you to return it."

"Sorry I didn't do it sooner. Thanks again for bringing us dinner that night—we were dog-tired from moving, and it was so thoughtful of you. Zach and I were hoping you might let us return the favor. Would you and Mark and the boys like to join us for dinner tonight? Nothing fancy, but it would give you a night off from the kitchen."

"That's very nice of you, but it's not necessary," Karen answered quickly.

"Please—it's no trouble."

"Um, we really can't."

"Another night this week, maybe?"

"I don't think so. Look, Addie." Karen shifted awkwardly on her feet. "I don't know how to say this without sounding like a terrible person, but—" She paused and looked around as though she were worried someone might be watching them. "You and Zach are only here for a while—you'll leave after this trial and go back to Charleston, and it won't matter anymore what might have happened here. But Mark and I have lived in this little town all our lives. It may not seem like much to you, but it's all we've ever known. It's home. Mark has worked for the same company since high school, and the boys go to school here and"—she stopped, big round tears sliding down her cheeks now—"it's just that—"

"It's just that you don't want a brick through your window too, or worse," Addie said, nodding. "It's okay. We understand."

"Thank you," Karen said, blotting at one cheek with her dish towel. "I wish there were something more we could do."

"Would you mind keeping your outside lights on at night for a while?" Zach asked, trying to steer things to something less upsetting for Karen.

"That we can absolutely do." She seemed relieved to be able to say yes to something.

"And maybe you could recommend a good carpenter to repair a window?" Addie asked.

"Try Joe Rogers," she said. "He has a little shop behind his house over in Forest Hills. Does nice work and his prices are reasonable."

"Thanks, we'll give him a call. And we'll be sure not to tell any secrets to Tiffany Sanders or Janet Monroe if we should happen to meet them," Addie joked, remembering Karen's account of the local gossip route.

"You're for sure right about that—or that Betty Smoak either, if you don't want it hitting the street faster than a Baptist hiding a liquor bottle," Karen said, nodding.

"*Mo-om*, I can't find my lucky socks!" came a wail from somewhere in the house.

"Oh goodness, sounds like I have a crisis situation on my hands." Karen rolled her eyes and wiped the last of her tears on the dish towel. "And, heavens, this towel has to go in the wash." She sniffed and made a sour face. "Um, if you don't mind—"

"No, of course, we'll get out of your hair."

They turned to leave, and the door closed a little too quickly behind them.

Addie made it back to the house dry-eyed, but barely. Zach wrapped his arms around her and pulled her close. Her face was to his chest, so he couldn't see her tears, but he could feel the quiver in her breathing that gave her away. Then came the sniffling. He rocked slightly from side to side and waited while she got it out.

"Want to talk about it?" he asked when she was finally still and quiet.

"I guess," she said, pulling out a chair. Zach pulled another chair close so they were face-to-face, knees touching.

"I responded to some horrific scenes when I was with the sheriff's office," she said, "and some of the cases you and I have worked on together had facts that were hard to grapple with. This is one stupid brick, but somehow it seems worse."

"Closer to home?" Zach prompted.

"Exactly. It wasn't that I didn't feel sympathy for the victims at those scenes—I did, and it was real. But I always got to go home after the bad stuff, back to a place I felt safe. Now . . . now my safe place doesn't feel safe. It's bad enough that some stranger out there hates us but now even the neighbors are scared to be seen with us."

"I feel it too, Adds." He pulled her hand to his lips and kissed it before taking it in both of his. "And it wasn't just a brick. It was the hate that was painted on it and the hate that crept through the dark and hurled through our window. That kind of hate doesn't grow out of anything rational. And what's scaring the hell out of me is that same hate is going to be slithering around in the courtroom—maybe even in the jury box—during Sam's trial. It's the same shadowy hate lurking around so many corners that Eli has had to deal with all his life. It's hard for me to even wrap my head around what that must feel like."

"I know, and it becomes a vicious cycle as the hated become the haters. I found some photos on social media of the demonstrators at the jail. There was anger and ugliness coming from both directions. And here we are, sticking ourselves right smack dab in the middle," she said, staring at the ugly scar of plastic and duct tape on the window.

"You mean *I* stuck us right here in the middle."

"No. I said what I meant." She pulled her hand away and wiped her face. "I'm the one who pushed you to take this on. And for the right reasons. There will always be good and bad, right and wrong on both sides, and racists come in all colors. But justice is worth standing up for. You have a gift, and you—*we*—will never have another moment's peace if you don't use it to help Sam. Even if it means we end up with a brick through every window in this house and not a soul wants anything to do with us."

"There's the fighter I fell in love with." Zach grinned. "Now, what do you say we go do something about it?"

"What did you have in mind?" Her sniffles were mostly gone now.

"I'm thinking I want to drive out to Cicada Road and have a good look around that old church. Will you come with me?"

"I dare anybody to try and stop me."

The old church was nestled in a sunny clearing, its white clapboard exterior bright against the shadowy grays and greens of the heavily wooded land behind it. The portico was topped by a modest pediment and bell tower with a cross pointing to the sky. A row of palmetto trees marched down each side of the small structure. Their size suggested they were planted long after the church was built, but otherwise, the church appeared to have stepped out of time.

Zach and Addie stood in front of the car as the ticks and hisses of the warm engine slowed to a stop, leaving a chorus of wild birds broadcasting their arrival. To the left, the dirt drive morphed into a makeshift parking area. To the right was a small cemetery enclosed by a picket fence—with more than a few of its pickets leaning or altogether gone.

"Wonder if it's open," Zach said, eyeing the church's arched wooden door.

"I'll bet he knows," Addie answered. She was watching a lone figure in the cemetery tossing pulled weeds and abandoned flower-pots into a wheelbarrow. As if he'd heard them, the man looked up and waved his arm as he began walking with long confident strides in their direction. They met him at the small gate.

"Sorry to disturb you. Are you the caretaker here?" Addie asked.

"Well, I suppose that's as good a way to describe it as any. I'm Benjamin Gatch, the pastor here—caretaker of grounds, graves, and souls, both lost and found—at your service," he said, extending his hand with an open smile that ushered welcoming crinkles to the corners of his dark eyes.

"I apologize, Pastor Gatch," Addie said, feeling her face grow hot.

"No need, child. And most folks here call me Pastor Ben—at least the ones who don't call me Preacher. We don't stand on formality around here. Ours is a small congregation, so we all pitch in at whatever needs doing. That includes me, as you can see. I try to get out to tend the graves as often as possible. How can I help y'all this morning?" he asked, turning to Zach with unmasked curiosity.

"We were hoping we might be able to see the sanctuary."

"Always happy to share our beautiful piece of history. Please, join me." Curiosity was still painted on his face, but he let it be for the moment, and they followed him to the oversized arched doorway and waited as he dug an impressive ring of keys from a pocket and unlocked the door. "After you," he said. He watched as Zach and Addie entered the small sanctuary and he laughed out loud as both of their heads immediately popped upward.

"Everyone does that the first time they come here," he said. "That's the beauty of the design. The room is not large, but the vaulted ceiling and the lancet windows with their long lines and pointed arches lead the gaze straight up every time. Sort of forces us to acknowledge the heavens," he said.

"May I?" Addie asked, gesturing to the wooden pew beside her.

"Of course. Please."

She sat and leaned back to take in the room. The stark interior emanated a solemn dignity and a quiet strength grown deeper over time. A peacefulness that felt transferable.

"The church dates back to the late 1800s," the pastor filled in the silence. "It was built by freedmen and was one of the first places of worship in this area that was built and owned entirely by emancipated Blacks. Those exposed beams you see in the ceiling are original to the structure as are most of the heart pine floorboards. The window openings are part of the original design, but the patterned leaded glass was added later as the membership was able to afford a few more material things. The church has changed denominations numerous times over the years as some congregations thrived and moved when they outgrew the sanctuary and others dwindled away. This old church has housed Pentecostals, AME, Baptists like us, and a few others who, over the centuries, have called it home. Regardless of denomination, there has been an active congregation here consistently since the building was erected. I grew up not far from here, and I've been pastor here for nearly thirty years now—back when this was black instead of white," he added, rubbing his wiry hair. He paused to let them reflect on the church's history.

"Do you mind if I ask what brings you here?" he asked. "I don't believe I've seen either of you here before, but you," he said, turning to Zach again, "you look familiar."

"Sorry—I clean forgot my manners." Zach reached his hand toward their host. "Zach Stander," he said, "and this is Addie Stone. If I look familiar, you may have had the misfortune of seeing my photo in the newspaper. I'm the lawyer representing—"

"Representing Sam Jenkins," Pastor Ben finished for him. "Now it makes sense. I've known Eli for many years. I tried more than a few times to convince him to join us at church, but Eli made it crystal clear that he was more at home talking to God in a field." Pastor Ben shrugged and smiled. "Over time, you learn to accept some things you cannot change." He sat down heavily as if suddenly very tired. "How are they doing?"

"About as well as could be expected, I guess. It's hard on both of them," Zach answered.

"I wasn't close to Sam by any means, but I watched him grow up, and I know the character of the man who raised him. What I know of him doesn't align with what happened to Jessie Gadsden. I can't bring myself to believe he could be capable of such a thing."

"Neither can I," Zach said.

"The thing that puzzles me most, though, is that Sam was here. I know why Jessie was here, but why in the world would Sam have been out here at that time of night—or at all for that matter?"

Zach shoved his hands in the pockets of his jeans and cleared his throat. "I know you want to help, but I can't discuss the details of Sam's defense. I can only tell you that we're working hard on it."

"I understand. In my line of work, I often have to keep secrets too. Sometimes they can be heavy to carry."

Zach nodded in agreement. "Right now, we're trying to piece together what happened, and hoping to find something that will help us uncover the truth."

"Uncovering the truth can be . . . ," Pastor Ben let his words trail off, as though he'd thought better of it. "Is there anything I can do to be of help?"

"There might be," Addie started and then stopped cold, her eyes fixed on the altar. "Is that . . . ?"

"No, no," he assured her. "The authorities still have our altar cross. That was loaned to us as a kindness by one of the larger churches in town, though it's virtually identical to the one used to . . . well, to ours. The only visible reminder now is a small stain in the floorboards near the altar that we couldn't quite get out. But that isn't what you wanted to ask me," he prompted.

"No, you're right," she said, tearing her eyes from the altar. "We were hoping you could tell us a little about Jessie Gadsden."

"Jessie? I didn't know her before she came to work on our projects, but coordinating with her to design and launch our social media ministry was a project I handled myself, and I came to know her fairly well. She was raised in the Episcopal church and addressed me as Father her first day here. When I explained that Baptists don't address clergy that way, she took to calling me Padre. I have no idea why," he laughed, "but it stuck."

Something pinged in the back of Addie's mind.

"To determine what we needed from social media, Jessie had to learn a lot about us, and she had a gift for that. She was engaging and curious, and she used snippets of information about herself to draw out details about us. I came to feel we were friends, but she was an enigma—a perplexing juxtaposition of contradictions," he said with a befuddled shake of his head. "She grew up the only girl in the family with a passel of brothers. She was something of a beauty, and I had the sense her father would have been perfectly happy to let her play the little princess, but she was determined to out-boy the boys. She had to shoot better, bag the biggest buck of the season, catch the biggest fish . . . you get the picture. She worked relentlessly to build a successful business, yet she came here to clean this old sanctuary twice a month for pennies—and she apparently didn't think I'd notice that an anonymous monthly offering more or less matched what little we paid her. She could be kind in surprising ways like that. But she was also headstrong and ambitious, and if something got in her way, I suspect she would push back. Hard. In the days since her murder, I've wondered if maybe she pushed something—or someone—a little too far."

"Is there anything specific you can point to?" Addie asked.

"No. Just sort of a sense for these things after a lifetime of trying to help others find their way in the world." He stopped talking and looked down at his hands. It seemed the subject of Jessie's personality was closed.

"Do you know if she had a boyfriend?"

"I had the impression she had a lot of casual friends, but not many close ones. She never mentioned a boyfriend."

"Did she have a set time to come and clean?" Zach asked.

"Usually Tuesdays. I know she always came after her regular business hours, so it would generally be evening, but I don't know if that would always have been the same time. Althea Jefferson might know if she did—Althea does some paperwork and administrative things for the church. I can see if she knows, if that would help."

"That would be great," Zach said, handing him a card. "Is there anyone else who knew she'd be here that night?"

"Well, most of the congregation knew she was cleaning for us, but I don't know of anyone other than Althea who'd have any reason to know when."

"Any chance you were here and saw what time she arrived that night?"

"No," he said, shaking his head. "As I told the authorities, I was here for a short while that morning but worked the rest of the day in the office at the parsonage. Sorry I'm not more help."

"When did you talk with the officers? Was it that night?"

"No, it was the next morning."

"Do you mind me asking what you talked about?"

"Obviously, they had questions—mostly the same questions you're asking now. And they wanted to know if I knew why Sam would be here or of any connection between him and Jessie. They also asked if I had any idea who might have done such a thing to her. The answer to all three is no."

"Do you know who owns that wooded land behind the church?" Addie asked, shifting subjects.

"The church owns it—but only because it isn't worth selling," he said. "The woodland only extends for the first ten yards or so, then it sinks into swampland—no good for building or farming. The gators seem to like it, though—every now and then one wanders into our little clearing for some sun. Gets some of my parishioners stepping a little livelier on the way into church than they usually do," he added, those merry crinkles coming back to his eyes.

"Is the parsonage here on the property?" Addie asked.

"No, it's the next structure you come to along this highway, but it's a little over a mile down the road. I live there alone, and it has a small office with a separate entrance that we use for church business."

"A mile toward town?"

"No—away. The only other building on this property is an old shed out back."

Zach vaguely recalled that Captain Chambers had testified about searching a shed. "What is the shed used for?" he asked.

"Mostly tools and such—like the wheelbarrow I was using in the cemetery. Which, by the way, I should be getting back to if there's nothing else you need."

"No, thanks for your time, though. Would it be okay if we hung around a few minutes to take some photos and some measurements?" Zach asked.

"That will be fine. I'll lock up after you're gone. I'll be outside if you need anything."

"Oh, one more thing?" Zach called back as he headed for the door.

"Yes?"

"Did you find anything Sam or Jessie might have left behind?"

"You mean like personal belongings?" He seemed confused by the question.

"Maybe, or anything that didn't belong here."

"No, I assume the police took all of that when they left."

"I was wondering if you found anything they might have missed."

"No, nothing." He stepped abruptly out into the late-morning sunlight, and the door closed behind him.

"I see now why Jessie loved this place so much," Addie said, looking around the sanctuary again. "What was it Sam said to you? Something about it being worse that it happened in a place she loved and felt safe?"

"We still talking about Jessie, or you now?" Zach asked.

"Both, I guess," she said, getting up and walking to the front of the church to take some photos. Then she used an app on her phone to take a few measurements. She turned back toward him and studied the room intently, arms crossed, head to the side. "These windows," she said finally.

"Mm-hmm?" Zach looked up from the back of the room where he was taking more photos. "You don't see clear leaded glass as often as stained in churches. Beautiful, aren't they?"

"No—I mean yes, they're lovely, but that's not what I meant. What I mean is there are so many of them—they let in an incredible amount of light, and they line the whole place so that light comes from every direction."

"And your point?" Zach smiled as he watched her slip into her zone.

"If Jessie called Sam at 8:38, it would have been almost dark then, and she was still fine. She obviously had time to set up and start cleaning, so by the time of the attack, it likely would have been full dark."

"And?"

"And Pastor Ben told us there is nothing along this road going in the direction of the parsonage for over a mile. We drove in from the other direction, and it was at least that far back to the last struc-ture we saw, maybe farther. That leaves only the land behind the church, and it's nothing but uninhabited swampland. Whoever attacked Jessie had to come by car, and as dark as it gets out here in the boonies, that would have been next to impossible without using headlights, probably the brights. Any headlights turning in here—or even approaching—would have been unmistakable through these windows. Jessie would have to have known someone was coming—meaning they couldn't have slipped up on her. Given what Pastor Ben told us about her, doesn't it seem likely she would have been on her guard and ready to fend for herself?"

"Maybe she thought it was Sam. She knew he was coming, so what reason would she have to be alarmed?"

"Or maybe"—her words were tumbling fast with excitement now—"she never saw any headlights to warn her. Maybe there were never any headlights to see."

"That doesn't exactly fit with your theory about the dark roads and the windows. Tell me what you're thinking, Adds."

"I'm thinking we need to go out back and take a close look at that shed."

CHAPTER 18

THE AIR IN THE OLD SHED WAS COOLER, AND IT HELD THE FAINT smell of gasoline melded with the earthy smell of a dirt floor and wood siding that stayed perpetually damp with humidity. They stood motionless just inside the door. The structure was larger than Zach had expected, maybe fifteen by twenty, with an oversized barn door that had opened easily when he pulled. There were windows, but Zach's eyes were adjusted to the bright daylight. He pulled on the cord strung from a single bare lightbulb to the door, and a yellow light filled the space, revealing dust-laden spiderwebs hanging above them. The center of the shed floor was clear, as if maybe it were meant to store a tractor for mowing.

There wasn't much of anything in the shed. To their right were shelves of flowerpots salvaged from graves and littered with remnants of faded ribbon. They were waiting to be recycled the next holiday or anniversary by some loved one left behind, and they struck Zach as both sad and hopeful at the same time. To the left, a rusty lawn mower sat in the corner next to the door alongside a gas can. The rest of that wall was lined with gardening and groundskeeping tools of various types, and an empty spot about the size of a wheelbarrow. The back wall was bare other than a few plastic storage boxes stacked one atop the other.

"Wait!" Zach reached for Addie's arm as she started to step farther into the shed.

"Worried about alligators and snakes?" she teased.

"No. Look closely for a minute. What do you see?" Zach asked, gesturing to the dirt floor and using the flashlight on his phone to point. There was a single set of footprints leading from the door to the empty space on the left wall. Then the footprints made a sort of three-point turn and came back to the door—only with a single tire tread as well.

"No big mystery there, Zach. Those tracks were made by Pastor Ben this morning. The empty space along the wall had to have been where the wheelbarrow was, and that single tire track is the front wheel of the wheelbarrow as he pushed it back to the door and out to the graveyard."

"Right," Zach said, feeling his pulse quicken. "Now—look straight down and behind you and tell me what you see."

"Eureka," she deadpanned, rolling her eyes, "you've discovered our own footprints from walking in the door. Anything else, Sherlock?"

"No. Nothing—nothing at all. That's the point, Addie. Look again—there are no other footprints or tire tracks or drag marks or anything else in the whole shed. Someone"—he paused to let it sink in—"someone has swept this floor clean, and fairly recently. We know these tracks here are Pastor Ben's from this morning. We need to know when he was here last. If it was before the night of the murder, someone else had to have been here in between. And that someone—"

"Maybe didn't want anyone to know they'd been here?"

"You got it. We need to find out if Pastor Ben can give us an exact date for when he was last here."

"Even if he knows when he was here last, for all we know, a parishioner could have come out to work on the grounds after that. Pastor Ben said they all pitched in," Addie pointed out.

"You're thinking a parishioner swept the dirt floor before they left?"

"A very neat parishioner?"

"Very funny. A neat freak who left all those spiderwebs?"

"You got me. So, where does our theory go from there?" Addie asked.

"Maybe someone else knew Jessie was coming to the church that night. That someone else could have arrived before Jessie did and pulled their car into this shed—there's more than enough room for a vehicle—and waited. After Jessie got settled in the church and began her cleaning, our someone crept around to the door, entered without warning, and attacked her."

"And how does that help us—couldn't they argue that was Sam?" Addie said.

"No. For starters, Sam pulled in and parked his truck in the parking area on the side of the church next to Jessie's car—not the shed. Captain Chambers testified at the prelim that's where they found it."

"He could have moved it before he called for help."

"With all that blood on him? No way. It would have been all over the seat of the truck," Zach said, shaking his head, "probably the door and the steering wheel too. And if the video evidence can establish it was Sam who left the office and set the alarm at 10:16, he couldn't have gotten here before she did and hidden his car in the shed." Zach squatted and took photos of the tracks on the floor.

"So how do we find our someone who parked in the shed?"

"Not sure yet," he said, "but I'm wondering if it could be related to our mystery caller with the burner phone, and I'm thinking our jurors might wonder that, too."

"What's going on here?" a sharp voice demanded. Startled, Addie gasped and grabbed for Zach as they spun to find themselves in the shadow of Pastor Ben standing in the doorway. The light behind him made it difficult to read his expression, but Zach could see enough to know there were no merry crinkles around his eyes.

"Oh shit, you scared me," Addie said and immediately put her hand to her mouth. "Sorry, Pastor, we didn't know you were standing there."

"That much was obvious. I understand why you needed to see the church, but what does the shed have to do with Sam's case?" He seemed perturbed.

"Maybe nothing," Zach said, "but you never know when something that seems insignificant can be the tiny piece of the puzzle that pulls the bigger parts together—or that the solicitor uses to pull them apart. With Sam's life on the line here, we can't afford to overlook anything."

"I didn't mean to bark at you like that." Pastor Ben's tone was more even now. "But we've had more than our share of thrill-seekers and curious idiots since the . . . incident. So far, the morbid interest has been focused on the sanctuary where it happened, and no one's made it back here as far as I know—we started leaving it padlocked after the murder. When I heard voices coming from the shed, I'm afraid I jumped to conclusions."

"No, not at all," Zach said, "you're right—we should have asked."

"So, the shed would have been unlocked the night of the murder?" Addie asked, catching Zach's eye.

"Yes. Until that night, it was always unlocked in case someone wanted a planter or something for one of the graves."

"Did the officers on scene come back here to the shed?" Zach said.

"I don't know. I would suppose so—they had the run of the place for a day or so, but I certainly didn't see them back here."

"And they didn't ask you anything about the shed?"

"No. Why would they? Jessie was murdered in the church."

"Pastor Ben, you were working in the cemetery when we drove up. Do you remember the last time you were working out there?" Zach asked. "And would you have come in the shed that day?"

"Ordinarily, I probably wouldn't recall, but this time it's easy. The last time I was clearing out the cemetery was Tuesday, July eleventh, the day Jessie was killed. I told the deputies the same thing I told you—I was here for a while early that morning, and then worked the rest of the day at the parsonage. And yes, I was in and out of the shed several times that morning. We don't keep tools anywhere else. I came in to get the wheelbarrow and I brought it back in. I stacked the flowerpots and containers against that wall to the right, and I put the wheelbarrow back in that space on the left before I went home—which is exactly where I found it this morning. I probably would have pulled a few hand tools from that wall and then hung them back later, but I'm not sure which tools I used that day."

"And you haven't been in the shed since then?" Zach asked again.

"No. I unlocked it when I arrived this morning."

"But that's been more than two weeks, and the grass in the clearing looks like it has been cut since then." Addie cocked her head as she considered that.

"Oh, I don't cut the grass. One of our members has a lawncare business. He cuts the grass as part of his gift to the church."

"Using that?" Addie asked, pointing to the rusty lawn mower in the corner.

"Heavens no," he laughed. "I doubt that relic even starts anymore. Joe brings over a riding mower and equipment he uses in his business—he wouldn't have any reason to come back here. But I'm confused. What in the world does any of this have to do with Jessie or Sam?"

"Pastor Ben, we were surmising that those footprints to the wall and back are yours from this morning. Can you confirm that?" Zach was zeroing in for the prize.

"Yes. I store the wheelbarrow along that wall—that's the tire track from where I wheeled it out this morning. Why?"

"How often do you sweep this floor?"

"Do I what? It's a dirt floor. Why would I sweep a dirt floor? Why would anybody sweep a—" He stopped midsentence as he looked down. "Holy cow," he said, staring dumbfounded. "Someone has swept this floor."

"When did you first padlock the shed?" Zach asked, working to keep the excitement out of his voice.

"The day after the incident—as soon as the sheriff's office let me know they were finished with everything. I locked the shed, the fence to the graveyard, and the sanctuary to keep out vandals and busybodies who might be curious after the murder."

"And they've been locked since then?"

"Yes, Zach, they've been locked ever since."

"Who else has a key?"

"There are several members who have keys to the church and the cemetery, but I have the only key to this new lock on the shed. And I haven't been in here since that morning. No one has." He paused and looked around as though he suddenly found himself in a foreign land and couldn't read the signage. "What do you think this means?" he asked finally.

"We're not sure, Pastor. We have some ideas, but we can't go into it."

"I understand," he said, still looking befuddled.

"I apologize for repeating the same questions, but I have to be sure. Are you certain the investigating officers never asked you any of these questions?"

"Positive. They never even mentioned the shed, and we talked for maybe thirty minutes."

"I obviously cannot tell you who to talk or not talk to, but would you mind keeping this to yourself for now?" Zach held his breath, hoping for the right response.

"Is that legal? What if the sheriff's office or the solicitor asks me?"

"Neither of them can compel you to talk with them. If they ask to interview you, you are within your rights to decline."

"What if they ask me why?"

"You don't have to answer that. But if you decide to talk to them you can't lie about it, and we would never ask you to," Zach said.

"Will it help Sam if I decline to be interviewed again?"

"It might."

"Can it hurt him?

"No."

"Fair enough then. I'll do what I can. Is it okay for me to keep using the shed in the meantime?"

"Yes—the sheriff's office has cleared the scene, and Addie and I took a lot of photos of the floor."

"Maybe I should take a few now too? Would that be a good idea?"

"Sure. It would be good to have another source just in case. And please don't throw away anything that is in here now. You never know what might end up being important."

"Have you seen everything you need to see now?" Pastor Ben asked as he pulled a phone from his pocket and began to take photos. There was a tremble to his hands that Zach hadn't noticed before.

"Yes, we're done for now," Zach said. "I hope we haven't taken too much of your time."

"Not at all, I hope I've helped. Please tell Sam and Eli they are in my prayers."

"That felt productive," Addie said as she kept her eyes on the odometer. She was clocking the distance from the church to the nearest structure as they drove toward town. "Can you use what we found in the shed in court?"

"I think so," Zach answered. "We can call the pastor as a witness. He would be allowed to identify the shed and walk through the sequence of facts he knows firsthand. That sequence shows that the floor was swept clean the day of the murder sometime between noon when he put the wheelbarrow away and the time the sheriff's office took control of the scene after Jessie was killed. We have the crime scene reports as evidence of what time that would have been. That's a tight window of time, and it seems too close not to be related. What I've been wondering, though, is why the deputies didn't go in there? If they had, their tracks would have been everywhere. You were a cop—what's your take on that?"

"The night of the murder is easy to explain. Their focus in searching would have been to see if anyone was still on the property. As soon as they opened the door, they would have seen that pull with their flashlights and turned the overhead light on like we did. The shed is empty enough that they would have seen it was empty without going in and trampling all over the floor. Once they saw the shed was empty, they would have moved on to the rest of the property before any more time lapsed that would have allowed someone to escape. After that, they would have been focused on the sanctuary. As for why they didn't go in the following day while they still had the scene, your guess is as good as mine. They had a shitload of blood splatters to follow and photograph from all kinds of angles and that would have taken a lot of time and manpower. Or maybe they had dogs working the scene. If the dogs didn't find any scent of Sam or Jessie going anywhere other than the sanctuary, that would have limited their focus to the sanctuary. For that matter, I'm not sure we would have noticed the floor if it were still swept entirely clean—the single set of tracks from this morning stick out like a sore thumb and made us notice there should have been more."

"I guess that all makes sense," Zach said.

"Oh—there it is," Addie said. "Two-point-one."

"What?"

"That house on our left is the first structure we've passed since leaving the church. It's two-point-one miles from the church. Not an impossible walk to get there, but it would be dangerous in the dark, and it would be tough to walk back and be off the road before the first responders came roaring by. Some of them would have noticed a pedestrian walking around way out here."

"I guess that fits with the theory about someone coming early and hiding a vehicle in the shed."

"Mm-hmm." Addie nodded in agreement. "Oooh, I like this one," she said, turning up the radio. She leaned back against the headrest as the sound of Adele's sultry voice filtered through the speakers. Suddenly, she snapped back up.

"Padre," she said, looking at Zach. "Pastor Ben said Jessie called him Padre."

"Odd behavior," Zach said, turning down the radio, "but what about it?"

"Sam said Jessie's last words were *my father*. Padre means—"

"Father," finished Zach. "Surely you're not suggesting that Pastor Ben killed Jessie?"

"No, but maybe Jessie saw him on the property or thought he could tell Sam something about what happened that night."

"It's possible, but Sam's not even sure that's what she was saying, much less what it might mean. The pastor said she grew up in a church where clergy are called Father. For all we know, she could have believed she was talking to the pastor in a last rites kind of thing."

"Maybe." Addie turned the radio back up.

Zach was starting to feel better about Sam's chances. Damn, he hoped the video Colleton was picking up proved Sam was still in town at 10:16 that night. Between that, the mystery burner, and what they'd found at the shed, reasonable doubt seemed closer than ever. There was no denying that racial prejudice was still a threat, but Sam was a clean-cut college-educated professional with no record—not even a speeding ticket.

"At least now we know the tax records Jessie wanted Sam to pick up weren't left in the church, and we know Sam never got them—that means they have to have been in Jessie's car," Addie said, breaking his reverie.

"What if they're not?" Zach asked as he stopped for a traffic light.

"Where else could they be?"

"Maybe they don't exist at all. At the risk of sounding like a broken record, I still think Sam is hiding something."

"So you've mentioned," she said, rolling her eyes.

"Colleton picked up on it too," he insisted. "And that business records story has always sounded sketchy. Even Eli questioned it at first. What if that's not the reason Sam was at that church?" Zach turned to look at her.

"Light's green," she said as a horn blew behind them. Zach threw up a wave to the other driver and drove through the intersection.

A few blocks later Zach pulled into their driveway and killed the engine.

"So if the business records don't exist, why do you think Sam would have gone to that church that night?"

"That's what I can't figure out."

"Well, we'd better figure it out soon. There's a trial coming like a freight train."

CHAPTER 19

ADDIE SAT ON THE PORCH IN THE COOL OF THE MORNING AND drank the last of her coffee as she watched Karen carry the trash out to the bins next door. They both waved politely, but Addie knew that would be the extent of it.

It had been over three weeks since she and Zach had gone out to the old church. She'd made offer after offer to help since then, but it seemed he and Colleton didn't need her. They were at the coroner's office this morning, looking at their reports and photographs. She knew she should be grateful that Zach had the benefit of Colleton's local contacts, but she was still feeling pushed aside, not to mention bored out of her mind.

She needed something useful to do and had an idea of what that something might be, but she would need the help of her friend at the Charleston County sheriff's office. She picked up the phone from the small table beside her and put the empty mug in its place. With any luck she might catch him between appointments, she thought as she scrolled through her contacts and hit on his cell number.

"I knew it—you're calling to tell me you made a terrible mistake and you're ready to put a uniform back on," he answered when her number flashed on his phone. "Tell me I'm right."

"Not exactly," she laughed, "but I would like to make a contribution to the cause. I'm going to need some help, though. Will you do me a favor?"

"Depends. What is it you have in mind?"

Smiling, she launched into her plan and explained what she wanted. "So, can you give a girl a hand?" Addie asked when she'd laid it all out.

"I'm on it. Give me a couple hours, and I'll let you know when I hear."

"Thank you so much. You know I think you're the absolute best, right?"

"I get that from women a lot," he said with a grin she could hear over the phone, and the call went dead.

Not more than an hour later, she heard the *ping* and saw the text:

10 this am. Cpt Wms. Say I sent u

I owe u

No shit

"Addie Stone," she said through the slat in the window at the front desk, "here for a ten o'clock appointment with Captain Williams."

"Sure. If you'll have a seat over there," the receptionist said. "I'll let someone know you're here."

"Thanks."

Addie settled into one of the burgundy chairs, picked up a newsletter, and skimmed through the recaps of community events. Looked like they stayed busy.

"Ms. Stone?" The deputy looked at her curiously.

"Yes?"

"If you'll come with me, I'll take you back now."

Addie followed the deputy down a short hall to an office door where he stopped and knocked softly.

"Yeah," a voice called through. The deputy opened the door, nodded to signal Addie to enter, then silently stepped away, closing the door behind him.

"Yes, I heard you, I just don't happen to agree with you." Captain Williams was speaking to someone on the phone and gestured for Addie to take a seat.

Sitting quietly, Addie glanced around the room at the various photos and clues into the character of the woman in front of her. Kate Williams was probably in her mid-forties guessing by the diploma dates on the wall—young to be a captain—and she could have passed for younger. She obviously knew where the gym was. Her dark hair was cut close to her head—not quite a crew cut, but bordering on it, and she had one of those angular faces with sharp cheekbones that pulled the haircut off well. There were no photos of children, but there were plenty of shots of two massive Labrador retrievers. Addie wondered briefly how tough it must have been to gain respect and rise to her rank as a Black female. Captain Williams's eyes were fixed on Addie as she listened to her caller, and Addie knew she was being sized up too.

"Sounds good—I'll talk to you then," Captain Williams said, ending her call. "Sorry about that," she said, and leaned across the desk to shake Addie's hand.

"No problem. Thank you for seeing me."

"Well, it isn't often I pick up my phone to hear the Charleston County Sheriff tell me one of his most talented former deputies is volunteering to work cold cases for free. That's a pretty impressive reference."

"Thanks. I'm a big fan of his, too. If it hadn't been for the political crap, I'd still be there. And yes, I would like to help out as a volunteer on some cold cases, but before we get too far down this road, I probably need to let you know that my fiancé is representing—"

"I know who you are," Williams interrupted. "But your sheriff assures me you are the consummate professional and will respect the boundaries we set to make sure there are no conflicts. He's right about that, I assume?" She looked at Addie expectantly.

"Of course, Captain."

"Call me Kate. And it's not like we can't use the help," she said, her voice revealing the weariness that comes from working long hours—even when you love what you're doing. Addie knew the feeling well. "We are so short-staffed right now. We have empty budgeted slots to fill, but it's getting harder and harder to find candidates who are interested in law enforcement right now. To tell the truth, I'm not sure I blame them.

"I can't remember a time it was so hard to be a cop. The high-crime neighborhoods complain that we are marginalizing them because we aren't visible enough. If we're visible, they argue we're profiling. One minute a group screams that we're not doing enough and the next minute the same group wants to defund us. Integrity and accountability are paramount, and I don't have a shred of sympathy for cops who break the law—those guys deserve what's coming to them. But a whole lot of us are out here just trying to do a good job."

"Hey," Addie said softly and leaning forward, "you're preaching to the choir here, and I want to help."

"I know, I know." Kate rubbed at her temples. "Thanks for letting me vent, though." Kate's voice trailed off for a moment. "Look, I'd love to ask you to lunch and go through all the professional niceties we enjoyed back in the good old days. But I'm stretched so thin I can see through myself. If you're ready to get started, I've got a long list of other things that are screaming for my time today too."

"Point me in the right direction."

"Okay, then." Kate looked relieved. "I've asked Records to pull a list of cold cases involving serious crimes. They put everything in a small conference room across the hall. I'll let you spend some time with that and, once you've found something you have an interest in or think you might be able to make some progress on, I'll hook you up with a deputy who knows something about the case and can get you the full file. Sound like a plan?"

"Sounds great," Addie said, standing up and smoothing her jacket.

Kate took her into the conference room. "There are some waters in the mini fridge in the corner if you need them," she said, pointing. "Otherwise, most of the materials are here on the table and the rest are in those boxes. I'm right across the hall when you're done. Anything else you need?"

Before Addie could answer, they heard the ring of a phone.

"Damn, that's mine," Kate said, tossing her hands up apologetically.

"Go—I've got this," Addie answered, already sitting down and pulling the first pile of documents toward her. She hardly heard the door close.

"Seriously?" Kate Williams's tone was incredulous. "This is what you want to work on?"

"It's a double homicide—what could be more worthy of another look?" Addie asked.

"It's a double homicide that took place thirty-four years ago—were you even born then?"

"No—not that it should matter."

"I vaguely remember this," Kate said, flipping through the first few pages of the file in front of her. "I was only eleven or twelve—probably six or seven years younger than the two girls who were killed that night—but I had siblings close to that age, and I remember all the parents freaking out. Every kid in town got stuck with early curfews and had someone watching their every move because the whole community was convinced there was a predator out there trolling for unsuspecting teenagers. It was such a strange story. It was all the news media talked about for weeks."

"And then?"

"Over time, it faded away. There were very few leads and none of them went anywhere. The consensus seemed to be that it likely was a drifter who had passed through and was gone. Eventually, life went back to normal without there ever having been any answers. Like it does all too often," she sighed.

"I doubt it went back to normal for those two families," Addie said.

"No, I'm sure you're right about that. So, what makes you think you can pick up a scent on a trail that's been cold for more than three decades?" Kate was giving her that same appraising look again, and Addie was determined to measure up.

"The last people to see them alive were teenagers at the time, probably scared to talk because they lied to their folks about where they were going that night or some other teenage bullshit. But they're not kids anymore. They're all in their early fifties now, and probably a fair percentage of them are still in the area," Addie said. "Whatever they might have remembered over the years they now see through the eyes of adults.

"Plus," she said, "if this was the act of a drifter, the same thing may have happened again somewhere else. We have access to all sorts of databases now that didn't exist back then, and new forensic tools can help connect remains that might otherwise seem unrelated."

"And you're sure this is what you want?"

"Absolutely."

"Well, at least one bit of timing went your way. The only guy still on the force who worked on the case when it was new handed in his notice to retire in three weeks. If you hadn't shown up now, you would have missed him."

"Must be my lucky day."

"I'll be interested in seeing if you still feel that way after working on this for a while," Kate said, picking up her phone. "Heather, could you please find Sergeant Bowen and send him in here ASAP? Yeah, thanks."

"Sergeant? After more than thirty years?" Addie asked.

"Yes, but not because Command Staff didn't try to promote him. He flat out refused to apply. Lee Bowen shares your disdain for the political aspects of the job, and all he wanted was to be left alone to be a cop. And he's been a good one, too. One of those guys born with a knack for it." She was interrupted by a rap on the frame of the open door.

"Yo, Cappy, you looking for me?" Then he spotted Addie. "Oh, excuse me, I didn't realize you had company. I thought Heather said you were looking for me."

"I am. What are you doing right now?"

"Well, I was planning to go to lunch. I mean, you didn't expect me to do any real work these last few weeks, did you?"

"Relax, Lee. You're still going to lunch—only now you have company. Lee Bowen—Addie Stone," Kate said, introducing them. Lee's confusion was obvious. "Addie's about to become your new best friend, Lee. She's reopening the old Edisto Beach double homicide."

The initial shock that flashed across his face was quickly replaced by a grin. "For that, I'm even buying."

CHAPTER 20

"What'll it be, folks?" the waitress asked as she put down the two sweet teas and placed paper-wrapped straws beside them on the checkered plastic tablecloth.

"I'll have the blue plate special," Lee said. "Addie?"

"What's good here?" she asked, looking up at the menu written in colored chalk on a blackboard.

"It's all good," Lee said, "but if you order anything other than the blue plate special, you'll probably regret it when you see mine," he warned her.

"That so?"

"Oh, yeah. Miss Tess can cook up a storm and nothing she fixes is bad, but when you let her choose whatever she happens to be inspired by at the moment, that's not mere food, it's an experience."

Addie looked at the waitress, who nodded enthusiastically.

"Make that two, then," she said. Addie had ridden with Lee in his cruiser and had already decided that she liked him before they ever sat down at the table. Kate had been right, of course; he came across as a cop's cop who just wanted to do his job.

"Not that it's any of my business . . . ," Addie said after the waitress left with their order.

"But?" His grin suggested he knew that wouldn't stop her.

"But you seem a little young to be retiring. For that matter, you seem a little young to have been working a case this big thirty-four years ago."

He laughed. "Thanks, I think. After high school, I got a two-year degree in criminal justice from Carolina, then I came straight here to the sheriff's office at age twenty-one. They sent me to CJA—the police academy—and then out on patrol. That first summer they assigned me to the beach—probably because I was only a few years older than most of the kids they expected me to keep out of trouble."

"So, why'd they give you such a big case?"

"Didn't—they put a senior sergeant on it, but I was assigned to work with him since I was working the beach and knew some of the kids who hung out here. He was all hyped up about it at first—liked the attention that came with a big case. But when the case dragged on for weeks and then months with no leads, he started pushing more of it my way until I finally ended up handling it mostly on my own and reporting to him."

"That explains why you got to work on a big case so early, but why retire now?"

"Under the state retirement system for police—PORS—officers who've been in the system as long as I have only need twenty-five years of service or to be fifty-five for full retirement. I hit the twenty-five-year mark years ago but wasn't ready to give it up. Last month I had my fifty-fifth birthday, and I decided this was a good time to hang up my spurs. Maybe see what else I might like to do for a while."

"Aren't you worried you'll miss it?" she asked.

"No. I've loved it, but I'm getting too burned out to do this anymore. I'm grateful for every kid we were able to bring home safe, and I'm glad we could at least bring closure to some families when we couldn't, but I'm tired of chasing bad guys. Besides, it's become so demoralizing lately. We can't seem to please anybody on any side of things, and I decided I've had enough."

Addie nodded, remembering Kate expressing some of the same frustration. And they were right—this was a hard time to be a cop.

"This case, though . . . they say every career cop has one he can't let go of. One that follows him around and haunts his dreams. This was that case for me. I worked on it day and night from the beginning. They finally made me move on when it became clear we were getting nowhere. Still, I'd drag it back out whenever I had some time to spare or saw something I thought might possibly be related. After all these years, I still think about it more than I care to admit." There was a resigned sadness in his eyes.

Addie was quickly finding herself drawn in by the case and it wasn't hard to understand why. Edisto Beach was a laid-back, no-shirt-no-shoes-no-problem kind of place, and Edisto Island itself was remote, primitive, and steeped in history—replete with stories of hauntings and mystery. The unresolved murders of two young women only added to the intrigue and made the story hard to shake.

"I read some of the initial reports, but those are dry facts," she said. "Can you walk me through it and add your perspective?"

"You might be sorry you asked. Once I start, I'm hard to shut up," Lee warned.

"I'll take my chances," she said, and Lee shrugged and leaned forward, putting his elbows on the table.

"It started with a party in May 1983. Most of the kids were seniors wanting a final blast before they headed separate ways. Internet and cell phones didn't exist. Their grapevine used landlines and meet-ups to spread the word, and they usually partied someplace private—not in clubs like kids in bigger cities. Maybe someone's parents were out of town, or someone lived on a farm. Maybe they were out in the woods—there were plenty of those around."

"I'm starting to feel I was born too late," Addie said as her cell phone vibrated for the third time since they'd sat down.

"Eighteen was the legal drinking age, which means they were drinking by sixteen or seventeen because older siblings or dates bought the beer. Cigarettes sold in vending machines to any kid with two quarters. Seat belts weren't required, no open-container laws, and nobody gave a rat's ass about speed limits on back roads. Kids weren't as linked-in to what was trending on the other side of the planet, but they had a lot more latitude here at home."

"I take back my comment about being born too late," Addie said. "I'm not so sure I would have survived with that much freedom that young."

"Sadly, that's how this ended, but then you know that already." Lee's expression grew heavier.

"That night, they were having their blowout on some private property that bordered the beach on Edisto."

"Somebody's beach house?"

"No, just land. It was owned by the Gadsden family."

"Buford Gadsden?" Addie's eyes widened at the mention of the name.

"No—this was thirty-four years ago. It would have belonged to his father. Anyway, God only knows where those kids told their parents they were going, but they all showed up with whatever alcohol they had, built a bonfire, set up some music, and were living the dream.

"The party was in full swing by nine that evening, with people coming and going. Somewhere around one in the morning, they started packing up. That's when they realized that Tara Godfrey and Cindy Crosby were missing. They rode to the party with two other girls—Julie Mathis and Sonya Beach. When they couldn't find them, they started to panic."

"So what did they do?" Addie asked.

"Are you familiar with Whaley's—the seafood restaurant on Edisto Beach?"

"Sure. The self-described seafood dive—great place."

"Back then, it was a filling station and convenience store—sort of a hub on the beach because there wasn't a major grocery store—and it was used as a base for an ambulance on the island. One of the girls—Julie—knew the paramedic. She went to him, and he pulled together a search party. What they didn't know was they were already on a recovery mission instead of a rescue."

"Why was the paramedic gathering the search party instead of calling for you?" Addie cocked her head.

"He did call us, but it was going to take me a few minutes to get back, and in cases with missing persons, we don't want to waste even a few minutes, so I asked him to get started."

"Edisto Beach is not a big place—where were you?"

"On Jungle Road. It doesn't look like much of a jungle today, but back then there weren't many houses in that area, and a jungle is what it looked like. We'd had complaints that someone was using those woods as a place to party—leaving trash and burning camp-fires that posed a risk. I was patrolling that night and spotted flash-lights, so I parked my cruiser and went to check things out. I got the call on my radio and had to run back through all that brush to get to the cruiser. I was pretty scratched up and dirty, but I made it back to Whaley's where they were gathering in the parking lot and joined them about fifteen minutes later.

"We found the first body—Tara Godfrey's—around 4:00 a.m. The tide had turned, and her body had drifted with the current to farther down the beach. There was trauma to her head, but on scene it wasn't clear whether the head injury came first, or she drowned and hit the rock groins as she washed up along the beach. And there was no way to know at that time if the head injury was accidental.

"Those questions were answered when we found Cindy Crosby's body. No question that wasn't an accident. She was found in the wooded area near the beach, facedown under a palmetto tree. There were finger marks and bruises around her neck—she'd been strangled."

"Two blue plate specials," the waitress interrupted as she placed the piled-high plates in front of them.

"Wow—what is all this?" Addie asked her.

"Fried chicken breast with a wild blackberry sauce on the side, mac and cheese with shrimp mixed in, and here you have collard greens," the waitress said, pointing to each in turn.

"What's this stuff on the collards?"

"If I told you, I'd have to kill you," she said, "but I guarantee you'll love it." She winked and turned to go. "I'll be right back with more sweet tea," she promised.

They were quiet for a moment as they both dug into lunch.

"You weren't kidding, this blackberry sauce is out of this world," Addie said.

"Told you," Lee said. "Sorry about the timing—not ideal conversation for lunch."

"Goes with the territory." Addie shrugged. "Speaking of timing, what did the coroner say about time of death?"

"They placed it between 10:00 p.m. and midnight for Cindy. They couldn't be sure with Tara since the body had been in the water. That would have affected the body temperature and complicated things in other ways too, but the body condition was not inconsistent with that timing, and their estimate was that they were both likely killed in that same time frame. The theory that made the most sense was that they were both attacked relatively close to where Cindy's body was found."

"And the cause of death for Tara?"

"The head trauma. They said it would likely have caused immediate death."

"Were they able to identify what she was hit with?"

"No. There were particles of the rock from the groins found in the wound, but that could have been deposited while the body was in the water. Same was true for trying to identify any foreign fibers that might have come from an attacker."

"Footprints? Signs of struggle?"

"No, any prints—or blood—on the beach had been washed away. With the other girl, Cindy, the forest debris around her body made it impossible to get any good prints, but there were broken branches and trampled plants that suggested she had been running in a northwest direction—and was being chased. There was tearing at everything within an arm's reach of where they found her. No question about it, that girl went down fighting."

"Was either girl sexually assaulted?"

"Both were fully dressed, and there was no evidence of sexual assault on either body. We found DNA under Cindy's fingernails, but no match in any of the databases we had.

"Cindy had a little cash in the pockets of her jeans. Both girls were wearing those gold herringbone chains that were so popular in the eighties, plus a few rings, earrings, and bracelets between the two of them—all there when the bodies were recovered."

"What about forensic toxicology reports?" Addie asked, placing her fork on her empty plate and pushing it away.

"They had been drinking that evening, but their blood alcohol levels were minimal. The specifics are in the file, but I don't recall them off the top of my head since there wasn't enough to suggest that contributed significantly. They didn't find evidence of any drugs for Tara, though the results might be less reliable because of the time the body was in the water—bacteria and all. Cindy's test results showed low levels of marijuana. All that was consistent with witness statements about what was observed at the party."

"Will there be anything else?" the waitress asked as she put the check on the table.

"No thanks, Sue. That's it for today," Lee answered as he handed her a few bills. "I don't need any change."

"Thank you, kindly. See y'all next time," she called back as she headed for another table.

"You mentioned witness statements—were you able to talk to them that night?"

"Only the two girls who went for help. The others had all gone home with no clue about the tragic turn things had taken. We got a list of names from Sonya and Julie of the people they remembered being there, and as we tracked those down, we asked for additional names from them. I think we had a complete list by the time it was over. Come on, let's head back."

As they left, Lee held the door for a group coming in, several of whom had heard about his retirement and made all the usual corny jokes accompanied by handshakes and slaps on the back. Watching the scene, Addie could tell their well-wishing was heartfelt and she suspected Lee was going to miss this more than he let on. She felt a little pang of jealousy over the camaraderie and realized she missed that part of it.

The car was hot from sitting in the sun, and Lee put down the windows as he backed out of the parking space.

"So, what did you get from the witnesses?" Addie asked as he pulled the car out of the lot and into the street.

"Lots of kids noticed that Tara and Cindy had left the party, but nobody seemed to think that was any cause for alarm. The biggest bombshell was that another kid—Logan Bennett—left the party around ten and came back around eleven."

"That coincides with the time of death," Addie said quickly.

"It does, and that got our attention. Nobody had seen him with the two girls, but it seems he and Cindy had been an item until a recent breakup that got ugly."

"Where did he say he'd been?"

"He wouldn't," Lee said, "which only raised our suspicions."

"I can imagine. Sounds like he was a serious suspect?"

"Sure was, we eventually arrested and charged him."

"Seeing as how this is still an unsolved case, that obviously didn't hold up. What happened?"

Before he could answer, Lee's cell phone rang. He glanced at the number and groaned.

"Bowen," he answered and then was quiet as he listened to the caller. "Yes, sir. On my way," he said. "Sorry, Addie, but I'm going to have to get back now. But go through all of the witness statements in the file. They'll give you a good idea who all the players were and what we know of what happened that night."

"What about Logan Bennett—is he still in the area?"

"Not sure. As you might imagine, he got a lot of unwanted attention at the time. After he was cleared, he moved around a bit. I kept track of him for a while, but I don't think he's in town anymore. Maybe one of the other witnesses will know. If not, we can help locate him through his driver's license."

Lee parked the cruiser, and they walked toward the building.

"The front desk can get you to the Records office to sign out the files," he said, holding the door for her. "Do you need any help getting them out to your car?"

"No, I'm good."

"Okay, then. Here's my card. They're going to let me transfer my cell number to a personal phone. Would you mind keeping me in the loop on what's happening with the case? I've been working it from the inside for so long, I'd like to see it through—and maybe I can help fill in any details that the files aren't clear about."

"Thanks—I'm going to need your help. I'm sure we'll be talking soon."

"And maybe you could slip me a scrap of detail on that other case you're working on," Lee said.

Addie rolled her eyes. "I should have known that would come up."

"Sorry, but you gotta admit it's a tantalizing case. I was at that bond hearing, and the preliminary hearing too," he added with a sheepish grin. "Half the town was."

"No kidding," she said.

The phone in Lee's hand buzzed with a text. "Duty calls," he said, looking at the screen.

"Go—and thanks for lunch."

"Don't mention it," Lee said, already heading for the hallway. "Oh, wait," he said, turning back. "The public defender who represented Logan Bennett at the time was Emma Hudson. She's not at the PD anymore—retired a few years back—but I think she opened a solo practice here in town after she left there. Back in the day she was on the other side, so we didn't have much contact with her. I've always wondered, though, if she might have some tidbit of information that could help. Maybe something she doesn't even realize is relevant. I don't know how privilege works after all this time, but it might be good to give her a call and at least see if she'll talk to you."

"Attorney-client privilege continues on after the case, so that sounds like kind of a long shot," Addie said, looking unconvinced.

"Addie, this case is more than three decades old—everything is a long shot." The phone in his hand buzzed again. "I'm coming already," he said, with a scowl, and waved as he disappeared down the hall.

CHAPTER 21

CLIMBING IN THE JEEP WITH THE FILES IN THE SEAT BESIDE HER and more in the back, Addie saw a missed call from Zach.

"Hello, beautiful, where are you?" he answered.

"Long story. I'll tell you all about it when I get home, but I saw you had called. What's up?"

"I got a call from Pastor Ben."

"Aka Padre Ben?"

"One and the same. Colleton and I were out there this morning walking through some theories and looking for possible problems with them."

Colleton again, she thought, remembering how seamlessly he'd taken over her hunch about surveillance cameras at the fast-food place.

"I left my sunglasses at the church. Pastor called to tell me he found them if I wanted to come pick them up. Says he'll be at the church between two o'clock and four today. Any chance I could talk you into swinging by there and picking them up? Colleton and I are here at the house working, and Eli stopped by."

Addie pictured the Maui Jim shades. They were one of the only little luxuries Zach had left after the fall. If he had to replace them, it would be at Walmart, and there was no way she was saying no. "No problem. It's almost three o'clock, so I'll head there now. After that, I'm going to run a few errands. I'll be home in an hour or so."

"Sounds good, see you then. Bye."

Addie started to release the brake but held off. What the hell, it would take her fifteen or twenty minutes to get to the church from here. She might as well use the drive time to call Emma Hudson's office. Addie Googled the number and dialed, then switched to hands-free as she backed up and turned in the direction of Cicada Road. Bluetooth automatically shut down the music, and the sound of Ms. Hudson's phone ringing came over the speaker.

"This is Emma Hudson."

Addie froze for a moment—she had expected to get a receptionist or some other staff person. "Um, yeah. Ms. Hudson? My name is Addie Stone."

Ms. Hudson didn't respond at first.

"I'm—"

"Oh, no need to explain, Ms. Stone. I know exactly who you are," Ms. Hudson replied in a voice that betrayed her piqued interest. "For that matter, every lawyer in this two-bit town knows who you are. You and Mr. Stander and that case of yours are the juiciest topic of conversation in every coffee klatch from here to the County lines." Her tone bordered on gleeful. "Please—don't keep me hanging. How can I help you, Ms. Stone? And call me Emma. It will absolutely make my day tomorrow to drop it on all the cronies that you and I are on a first-name basis."

"I hate to disappoint you but, as it turns out, I'm not calling you about the Jenkins case," Addie said. "Sergeant Lee Bowen suggested I call you about a cold case I'm working on—a double homicide on Edisto in 1983. Lee tells me you were involved?" Addie couldn't see Emma's face over the phone, but the pregnant pause that followed suggested raised eyebrows and a dropped jaw. "Are you still there, Emma?" Addie asked, trying not to sound like she was enjoying this as much as the other woman.

"I assume you're talking about my representation of Logan Bennett in the Godfrey-Crosby murders." Her tone was not quite as warm now.

"I am."

"You understand that the attorney-client privilege continues after charges are dropped, right?"

"I do, but not everything in your file would be privileged," Addie answered. "You might have third-party witness statements or other information that isn't in my file that could be helpful."

Another long pause.

"Addie"—Emma was suddenly laughing—"I doubt I have any information that would be the least bit helpful to you, but there is no way in hell I'm turning this invitation down. Hell, I'll be the newly crowned queen bee of the diner tomorrow just for telling them you called—which I will do repeatedly. When would you like to meet?" Emma's laugh was infectious, and Addie felt herself joining in.

"Better sooner than later," she answered. "Would tomorrow work?"

"Let's see—August eighteen, I have a hearing at nine," Emma answered. "How about if we meet at my office at eleven o'clock?"

"Perfect. See you then," Addie said, and ended the call.

Moments later, Addie pulled into the old church lot. There was a single car parked off to the side, but no sign of Pastor Ben on the grounds. *Must be in the sanctuary*, she thought as she closed her door and studied the church. The afternoon light gave the place a different feel than it had yesterday morning. The church faced east, so the morning sun yesterday had cast it in a gleaming white against the softly grayed woods behind it. Now, with the afternoon sun sinking lower in the west, the facade was darkening, and the shadow of the tree line had crept up around the building. The word *brooding* filtered through Addie's mind.

The door was unlocked and swung open without a protest. Stepping inside, Addie was immediately struck by the relative light. The tall windows drank in and amplified every ray of light such that the interior appeared brighter than the exterior from which the light was coming. She knew she was right about the similar effect that car lights would have after dark.

"Addie," the voice boomed startlingly close behind her. "I was expecting Zach. What a nice surprise to see you."

"Pastor Ben," she said, managing to cover her reaction with a smile. "I didn't see you—did I walk right by you?"

"No," he said. "I was out back when I heard your car and walked around. When I didn't see you outside, I assumed you were in here. I hope I didn't startle you."

"Not at all," she lied. "Zach said you found his sunglasses?"

"Yes, yes, they're right there on the end of that first pew. The one on the left."

Addie turned and walked to the front of the sanctuary. As she leaned down to pick up the glasses, the small dark stain on the floor near the altar caught her eye.

"Thank you so much for calling about these."

"It was no trouble," he said. "Is there something else you wanted?" he asked when she didn't leave.

"If you have a minute, yes, but it's not about the Jenkins case."

"Well, now you have me curious. What is it?" He sat down and leaned back against a pew, crossing one leg over a knee and gesturing for her to have a seat.

"It's about a cold case I'm working on for the sheriff's office," she said, perching on the edge of the seat. "It's an old case—more than three decades ago—but you mentioned yesterday that you grew up here, so I was wondering if you might remember anything about it. It was a double homicide on Edisto Beach. The victims were both teenaged girls."

"Why would something that old be reopened?" He was visibly surprised. "Have they found some new lead?"

"No," she said. "But I'm intrigued by the story and think it deserves another look. Did you happen to know either of the girls or their families?"

"No, I remember the incident—it was the lead story in all the local news sources for weeks, maybe months, and it shook this sleepy little town to its core. But I was a good bit older than those girls, and I certainly didn't know them."

"What about their families?"

"Addie"—he hesitated, searching for the right words—"it may be hard for someone from your generation to understand how different the world was then, especially in a small town. Those families were white—not Black like me. Schools were integrated by the eighties, but that was about it. Our little congregation here isn't exactly diverse now, and it was even less so then. Except for the occasional funeral, it would have been rare to see a white person at one of our services. To be fair, not many of us would have cared to visit white churches either. The same was true for most other aspects of daily life as well. It's not something for any of us to be proud of, but it doesn't help to pretend differently now."

"Sadly, some things haven't changed," she said as she stood to leave. "I'm sure it hasn't escaped you how much race will factor into Sam's case."

"You're right about that. A lot of people will see a young Black man and not a hardworking young accountant sitting at that defense table. I hope your Mr. Stander is up to the challenge."

"Have a little faith, Pastor," she said, smiling.

There were still trucks in the yard when Addie pulled in, which was what she'd been hoping for. Colleton's connections may have been edging her out of the Jenkins case, but they would be an asset to her new project. He and his family had been around forever, and, as a criminal defense lawyer, he would have been paying close attention to the Edisto murders—and his talent for soliciting gossip would have had him in the thick of it.

Buck, who was on the porch waiting for Eli, wagged his way out to meet her as she pulled a box of files and a bag of groceries from the seat. "Sorry, Buck," Addie said as she made her way in, leaving him exiled, "but something tells me you and Elvis would not be the closest of pals." Inside, she found Zach, Colleton, and Eli huddled together over maps and numbers.

"What's all this?"

"We're trying to nail down the alibi argument," Zach answered with his eyes still glued to the numbers. "Colleton got the security video from the place across from Sam's office. We hit a home run. One of the cameras caught Sam leaving the office and punching the keypad at 10:16, and then pulling out of the lot to the left. That was a great find," he said, giving Colleton a fist bump.

You're welcome, she thought, but held her tongue.

"We mapped out all the possible routes Sam could have taken to the church that night and then Colleton, Eli, and I took turns driving them to get an idea of the potential range of travel time. Now that we have a good idea of what the possible range is, Colleton and I will try to identify a witness who can repeat the tests and testify at trial."

"Like an expert witness?"

"I'm not sure we'd need to qualify the witness as an expert, but that's something we'll need to think about. Based on our trial runs, it's looking like there could have been as little as two minutes for Sam to get out of his car, enter the church, and call EMS. That doesn't leave time for the kind of physical action it would have taken to inflict the wounds that poor girl had."

"Sounds like you're making progress. What can I do to help?" She recklessly fanned a tiny spark of hope to life.

"Thanks, but we've got it," Zach said.

The little flame died a quiet death. Addie shrugged—more for her own benefit than anyone else's—and began putting the groceries into the refrigerator. Zach may have been oblivious to her disappointment, but she caught a guarded glance between Eli and Colleton.

"Why the bankers box?" Zach asked, finally looking up.

"That's my new project. There are more in the Jeep," Addie said, making a show of intense focus on the groceries. "I'm working on a cold case for the local sheriff's office. It'll give me something to do."

The unspoken message hit Zach with the subtlety of a Louisville Slugger to the gut. "Oh." His voice sounded small.

"Well, don't keep us in suspense," Colleton said, trying to drag Zach to safety. "Tell us about your case. And is that beer you're putting away?"

"Want one?" she asked.

"Hell, yes."

"Me too," Eli said.

"Make it three."

"So?" Colleton prompted again as he took two of the bottles from her and handed one off to Eli.

"It's a double homicide from 1983. Two girls were murdered at Edisto Beach when they wandered away from a party."

"From 1983? Are you serious?" Zach's bottle stopped halfway to his mouth.

"I remember when that happened," Eli said.

"Did you know anyone involved?" Addie asked, hoping for a lead.

"No, they were all a lot younger than I was—and white. Not a circle I would have been part of. But I remember the media frenzy about it. Sometime after the murders, they arrested a kid they thought might have done it. Only he came up with an alibi that involved buying drugs from Buford Gadsden at the time of the murders."

"Hold on, was that when Buford was arrested and did time?" Zach asked, remembering the rest of the story Eli had told him at the diner.

"When the alibi came out, yeah, I think that's when Buford's moonlighting gig came to an abrupt end. I reckon if you look at it from that angle, I did know someone involved," Eli said with a chuckle.

"And you, Mr. Burns." Addie turned her attention to Colleton. "You've been uncharacteristically quiet during all this. With your lust for gossip and uncanny ability to get the juiciest of it, I'm counting on you to give me the lay of the land and tell me who the players would have been."

Everyone looked expectantly at Colleton.

"Sorry to disappoint y'all," Colleton said, throwing up his hands, "but I don't have much to offer this time."

"Yeah, right, like we're going to believe that," Addie said.

"No, I mean it. I remember when it happened, of course—it was all anyone was talking about. Those girls were younger than I was, and I didn't know either of them. I knew some of their family, but not that well, so I didn't get any inside news. I do remember that every parent in town with teenagers was freaked-out about where their kids were all the time for a while after that."

"Come on, surely you were hearing some of the details on the street," Addie said.

"At the time, I was working on a big case of my own that was getting close to trial. Nothing as big as a double homicide, but big for that point in my career. I didn't have much time for gossip that summer. Sorry to let you down." He shrugged apologetically. "Truth is, I've always been curious about it, though. Promise you'll share the juicy details as you get further into it."

Addie caught Zach's gaze, and she could see that hers wasn't the only bullshit alarm going off, but she let it drop.

"I should probably get going," Eli said, looking at his watch. "It's getting close to Buck's suppertime, and if I don't feed him, he's likely to start gnawing on your porch furniture."

"Seeing as how it's not even our porch furniture, we appreciate that," Zach said.

"I should be going too," Colleton said. "Zach, I'll see you tomorrow. Addie, thanks for the beer—and I was serious about wanting to hear the scoop on your cold case. That was one of the most shocking events we'd had around these parts."

Addie was in bed reviewing a file of witness statements when Zach came out of the shower.

"Anything helpful?" Zach asked, eyeing the file.

"At this point, it's all helpful since I know so little. And the small-town factor still makes my head spin."

"What do you mean?" he asked.

"You're defending Eli's grandson on charges of murdering Buford Gadsden's daughter, and I pick up a cold case involving a double homicide near a party on Gadsden family land that had a ripple effect of landing Buford Gadsden in jail for selling drugs—and one of his 'customers' was Eli. It's like everyone here is connected, and chance meetings create secrets between the most unlikely people. Doesn't the connection here seem strange to you?"

"It crossed my mind, but the more I think about it, it's not that strange."

"No? Then why did it jump out at both of us as?"

"I think it's called selective distortion," Zach said, "taking new information—like your new information that there was a double homicide on Edisto Beach—and trying to make it fit with information or a perception you already have. We've been hyper-focused on Sam's case, and that necessarily includes Buford's daughter and Eli's grandson. When Eli reminded us that he and Buford both had some remote connection to that old case, we tried to make it fit somehow with the current case. But, as far as I can tell, it doesn't."

"I guess that makes sense."

"The thing that puzzles me more is that someone as nosy as Colleton didn't know more than he did."

"We're on the same page there. I'm betting Colleton knows more than he's telling. The question is why."

"Afraid I'm no help there—I'm as clueless as you are," Zach said.

"You planning on working late there?" He gestured to the file.

"I'm thinking I've probably had enough for one day," she said. "Why? Something else you'd rather I do?"

"Turns out there is," he said, reaching for the lamp.

She smiled into the darkness as she heard his towel hit the floor.

CHAPTER 22

FUCK, FUCK, *FUUUCK*! THERE MUST BE HUNDREDS OF COLD cases rotting away in moldy boxes in the bowels of the sheriff's office. How in the hell did Addie Stone manage to land on that one? I don't know how I managed to hold it together when I heard she was reopening the Edisto Beach thing. I remember thinking I sounded normal while we were talking, but I was trying so hard to choose my words carefully I can't be sure.

When I left Jessie Gadsden on the floor with her miserable life oozing out of her, it never dawned on me that Samuel Jenkins—or anyone else—would find her so soon. Sam's arrest does have advantages. He didn't just call for help—he got down and wallowed around in the gore and trampled up the scene. Jesus, what was he thinking? No complaint from me, though—as long as the powers that be are convinced they have the killer behind bars, they won't come looking for me. Hat's off to the BLM protesters on that point—they are 100 percent right about Sam being railroaded. Neither the cops nor the solicitor are even thinking about any other suspect, much less looking for one.

On the other hand, Sam's arrest means there will be a trial, and a trial means there will be two sets of lawyers rooting around in the evidence, taking a closer look. Not good.

I've known since Sam's arrest that I would need to worm my way into some inside information on his case. Now, with the old case reopened, I'm going to need to keep an eye on that one too. At least

Addie gives me an inside track on both cases. But if Addie connects enough dots to see the connection between that old Edisto case and the new one, that will not be good for me. It will be a hell of a lot worse for her.

Because I am NOT going to jail.

CHAPTER 23

EMMA HUDSON'S OFFICE WAS IN AN OLD GOVERNMENT BUILDING across from the courthouse that had been repurposed as shared office space for solo professionals and entrepreneurial start-ups. The perimeter of the building was lined with small offices with windows and the interior had common space conference rooms, breakrooms, etc. It was modest but respectable. A shared receptionist at the front desk gave Addie Emma's suite number, and Addie walked down the hall to find the door slightly ajar and Emma typing furiously on a computer.

"I hope I'm not too early," Addie said, knocking lightly on the door.

"Not at all, come in," Emma said, looking up. She had let her graying hair go natural, and her face was deeply tanned and heavily lined as though she'd lived her life out in the sun. The combination of the white hair against the deep tan lent a startling intensity to her bright blue eyes. "Have a seat," she said, extending an arm toward the chair on the other side of the desk. "I was about to step across the hall and grab myself a cup of coffee. Can I get you one too?"

"Thanks, that would be nice. Black."

"Ah, common ground already. I'll be right back."

Addie took in the shelves of tennis trophies and photos of a young Emma with ponytailed chestnut hair holding up silver cups and engraved plaques. One of the photos had a familiar-looking face in the background. If that wasn't Colleton Burns, he had a doppelgänger.

"Here you go," Emma said, handing her a steaming cup and closing the door before sitting at her desk.

"Do you still play?" Addie asked, nodding toward the trophies.

"Not at the level I could when I was younger, but I still play. Believe it or not, there's not a lot to do in Walterboro, and it keeps me active."

"Is that Colleton Burns in the background there?" Addie asked.

"Of course it is." Emma laughed. "If there was a team of young women in short tennis skirts, there was a good chance he was around somewhere. To be fair, though, it was also because his well-heeled mother sponsored a lot of our teams, and Colleton would show up to hand out the trophies. That was taken not long after I moved here— it was the last year I played competitively. After that, I helped coach the high school team for a while."

"Looks like you were successful at that too," Addie said, noticing a later photo with Emma surrounded by a circle of younger girls. One—a perky blond with a pretty smile—was holding up a plaque.

"I did okay." Emma's blue gaze stared intently over the rim of her cup as she raised it. "But you aren't here to ask about my long-gone glory days."

"No, I'm not. Like I said on the phone yesterday, I'm working with the sheriff's office on a cold case—a double homicide on Edisto Beach."

"I heard you were Zach Stander's investigator. Is the Jenkins case not keeping you busy enough?"

"Legal cases don't work the same way in real life that they seem to in the movies—the work comes in fits and starts, and it's not all over in a few days," she answered, diplomatically avoiding the subject of Colleton's coup.

"You're not telling me anything new there," Emma said. "I spent almost thirty years with the public defender's office before retiring and starting this sleepy little private practice."

"Actually, it's your time with the PD I want to ask about—I understand you represented Logan Bennett when he was charged in the Edisto murders."

"That's right. A lot of what I know would be privileged, but I'm happy to share what I'm allowed to. I can't imagine how any of it would help, but, as I admitted when you called, I have ulterior motives for wanting to meet you," she said with a wide grin.

"Fair enough."

"So, fire away, Addie Stone. What is it you want to know?"

"Let's start with this: the night of the murders, Logan left the party for an hour or two at about the time the girls did. There were at least thirty witnesses who gave statements, and almost every one of them mentioned that. It's been a while since I was a teenager, but, if memory of similar parties serves me, there would have been a lot of kids coming and going—probably in couples. It seems odd that so many people would even notice, much less think it was unusual that one guy left for a while. What am I missing?"

"Logan was handsome and a bit of a daredevil. He was popular with the other kids, and you know how teenagers are. They all want to be popular, so they idolize the ones who are and emulate everything they do. Cindy didn't have that same level of popularity, but she had a reputation for being a drama queen, and she supposedly made a big public scene when their little fling ended badly. When an 'it' kid like Logan leaves a party, it gets noticed. Then all the others look around to see who else is missing that might be with him. That led to noticing Cindy was gone, which led to Tara since they were best friends.

"Then there was the timing thing since Logan was unaccounted for during the window they estimated for time of death. To add fuel to the fire, when the investigators asked him where he'd been, he flat out refused to answer. Throw in the fact that public pressure was hot, and the cops didn't have so much as a scrap of another lead, and Lee Bowen and his team were all over Logan."

"Sounds like you don't think that was justified. Is there some bad blood between you and Bowen?"

"No," Emma said after an awkward pause, "nothing personal. Lee and I started our careers at about the same time, and he seems like a decent guy. It would have been reckless not to seriously consider Logan under those circumstances. But I knew they weren't putting much effort in searching after they arrested Logan. That changed after he was released, of course, but they wasted valuable time they could never get back. If they'd stayed hard on the trail while it was still hot, we might have answers today instead of another cold case. But they didn't. They were convinced it was Logan, and I ended up defending him."

"Any chance you took statements from any witnesses that you can share?" Addie asked.

"I thought you might ask. After our call I looked through my file and found a summary I put together of the most salient facts from the more detailed statements. Technically, it would be attorney work product, but the information isn't privileged, so I can give it to you." As she talked, she reached for her mouse and printed a document that she handed across the desk.

"Impressive," Addie said. "I was guessing we'd have to go through an old box full of mildew and silverfish."

"In this shoebox of an office? There's not much space for storage. It eventually forced me to go paperless. I admit, though, I put it off for a long time, especially scanning this old stuff. Old dogs, new tricks, and all that."

"Thanks for this," Addie said, putting the papers in her backpack. "There's something else I wanted to ask about. Please don't take this wrong, but thirty-four years ago, you couldn't have been more than a few years out of law school. I'm sure you were—are—a good lawyer, but how does a baby lawyer get assigned to a double homicide?"

"And a girl lawyer at that, right?"

"That wasn't what I meant."

"I know, but trust me, it was a significant factor three decades ago in this little town," she said with an air of resignation. "Besides, they didn't assign it to me initially. Instead, they quite sensibly gave it to a lawyer who was far more senior and had some murder cases under his belt. Crazy thing was that Logan wouldn't have it. He insisted they reassign it to me. As you might imagine, the guys at the top explained to him that he didn't get to pick because they knew who was best for what case and he would have to accept the counsel they assigned if he wanted to be assigned a defense attorney." She paused and smiled as if picturing the skirmish.

"Next thing we knew, Logan—in typical Logan fashion—told them all to go fuck themselves. Said it was his ass on the line and he'd have me or no one. They called his bluff and said it was his right to refuse counsel, figuring he'd relent in a day or so. When he didn't, I finally went to my boss and begged him to assign me with the condition that I would report to the more senior lawyer and get his help at every stage, and we'd try the case together if it came to that."

"And they agreed to that?"

"Hell no—they were no more inclined to let a baby lawyer tell them what to do than to let Logan, but the families and the public were screaming for action. The judge was passing that heat along to the PD because circuit court judges are elected by the legislature for terms, and the last thing the judge wanted was to have his name on a conviction and sentencing that was kicked back on appeal on a high-profile case. My bosses finally caved and put me on it."

"No offense, but why would Logan want a less experienced lawyer?"

Emma sighed. "Logan and I had a bit of a history."

"A history?" Addie's jaw dropped.

"No, not a personal history, a legal history." Emma seemed amused by Addie's reaction. "Like I said, Logan was a daredevil and didn't exactly think the rules applied to him. This led to a few brushes with the local authorities—the kind of lesser offenses that are assigned to a young, less experienced lawyer. I can't tell you details since most were removed from his record because he was a minor. I can tell you they were typical teenager stuff."

"Like underage drinking?"

"Along those lines," Emma said with a noncommittal shrug and an impenetrable poker face. "If you looked up his criminal record, you'd find at least one of the arrests because he was already eighteen. It was for trespassing. One of our more prominent local citizens had a swanky backyard setup with a swimming pool, colored lights, and a refrigerator full of beer—and a lousy hiding place for the key to the padlock. He woke up one night to noises coming from the backyard. When he went to investigate, he found Logan skinny-dipping in his pool and drinking his beer."

Addie couldn't help but laugh. "I get why the guy was pissed off, but that sounds more like something most people would have dealt with Logan's parents about rather than press charges, especially back then."

"Sorry—did I forget to mention Logan was skinny-dipping with the guy's beautiful teenaged daughter?"

Now they were both laughing.

"What happened?"

"By the time the police arrived and fished a drunken Logan out of the pool sans pants, it had occurred to the citizen that if he pursued it to trial, his daughter would be the subject of gossip for years. After I was appointed to represent Logan, I met with him, and we worked out an informal deal. The citizen agreed not to pursue prosecution—which the authorities were only too happy to agree to with so many bigger fish to fry. In return, Logan agreed to stay at least five hundred feet from the daughter and their residence, reimburse him for the beer, and check in with me once a month for six months to confirm he was staying out of trouble. It wasn't a formal pretrial intervention, so the arrest is still on his record, but it only shows as an arrest for trespassing that was dismissed.

"God," Emma said, "I haven't thought about that fiasco in years. How did we get off on this tangent?"

"You were telling me about Logan insisting his case go to you."

"Ah, yes. At first, Logan wouldn't tell me where he'd been either. Finally, after my incessant begging and cajoling, he admitted that he had left the party for a while to buy some drugs. I tried to explain that any sentence for drug charges would pale in comparison to what was going to happen if he were convicted of murder. His take on it was that he hadn't murdered those girls so it wouldn't be possible for anyone to prove he did."

"If only that were true," Addie said, thinking about Zach and Sam.

"*If only* is right. Logan finally agreed that I could tell the solicitor what he'd been doing, but he still refused to say who the dealer was. I talked myself blue in the face trying to convince him that wouldn't get us anywhere, but he never gave in. I've always wondered if he was more afraid of the dealer than he was of jail, but who knows. I did go to the solicitor with what Logan would let me say and tried to bluff my way into making him believe we'd give up the name at trial, but he wasn't buying it."

"Then how did you get Logan out?"

"That's just it. I didn't. After weeks of beating my head against a wall, I still had nothing. Zilch. In the end it was pure luck. The sheriff's office received an anonymous hotline tip that Buford Gadsden had been selling dope from a shrimp boat docked at Edisto Island. Even gave a date he'd been selling."

There was Buford Gadsden's name again.

"I think the cops thought the tip was sketchy, but they checked it out anyway. The K9s alerted on the pot, but it had been weeks since the date identified in the hotline tip. What was left wasn't enough to warrant a trafficking charge, and nobody really cared. But Logan's big break came when they turned over a cooler lid and out dropped a leather wristband."

"A what?"

"A leather wristband. They used to sell them at cheesy kiosks at Myrtle Beach and places like that. They had names tooled into the leather. They were all the rage with some of the kids for a while—especially in the seventies. They had gone out of style by the eighties, but a few still hung around. Anyway, this one fell out of a seat on Buford's boat—and guess what the name was."

"No way," Addie said.

"Way. And guess what date the caller gave."

"The date of the Edisto murders."

"You got it. Suddenly Logan Bennett had an alibi."

"Now that's a story."

"Yeah—my first big win was one I can't take any credit for," Emma joked. "I don't suppose you could tell me a bit about your case now?" she added.

"You know better."

"I know the solicitor hasn't announced whether he'll be asking for the death penalty. Has he given Zach any feel for how he's leaning?"

"Not yet," Addie said.

"Want my take on that?" Emma asked.

"Couldn't hurt—you've known him a long time."

"I've spent a lot of time across the courtroom from Jake Barton, and there are a lot of unflattering things I might call him," Emma said, "but stupid isn't one of them—he is as smart as they come. He knows this is going to be one of the highlights of his career, and he will not risk losing even on one point. The death penalty is not as unpopular in this part of the country as it is in others, but there are still plenty of people who balk at making that call."

"You don't think he's worried about the optics of not going for the death penalty—looking too soft on the crime?"

"No. If he gets a guilty verdict, there might be a few diehards out there thinking he should have asked for the death penalty, but there will be more people who see the decision as smart. On the other hand, if he asks for it and misses, he looks like he failed at something he set out to do. Trust me on this if nothing else—Jake Barton has aspirations for higher office, probably governor. This case will get the kind of publicity he needs to extend his local name recognition to a bigger playing field. He won't go for the death penalty unless he thinks he has a sure thing."

"Interesting theory."

"That's all you have to say?"

"Come on, you know I can't say more. Everything I know that isn't already public information is privileged."

Emma let out a huff. "Could you at least throw me a bone and let me buy you lunch at this cute little place I like on Main Street?"

"I'd love that," Addie said, "but how is letting you buy me lunch doing you a favor?"

"Are you kidding? The place will be packed, and some idiot with a phone won't be able to resist taking our photo and posting it on

Facebook tonight. By tomorrow, I'll be the most sought-after lunch date in town. Game?"

"Sounds like it's the least I can do."

Emma was right, the lunch place was cute. And Addie had spotted several people clandestinely taking photos. So, this is what celebrity felt like.

"Did you grow up here?" Addie asked while they waited for the check.

"No, I was raised on Georgia clay. I went to University of South Carolina for law school, and decided I liked it here. I had clerked for the PD, and they offered me a job; I took it. Somewhere along the way this became home."

"Good for you. Is there a Mr. Emma Hudson?"

"That never happened for me. When I first came here, there weren't many female lawyers, and most people acted like I was some kind of an alien. I thought I'd keep my head down until people got to know me. Then I wanted to put off a relationship until I got my career established. By the time my career was in full swing, I didn't have time for a relationship. Then one day I looked up and all the good ones were committed to someone who wasn't waiting for something else. A decade later, they all divorced, and it dawned on me that I may have been spared more than I missed."

"And now?"

"Now I'm too set in my ways. I sleep in the middle of the bed, I hate to share the remote, and I don't want to see another human before I've had my first coffee. I think single life suits me."

Addie nodded, but something about Emma's smile seemed sad. Addie couldn't help but wonder if there was something else driving Emma's choices. A bad breakup? Betrayal?

Emma handed a credit card to the waitress who brought the check.

"Be right back with that," the girl said.

"What about you? You and Zach headed for the altar?"

"Eventually. For now, we're sort of waiting."

"Waiting for what?"

"I wish I knew," Addie said, finishing off her Diet Coke.

"Let's go," Emma said as she signed the credit card receipt.

They wandered back down Main Street, moving slowly in the August heat with Emma pointing out some of her favorite spots. As they turned the corner, they heard shouting and chanting coming from a crowd camped on the courthouse lawn.

"Want to make a bet on what that's about?" Emma asked.

"I think we both know what that's about," Addie answered.

"According to the court's roster, Sam's first appearance—roll call—is set for August twenty-first. That's Monday," Emma said. "That's a routine hearing for scheduling, but I guess it's enough to stir things up."

"Or somebody's trying to stir things up to get a bigger crowd on Monday. Zach filed a motion asking for bail that will be heard at the hearing too." Addie took in the scene as they drew closer to the demonstration. The rhetoric was the same, but the crowds on both sides seemed to have grown since last time and the intensity was building. Addie spotted JB waving a sign, and she felt sick as she recalled the brick smashing through their window. Had he been behind that? What more was he capable of?

"This case of Zach's is getting hotter," Emma said.

"Tell me about it," Addie said, "and it's going to get worse."

Colleton's Tahoe was in the drive when Addie pulled in after leaving Emma's office, and Addie found Zach and Colleton at the table going over some notes.

"Hey," she said with a smile. Two grim faces stared back at her, but neither man spoke.

"Oh," she said, registering their expressions as the smile faded from her own face. "I take it you've heard about the ruckus outside the courthouse."

"We did," Zach said, "but . . ."

"But what?"

"There's been something else," Zach said and pointed to a kraft envelope lying on the table. "Colleton found it propped on one of the front steps when he came to the door."

Addie looked at the envelope. It was blank, without an address or any other marking on the outside. "What time did you find it there?" she asked Colleton.

"I got here around 10:25."

"Odd. I didn't leave until a few minutes before ten, and it wasn't there then. What's inside?" Addie asked, feeling an uneasiness building in her chest. Zach held the envelope by its edges and dumped its contents, and Addie gasped as a small noose landed in front of her. The message was clear.

"Did you report this to the city police?" Her eyes were full of fire, now. "This isn't like the brick—they can lift prints from a paper envelope."

Zach nodded. "I called Officer Mixon and texted him a photo of the envelope and noose. He's going to come by this afternoon and pick it up."

"Well, we know our friend JB has been less than a mile from here today—I saw him on the courthouse lawn with the crowd."

"That doesn't prove he did it," Colleton said.

"No, but his prints on that envelope could. And even if there aren't any prints, I know he's behind this and that brick. Sooner or later, I'm going to catch his ass."

"Be careful what you wish for, Addie," Colleton said. "If you catch him, you might wish you hadn't."

"I can take care of myself," she said.

"I know, I know . . . I'm only reminding you that if this keeps escalating, it raises the stakes."

"And you thought I missed that?"

Colleton threw up his hands in surrender.

Zach was trying to play it cool, but the look on his face gave him away. This had shaken him, too.

Addie scrunched her face in disgust as she looked again at the noose on the table.

"What were you two working on this morning?" She changed the subject, determined not to let the bastards mess with her mind any more than they already had.

"We've been tossing around the idea of asking for a change in venue," Zach answered.

"To where?"

"That's the problem—the alternatives aren't any better. Sam's case has gotten so much publicity, we'd have the same worries about juror bias anywhere else in the state, and we could end up in another conservative county with a history of more convictions. For that matter, we could land in another county in this same circuit, where Barton's name will be as big as it is here, but no one will know Eli or Sam."

"Or me," Colleton added. "I don't have the same relationships that could help us in the other counties. I wouldn't have access to as much information about potential jurors either."

"So, no change in venue?"

Zach and Colleton both shook their heads.

Addie looked out the window, sorting through what they had said.

"What about you?" Colleton asked. "What kept you busy this morning?"

"I met with Emma Hudson to see if she could shed some light on my cold case."

"The Edisto Beach thing? Was she helpful?" Zach asked.

"She had plenty to say about Logan Bennett—the kid who was the only suspect. She represented him, and she filled me in on enough to convince me he didn't have anything to do with the murders. She didn't have any information that jumped out at me as a clue about who did, though."

"That must have been a long talk if you left here around ten, and you're just getting back," Zach said.

"Not really—we went to lunch after."

"Sounds like the two of you hit it off."

"We did—she's an interesting person. If nothing else, she's a good source for insight if I do find anything."

Colleton hadn't said anything, but he had stopped what he was doing and was watching Addie intently as he listened to the conversation about the old case. She opened her mouth to ask if he had remembered anything else about the case when they were interrupted by the buzz of Zach's cell phone.

"Zach Stander," he said, taking the call. "Oh, hi, Serena. What can I do for you?"

Addie looked questioningly at Colleton, who mouthed *solicitor's office*. They both waited while Zach listened to Serena on the other end.

"Thanks for the heads-up," Zach said, his expression stony. "Sure, you too." He ended the call with one hand while he groped for the television remote with the other.

"What is it?" Colleton asked.

"Jake Barton is making an announcement about the case," he said, powering up the television and turning to local news.

"Looks like he gave the media more of a heads-up than he gave us," Colleton said as he took in the crowd of media jockeying to get their cameras in the best positions.

"Somehow I don't think whoever organized that protest group was entirely in the dark, either," Addie said.

"This guy is pissing me off," Colleton said.

"Shhh, both of you." Zach's face had gone pale.

The cameras turned toward the courthouse entrance and the commotion there as Jake Barton strode through the door with a posse of young assistant solicitors following a few feet behind in a show of force. The banter of the protesters on both sides rose briefly and then died down as Barton stepped up to the outstretched arms holding microphones.

"As all of you know," Barton opened, "my office is charged with the prosecution of Samuel Jenkins for the murder of Jessie Gadsden, July 11, 2017. There is no crime more grave than the crime committed that night. A young woman was robbed of her life in a vicious and brutal attack that was made more horrific by the desecration of the sanctity of a place of worship.

"Part of my responsibility as solicitor is to make a decision as to whether the state will seek the death penalty." Barton paused for effect, not that the situation needed any more drama. "There is no decision more difficult for any prosecutor than whether to seek a life for a life, and it cannot be made lightly. But I believe the evidence in this case is compelling and beyond all reasonable doubt. In light of the presence of aggravating circumstances and the heinous nature of this crime, my office will be seeking the death penalty. The brutality of this crime threatens the very fabric of society, and Jessie Gadsden deserves justice.

"Thank you," he said, giving the camera his practiced solemn gaze.

As Barton turned from the cameras, the cadre of young lawyers behind him parted like the Red Sea to let him pass and then closed ranks and fell in with him as he withdrew into the courthouse without answering any of the questions reporters were shouting frantically from the lawn. Within seconds, those questions were inaudible as the yells of demonstrators drowned them out.

Zach clicked the remote as he collapsed back into the chair, and a heavy silence swallowed the room.

"It's no coincidence that he announced before the motion for bail will be heard next week. Putting the death penalty on the table raises the flight risk analysis and the amount of bail set," Colleton said.

"You're right," Zach said. "I'd better call Eli before he hears this from someone else. Then I'll go to the jail and talk to Sam." He sounded tired, and Addie wanted to tell him it would all be okay, but she didn't have any idea whether that was true.

"Want me along for moral support?" Colleton volunteered.

"No, thanks. This is my job."

"Okay, then, I'm going to head back home. I'll be back in the morning, and we can pick up where we left off."

Zach held the door for him and stood on the porch until Colleton's Tahoe pulled away.

Addie watched through the screen door as Zach plugged in the number and waited.

"Eli? It's Zach. Listen, there's something we need to talk about."

Zach left the porch and walked around the yard as he talked, so Addie didn't hear the conversation. She didn't need to hear—she could tell from the slump of Zach's shoulders that the old man wasn't taking this well. But who would?

As she retreated to the silence of the empty room, Addie felt the weight of Emma's words: *Barton won't go for the death penalty unless he thinks he has a sure thing.*

The stakes had definitely been raised.

CHAPTER 24

THE MORNING AIR WAS UNUSUALLY COOL FOR LATE SEPTEMBER, AND Addie drove with the windows down and the sunroof open. This was still the tail end of dog days, and by midday it would be sweltering again, so best enjoy it while she could.

Sam's second appearance hearing—like an arraignment, at which a defendant tells the court whether he wants to plead guilty or be tried by a jury—was about a month away. That played into why Barton had made a show out of his death penalty announcement before the first appearance last month. He had intended to turn up the pressure, and it had worked. The circuit court judge had set bail at $750,000—making a bond out of reach for Eli and Sam. Zach and Colleton had been working nonstop on Sam's case, but despite her constant offers, both insisted there was nothing Addie could do.

If there was a silver lining, it was that Zach had rediscovered his passion for practicing law. She loved seeing him back in his groove. She just wished she could be part of it, and she couldn't help but feel a sting of resentment at being pushed aside after she'd been there for him through all the crap. She was trying to put up a good front, but she knew Zach sensed how she felt, and it was creating tension between them.

She and Emma had become casual friends, which led to the occasional lunch or happy hour, but that could take up only so much time. If it hadn't been for the Edisto Beach case, she would have lost her mind. Edisto was where she was headed this morning.

According to Facebook, Julie Mathis was living on Edisto Beach. Julie had been the one to go for help when she couldn't find her friends that night. She was in her early fifties now. Even after all those years, the trauma of that night wasn't something she was likely to have forgotten, and Addie was hoping she would be willing to share.

She turned right off Highway 17 and drove through Adams Run—barely more than a crossroads—and then across the Dawho Bridge to Edisto. From the bridge, the landscape looked much as it had centuries ago. An osprey soared above the river, scouting for prey.

It had been years since she'd been to Edisto, and she'd forgotten the lure of its unspoiled beauty and rich, layered history. The island's forests had once been hunting or winter planting grounds for the Edisto and Oristo native tribes. Towering live oaks that had provided shade for English colonists and later for American revolutionaries now formed a canopy over the road and shaded historic churches and storied graveyards that had stood witness to slavery, union troop occupation, and all that came after.

At last, she crossed Scott Creek to Edisto Beach. Though the inevitable pockets of gentrification had crept in, much of the beach still boasted the shabby chic of yesteryear. A gentle undercurrent of Gullah Geechee culture flowed through its veins, and the vibe was still undeniably southern. A little line creased her brow as she wondered how much longer that would last.

Julie Mathis worked at Whaley's restaurant. The tone of her cigarette-graveled voice had toggled between leery and curious when Addie called and asked to meet her. Eventually the curiosity won out. The restaurant started serving lunch at eleven-thirty, but Julie was scheduled to open today, and if Addie could get there by ten, Julie would have a little time to talk before the others arrived.

Addie pulled in at 9:48. The sign on the door said closed, but she knocked as Julie had told her to, and a woman who looked to be in her early fifties quickly came to the door.

"Julie Mathis? I'm Addie Stone."

"I figured," the woman said, nodding. "Wait here a second while I get my smokes and we'll sit outside if that's okay."

"Sure, whatever works best for you." Julie disappeared into the back, and Addie took a quick look around the place. A sign on the wall read: WEEKEND FORECAST: *ALCOHOL*LOW STANDARDS*POOR DECISIONS. The place was small and unpretentious and had that local feel.

"This way." Julie returned and gestured toward an outside table with an umbrella where they took their seats.

"Thanks for seeing me, Ms. Mathis."

"Oh Jesus, nobody ever calls me that. Just plain Julie is fine."

"Thanks. Call me Addie."

"Sure thing. Mind if I smoke?" she asked, holding the lighter in front of the cigarette already between her lips.

"Not at all." Addie knew better than to jump to conclusions about people, but it didn't take a clairvoyant to see that life had not been easy for Julie Mathis. Telltale gray roots edged the home-dyed blond, and she was quick with a smile, but it came across more as a defense and never quite made it to her eyes. Addie knew from the file that she was fifty-one. That was still a long way from being old, but there's a reason that so many of the workers in food and beverage are very young. Long hours of standing on your feet and carrying heavy trays takes a toll on a body—it was no place for sissies.

"So"—Julie blew out a stream of smoke that curled briefly around her face before the breeze carried it away—"why is the sheriff's office reopening this case now, after almost a lifetime?"

"It's a long story. My fiancé, Zach Stander, is defending Sam Jenkins, in Walterboro, and—"

"I know who you are"—Julie stopped her—"small town and all," she added with a dismissive shrug. "What I want to know is what the Jenkins case has to do with what happened to those two girls all those years ago."

"Nothing," Addie said, "other than that's what brought me to Walterboro. I needed something useful to do and, since I used to be in law enforcement, I volunteered to help out with cold cases."

"And they asked you to work on this one?"

"No, they let me look through records on old cases, and I asked them to let me reopen this one."

"You random picked it out of a box?"

"Not exactly. There was something about it that tugged at my heart. Two young girls murdered and still no answers thirty-four years later? I don't know whether I'll be able to find anything new on a case this old, but it seemed to me they deserved another shot at justice."

"Justice?" Julie seemed skeptical.

"I know it won't bring them back, but maybe I could at least bring closure to the families and friends they left behind."

"I'm not sure closure is all it's made out to be, but sure. If I can help, I'm happy to. What is it you want to know?" She took another drag off her cigarette.

"Tara Godfrey and Cindy Crosby rode with you to the beach that night, right?"

"Yes, and Sonya Beach. Surely you got that from my statements."

"I did, and I'm guessing that means you were all friends, but how close were you?"

"Sonya was my cousin somewhere down the line. I think my mother and her mother were first cousins. Not sure what level that made us—all that second cousin and first-cousin-once-removed stuff always confused me. Anyway, we grew up together and were like sisters back then."

"Not anymore?"

"Not like we were. After that night, Sonya's mom wouldn't let her come over for a while. We had lied about where we were going—like everybody else—and her mom got it in her mind that because I was driving, it was my fault we were there. She and my mom had a big row over it. It blew over after a couple months, but it wasn't the same after. I guess none of us were really the same after." Her voice trailed off.

"So, what about Tara and Cindy—were you close with them?" Addie prompted.

"Tara and I were good friends, but not super close. I think most of us thought of Tara as a friend. She was one of those people who could get along with all kinds. Cindy, well, not to speak ill of the dead, but I didn't much care for her. She and Tara were close, though I never understood why." Julie took a last drag, stubbed her cigarette out in the gravel, held up her hand in a *hang on* gesture, and carried the butt to a long-necked outdoor ashtray.

"What was the rub with you and Cindy?" Addie asked as Julie slid back onto the blue metal bench seat.

"It wasn't that we didn't get along. She was a bit of a drama queen, though I'm not sure we used that term back then. You know the type—loud, showy, always talking and waving her hands around. Life of the party and all that. Everything was over-the-top fantastic or simply too awful to bear. There wasn't a lot of plain old stuff as far as she was concerned. She was fun in small doses, but she needed a lot of attention, and I didn't have the patience for it."

"And Tara did?"

"Tara was patient with all of us. She was the kid that parents *and* kids liked. She got good grades, but she worked for them. Same with sports—she played them all well, but she was always cheering on the other players. She had a scholarship to the College of Charleston—was excited about living away from home, but still being only an hour away. She wasn't a Goody Two-shoes, but she had enough common sense to stay out of trouble. Maybe it was because she'd been through so much."

"Been through what?" This was the first Addie had heard of this.

"She was nineteen—a year older than most of our class. Her mother was dying from cancer when she was supposed to start first grade, and they held her back to be with her mom. She seemed—I don't know—mature for her age.

"I think that's part of why it was such a shock about her. Most of us could imagine Cindy Crosby making the mistake of pissing off the wrong person, but it seemed impossible that anyone would want to hurt Tara Godfrey."

"When did you first notice that Tara wasn't at the party anymore?"

"That's easy—she came and told me. The party was starting to get pretty wild, and she said she was going for a walk down on the beach to take a breather."

"Why would she bother to tell you she was taking a walk?"

"I was her ride home. I remember her giving me a friendly hug and saying don't leave before I get back. I promised her I wouldn't. That was the last time I saw her."

"Was Cindy with her?"

"Not when she came to tell me. I didn't notice Cindy being gone at all, to be honest."

"What about Logan Bennett—did you notice him leaving?"

"No, but he was popular and eventually I heard somebody asking where he was. He came back, though—I remember seeing him later that night. He was helping put the bonfire out." She laughed and put her hand over her mouth.

"What?"

"Before they dumped buckets of water on it, he and some other guys dropped trou and tried dousing it with something else." She pursed her mouth, trying to suppress another laugh. "Sorry, they were boys being boys."

"I have three brothers," Addie said. "Can you tell me anything about Logan and Cindy?"

"They had a thing for a while that year. It ended badly, but everyone saw that coming."

"I understand she made a scene when it ended."

"Cindy's whole life was a big scene."

"Do you remember the details of the breakup?"

"No, but I heard a rumor she found out he'd been skinny-dipping with some girl from the private school. That part was hush-hush, and I never knew the other girl's name."

Now it was Addie's turn to suppress a smile.

"How well did you know Logan?"

"I wasn't part of the popular crowd he ran with if that's what you're asking. We had a few classes together, and I got to know him a little. He was rock star good-looking, and he was the kind of kid who never turned down a dare. But he was also incredibly smart, though he worked hard not to let that show. I think that was part of his cover—a self-defense thing."

"Why would he need cover?"

"Logan didn't exactly have it easy at home. His father was an alcoholic, and his mother took solace wherever she could find it, if you catch my drift. He was an only child, and I got the impression he had been taking care of himself for a long time. Maybe it was easier to slide by when he played dumb."

"I'd like to talk to Logan, but I hear he left the area."

"Who told you that?" Julie sounded puzzled.

"Lee Bowen—from the sheriff's office. I assume you know him since he worked the case from the beginning. He says he kept up with Logan for a while but lost track of him."

"Yeah, I know Lee. He worked the beach back in those days. He wasn't much older than us, so he'd always try to play that angle—act like our buddy to try to keep an eye on what we were up to. We didn't buy that, but he was kind of cute, so we'd play along—at least the girls anyway." She cocked her head. "Seems odd Lee couldn't find Logan. Logan is right here and has been for years. As far as I know it's no secret—certainly not something the sheriff's office couldn't find out."

"Here as in here on Edisto?" Addie's pulse quickened.

"No, but close. He's living over near Green Pond. He's still handsome for a man his age, but you wouldn't recognize him otherwise—the daredevil is gone. He seems downright calm. We don't talk often, but we've kept in touch here and there over the years. From what I can tell, he keeps to himself mostly, not that I blame him. He got a lot of attention after . . . what happened. It followed him around like a bad luck charm. I guess he finally decided to drop out."

"Could you give me his cell number?" Addie asked.

"I'm not sure. Would you mind if I get in touch with him and give him your number? Then he can call you if he's willing to talk." Julie's wariness was back.

"Sure, that's fine." Addie tried to hide her disappointment. It was much easier for a witness to put off making a call than it was to say no in person.

Both women turned their heads at the crunching of gravel as a beat-up Chevy painted various shades of body shop blue pulled up. Julie raised her hand in a wave.

"That's my friend Celia. She's working this shift with me. She's my roommate, too, now that my ex threw me out." Julie's hand drifted to a small pink scar on her arm, and Addie wondered if the ex did that too. "Sorry, but I gotta go now and help prep for lunch." She stood to leave. "You'll let me know if you find out what happened to them?" Her tone was almost childlike in its vulnerability, and Addie wondered how different Julie's life might have been if her friends had returned to the party that night.

"I promise. Thanks for seeing me," Addie said. Julie nodded, but she was already on her way back in, and Addie watched her disappear through the door with her friend.

As Addie climbed back in the Jeep, she checked her phone and saw she had missed a call from Emma. She listened to the message.

Hi, want to hit Bud's for happy hour tonight? I can pick you up at your place at four-thirty. I made sure it's not karaoke night this time.

Addie laughed out loud. The last time they'd gone to Bud's they had unwittingly walked into a karaoke "classics" nightmare that hit a crescendo with three good ole boys with mullets and tight jeans doing a rendition of Billy Ray Cyrus's "Achy Breaky Heart"— complete with the line dance.

Addie was hesitant to return the call since she didn't know if Emma might be meeting with clients, so she sent a text: *Sounds good—see you at 4:30. We can go over what I learned from Julie Mathis. Maybe it'll spark something you didn't think of before.*

Before she could put the phone down, a text pinged in. *That was quick*, she thought, but it wasn't Emma. It was Lee Bowen. She wondered again why he hadn't told her Logan was local.

How did it go with Julie?

Addie touched *contact* to call, and Lee picked up on the first ring.

"So, how did it go?" he asked immediately.

"Good, I think. I did get one piece of useful information. Turns out Logan Bennett is living in the area—according to Julie, he has been for years." She waited.

"Damn." Lee sighed after a long pause. "I guess after thirty-four years, I got a little lax on keeping up with the witnesses. I hate I missed that." He sounded sincere.

"Don't be too hard on yourself. That's part of the reason for putting a fresh set of eyes on an old case," Addie said, recalling his passion for the case when they first met and feeling a twinge of guilt for embarrassing him now.

"I guess so," he said, sounding tired. "Well, thanks for keeping me in the loop. If you talk to Logan Bennett, will you let me know how that goes?"

"Of course."

"Thanks," he said, ending the call.

Addie stared at the screen for a moment, digesting the call. That was a pretty lame explanation, but sometimes things just get missed—like the cops had missed the clean-swept floor in that shed on Cicada Road.

Addie sent one last text letting Zach and Colleton know she had met with Julie and was leaving the beach in case they needed anything. They wouldn't, though, she sighed. Then she tossed the phone on the seat beside her, pointed her Jeep toward Walterboro, and let her mind wander back to her case.

Who killed Tara Godfrey and Cindy Crosby on the beach that night, and why? And how did the killer disappear without a trace?

CHAPTER 25

I HADN'T EXPECTED TO RUN INTO TARA GODFREY THAT NIGHT.
It was years ago, but the image is still so clear in my mind that it
might as well have been last week. I was walking on the beach, not
headed anywhere in particular, when I noticed the glow of a bonfire
off in the distance and heard the faint sound of music playing. A
party maybe? I was too far away to tell. Then I saw her.

She was sitting alone on the rocks of one of the beach groins.
We'd been spending more time together, and I was smitten. I was
a bit older than she was, but it didn't seem to matter to her, and it
certainly didn't matter to me, especially since she was headed for college only an hour away and wouldn't be living at home. I was sure she
felt the same—all the signs were there. A laugh at a joke that wasn't
funny, a brief touch of a hand, warm gazes . . . Now, here she was.
Sitting there against the backdrop of a full moon with ocean breezes
lifting her hair. She smiled as she recognized me and waved me over.
I thought it must be fate, and I didn't give myself time to chicken
out. I just blurted it all out.

It was fate all right, but not the way I was expecting.

How could I have been so stupid? I felt like an absolute fool
standing there when she finally stopped me. The look on her face—
embarrassment? Pain? Pity? Whatever it was, it wasn't what I'd hoped
for. I would have given anything to have the ground open up and
swallow me. But it didn't, and I had to stand there feeling naked to the
world. She told me I was important to her as a friend, but she didn't
like me that way.

Didn't like me *that* way? Then why had she led me on? I went from hurt to angry in seconds. She was being gracious about it to my face, but what about later? She could tell everyone, and I would be an ugly joke for thinking someone like her could fall for the likes of me. The Main Street gossips would have a feeding frenzy. Tara was prattling on nervously saying something trite about still being friends, but I was so angry I could barely hear her. I wanted to hit something or throw something. I picked up a rock that had broken free from the groins and smashed it down to the ground. How was I to know she would lean in right at that moment? Who the hell could have predicted that? I remember being surprised that there could be that much blood that fast. It pooled for a moment before it started to seep into the sand and the moon reflected a deep red. She hadn't seen it coming either—there was still something like a smile frozen on her face, only now it was grotesque, and her eyes that were so full of life seconds ago looked flat and empty.

My breath was coming fast, and my head was reeling so wildly I almost didn't register the scream behind me.

Almost.

I turned to find Tara's friend, Cindy Crosby, though I didn't know her name at the time. She clutched her hands to her chest as the horror washed over her face. She had seen everything, and clearly didn't think it was an accident. Oh, God! I had to explain before she told anyone. I started toward her, but she turned and ran. Next thing I knew, I was running too. I had to catch her in time.

Cindy must have been disoriented by the shock because she turned and ran the opposite direction from the party. If she hadn't, I doubt I could have caught up with her before she got there. I was surprised at how quick she was—skittling around trees and through brush as though she didn't even feel the scratch of the branches. Fate caught up with her too, though, and she tripped over something and landed facedown at the base of a palmetto tree. As she was scrambling to her feet, I grabbed an ankle and dragged her back down. She was smaller than I was, and once I had her, she never had a chance.

I only intended to explain things when I caught her and pinned her to the ground—tell her it was all an accident. I thought I could make her understand. But she wouldn't listen. She was hitting and kicking and trying to scream. She was so scared I knew I'd never convince her it wasn't how it looked. Nobody would believe me that it was an accident—especially now that I'd chased her down and she was all scratched up.

Some dark thing inside me took over, and next thing I knew, my hands were around her throat. She was gagging and flailing her arms, reaching for something, anything, clawing at the ground and me. It wasn't pretty. Her body convulsed under my weight, and she peed herself before she finally grew still.

The dark thing inside me screamed: *Run!*

There was no way I could leave along the beach or the road—people would see me. My shirt had ripped on a branch as we struggled, and I was covered in bloody scratches and dirt. Anyone who saw me would know something was up. Once those bodies were found, they would figure out what. That part of the beach edged up against wooded land owned by the Gadsden family, and I instinctively headed for the woods. I ran so far and so hard I thought my lungs might explode. Thirty minutes later, I came across a path leading out to the road. This was far enough out to safely cross the road and go the back way without being seen. I stopped to catch my breath. I couldn't imagine anyone else being out that deep in the woods this time of night, but I crouched in the brush just in case. Good thing I did—seconds later I heard a twig snap and the rustle of dead leaves as a man approached along the path. He was headed for the road, coming from the other way—from the direction of the docks where the Gadsdens kept their boats. He walked right by without ever seeing me in those bushes.

I got a good look at him, though. It was Buford Gadsden.

CHAPTER 26

EMMA DROPPED ADDIE OFF AT 6:45 P.M., AFTER HAPPY HOUR.

"Looks like you've got company," Emma said.

"Colleton—that's his Tahoe. The Camry is Zach's. Say, as long as you're here, do you have a minute to come in and meet Zach?"

"I'd like that," Emma said, killing the engine and opening her door.

Zach and Colleton were in their usual spot, buried in work, when Addie and Emma walked in. It was Zach who first raised his head, looking questioningly at Addie.

"Zach, before she takes off, I wanted to introduce you to Emma Hudson," Addie said. "Colleton, I think the two of you have already met."

"We have, but it has been a long time—too long," Colleton said. "You look great."

"Liar—but charming as ever, I see. Please don't get up," she added as they moved to stand, "I can't stay.

"And you, Zach Stander, hardly need an introduction—I'm sure you realize you are the talk of every gossip pool in town."

"Ten bucks says none of it's true."

"If you'd like to let me in on some scoop about your case, I'd be happy to spread it and clear things up," she offered with a conspiratorial wink.

"Great—you can assure everyone my client is innocent."

"Aren't they all?" Emma laughed. "Well, I really do need to go—just wanted to meet you, Zach."

"Are you sure you can't stay?" Colleton asked. "Addie tells us you've been working with her on the old Edisto Beach case. I'm dying to hear more about it."

"Sorry—not tonight. Besides, I'm sure Addie is filling you in," Emma answered.

"Another time then," Colleton said, looking disappointed.

"Zach, I'll be watching that case of yours—along with everyone else in town." She gave a little wave and turned back to the door.

"I'll walk you out," Addie said, holding the screen door and following her onto the porch. Both women looked up as another vehicle pulled in.

"Well, this is certainly the place to be tonight," Emma said.

"That's Eli Jenkins—Sam's grandfather," Addie said. Eli pulled his truck around the other vehicles in the drive and parked in the grass. He climbed out alone, leaving Buck in the truck.

"Hey, Eli," Addie called as he came closer.

"Evening, Addie," Eli said, casting a curious glance at Emma.

"This is Emma Hudson," Addie said. "Have you two met?"

"I don't think so."

"I'm quite sure we haven't. Nice to meet you, Mr. Jenkins," she said, taking the hand Eli extended.

"Likewise, ma'am," Eli said, nodding politely.

"See you later," Emma said, turning back to Addie. "Maybe we can catch lunch one day next week?"

"Sounds good—shoot me a text and let me know what day works. And thanks for the ride tonight." Addie waved to Emma as Eli stepped up on the porch beside her. This time of year, it was still light at 7:00 p.m., and they stood for a moment, listening to crickets trilling as the light softened and the air cooled. Addie took Eli's arm and led him toward the door. "What brings you over this evening?"

"Got something important to tell Zach. Looks like Colleton's here too?"

"He is."

"That's good, I can tell 'em both at the same time." Addie's curiosity was raised, but she knew better than to ask. Eli would say what was on his mind when he was ready.

"Look who I found," Addie said as they walked in.

"Eli!" Zach and Colleton greeted him in unison.

"Wasn't expecting to see you here. What's up?" Zach asked.

Eli didn't waste any time. "I wanted to show you this right away," he said, reaching for his pocket. "Found it in Sam's Tacoma and thought it might be important." Eli pulled the object from his pocket and held it out at arm's length as though it might be something dangerous.

The room went as quiet as a tomb.

"Did you say you found that in Sam's Tacoma?" Zach asked when he finally found his voice.

Eli nodded.

"Who else has access to the vehicle?"

"Nobody." Eli shook his head. "It's been locked in that barn since I picked it up from the sheriff's office and took it home for Sam."

"That's not possible," Colleton said. "Zach and I combed through it weeks ago. That wasn't there then."

"And the sheriff's department searched the Tacoma while they had it. They would surely have taken that if it had been in the truck then," Zach said. His eyes were still glued to the cell phone in Eli's hand, and his mind flashed back to Sam's fixation on getting his truck to Eli that first day in jail.

"I'm not too sure about that," Eli said, his hand still held out. "I went out to the barn to charge the battery since nobody's driving the Tacoma right now. I had to climb in to make sure it was cranking, and I got clumsy and dropped the key down beside the seat. When I reached to pick it up, my hand caught on something, so I got out and crouched down on the ground beside the open door to look closer. Someone—Sam, I reckon—had opened up a seam on the side of the seat cover and made a little pouch. The seam was closed back up with Velcro. If you didn't know it was there, you'd never find it. It was a fluke that I stumbled on it. Anyway, when I slid my hand flat and stuck it in the opening, I found this hidden there."

Realizing that no one was going to take it from his hand, Eli put the cell phone on the coffee table where Zach and Colleton were standing.

"Does it work?" Zach asked, reaching for the phone and turning it over in his hand.

"Don't know," Eli said, "it's dead as a doornail now and my charger didn't fit it."

"Hang on," Addie said, already heading for the other room. "One of the kitchen drawers is full of old chargers. Maybe one of them will work." A moment later, she was back with a tangle of cords in her hands. "Here," she said, taking the phone from Zach and comparing the port to the chargers in her hand.

The others watched in silence.

"We've got a winner," she said finally. "Colleton, plug this in that outlet," she said, handing the phone and charger off to him. He shoved the plug in and watched the screen blink to life.

"What now?" he asked, sounding like he didn't really want to know.

"Dial my number," Zach said, pulling out his own phone. Colleton punched in the numbers and, seconds later, Zach's phone began to ring.

Zach tasted bile in the back of his throat, and his head started to spin. He turned the phone—still ringing—so that the others could read the number on the screen.

"Oh, fuck" was all Colleton could get out.

"What?" Eli hadn't quite caught on. "What?" he asked again when no one spoke up.

"That's the number," Addie said, hating that they had to deal this blow to the old man. "The burner phone that Jessie had all those calls with. The one we thought would lead to whoever . . ." Her voice trailed off as she watched Eli's whole body slump under the weight of her words.

"Oh, fuck," Colleton said again.

"Oh, fuck is right," Zach said as he grabbed his keys and headed for the door. "Colleton, would you mind moving the Tahoe so I can get out? You're parked behind me."

"Where're you going?" Eli asked, still not looking up.

"Where the hell do you think I'm going? I'm going to the jail to ask my client why he's been lying his ass off to me since day one. Colleton—the Tahoe. Now."

"Better yet, how about I drive us there?" Colleton was pulling his keys from his pocket.

"Fine, just get your big ass moving."

"I'm coming too." Eli was standing straight again and looked ready to walk through a wall of fire if he had to.

"Eli, we've been through this before, and I don't have time to waste standing here explaining it all again."

"What? That privilege shit? Are you kidding? I found the phone, remember? I already know it's the burner number on Jessie's bills, and I know he kept it hidden."

"Yeah, and that's bad enough. At this point, you can't testify about how it got there or what it means, because you don't know. Let's keep it that way."

"Maybe he has a good explanation." The desperation in Eli's eyes had made its way to his voice now.

"He damn well better."

Eli looked ready to make this a bigger fight, and Addie put a hand lightly on his arm. "Eli, Zach's right—let him do his job."

"But—"

"Wait here with me. If there's something they can tell you, they'll tell you when they get back."

"I need to be there for Sam."

"What Sam needs is for you to let Zach do his job."

Eli glared at Zach and Colleton.

"We're wasting time," Zach said.

"Go," he said finally.

Colleton was surprisingly fast for a man his size, and he already had the truck in reverse as Zach went to close his door.

"Hang on a sec," Zach said, and leaned out the door as his gut finally made good on its threat.

"Thanks for the warning," Colleton said, eyeing his floor mats.

When he finally stopped heaving, Zach sat back in the seat and closed the door behind him. "Hit it," he said, wiping his mouth.

"Here," Colleton said, lifting the console cover and pulling out a pack of gum as he backed out into the street.

"Thanks," Zach said, putting several sticks in his mouth.

"Sorry—I'm fresh out of beer in here."

"No problem. I'm not sure it would stay down right now anyway, but something tells me I'm going to want several by the time this night is over."

Zach and Colleton were already in an interview room when the detention officer brought Sam in. He was limping slightly this time, but Zach was too angry to risk opening his mouth while the officer was present to ask what happened.

"Cuffs?" the officer asked.

"Off," Colleton said when Zach didn't answer.

With the cuffs still in his hand, the officer motioned toward the buzzer by the door. "You two know the drill."

"Got it," Colleton said, and the officer left, closing the door behind him.

"Wasn't expecting to see you two tonight," Sam said as he joined Colleton at the small table.

"Wasn't expecting to be here," Colleton said. Zach was still standing and still silent.

"You're mighty quiet tonight, Zach."

"Yeah, well, I'm busy thinking. Remember the first day we met, Sam?" Zach's voice was measured for the moment.

"What do you think? I'd been thrown in jail for a murder I didn't commit. Not the kind of day you forget."

"Remember asking me about your Tacoma? Asking me to make sure Eli took it?"

Sam nodded.

"Do you remember why you told me you wanted him to have it?" Sam opened his mouth as if to answer, but Zach cut him off. "Because I sure remember that. You told me Eli's old truck was broken down more often than it ran, and you wanted him to be able to use your newer one." The measured tone of Zach's voice was starting to slip.

"The first time I saw that truck of his, I thought that might be right. Funny thing, though, he turned that key, and it started right up. That day and every time I've seen it since. Hell, that old truck runs so good, he hasn't even once used yours. But then you expected that, I'm thinking. He put your Tacoma in the barn for safekeeping. You expected that, too, didn't you, Sam?"

Sam didn't try to answer this time. The puzzled look in his eyes had been replaced by something darker, and he leaned back, as though trying to put distance between himself and Zach. There was nowhere for him to go in the tiny room.

"But what you didn't take into account, Sam, is how much Eli—*Lija*—cares about you. Worries about you. Wants to take care of you."

"I don't need you to tell me Lija loves me."

"Is that so? So, tell me then, smart-ass, this afternoon, after working all day and probably being tired as hell, what do you think Eli did? Sit down and take it easy? No, he was worried your battery might need charging since it's not being used. So he trekked out to the barn to see if it would crank. But the key slipped out of his hand. He slid his hand down the side of the seat, reaching after it. Only it wasn't a key he found, was it? It was a hidden pocket. And what was in it, Sam?" Zach's voice was booming.

Sam closed his eyes as though he could wish it all away.

"Answer me!" Zach slammed his hand on the table and Sam jumped as though he'd been hit.

"He found a phone," Sam said, in a voice barely more than a whisper.

"*A* phone? How about a *burner* phone. And guess what else we have now?"

Sam was quiet again.

"We have Jessie Gadsden's phone records." Zach paused and watched Sam's eyes as that information sank in. "Yes, exactly," Zach said as the panic spread across Sam's face. "We know you were calling Jessie every day—at all hours of the day—from that burner phone. You swore you barely knew her, said you just did her accounting. You. Lied. To. Me. Over and over, from day one. Why?" Zach knocked over the empty chair and the metal hit the floor with a racket that filled the room.

"Easy," Colleton warned, looking at the door. "They aren't supposed to be listening, but if you make enough noise to hear in the hall, they're going to check on us, and they're likely to cut us short for the night if they see the expression that's on your face right now."

Zach gave Colleton a look that said *fuck off,* but he took a deep breath and lowered his voice. "Why did you lie to me?"

"I didn't see any other way . . . ," Sam started and then stopped.

"And what did you think would happen when we got the inventory of Jessie's car?"

Colleton caught Zach's eyes. Zach was bluffing now, and Colleton knew it. Zach gambled that Colleton would keep his mouth shut. Zach needed to hear this part from Sam.

"Tell me what wasn't there when we got that inventory, Sam."

"There were no business records for me to pick up," Sam said. "There never were. I made that up to explain why I was there. Only, I guess I wasn't thinking clearly after finding her that way, and it didn't occur to me until later that you'd find out there weren't any. I still thought it could work, though. I knew I didn't kill her, so I thought if I kept my mouth shut for a while, they'd find whoever did this, and no one would ever know about—"

"Never know about what? Dammit—say it."

"I thought no one would ever have to know we were lovers," Sam said. He was crying now.

"Did anyone know other than the two of you?"

"Not that I know of. Jessie said it had to be that way for now. She wasn't sure how her father would handle . . . the race thing. But she knew for sure that some of his buddies—that JB guy in particular—would raise a ruckus. The little house she lived in is one her daddy owns, back on some of their property, and she didn't want to rock the boat. We were never together in public. She bought the burner phone—used cash to buy it and those cash-paid credit cards you buy at gas stations to add minutes. She said it couldn't be traced."

"And what were you planning to do if things got more serious?"

"We weren't thinking that far ahead. We weren't thinking at all. I saw her at a Walterboro Rice Festival concert and recognized her. We'd only met once at the office, but she had the kind of looks you didn't forget. I said hello and we started talking, mostly about work at first—we were both ambitious. By the end of the concert, we had a connection and I ended up at her place. I figured it would be a one-time thing, but then she called me later that week. From there it just happened. I was crazy about her—she said it was mutual."

Zach leaned over to pull the chair back to its feet, pushed it nearer to the table, and sat down heavily. He ran his hands through his hair, his mind racing. Suddenly Barton had a potential motive— the kind of motive that would resonate with a jury.

"Doesn't it help us that I loved her?" Sam asked. "I could never hurt her."

"Surely you can't be that naive. Haven't you ever noticed how frequently it's the spouse or the lover?"

"But I called for help."

"Barton will say it was remorse for what you'd done."

"Can they force me to tell them about our relationship?"

"No, but were you not listening when we told you they'd search your apartment? All it takes is a single hair on a pillow, a used washcloth, fibers from her clothes."

"Jessie was never in my apartment—never once."

"Maybe not, but you were at her place," Zach said.

"Well, yes. That's where we always went. Would they search that too?"

"What do you think? Hell, yes, they searched it, and from the sound of it, your DNA was all over the place. When was the last time you were there?"

"I stayed over the night before she died. I left early to go to work."

"Did you have sex that night?"

"That's kind of a personal question."

"No fucking kidding—get used to them. There will be a lot more if you testify at trial. When was the last time you had sexual intercourse with Jessie Gadsden?"

"That next morning before I went to work—around six-thirty. The day she was murdered."

"Did you use a condom?"

"Why the hell would that matter?"

"Why do you think? I'm asking about DNA evidence."

"Oh." Sam's face finally registered understanding. "No. She was on the pill."

Zach looked at Colleton as both their faces fell. "Barton probably knows about the sex from forensics," Zach said. He felt his stomach turn over again. Colleton nodded, and Zach knew they were thinking the same thing—Barton made his death penalty announcement because he already had this bombshell, and he saw it as a sure thing.

"What?" Sam was in full panic mode now.

"Mind if I take a shot at this?" Colleton asked.

"Please, work some magic."

"There are pieces that don't fit here, Sam," Colleton said. "You had the burner phone—why did she call you on your work phone at 8:38 that night? Why wouldn't she have called the burner? And since you did talk to her on the work phone, why did you call her back later on the burner?"

Sam sighed. "It's complicated. She did call the burner first. But I never took that phone in the office—I was afraid I'd get the phones mixed up or leave the burner lying around. She knew that. When I didn't answer the burner, she figured I was in the office, and she called my work phone. Like I told you earlier, I told her I had to get something filed and then I'd come out there. The call I made later from my burner to her was when I was in the car, to let her know I was on my way. She didn't answer. Now we know why."

Colleton shook his head. "But why did she want you to come to the church? You said you were never together in public places. Why not meet her at home?"

"She didn't want to wait that long. She was—well, spooked, I guess you'd say."

"Spooked? By what—being in that old church at night?"

"God, no, she loved that place. It would never frighten her to be there."

"Then why was she frightened that night? That's another piece I can't make fit," Colleton said.

"I don't know all the details, but I know it had something to do with a project she'd been working on."

"A project? Something for work?"

"Not exactly." Sam's tone was evasive again.

"Oh, for fuck's sake—is there something else you're hiding? So help me, if I catch you lying to me again, you can find yourself another lawyer. I'm not going into a murder trial blind with a solicitor who's locked and loaded. Especially when it's my own client keeping me blindfolded." Zach was getting close to his breaking point.

Sam looked like a deer caught in headlights. "You'd really cut out on me?"

"Start talking or I'm done."

Sam wiped his face and looked up at the ceiling as if he were arranging notes in his head.

"It would help if you knew Jessie," he said. "She could be sweet when she wanted to, but she was also fierce. And once she set her sights on something, she was hell-bent on getting it. She had a bunch of brothers, and she was determined to keep up with everything they did, maybe even do it better."

Zach nodded. This sounded a lot like Pastor Ben's description.

"Her family owns hundreds, maybe even thousands, of acres of land—and a hunting lodge. They had a big hunt at the end of the year, before the end of deer season. They stayed out there for a week—hunted all day and drank around the campfire all night, it sounds like. Anyway, one night Jessie was asleep, or at least she let them think she was, and JB started talking about something that happened a long time ago—some kind of mystery or a secret or something. They must have suspected she was awake, so they shut up, but she'd heard enough. She got it in her head that she was going to solve the mystery.

"She wouldn't tell me any details—said it was better if I didn't know. Jessie had a flair for drama, and that's all I thought her secrecy was. I wish now I had pressed harder. All she would tell me was that they'd mentioned somebody they suspected knew the answer or the secret or whatever the hell it was. From what she said, she was spying on that person."

"Spying?" Colleton asked. "Like how?"

"Like maybe she pretended to be a friend to get them to talk to her about things? I'm not sure, but she must not have been careful enough, because that night when she called me to come to the church, she was convinced she'd been caught. And she sounded scared—real scared."

"Wait." Zach sat up as a surge of energy set his cells on fire. "Are you telling us she was scared someone would harm her? As in physical harm?"

"She made it sound like that," Sam said. "But, like I told you, she had a flair for drama, and I didn't realize how serious she was—or I would have gone sooner."

"Jessie thought someone meant her harm and a few hours later she was lying dead in the church? Sam, this is huge. Who was she afraid of? Didn't she tell you anything that might give us a clue?"

"Don't you think I've been racking my brain for that every day since then? Shit, Zach, I'm going to trial for a murder I didn't commit. If I knew who did, I'd be shouting it. That's what I'm trying to tell you—I don't know." Sam had started to cry again. "I know I shouldn't have kept all this from you."

"Lied to me," Zach corrected him.

"You're right, I lied to you, and I know it must be hard to trust me now, but I swear I'm not lying now." He put his head in his hands.

"Let's focus on what we do know." Colleton was trying to salvage the situation.

"Focus on what?" Sam looked up.

"Maybe we could figure out who she was spying on if we knew something about the secret. Did she say anything about that?"

"Only that it was old—from a long time ago."

"Do you know what the secret was about?"

Sam put his palms on the table and leaned forward.

"Her father," he said.

CHAPTER 27

It was almost 9:00 p.m. when Zach and Colleton pulled the Tahoe back in the drive. Eli's truck was still in the yard. "Thought about what you're going to tell him?" Colleton asked, nodding toward the truck.

"I don't think I can tell Eli about the affair. I doubt the solicitor would call Eli as a witness, but I can't risk him taking the stand with that knowledge. I can tell him that Sam gave us some information we think might lead us to someone who had a reason to harm her." Zach shrugged. "Maybe that will at least give Eli something to hope for. I think that's the best I can do right now."

"Want me to come along? He may not take this well." Thunder rumbled faintly in the distance.

Zach shook his head. "Thanks, but I signed on for this. You head on out before that storm gets here." Zach opened the door to exit the truck.

"Careful where you step," Colleton said with a chuckle.

"Ugh, thanks. I'll get the hose and clean that up in the morning."

At some point since they'd left earlier, Buck had been let out of the truck and was lying on the porch. Zach heard the jingle of his tags as the old dog stood and shook himself.

"Hey there, fella," Zach said, holding out a hand. Buck gave him a gentle nudge with a cold nose, then settled back on the floor.

Eli and Addie were on the couch talking when Zach walked in. The television was on with the sound turned down. Addie's eyes flew immediately to Zach's, and he could tell she already knew the news wasn't good.

"Shit, you look like you could use one of these," Addie said, holding up the beer in her hand.

"He looks like I might need one, too," Eli said.

Zach didn't answer, just sat down across from Eli as Addie got up to go to the kitchen on a beer run.

Eli slid to the edge of his seat. "Tell me Sam has an explanation that makes all of this go away," he said, his voice pleading.

Zach shook his head. "It isn't good."

"But you aren't allowed to tell me," Eli said, putting it out there so Zach didn't have to.

"Something like that," Zach said, reaching to take the beer Addie was holding out. She folded herself up on the corner of the couch and handed the other beer to Eli, who wasted no time turning it up.

"I'm sorry, Eli, I know this is frustrating for you." Zach was expecting a fight, but that wasn't what he got.

"It's okay, Zach." Eli was trying to comfort him, and Zach hated that he couldn't do the same.

"I'm old," Eli went on, "but not so old I can't remember the only reason a man Sam's age would be calling a woman all hours of the day and night. And I'm not color-blind either—I understand why they kept it quiet, especially in this small town.

"Those business records Sam said he drove to the church to fetch—that always sounded like bullshit to me. I'm guessing he's finally admitted there were never any records?"

"He has," Zach said. The solicitor already knew what was and was not in Jessie's car—no privileged information there.

"I 'spect you're pissed off at Sam, right about now," Eli said, draining the rest of his beer. "And I can't say as I blame you for that.

Sam was dead wrong to lie to you, but that doesn't mean he murdered that girl." Eli put the empty bottle on the coffee table and looked up at Zach.

"You can be as mad as you like—he deserves it. But promise me you'll stick with my Sam, and you won't give up on this trial." Eli locked eyes with Zach and didn't look away.

"I won't lie to you, Eli," Zach said, holding the old man's gaze. "I've given some serious thought tonight about whether I'm still the right person to take this to a jury."

"You can't mean that, Zach. Sam needs you. I don't know much about your life, but I'm betting you had a mother and a father who believed in you and encouraged you—gave you a good word when you needed it and a strong one when you needed that, too."

Zach felt a sting. The old man had no idea how much Zach and Sam had in common.

"You probably had others supporting you too. Maybe a sibling or an aunt . . . somebody who believed in you. But Sam? Sam never had any family but me. He never knew his mama or his father. Hell, I barely remember his mama, and I don't have a clue in the world who his father might be—maybe she didn't either. I remember my old man, though, and he was as useless and hateful as an old mule with a bad leg. It wasn't bad enough that he never did anything good for me. No, he had to make a special effort to make things worse. Beat the crap out of me every time he took a notion. Seemed notions came to him right regularly.

"Sam's mama didn't even say goodbye. I came home and found him on my living room floor in a cardboard box with a blanket like an unwanted puppy. Left a note saying she was gone, but not a word about where to. I promised him—and myself—it would be different for him. Promised even if he never had another soul in the world, he'd always have me, and I've kept my word." Eli stood up in front of Zach, and Zach stood to match his gaze, as Eli finished pleading his case.

"I made sure Sam knew right from wrong, but I never raised a hand to him. Didn't want him to grow up thinking it was okay to hit someone you're supposed to protect. For the same reasons I never raised a hand to him, I can't close my heart to him now. I know he did wrong to lie to you, but I also know he felt like he had reason. Most important, I know in my bones he didn't kill that girl. Please, Zach, I can't help him alone this time. You may be our last chance."

Eli's eyes were dry, but the tremor in his voice gave away his pain. From the corner of his eye, Zach could see tears slipping down Addie's face, and he knew better than to look at her if he was going to have any chance of holding himself together.

"Eli, I'm not sure what I think about Sam right now, but I'm sure about you." Zach swallowed hard. "I trust your moral compass more than I do my own where Sam is concerned. You believe in Sam's innocence, and I believe in you. That's all I need to know. I can't make any promises about how the trial will go, and you need to understand things could go very badly. But I promise I'll be there for whatever comes. And if the verdict isn't the right one, I'll be there for the appeal and any appeals that come after. I'll stick with you until you tell me it's time not to."

"I believe in you, too," was all Eli said before he turned and headed for the door.

Zach watched through the screen door as Eli and Buck made their way to the old truck. Buck usually bounced ahead once he saw Eli was going to the truck, but tonight was different. Tonight, Buck hung back and walked slowly at Eli's feet, as if he knew Eli needed him there. Reaching the truck, Eli opened the door and waited while Buck jumped up onto the seat. Then he raised one arm to Zach and climbed in.

Once again, the old truck started the first time, and Zach closed the door.

"You must be starving—I know I am. How about I make us a sandwich?" Addie's eyes were pink, but she had wiped her face dry and was making a brave attempt at a cheery smile.

"Only if it comes with another beer," he said.

"That works. Come out to the kitchen with me."

"How about I meet you in there in a minute? I seriously need to brush my teeth right now." Addie cocked her head.

"Don't ask," he said, "and be careful going out to the car in the morning."

A few minutes later he went to the kitchen to find Addie at the counter putting dinner together.

"Sit," she said, pointing toward the table where she already had a beer waiting for him. "I've got this. Roast beef or turkey?"

"Roast beef."

"Cheddar or provolone?"

"Cheddar," he said, taking a long pull from his beer.

"You didn't say as much, but I'm guessing Eli was right about the reason Sam had all those calls with Jessie."

"He was, and he was right about the reason they kept it hidden. According to Sam, the burner was Jessie's idea, and she bought it with cash."

"Do you think Barton knows?"

"Barton may not know about the affair, but he knows enough. That probably prompted his dog and pony show at the courthouse. Sam said he had stayed over the night before the murder. They had sex the next morning, so Sam's DNA would be on the body, and Barton could have had enough time to get those results back by the date of the announcement."

"Well, shit," Addie said.

"Shit is right."

Addie glanced out the window as a trace of lightning flashed briefly on the horizon. "That storm's getting closer," she said as she carried sandwiches to the table and sat down in front of Zach. "I assume Sam finally admitted he wasn't at the church to pick up business records?"

"There might have been some bluffing to get that out of him, but, yes, he finally came clean on that, too." Zach took a bite of his sandwich.

"Then why? Why did he go to the church that night?" she asked.

Zach filled her in on Sam's story about Jessie spying on someone she'd befriended, trying to solve a mystery about her father, and about Jessie being frightened when she asked him to come to the church.

"That's quite a story," Addie said when he'd finished. "The connection between a secret about her father and her dying words to Sam is intriguing. Do you think there's any admissible evidence or is it all hearsay?"

"Well, if we put Sam on the stand, I think he could testify about her last words to him."

"And the rest of it?" she asked.

"The call that night saying she was frightened and asking him to come might qualify as an excited utterance or a statement of her emotional condition, maybe even a present sense impression. But none of that can happen if we don't put Sam on the stand."

"You don't sound convinced that's the way to go."

"Let's say my experience with Sam thus far is leading me to question whether he's telling the whole truth and nothing but the truth. If the jury doesn't believe him, it will backfire."

"The part that sets my alarms off is the scheme that starts it all. I mean, she hears something about an old secret and thinks she can trick someone into revealing what it is? That all sounds sketchy to me," Addie said.

"You're right. We need a lot more detail."

"Any idea how to get it?"

"Not yet, and, honestly, I'm too tired to think any more about it tonight. I'm ready to call it a day."

"Okay, babe. Go get your shower. I'll put everything away in here and be in shortly."

Twenty minutes later, Zach was easing into bed to the sound of the shower in the next room and the pounding of rain on the roof. The slow-moving storm that had been creeping up all evening was finally here.

"Shit—that was close!" The water shut off abruptly as lightning flashed and thunder rattled the windows. "Honey? I think I left my laptop on. Could you power it down and unplug it before this storm knocks it out? It's there on the desk."

"Got it," he answered, hoisting himself up and leaning over the desk. An email flashed on the screen as he reached for it. "Hey—you got a reminder for an appointment with Dr. Burgess," he said.

"Thanks," she said, a little too lightly, as she came into the room.

"Isn't that your ob-gyn?"

"Mm-hmm." She didn't make eye contact.

"Everything okay?"

"Sure—just a checkup."

"This isn't the time of year you usually do that—you sure you're okay?"

"I'm fine. I want to talk with her about vaccines and vitamins and birth control—things to think about before you think about getting . . . you know." She still hadn't looked up.

"Getting pregnant? Dammit, Addie, are you really bringing this up now? While I'm up to my ass in a high-profile murder case—with a client who seems to be working against me and the whole world watching to see if I go down for the count? My checkbook's a joke, my practice is in shambles, and you thought this would be a good time to consider getting pregnant?"

"If not now, when? There's always some reason and then another." She finally turned to face him. "I've been straight with you from the start that I want a family. You said you did too. Zach, I'm thirty-three. If we started trying right now, there's no way to know how long it might take. It doesn't always happen the first time, despite that crap they told us in high school. You know I love you, but . . ." She was crying now.

"What I know is I feel like I've been hit by a train twice tonight. What I know is I've had all I can take right now, and what I know is I'm going to sleep on the couch." He grabbed his pillow and turned for the door. "And," he said, spinning around and yanking the quilt from the bed, "I'm taking this with me."

The slam of the door shook the room.

CHAPTER 28

ELI POURED ANOTHER TWO FINGERS OF JACK DANIELS AND PUT THE bottle back on the floor. Thunder rolled outside, and Buck raised his head, eyes pinned to the south wall. Probably just the storm, but Eli wasn't one to ignore Buck's instincts. He turned off the lamp and eased to the south window, pulling back the edge of the curtain. Buck followed, his hackles up. The porch light didn't reach very far in this direction, but a flash of lightning lit the sky like noon, giving a clear view.

"Not a thing out there, Buck," Eli said. But he took the rifle—another trusted friend—from the rack and put it by the door just in case.

Eli returned to his chair but left the lamp off. Tennessee whiskey tasted the same in the dark. Besides, he liked the way the lightning lit up the room. Buck abandoned his vigil at the south wall and curled at Eli's feet.

Eli's thoughts raced. It wasn't that Sam had a girlfriend Eli didn't know about. Hell, most kids kept stuff like that to themselves, but in a million years he never would have guessed his grandson was having a go with Buford Gadsden's daughter. Eli and Buford had crossed paths a few times, but they were from different worlds, and in those days, there had been no way to step from his world into that white one. Given how things had turned out for Sam and Jessie, maybe there still wasn't.

Eli had known when he discovered the hidden phone that it wasn't good, but it never entered his mind that it was the thing that would link Sam to Jessie—certainly not that it was the burner they'd been talking about. What would he have done if he had realized what he'd found? Taken it to Zach anyway? Or destroyed it and never told another soul?

He was thinking it would have been the latter. No man liked to think he would deliberately do something wrong. But what was wrong and what was right? It sure as hell wasn't right for Sam to lose his life for something Eli knew he couldn't have done, or that Sam's trial would be tainted by the color of his skin and the color of the victim's.

Buck roused again, only this time his focus was to the east— at the front door. A low rattle filled his throat. Not quite a growl, but something had his attention. Eli put his glass down and moved toward the door, reaching for the rifle. There was a narrow opening between the curtains over the glass pane in the door, and he peered out. The reach of the porch light was farther in this direction, and Eli chuckled when he spotted the patch of gray and brown fur that had Buck all bowed up. The storm had sent a raccoon scuttling for shelter, and Buck clearly did not cotton to this critter on his turf. The dog whined and put a paw to the door—his signal for out. Eli put the rifle back by the door and knelt to rub Buck's wiry fur. The dog was all muscle and wriggling with excitement.

"Buck, you got no business out in that storm, and that old coon will give you more than a fair fight. You'd best stay inside with me." Buck disagreed. He put his paw back on the door and barked—his signal for *out now*. Eli took both hands and ruffled Buck's fur and laughed as the dog huffed, shook him off, and pressed his paw back to the door.

"All right, buddy, I'm gonna give you what you're asking for. But if you chase that blasted thing so far out in the woods that you don't get back till after I'm gone to bed, your crazy ass is out for the night. You understand?" Eli could have sworn the dog grinned. He patted him on the rump one last time and opened the door, and Buck shot out like a bullet. Eli watched, chuckling, as the raccoon disappeared into the woods with Buck hot on his heels. Damn fool dog.

God, I wish I had half his energy, Eli thought as he settled back into his chair and reached for his glass. His thoughts went back to Sam and Jessie and what this might mean for Sam's trial. A new question came to him: did Buford know? Could he have known earlier? His next thought made his blood run cold: did JB know? Could he have something to do with what happened to Jessie? Eli had long suspected JB was capable of that kind of violence. What if . . .

Lightning cracked so loud that Eli jumped and the last of his whiskey spilled across his lap as the glass fell to the floor. That wasn't just close, it hit something. Eli hurried to the window.

Sure enough, the lightning had struck a small toolshed and started a fire. With everything so wet, he wasn't worried about the house, but the truck was parked between the shed and the edge of the woods. He grabbed for his keys to move it away from the fire. It wasn't until he was down the steps and running in the direction of the truck that it hit him—the flames weren't coming from the roof of the shed where lightning would have hit. They were down around the ground and running along a line like they were fueled by a streak of something flammable sprayed along the edge of the shed. This fire was man-made, and no accident. As that thought hit him, he heard the distant slam of a truck door, and then another, and, like Buck's, Eli's own instincts kicked in.

He ran back for the rifle and pulled it to his shoulder. Seconds later he saw taillights and heard gravel scattering. Eli's sniper skills were rusty but still there. One of the taillights shattered, then they were out of range. *Oh no you don't, you fucking cowards. You ain't getting off that easy.* He ran for the truck. He would chase those bastards down and put an end to this shit now.

He hadn't run more than a few yards before his foot snagged on something that sent him sprawling face-first to the ground. The impact sent a sharp pain through his hip, snatching his breath away, and he lay motionless for a moment waiting for the pain to ease. Slowly, he regained his senses, and a few cautious attempts confirmed he could move his leg. The hip wasn't broken. The ground was soaked, and mud had caked the side of his face and his clothes. Moving gingerly, Eli raised himself up onto all fours. Damn if his fall hadn't given those fuckers time to get away. He'd never catch them now—no sense trying. The rain was pelting down harder, and he couldn't see more than a few feet. What the hell had he tripped over, anyway? He turned and groped his way through the muck. At first, he could only feel mud and wet. Then his hand brushed against the unmistakable wiry hair, still warm. Eli heard a low keening, but it didn't quite register with him that it was coming from him. He crept closer and gently lifted Buck's limp body into his lap. A hole was torn through his old friend's chest.

No. No! No, no, no, please, God, no, he begged. *Don't let it be.*

But it was. Lightning hadn't hit the shed, and it wasn't a crack of lightning he'd heard at all. It had been the crack of a rifle. Buck must have circled back from the woods when he'd heard the intruders come into the yard. With the heart of a warrior, Buck was hardwired to protect what he loved—and that had cost Eli's faithful friend his life.

The old man lifted his face to the sky as the rain punished the ground, and his howl rivaled the thunder that followed.

Zach was dead to the world when the phone rang, and he struggled to make sense of where he was as he sat up against the coarse material of the couch. Oh. Right.

He groped for the phone. Colleton. What the hell did he want this time of night?

"Colleton? You all right?"

"Yeah, but I'm worried about Eli."

"He took the news better than I'd expected," Zach said, thinking Colleton was talking about Sam.

"No, I mean this storm. It's pretty bad out here."

"Yeah, it had a punch to it when it rolled through town, too, but Eli's weathered worse storms, and—"

"Lightning must have hit something over on his farm," Colleton interrupted. "I can see the glow over the back tree line. It doesn't look big enough to be the house, but it's big enough to have me worried, and he's not answering his phone. I've called and called, but it just rings. I'm getting dressed to drive over there, but it's not possible to drive through the woods—I'll have to drive the long way around and it will take me a while. You could get there faster from where you are. Would you mind meeting me over there?"

"On my way," Zach said, already up. "Do you think I should call the fire department?"

"Already called," Colleton said. "Just get over there. Call my cell as soon as you get there and let me know what's going on, okay?"

"Got it," Zach said, ending the call. He had left his clothes hanging on the back of the desk chair in the bedroom, so he opened the door quietly and grabbed them. If Addie was awake, she didn't say anything, and that suited him fine right now. He went back to the living room, dressed, and was in the car seconds later.

By the time Zach turned down the long dirt drive to the farmhouse, the rain had doused the fire, though smoke still hung in the air. Pulling around the house he could see it had been a shed that burned. The house looked fine. He dialed Colleton's number.

"Hey," Colleton answered. "I'm still a few minutes away. What's on fire?"

"Nothing anymore," Zach told him. "It looks like lightning hit a shed. The rain put it out, though. You can tell the fire department to call their truck back."

"Okay. Where's Eli? Why didn't he answer the phone?"

"No sure yet, the house is dark, so maybe he's sleeping. The drive is a muddy nightmare, so I'm still making my way up there. I'll bang on the door and wake him up."

"Thanks—I'll be there shortly." Colleton hung up.

Zach turned the car so the headlights would light a path to the house. It was only then that he saw the lone figure on the porch.

"Eli? Eli!" Zach was out of the car and running. Eli was sitting motionless at the top of the steps with something dark cradled in his arms. He didn't answer or even turn his head. Zach stopped in his tracks at the bottom step, finally able to make out what Eli held.

"Eli?" Zach kept his voice soft and low. "Eli, did Buck get hurt in the fire?"

Eli shook his head.

"Did he get hit by the lightning?"

"Wasn't no lightning," Eli said simply. "Wasn't no lightning that started that fire, and wasn't no lighting killed Buck, neither." Eli sounded like he was about to break.

"Can you tell me what happened?"

"What does it look like happened? Those hateful soulless fuckers shot my dog. They snuck in the yard like cowards in the dark and set fire to my shed and they Shot. My. Dog."

"Did you see who it was?"

"No. By the time I got out here, they'd run back up to the road where they left the truck."

"Did you get a good look at the truck?

"No, but it was a dark color—and now it's missing a taillight."

"You shot out a taillight from way back here?" Zach asked, looking back toward the road.

Eli wasn't answering. He was bent over Buck, and it wasn't until Zach saw the convulsing of his shoulders that he realized Eli was sobbing.

"Eli, I don't know who did this. But I aim to find out. And when I do, I promise I'll make them pay."

Eli's sobs had stopped, and he looked up with a quiet rage. "If you plan to settle this score your way, Zach Stander, you'd better find them before I do."

CHAPTER 29

Zach was gone the next morning when Addie woke up. He hadn't spoken to her since last night, but she'd heard him on the phone earlier about what had happened at Eli's last night, and it made her sick inside. The police hadn't found any prints on the envelope with the noose, but she still suspected JB and wondered if he'd been the culprit last night as well.

She'd also heard Zach say something about working at Colleton's place today. She suspected that part was a last-minute plan so Zach could avoid her after last night's fight.

She padded to the bathroom and grimaced at the puffy pink eyes that stared back from the mirror. She ran cold water over a washcloth and pressed it to her face and stood there a moment relishing the cool of the water. Her phone rang. Zach? She lowered the cloth to look at the screen. It wasn't a number she recognized, and she started to let it go to voice mail. *What the hell,* she thought, *any voice would be welcome right about now.*

"Ms. Stone?"

"Yes." She didn't recognize the voice.

"I got your number from Julie Mathis—she said you wanted to talk to me about . . . about the Edisto murders."

"Logan? Logan Bennett?" She couldn't believe her luck.

"That's me. What is it you wanted to know?" he asked. Addie didn't want to have this conversation over the phone—she wanted to see his face and body language.

"Could we meet somewhere? Maybe for coffee?"

"I'm not too keen on coming into town when I don't have to . . ." His voice trailed off.

"I could come to you in Green Pond," she suggested. "What's your address?"

"I'd rather you not come to my place—nothing personal. Do you know where the old Sheldon Church is, in Yemassee?"

"The old Greek revival ruins? Sure—do you want to meet there? Say in an hour and a half?"

"Yeah, that works. See you then."

"Okay, bye," she said, but he was already gone.

She leaned in and started the shower—she wanted to get there early. The last thing she wanted was for him to be waiting around and get cold feet.

Sheldon Church was burned by British troops in 1779, rebuilt, and burned again by Sherman's 15th Corps in 1865. Now only its exterior redbrick walls and perimeter of towering columns remained, surrounded by ancient grave markers and live oaks. Despite its tragic history, on a sunny morning the picturesque ruins evoked a calm that bordered on hypnotic.

Arriving fifteen minutes early, Addie was surprised to find Logan already there. He had parked his truck and was sitting on the lowered tailgate looking very much at ease in the middle of nowhere. Julie had apparently been right about his preference for staying away from crowds. As Addie walked toward him and got a closer look at his face, she realized Julie had been right about that, too. There was no doubting he would have been a heartthrob as a teenager.

"Logan Bennett, I presume," Addie said.

"Come on, I couldn't have been that hard to find." He smiled.

"You do seem to have been off the grid for a while."

"I didn't have much choice. You're interested in this case after more than thirty years. Imagine what it was like back then." He shook his head as he searched for words. "People were angry about what happened and scared it might happen again. They wanted answers and they wanted to feel safe and, maybe more than anything, they were desperate for someone to blame—anyone. And there I was. The mere fact that I happened to leave the party during the time period they were killed was enough to land me in jail for two murders I didn't have anything to do with."

"You didn't exactly help yourself by refusing to say where you were," Addie said.

"Maybe not, but even after they found proof of my alibi, there were people who refused to believe it. They convinced themselves I somehow killed those girls and hoodwinked everyone into believing I was somewhere else. I got a lot of hate mail, and then the threats started coming a little closer than my mailbox, if you know what I mean."

"I do," Addie said, thinking about the brick through the window and the noose left on their doorsteps.

"I was scared for myself, and, worse, for any friends I might still have, so I dropped out of sight for a while. I hadn't planned on it being permanent, but eventually, I came to realize I liked the peace and quiet. I guess you could say it works for me."

Something was sure working for him, Addie thought as an image of Julie Mathis flickered in her mind. The man with her this morning looked comfortable in his own skin and seemed to have made peace with what happened far better than poor Julie had.

"Julie told me about her talk with you, and that you have all the sheriff's office files. I'm not sure what I would have to add to that," he said. "What is it you wanted to ask?"

"I know your alibi was being on a shrimp boat with Buford Gadsden on another part of the island that night, but that information only came out because someone else called in an anonymous tip. According to Emma, you wouldn't say anything at the time other than you were buying drugs. Let's start with why you were so reluctant to tell the details."

"I didn't want to get anyone else in trouble."

"Some kind of honor among thieves?"

"I had a damn good reason to tell on myself. That didn't mean I should rat out the others."

"Surely you weren't going to take the rap for two murders just to protect someone who was selling drugs."

"I seriously doubt that, but I guess we'll never know for sure," he said. "At the time, I was convinced that whoever killed them would mess up and get caught, and I'd be out without having to involve anyone else. It didn't happen the way I imagined it would, but at least the truth came out on its own."

"Emma told me the basics of your alibi—what was in the news— but anything else she might have known would be privileged. She can't tell me, but you can. Now that all these years have passed, can you tell me the details?"

"You talked to Emma?" His face lit up. "I haven't talked to her in years—decades. How is she?"

"She's good. Retired from the PD's office and has a small private practice."

"Good for her," he said. "She was good to me, and she believed my story was true when no one else did." He had deflected her question.

"May I?" Addie asked, patting the tailgate with her hand.

"Sure," he said, sliding to one end and leaving her the other.

"So, about my question."

"Which question?"

"The one about your alibi. Can you walk me through where you were and what you did during the time you were missing from the party?"

"How is that going to help find who killed Tara and Cindy?"

"Maybe it won't," she admitted, "but the more pieces of the puzzle I have, the better my chances of spotting something they might have missed years ago. Especially if it's a detail you hadn't told anyone at the time."

Logan studied her intently before he answered.

"What is it you want to know?"

"I already know other witnesses noticed you were gone at around ten o'clock."

"That sounds about right."

"Let's start there—where did you go when you left the party?"

"I drove my car to another part of the island. I parked and walked down to where I knew a shrimp boat would be."

"Why did you drive? Was it too far to walk?"

"I could have gone on foot, but it would have taken at least thirty minutes one way—and that would probably have been running pretty hard. I wanted to get back to the party with my friends, so I drove."

"Did you tell anyone where you were going?"

"No, Miss Stone." He didn't even attempt to hide his amusement. "I had the presence of mind not to make an announcement that I was going to buy an illegal substance."

"So, you drove to where you knew the boat would be." She ignored the jab. "How long was the drive?"

"The distance was farther by road than straight through the woods, but it didn't take more than fifteen minutes. And it wasn't possible to drive right up to the boat. I had to park near the road and walk down a path."

"How far of a walk—how long did that take you?"

"Not far. Maybe five minutes—more or less."

"Did anyone else see you there?"

"Obviously, whoever I bought the pot from saw me. I don't think anyone else did, but I guess I can't be sure."

"That was Buford Gadsden?"

"I never revealed that, but, yes, he eventually admitted to it."

"And how long were you with him?"

"I'd guess fifteen minutes. Then I paid for my stuff, went back to the party, and had a good time. I didn't know about Tara and Cindy until the next morning. I think you know the rest."

Addie did the math as she listened. His timeline matched closely with the hour witnesses estimated he was gone.

"Emma told me about the sheriff's deputies getting an anonymous tip about Buford and then finding your leather wristband on his boat. Any idea who called in that tip?"

"It sure as hell couldn't have been me—I was in jail, and all my calls were recorded."

"But the leather band with your name on it . . . how would the caller have known about that?"

"I never heard anything to suggest they did. I think that was just the one time in my life when Lady Luck didn't fuck me over."

"You really think luck explains it?"

"If you can believe that I had the incredibly bad luck to leave a party—where I had all of those witnesses to my whereabouts— during the exact time period that my two friends were murdered, why is it such a stretch to believe I also had the incredibly good luck with the leather wristband? Luck is random, isn't it?"

"Maybe." Addie sounded less than convinced.

"It's funny, though, how your mind can play tricks when you try to remember details."

"Like what?"

"Like when they first told me they'd found my wristband on Buford's boat."

"What about it?" she asked.

"At first, I didn't think that could be possible."

"Why not?" Her pulse quickened with anticipation.

"I knew I had lost the wristband, and I knew it happened the day of the party."

"That all sounds consistent."

"Before I heard they found it on the boat, I thought I had lost it earlier that day. I could have sworn I couldn't find it when I was getting ready to go to the party that afternoon. Like I said, the mind plays funny tricks."

CHAPTER 30

Sᴀᴍ's sᴇᴄᴏɴᴅ ᴀᴘᴘᴇᴀʀᴀɴᴄᴇ ᴄᴏᴜʀᴛ ᴅᴀᴛᴇ ᴡᴀs Tʜᴜʀsᴅᴀʏ, Oᴄᴛᴏ-
ber 26—four days away. Those were usually set on Fridays, but
the judge set Sam's a day earlier rather than risk the media circus
disrupting the other hearings that were scheduled for Friday. Second appearance was the hearing at which Sam would be required to
tell the court whether he wanted to plead guilty or not guilty and
demand a jury trial—in some states it's called an arraignment. It also
was why Zach hadn't been the least bit surprised to receive a phone
call inviting him to Jake Barton's office that morning. Barton would
likely offer Sam a plea bargain, and doing it only a few days before
would set a short deadline to apply pressure. What a great way to
start a Monday.

"Have you seen my red and blue striped tie?" he asked as Addie
came into the room.

"It's hanging on a hook on the left side of the closet," she
answered, sitting on the bed watching as he got ready to leave.

They had reached something of a détente, so they were at least
speaking again, but their conversations were terse.

"Is Colleton going with you to meet with Barton?"

"He is," Zach answered, knowing it would stick in her craw, but
not particularly caring.

"Anything I can do to help?"

"No," he answered, standing in front of the mirror as he knot-
ted his tie. He watched her reflection in the mirror as she lowered

her head. She opened her mouth to say something else, but closed it again, apparently deciding now was not the time.

"Good luck then," she said, getting up and leaving the room.

We'll need it, he thought. Outside he heard a horn blow as Colleton pulled into the drive. Zach hadn't told him the details, but Colleton knew enough not to get stuck in a room alone with Addie and Zach right now.

"Damn, who are you, and what have you done with Colleton Burns?" Zach joked as he climbed in the Tahoe. Colleton's usual appearance was half man, half bear in cargo shorts, but this morning, he was decked out in a gray pin-striped suit and a teal Hermès tie with an impeccable knot. His hair was slicked back, and he had shaved. The transformation was impressive. "Say, is that Brylcreem? A little dab'll do ya . . ." Zach reached out to touch Colleton's hair.

"Fuck off," Colleton laughed, slapping his hand away.

"What kind of deal is Jake Barton planning to offer us this morning?" Zach asked, his mood sobering quickly.

"My guess is he's going to offer to take the death penalty off the table in return for a guilty plea," Colleton said. "He gets political points for quickly putting a murderer away, and he can still keep his PR points by puffing up and reminding everyone he started with the harder line but offered a plea only to spare Jessie's family the trauma of a gruesome trial."

"But he has a real problem with the death penalty," Zach said. "The South Carolina statute doesn't allow the death penalty unless there was at least one statutory aggravating circumstance. He doesn't have that here."

"I know—I've been wondering about that ever since his announcement. But Barton is too smart and too savvy not to have thought about that same issue. That worries me. He has something up his sleeve."

"Like what?"

"Beats the hell out of me, but we're about to find out," Colleton said, snagging a street spot and parking the Tahoe. The solicitor's headquarters was in Beaufort County, but he had an office in each of the five counties in the Fourteenth Circuit. The Colleton County office was on the second floor of the courthouse in Walterboro—the county seat.

As they made their way up the sidewalk, Zach glanced down. "Seriously?" he asked, spotting Colleton's duck shoes.

"What? It was muddy out at the camp, and I didn't want to muck up my dress shoes."

"And it didn't occur to you that you could change shoes in your car?"

"It's a truck. And I'll bet you twenty bucks that Jake Barton will be too busy admiring himself to so much as look at my fucking shoes."

"Twenty bucks? You're on." Zach held open the courthouse door.

"He'll see you now," the soft-spoken receptionist said, putting down the phone receiver and gesturing toward an office door.

"Mighty fucking big of him since he's the one who asked for this meeting," Colleton muttered under his breath as he hoisted himself out of the chair. Zach shot him a warning look as the solicitor appeared and held the door open.

"Good morning, gentlemen, please come in," Barton said, with the smuggest of smiles on his face.

"So nice of you to summon us." Zach smiled politely. "To what do we owe the pleasure?"

"I think you know the answer to that, Zach, so I'll skip the pleasantries and get right to the point."

"Dang. Were the pleasantries going to include refreshments?" Colleton asked. Zach shot him another menacing look.

"No," Barton replied, and turned his attention back to Zach.

"According to my calendar, Sam Jenkins's second appearance hearing is later this week—Thursday afternoon."

"What a coincidence," Zach said. "My calendar shows that too. And?"

"As you might imagine, the brutal murder of their daughter has taken a toll on the Gadsdens."

"Being plucked out of his law-abiding life and incarcerated for a murder he didn't commit has taken a toll on my client as well."

"I suggested this meeting to explore whether we might save the Gadsden family the trauma of sitting through a trial by negotiating a plea deal. I generally am not in favor, but given the desires of the family, I'm willing to discuss it."

"Why on Earth would my innocent client—who's never had so much as a parking ticket—plead guilty to a murder he didn't commit?"

"If this were a murder he didn't commit, you might have a point."

"What, you're the jury too now?"

"Zach, we both know you knew what this meeting would be about before you got here. You came because you want to hear what the offer is."

"I'm here because I'm ethically required to keep my client advised so that he'll be making an informed decision when he gives me the go-ahead to tell you to shove your so-called deal up your—"

Colleton cleared his throat loudly and stared at Barton. "Whatever happened to getting to the point? Tell us your offer and let us get out of here."

"Fine. I'm willing to drop pursuit of the death penalty in return for a plea. I know a lot of people will be disappointed in that decision, but the reality is that sitting in a trial and listening again to how their beautiful daughter died will be torture for the Gadsden family—especially her mother, who has taken this badly."

"And instead of the death penalty?"

"My office will recommend the court sentence him to life in prison instead, without the possibility for parole or release under any terms as the statute requires."

"Life? You've got to be fucking kidding me. Maybe that would be an offer if you had any chance in hell of getting the death penalty, but that isn't even remotely possible in this case. You know damn well, the death penalty isn't available in South Carolina unless the jury—and that means all of them—not only finds Sam guilty of murdering Jessie Gadsden, but also makes a separate finding of evidence beyond a reasonable doubt of statutory aggravating circumstances." Zach was sitting on the edge of his seat and his voice was raised. "You know what those are and they're specific—murder that was committed by a defendant with a prior murder conviction, murder for hire, murder committed in conjunction with another serious crime like sex trafficking, kidnapping, criminal sexual conduct, drug trafficking, armed robbery, arson first . . . you know the list as well as I do, and you don't have that in this case."

"Oh, but I do." Like pulling an ace from his sleeve, Barton slid a document across the desk toward Zach.

"What's that supposed to be?"

"That is a direct indictment from the grand jury."

"For?" Zach asked.

"Charges of criminal sexual conduct. A statutory extenuating circumstance."

"You've got to be kidding."

"I'll let you read it on your own time."

The solicitor stood and walked to the door. "Gentlemen, I'll see you in court Thursday. Mr. Jenkins has until then to accept my offer. If he pleads not guilty, it will be withdrawn." Barton opened his office door and stood back so they could exit.

"I can't believe you wasted our time with this crap," Zach said, yanking the document from the desktop as he walked out.

"Oh, and Colleton?" Barton called out as they were stepping through the outer door into the hallway. "Nice shoes."

"Thanks—I had a premonition I'd be wading through bullshit." Colleton closed the door behind them.

"You owe me twenty bucks," Zach said as they headed down the stairs.

"Fuck off."

As they walked across the courthouse lawn, Zach heard someone calling his name and turned to see a young Black woman in a suit and heels walking hurriedly toward them. He shot a questioning look at Colleton, who whispered "Serena Davenport—the assistant solicitor you've been talking to on the phone." They waited while she caught up to them.

"Zach," she said, catching her breath, "I was in the next office and heard most of the conversation."

"I think it's safe to say it didn't go well."

"Look, he's not going to say this, and I'm definitely not authorized to change his offer, but I know he would be willing to back off of the life position. I suspect he might even be willing to offer to recommend thirty years—that's the absolute minimum under South Carolina's murder statute."

"And why would he be willing to do that if he thought his case was as strong as he wants me to believe it is?" Zach thought he smelled a setup.

"Because the Gadsden family is a big deal in these parts, and so is the solicitor's family. You do the math," she said. "Jessie's mother is an emotional mess after losing her only daughter, and Buford is worried about what a trial will do to her. Buford has a lot of pull with Barton, and he'd like this over sooner rather than later."

"That's all well and good," Zach said, "but a mandatory thirty years in jail for a murder he didn't commit is not exactly a good deal for Sam Jenkins. How do I even try to justify that to him?"

"He'd be fifty-four at the end of the sentence, with years left in him," she said, "and with Barton's sway, he might even be able to help with where he spends that time."

"Like there are any good state prisons."

"Some are worse than others," she said with the air of someone who'd seen the worst of the worst, "and he'd still be alive."

"Alive with no life to go back to."

"Whatever. I thought you should know what might be possible." She shrugged. "I don't share your optimism that Sam Jenkins is innocent. But if you're right and he didn't murder that girl, someone else did. If you can keep your client alive, maybe they'll find the real killer, and Sam would be released from prison."

"Find the real killer?" Zach's voice was raised again. "They aren't even looking now—before the trial. They sure as hell won't spend any time looking after he's locked away for decades."

"Criminals mess up sometimes. If there is someone else out there who did this, there's always a chance they'll tell the wrong person or say the wrong thing and get caught. But, Zach, that will be useless if Sam's been executed. There's no early release from being dead." She turned and left.

"Once again, she gets the pithy line at the end," Zach said.

"Let's get out of here," Colleton said. "We need to have a conversation with Sam, and it won't be easy."

Sam had listened quietly as they explained his options, and then told them to ask Eli to come and see him. This was the hardest decision he'd ever had to make, and he wanted Eli's advice. After calling Eli, Zach and Colleton hunkered down at the camp, ruminating over a bottle of bourbon. Despite the sunny skies and mild October weather, their moods were dark.

"This is fucking great," Colleton said, scowling at the indict-ment Barton had given them. "They found semen on Jessie's body. It matched the DNA profile of the buccal swab they took when Sam was booked and the DNA they recovered when they searched Sam's apartment."

"Not exactly a big surprise. The notice they left after the search disclosed that they took the laptop and DNA, and Sam already told us they had sex that morning. It was only a matter of time until Bar-ton had the results," Zach said. "That explains how he plans to get the death penalty—he'll try to convince the jury there was criminal sexual conduct."

"There was no suggestion of rape at that crime scene."

"Doesn't need to be. The offense could be third degree—which doesn't require anything greater than coercion to have sex."

"And what evidence is there of that?" Colleton asked.

"None, but he won't need any evidence if he gets that far. Once a jury has decided a defendant is guilty of murder and they have sci-entific evidence of sexual conduct, they will convince themselves it was criminal, especially after the judge explains that it doesn't have to be rape. You know that—you've seen those same case studies." Zach drained his glass and plunked it down, and Colleton sighed as he reached for the bottle to refill it.

"Easy there." Zach put a hand over the glass. "I'll never be able to drive home if we keep this up."

"No need to. Betty's got a couch inside that's built for passing out on—tell Addie you're crashing here tonight. I'll pull some veni-son steaks out of the freezer, and we can work until it's time to throw 'em on the grill."

"That's an offer I can't refuse," Zach said, rubbing his eyes. He and Addie were barely speaking, and the tension had been suffocating the last few days. He couldn't resist a chance to lighten up and get wasted. He'd been driving around with an optimistic gym bag in the back seat the last few days, so he had shorts he could change into.

"Looks like I'll take that refill after all." Zach pushed his glass back toward Colleton, who promptly poured another while Zach sent a terse text to Addie: *Planning to work late with Colleton. I'll crash here tonight.* He knew that wouldn't get a warm reception, but right now he didn't care.

While Colleton was inside rummaging through the freezer for the steaks, Zach fished his gym bag out of the trunk. *Yet another great thing about a man camp way back in the woods,* he thought as he started changing by the car.

"Whoa—it wasn't that kind of invitation."

Zach flipped Colleton off and followed him to the big table.

"So, what are you thinking about this trial?" Colleton asked. He had replaced his suit with his usual cargo shorts, and he was leaning his chair back on two legs with his feet propped on an overturned crate.

"You mean other than that we are royally screwed after Sam's revelation?"

"Succinct assessment, and possibly accurate. Have you given any thought to whether to put him on the stand?" Colleton asked.

"I have trouble thinking about anything else. Barton can place Sam at the scene with Jessie's blood all over him and scratches on his arm with his DNA under her nails—in an old church out in the middle of nowhere in the dark of night with no other obvious reason to be there. Oh, and then there's the semen. If Sam doesn't testify, the jury will have no other explanation for any of that, and

I'm not thinking that will go well for Sam. Especially since refusing to testify screams *I'm guilty* to some jurors no matter how many times the judge charges them otherwise." Zach ran a hand through his hair. "On the other hand, we know Sam hid a lot of critical information from us from day one, which means we can't rule out the possibility that he's still holding out. If he takes the stand and Barton gets testimony from him on something we don't know about and without our getting a chance to put everything in context, that could be disastrous.

"Thankfully," Zach added, "whether he testifies can be a game day decision. But, as any trial lawyer knows, what options we'll have at trial depends a lot on what steps we took before we got there. That's where we are now."

"On that note," Colleton said, "I have an idea I think has potential." Colleton's chair was still back on two legs, and he'd started to gently rock it back and forth. The chair groaned in protest, and Zach considered warning him.

"Don't keep me waiting—let's hear your brilliant idea," he said instead.

"Rule 5 requires certain minimal discovery—the prosecution would be required to provide us copies if Sam had given any statements, and if he had a criminal record, they'd have to give us a copy of that too," Colleton said. "On the flip side, we would have to tell them if we were going to present an insanity or mental illness defense, the same way we're required to disclose that we have an alibi argument. Beyond that, no further discovery is required from either party unless the defense elects to start that process. In other words, we can get the evidence they have and reciprocate by giving up the evidence we intend to use in our case in chief, or we can get nothing and give nothing. Either way—the decision is up to us. Maybe we should choose to exchange nothing."

"Are you suggesting we go into this trial with both sides blind about what the other has? I know Rule 5 makes that an option, but I've never used it. Never even seen anybody else use it. Have you ever tried it?"

"Only once, back in the nineties," Colleton said, "but it worked. My client had a messy breakup with his train wreck of a girlfriend—not that he was any prize either—and, after she chased him around her house with a crowbar, she kicked him out without any of his stuff and changed the locks. My client, being resourceful and needing his clothes back, climbed through an open window one day while she was shopping, collected his things, and took off. She came home and found his stuff gone and told the police he also took an expensive diamond necklace. Footage on a neighbor's security cam showed him going in the window and back out with a trash bag. Of course, he swore he only took his shit and didn't touch her necklace."

"What a surprise."

"Not long after, my client got a tip that the train wreck had worn the necklace in question and not much else to a party. By means unknown to me"—Colleton raised his eyebrows in mock innocence—"my client obtained a photograph of her at the party wearing said necklace. I didn't make any discovery requests so I wouldn't have to disclose the photo. At trial, I got her to describe the necklace in detail and confirm when it was stolen. Then I ambushed her with the photo. After a lot of sputtering and wide-eyed blinking, she claimed the photo was taken before the theft. What she failed to recall was that it was taken at a hurricane party—and there was no disputing the date that storm came through. Let's just say the jury didn't have time to eat their free lunch before coming back with a not guilty verdict."

"Great war story," Zach said, laughing, "but with that kind of evidence in hand, why not simply disclose it to the solicitor and be done with it? You might have avoided trial altogether."

"Come on, you know that's not what would have happened. The solicitor would have tipped her off to the photo, and she would have come up with a different story—a different necklace missing—and with time to plan it, she might have been convincing to a jury. Instead, when I asked about the necklace, she followed me down the path like a little lamb because she thought she was getting away with something. Once she dug herself in deep under oath and in front of the jury, there was no walking that back. Showing the jury her first unrehearsed reaction to that photograph was crucial.

"The point is, I protected the one game-changing piece of evidence we had—and they didn't—and we saved it to use it where it most mattered. That same tactic might work here—or at least be Sam's best chance."

"I think you're overlooking something important—that was the early nineties when cell phones weren't a consideration, and that old case didn't involve the kind of DNA evidence this one does. Colleton, I'm worried that failing to get that information might be failing to do our job in this case. Malpractice."

"I'm not overlooking anything—what you are missing is we already have everything Barton has."

"Come again?"

"Granted, we don't have the paper reports, but we know what they say. They will have tested the blood on Sam's clothes from the night of the arrest and confirmed it was Jessie's. They will have test results showing his DNA under her fingernails because Sam admits she clawed at him when he knelt over her. Because of the direct indictment Barton gave us today, we know they found semen when they examined the body, and we know from Sam it was his. I guess we don't know for sure whether they tested any hairs or fibers at her place, so we don't know whether they know Sam was ever there, but we already know he was. If it comes up, it's not a surprise we're not ready for. They have records from Jessie's cell phone and Sam's work phone, but so do we. They have the 9-1-1 recording, but we've heard that, and it didn't have any surprises. Bottom line is, we don't stand to gain much, if anything, by asking for disclosure—we already know what they have."

"And what do you think we gain by not disclosing?" Zach asked.

"I think the shed floor being wiped clean that night is strong. If we point it out now, they'll have time to come up with something, some theory to lessen the impact. If it hits them for the first time when the jury hears it, they'll be scrambling. We can prepare the preacher so that his testimony highlights the implications and gets the jury wondering who else was there that night. And don't underestimate the value of a preacher as a witness in a small-town courtroom."

"How do we know for sure the cops didn't notice the shed floor?"

"Captain Chambers testified at the prelim there was no sign of anyone having been there. What are they going to do now, call his credibility into question right before they call him as a witness at trial? I don't think so."

"Do you think there's any chance the officers swept it clean while they had the scene?" Zach asked, the idea occurring to him for the first time.

"And destroyed evidence?" Colleton sounded surprised. "Not with Chambers in charge of the scene. There are some others I might suspect of playing dirty, but he strikes me as being on the up-and-up."

Zach paused, trying to work through Colleton's proposal. "There's another piece of evidence we could keep to ourselves until the last minute that could matter even more," he said, thinking aloud.

"You're thinking about that burner phone," Colleton said.

"Hell, yeah. Think about it. If it looks like the jury is buying into Barton's theory about sexual criminal conduct, we can put Sam on the stand and let him testify they had an ongoing relationship and use the phone as powerful proof of that. Imagine Barton getting hit with that bomb in the middle of trial with no time to plan his response."

"Now you're thinking," Colleton said. "And, on the other hand, if things are going our way and we don't want to risk putting Sam up, we have no obligation to disclose that phone—no one else has to know it exists. And the beauty of it all is that we get to hear all of the State's case and can wait until the very last minute of our own—watch how the jury's reacting—before we make a decision about whether Sam should testify."

"This could work after all," Zach said.

"It could. We still have months before trial. If something comes up that makes us reconsider, we can always serve discovery requests later. But, if we do that now, there's no taking it back, and we lose this option forever."

"Good point. Let's go with it for now. Re-evaluate later if we need to."

"Sounds like a plan. Meanwhile, we see what else we can dig up."

"What we desperately need is a lead on who was in that shed. I wish Sam knew more about who Jessie was suddenly afraid of that night," Zach said. Colleton had finally settled his chair back on all fours without a spill. Zach couldn't decide whether that was a relief or a disappointment.

"Sam was in panic mode last night. Once he's settled down, we'll talk to him again. Maybe he remembers something he doesn't realize is important."

"Maybe."

Both men were quiet as they mulled the situation over. Zach could feel the alcohol starting to soften his senses, and he settled back in his chair as he listened to the rustle of leaves in the afternoon breeze and the raspy bark of a squirrel in the tree above them. The groan of Colleton's chair broke his reverie, and Zach cast a sideways glance as Colleton leaned his chair back again.

"You can stop worrying about this chair," Colleton chuckled. "It's as strong as an oak. That one, however . . . ," he started, gesturing toward Zach.

"Very funny," Zach said, leaning his own chair back and resting his heels on the table. Too late, he heard the crack.

CHAPTER 31

THE PUBLIC DEFENDER'S OFFICE WAS ON LUCAS STREET AND EASY to find. Addie entered the lobby and checked in at the desk.

"Addie Stone to see Dan McGuire," she said to the woman at the desk.

"I'll let him know you're here."

Addie sat down and pulled out her phone to switch it to silent mode. As the screen lit up, she saw the still-open text Zach had sent yesterday saying he was staying the night at Colleton's place. He claimed it was so they could work late, but she knew better. He wanted to get away from her. Things had been tense since their fight. She knew Zach was under pressure, but he was taking this way too far. It was starting to piss her off.

"Addie?"

"Yes," she said, standing. "You must be Dan."

"My friends call me Danny," he said with a smile. "Come on back."

She followed him to a small office with a battered desk and tangled mini blinds. Yet the room glowed with the warmth of a lively array of photographs—smiling figures she guessed to be grown children and small grandchildren.

"Big family," she said, reminded of the one she grew up in.

"Joy of my life." He nodded, turning the desk chair to face the photos behind him.

"And that one?" She gestured toward a photo of Danny between two Black men—all three sporting big smiles.

"That was a big win," Danny said. "As a public defender I use character witnesses to present my client as a person—not just a defendant. Preachers can be especially persuasive. That day Reverend Gatch saved the day for my young client."

"Ben Gatch—from the church on Cicada Road?"

"One and the same," he said, spinning the chair back to face Addie.

"Thanks again for seeing me," she said. "I know you don't know me, but—"

"No, but I know who you are. The whole criminal bar knows who you are," he added. "Sam Jenkins's case is the biggest thing to happen around here in a while. And the facts are so . . . well, it's one of those things you hate to look at but can't quite look away. A beautiful young woman bludgeoned to death in a church, and . . ."

"Oh," he said, suddenly putting the pieces together. "That's how you knew Reverend Gatch was from that church."

"Yes," she said, nodding. "He's been very generous with his time. It's a sensational case, that's for sure, but that's Zach's case. Well, Zach's and Colleton's," she said.

"I heard Colleton had ventured out of that hideout of his to work on this case," Danny said, with a look of pure glee. "That alone would make it interesting—he's always been eccentric and larger-than-life. You should have seen him in the courtroom back in the day. He was in private practice, but most of us here with the Public Defender considered him a comrade-in-arms. I haven't seen him in ages. Please say hello for me."

"Will do," she said, hoping her tone didn't give away how un-enamored she was with Colleton at the moment. "But I was hoping we could talk about the 1983 Edisto Beach double homicide," she said.

"Yes, I played your message twice, thinking I must have mis-understood. Not that it doesn't deserve the attention, but I haven't thought about that case for years. What prompted them to reopen it, if you're at liberty to say?"

"With Colleton helping Zach on the Jenkins case, I had time on my hands, so I volunteered to work on cold cases. This one caught my eye. Emma Hudson has been helping me get up to speed on the background."

"You've met Emma too?" Danny's face lit up.

"Yes, she's been a huge help."

"That doesn't surprise me, she's a good lawyer. I was hired on here only a few years after she was, so we came up together in the ranks and worked a lot of cases together. I've missed her these last six or seven years since she left and opened her own shop. You're lucky to have her."

"I know. She told me she represented Logan in some minor skir-mishes before he was arrested in the Edisto Beach thing. She filled me in on what she could remember, but I was thinking your office might still have some of those old files. I know they weren't related to the murders, but you never know where you might find a stray fact that puts something else in context." She pulled out a pen and small pad to take notes.

"You're right about that," he said, "but I am glad you called ahead. I had to climb over a wall of old crap to find them. And what is it about seeing one spider that makes you feel like they're all over you the rest of the day?"

"Sorry for putting you through that. At least Emma had her files scanned so all she had to do was hit print."

"She did? I'm impressed," he said. "Despite my heroic efforts, I'm afraid I didn't find much I can share. Most of the cases were from when Logan was a minor. There was only one that I could even con-sider and, of course, I had to pull the privileged information out of that one. This is all I ended up with," he said with an apologetic smile.

"Thanks for trying," Addie said, reaching for the thin file. "Is this my copy?"

"All yours."

"Nice of you to go out of your way for me. If the file doesn't spark any ideas for me, maybe I'll run it by Colleton, or better yet, Emma or Lee since they know all the old background."

"Lee Bowen?"

"Mm-hmm. You know him?"

"Sure. He was always on the other side, of course, but I found him easy to work with, and we were friendly. I thought I'd heard he retired from the sheriff's office, though."

"He did, but he was still there when I picked up the case, and he asked me to keep him in the loop."

"I don't doubt that," Danny said. "Lee was obsessed with this case. Worked it night and day from the beginning. Almost seemed like he didn't trust anyone else with it—tried to do it all himself."

The desk phone rang, and Danny let out an exasperated sigh. "Give me a second," he said as he looked at the number. Addie nodded and he took the call.

As Danny spoke with his caller, Addie looked around the room, tossing his last comment around like a ball in her head. Why would Lee want a monopoly on the case? And what had Emma said about Lee letting the investigation sit and the trail grow cold while Logan was in jail? There was something else, too, something about seeing flashlights and running through brush on Jungle Road that night. The story made sense, but it was conveniently unverifiable . . .

"Sorry about that," Danny said, hanging up the phone. "You were telling me you were working with Lee on this case. I'm sure he was excited to see it reopened."

"Sure seemed to be," she said, getting up to leave. "Thanks again," she continued, "for going out of your way to get those old files for me, but I've taken up enough of your time."

"Colleton Burns, Emma Hudson, Lee Bowen, Reverend Gatch . . . you're spending time with all my old pals, Addie. I have to admit I'm envious of you," he said as he walked her out.

"What a nice thing to say. It speaks well for all of you. Mind if I pass it along?"

"Not at all—I'd appreciate that." He held the door and watched as she crossed the parking lot.

CHAPTER 32

IT WAS FIVE O'CLOCK, AND DANNY MCGUIRE'S TUESDAY HAD finally come to an official end. He put a few things away and tugged the rumpled suit jacket from the back of his desk chair. As he reached for the light switch, he stepped on something and looked down to find a pen on the floor. He picked it up and turned it over in his hands. With a PD's salary, he didn't own any expensive pens—all of his were plastic, disposable, and came from a box in a rickety metal supply cabinet. This one felt hefty and looked to be silver. It struck him as the kind of gift one might get for a graduation or a new job, and he was guessing Addie would want it back.

He went back to his chair and listened again to her message. She hadn't left a phone number or email, and he hadn't thought to get one today. Then it dawned on him—she'd rattled off the names of four people he knew who would know how to reach her. This was the perfect excuse to get back in touch with some old friends.

Going into Outlook, he clicked on *New Email*. He'd start with this one, he thought, as he typed in the address. In the subject line he typed: *Surprise!*

> Hi stranger, it's Danny McGuire, a blast from your past!
> I met a friend of yours today—Addie Stone. You could
> have knocked me over with a feather when I heard she
> was working on that ancient Edisto Beach double homi-
> cide! She wanted to see some old files on Logan Bennett.
> After she left, I found a pen she dropped. Normally, I would
> chuck it in my desk drawer, but this looks like a nice one

that she might want back. I didn't get her contact information. Would you mind letting her know it's here? Thanks— and let's get together for lunch or coffee and catch up sometime soon. It's been far too long!

He read it over and hit send.

Danny closed out his email and put the pen on his desk. He flipped off the light and left, smiling as he wondered what his old friend's reaction would be to find his email in the inbox.

CHAPTER 33

THAT WAS A SURPRISE, ALL RIGHT, BUT NOT A GOOD ONE. NOT THAT it wouldn't be great to catch up with Danny, but if Addie is going that far afield of the old investigation, who the hell else is she talking to? Danny doesn't know anything that could point to me, but who might?

They say all criminals make some little mistake—something they don't even realize they've done until it comes back to bite them in the ass. That shed behind the church was a good example. I'd put my bloody clothes in a plastic bag and backed the car out. As I went to close the shed door, my headlights shone across the floor. It was dumb luck that I even noticed. The dirt floor was topped with sand to help with drainage. Sand doesn't compact like dirt, and the surface held tracks and prints. My footprints might've blended in with others, but the tire tracks were a dead giveaway that someone else was there on Cicada Road that night, and that would have been enough to make them look closer for who that might have been—even with Sam in jail. Luckily, I spotted one of those old wooden yardsticks and used it to scrape the sand smooth, getting rid of the tracks; then I tossed it in the back and destroyed it later with the other stuff.

If I almost missed something that obvious on a night I had meticulously planned, there's no telling what I might have missed that frantic night at the beach. Just because nothing came to light three decades ago doesn't mean it couldn't happen now with Addie stirring that old case up.

I need a way to shut this down. Soon.

I've been able to keep up with some of what Addie's doing, but I only get bits and pieces. I need to find another source of information.

Maybe I'll take Danny up on that invitation after all.

CHAPTER 34

Zach's car was in the drive when Addie pulled in Tuesday evening. Colleton must have run out of liquor. She lifted the grocery bags and went inside. Zach was back in the little office—she could hear him talking with someone on the phone as she went to the kitchen and started pulling things together for dinner. She was making Italian, his favorite. Plan A was to share a romantic dinner and try to turn this thing around. Plan B . . . well, Plan B would likely be reviewing the file she'd picked up from Danny McGuire while she ate alone. It might also mean her going back to the Charleston apartment for a while. Zach hadn't so much as touched her since their fight, and she'd had about as much of this shit as she planned to take.

An hour and a half later, the air was thick with the warm acidic smell of tomato-based sauce and sharp Parmesan cheese. She heard the quiet pad of bare feet but didn't turn around from where she stood working over the sink.

"Wow, that smells heavenly," Zach said.

Addie turned to find him leaning against the small kitchen island with his hands in his pockets. She crossed her arms and gave him a good long look. His hair hadn't been brushed and he looked a little peaked. She knew a hangover when she saw one.

"It's lobster and cheese-stuffed pasta with spinach and Parmesan marinara sauce. There's warm focaccia in the oven."

"Sounds as good as it smells," he said. He was doing his best hangdog now. "Don't suppose you'd be willing to share . . ."

"I might. But it comes with strings."

"Like what?"

"Like you have to be nice to me. And talk to me, for starters."

"I think I can manage that. What else?"

"I know my timing was bad on bringing up a family, but if you won't talk about it at all, it's impossible to know when the right time is. I'm pretty fucking smart, but even I'm not a mind reader."

That last part brought a smile to his face. "I guess it is a tad hard to be humble when you're a goddess," he teased.

"This is your idea of being nice to me?" She was smiling too, now.

"No," he said, taking his hands out of his pockets and stepping toward her, "this is." He put a hand gently against her face and tipped it forward for a soft kiss.

"That's closer to what I had in mind," she said, "but maybe you should try again."

This time the kiss was longer and more insistent.

"You're getting there."

He wrapped both arms around her and pulled her close. "Adds, I love you, you know I do," he breathed into her neck. "I know you're ready to talk about babies and weddings, but can that part wait until I get through this trial? My case has been circling the drain since Eli found that burner phone in Sam's truck, and I don't have it in me right now. Could we please go back to how we were for a while longer? I promise when this trial ends, we'll sit down and talk about those things. Please?"

"And what if it ends badly, Zach? What if the trial ends badly and your practice is still struggling? Because after the bombshells Sam dropped the other night, that is a very real possibility. I love you, but if I want a family, I can't wait forever."

"You won't have to. When this trial ends—no matter how it ends—it will be our turn, okay? Please?"

"I guess I can live with that," she said, pulling away so she could look him in the eye. It may not be as much as she'd hoped for, but it was a step in the right direction, and damn sure better than her Plan B.

"So, are you going to feed me or not?" he asked.

"I am. There's a bottle of Chianti behind you if you think you're ready for a little hair of the dog."

"That sounds like exactly what I need."

Hours later, they were lying in bed, twisted sheets strewn off the end.

"What happened to my pillow?" Zach asked, crawling to the edge of the bed and peering over.

"Wherever you find it, look to see if my panties are there too."

"Ah, found it," Zach said, tossing the pillow back to the head of the bed and flopping himself down beside her.

"And my panties?"

"Nope. Guess you'll have to go without."

"Well, it's working so far."

"It is at that," he said, planting a kiss on her lips.

"How did your meeting with Jake Barton go yesterday?" she asked. They had been barely speaking lately, and they had some catching up to do.

"Not well."

"Did he offer a plea bargain?"

"He made an offer, but it was no bargain. He said if Sam would plead guilty, he'd take the death penalty off the table."

"And replace it with what?"

"Life without possibility of parole."

Addie drew in a loud, short breath. "You said no, I assume?"

"It's not my call, it's Sam's. But that wasn't all Barton had on his agenda."

"Meaning?"

Zach filled her in on the direct indictment for criminal sexual conduct and the new evidence. He finished off with Serena's suggestion that Barton might be willing to better the offer at Buford's request to avoid a trial.

"Do you believe her?"

"I'm not sure what to believe anymore, Addie. Anyway, Sam wanted some time to think about it. I'm supposed to meet with him tomorrow."

"Tomorrow's Wednesday. Isn't your hearing set for Thursday?"

"It is—Thursday at one o'clock. Sam will need to decide fast." He was quiet for a moment. "So, what were you up to today? That looked like a new file on the counter."

"It is. I went to the public defender's office to see what they had on Logan's old cases. Those are copies of what they could let me see."

"Weren't those all before the Edisto Beach murders? What would one have to do with the other?"

"Probably nothing, but I hoped they might give context to something. That's how desperate I'm getting, Zach. I'm running out of ideas. I haven't wanted to distract you with details that you don't need crowding your mind right now, but I'm coming to a dead end. I've talked to witnesses from the party, to Logan, with Emma and with Lee, I even managed to have a phone call with Cindy Crosby's mother—that was bleak, by the way—and nothing leads anywhere. The sheriff's office helped me run down some information on crimes in neighboring states with similar victims. Nothing matched or even came close. I'm afraid I might have to leave this one as much a mystery as I found it."

"Don't beat yourself up over it, Addie. All you can do is your best. The sad truth is that not every case ends in something you can call justice."

"Are we talking about my case now, or yours?"

"Maybe both," he said as he pulled up the sheets and wrapped an arm around her. "Right now, I can't think about either. I'm beat."

"Get some sleep," she said, but he was already out, and she was left with her thoughts. She was glad they felt close again, but they weren't any closer to a decision. His promising to talk about it after the trial was a long way from saying he'd be ready to make a decision. She'd already made hers, though. She would not be waiting forever.

Wednesday morning, Addie had a quiet house to herself while Zach and Colleton met with Sam about the plea offer and tomorrow's hearing. Settling in with coffee and breakfast, she opened the file from Danny. It was limited to the skinny-dipping incident, and there wasn't much to see. The police report narrative had been sanitized compared to the story Emma had told. Most of the other documents were internal administrative things. There was a copy of one of those old pink pads offices used to write phone messages on. Addie shook her head when she realized it wasn't even remotely related—it was a message about a canceled appointment.

The last document confirmed Emma's story that Logan had to check in with her once a month for six months to placate the girl's father. It was a typed schedule of projected meetings. There was nothing indicating whether any of the dates might have been rescheduled, but Addie blinked and looked a second time at the last date. It was the date of the Edisto murders. That was a hell of a coincidence. Neither Logan nor Emma had mentioned that they'd met earlier that day. Then again, maybe they hadn't—maybe that date was changed somewhere along the way. Still, she should follow up with Logan to see if that jogged any memory for him. She reached for her phone and pulled up the number. He answered on the third ring.

"Good morning, Addie."

"Hi, Logan. I hope I'm not interrupting anything."

"No, it's fine. What's up?"

"Is there any chance we could get together for a few minutes today? I have a few more questions." She wanted to talk in person, see his expression. "I'd be happy to drive out there."

"I'm tied up today," he said, "but I need to come to town tomorrow morning if that would work?"

"Perfect. Where should I meet you?" she asked.

"There's a coffee shop next to the Feed & Seed. It's small, but quiet."

"Feed & Seed?"

"Hey, my chickens have to eat too," he said. "Think you can find it? Say around eleven?"

"No problem. Thanks. See you then."

Addie put the phone down and flipped through the file one last time before she put it aside. She gazed out the window, savoring the last of her coffee. She knew she was grasping at straws—so what if Logan had met with Emma the day of the party? Still, it seemed odd that neither of them had mentioned it. Either way, she'd find out tomorrow.

It was late when Zach got home.

"How did it go with Sam?" she asked, as he sat on the couch beside her.

"I wish I knew," Zach answered. "He changes his mind every few minutes. One minute he's adamant that he isn't going to prison for something he didn't do. The next, he's as scared as anyone facing a possible death penalty would be, especially since Serena suggested Barton might be willing to offer a prison term of less than life."

"The hearing's tomorrow at one, right?"

"Right. But he has until the last second to decide. I guess I'll find out when everybody else does."

"That's intense," she said. "Sounds like you're in line for an interesting day tomorrow."

"No kidding. Can you be there? Eli could use someone to sit with him for support."

"Of course—I wouldn't miss it. I'm meeting with Logan Bennett in the morning, but I'll have plenty of time to get to the hearing after."

"I thought you already interviewed Bennett."

"I did, but something new has come up that's bothering me."

Zach shot her a questioning look.

"The file I got from the PD shows that Emma had a meeting with Logan the same day of the murders—just a few hours before the party."

"So?"

"So why didn't either one of them tell me that? Logan forgetting to mention it, maybe. But Emma? That doesn't quite fit. She has seemed so helpful, but now I'm getting the feeling maybe she was keeping something from me. And I'd like to know what, and why."

"Sounds like tomorrow will be an interesting Thursday for both of us."

CHAPTER 35

DANNY MCGUIRE WAS PREPARING FOR COURT THURSDAY MORNING when the reply email popped up with the *Surprise!* subject line.

> Surprise indeed! Great to hear from you and nice of you to let me know about Addie's pen. Can I stop by late this afternoon and pick it up for her? We can catch up while I'm there. Tell me what time would work best for you . . .

Danny hit reply and started typing:

> Sorry, but I have hearings over in Hampton County this afternoon. I'll be stuck there till the end of the day, but I don't need to leave the office until noon today. Could you get here around 11:00?

Seconds later:

> I can make that work. See you at 11:00.

CHAPTER 36

ZACH PARKED NEAR THE COURTHOUSE AT ELEVEN THURSDAY
morning. The hearing wasn't until 1:00 p.m., but he wanted to meet
with Eli to let him know what to expect, and a kind soul in the clerk's
office had helped him score a small meeting room. He'd also thought
they might avoid the media circus by coming early. No such luck.

A second appearance is a routine proceeding and not something
that would normally get much attention, but the public commotion
over this case had changed that. The local television trucks from
Charleston were lined up along the street, and their news person-
alities were jockeying for positions on the courthouse lawn. The
hearing might still be two hours away, but there was no lack of pan-
demonium to keep them occupied. Demonstrators had staked out
their opposing positions on either side of the walkway leading to
the courthouse doors. The local crowd had grown, and now they
were joined by some out-of-town groups looking to get their share of
attention. There were a few exceptions, but, for the most part, they
were divided along race lines.

The presence of television cameras had raised the level of enthusiasm significantly. Signs and posters were bigger, chanting was louder,
and some of the demonstrators were standing on stools and boxes to
hold their signs up above the throng. They had learned that a single
chant in unison packed more punch and each side had latched on to
a few short words to shout. The apparent goal was more to drown out
the other side than to truly be heard.

Walking the gauntlet between the two sides, Zach was suddenly hyper aware of his race, and the effect of "his side" not looking like him was subtly disconcerting. Someone threw a water bottle. It hit the pavement well in front of him, but he picked up his pace and felt a wash of relief when he ducked through the doors to the relative quiet of the courthouse. He spotted Eli leaning anxiously against a wall.

"Where's Colleton? Isn't he supposed to be here?" Eli asked.

"He'll meet us at the hearing—said he needed to stop and see someone first," Zach said. "This way," he said, gesturing for Eli to follow him to the meeting room. They closed the door behind them, and Zach did his best to explain what would happen today, but some things defy explanation.

CHAPTER 37

THE COFFEE SHOP WAS INDEED NEXT TO THE FEED & SEED, AND aptly named The Coop. Walking in at eleven, Addie found Logan Bennett at a small table. He had been right about quiet—the place was empty. She ordered a coffee at the counter and joined him.

"Sorry to keep you waiting," Addie said, sliding into a chair across from him and putting her cup and a file on the table.

"No problem. Chickens are patient, and they're all that's waiting for me. What did you want to ask about?"

"Emma told me she had represented you before the Edisto murders on some other charges," Addie said, jumping right into it.

"She did." He nodded. "Mostly dumbass kid stuff. The last time was for breaking into a backyard pool and having myself a party with the owner's cold beer and hot daughter."

"That's exactly the one I wanted to ask you about."

"What would that have to do with the murders?"

"Probably nothing, but humor me. According to Emma, she got you a deal on that last charge, and you had to meet with her once a month for six months as part of the deal."

"She's right, though that likely was more punishment for her than me."

"Do you remember when any of those meetings were?"

"Are you asking if I remember the dates of six meetings thirty-odd years ago? Of course not. Who would?"

"Maybe this will help," Addie said, opening her file. "This is a list of the dates you were scheduled to meet," she said, sliding it across the table. "Most of them were meaningless to me, but take a look at that last one." She watched as he ran his finger down the list and stopped on the last date. The significance registered on his face immediately.

"Holy shit, that's the afternoon of—" He looked up and she studied his expression. His surprise seemed real, but she couldn't be sure.

"I didn't see that in your statements," she said.

"Why would it have been? Nobody cared where I was before the party, and I haven't thought about it since. The things that happened later crowded out everything else. Honestly, if you hadn't shown this to me, I don't think I ever would have connected the two."

"That looks like a schedule made in advance for the whole series. Is it possible a meeting was set for that date but then changed later?" she prompted.

Logan looked out the window, rubbing the stubble on his chin. "Maybe, but, crazy thing is, now that this reminded me, I think I remember that meeting. She was wearing jeans."

"Jeans? Why would you remember that?"

"Because she always wore a suit. She was the new kid and trying to look the part. I remember asking her what the deal was that day, and she said I was her last appointment, and then she was knocking off."

"Says here you met at 2:00 p.m. Kind of early to knock off if you're new and want to look the part, isn't it?"

Logan didn't answer. His gaze wandered out the window again, and she stopped talking to let him work through whatever was coming back. Her peripheral vision caught the clerk disappearing around a corner in search of supplies or maybe a smoke break.

"I definitely remember a meeting with her wearing jeans, but maybe I'm wrong about it being *that* meeting. I know for sure the one I recall now was on a Friday. Were all the dates on that list Fridays?"

Addie pulled up a 1983 calendar on her phone and compared it to the dates on the list. "No, that last meeting with her was the only one that fell on a Friday. Why is that important?"

"Because the day Emma was wearing jeans was a Friday. She wasn't just going home for the day, she was leaving for the weekend. Are you sure that last date is the only Friday on the list?"

"I'm looking at a calendar, and yes, I'm sure. Why?"

Another minute ticked by. Was he trying to remember details, or make them up?

He turned to her with an expression she couldn't read— something that felt off. The clerk still hadn't returned from wherever he'd disappeared to, and it occurred to Addie that she knew very little about Logan Bennett or what he might be capable of.

"Why?" she asked again, her tone more insistent this time.

Logan's answer was one she could not have anticipated. Suddenly the picture had changed.

CHAPTER 38

DANNY MCGUIRE WAS WORKING AT HIS DESK AT 11:00 A.M. THURSDAY when he heard the knock on the frame of his open door. He looked up and his face broke into a wide grin at the sight of his old friend.

"Oh my God! It's so great to see you. Sit, sit down," he said, gesturing at the chair on the other side of his desk. "Toss that book on the floor."

"Thanks, it's good to see you again, too. How long has it been?" The book hit the floor with a *kerplunk* as his visitor sat down.

"You know, I was asking myself the same question," Danny said, "and I can't even remember. I think we might have run into each other at the courthouse when I was working the Tinkler case."

"Gosh, that was a long time ago, but you might be right. Time flies, doesn't it? I see from the photos behind you that you've had some new additions to that tribe of yours."

"We have for sure," Danny said, turning around to face the shelf. "These two are Sean's kids, and all four of these are Mary's," he said, pointing. "And this wriggly little thing is the newest— Kirsten's first. Six months old last month, but about three months in that picture."

"Congratulations—they're all beautiful."

"Thanks. Before I forget," Danny said, reaching across the desk, "here's Addie's pen."

"Right. Thanks again for getting this back to her."

"No problem. Gotta tell you, though, I was stunned to hear she was working on the old Edisto double homicide. That case was always such a mystery. It would be great if she could find something to crack it," Danny said.

"Wouldn't it? If you don't mind my asking, what was it she wanted here?"

"Don't mind at all—in fact, she mentioned that she might run it by you, so when I got your email saying you were coming by today, I made another copy," Danny said, sliding a folder across the desk. "I didn't see anything that jumped out at me as being helpful but maybe you will. Who knows, right?"

"Right—you never know. Well, look, I hate to run, but the Jenkins hearing is today."

"I know. Every criminal lawyer and cop in town will be there. I was hoping to go myself, but I'll be stuck in Hampton County instead. Maybe you can give me the play-by-play at lunch sometime soon?"

"Sounds great, shoot me an email with some dates."

Danny came around the desk to walk his visitor to the door. After a warm handshake and mutual promises to get together soon, Danny waved as his friend crossed the parking lot and drove away.

CHAPTER 39

IT WAS EVERYTHING I COULD DO NOT TO RIP THAT FILE OPEN AND
tear through it the second he handed it over. How I managed to get
out of there without screaming I'll never know. I drove around the
corner and parked at a strip mall and went through it in a frenzy. I
began to breathe a little easier as I flipped the pages—the file Danny
gave Addie was nothing but administrative forms and routine crap
no one would care about.

Then I spotted the copy of the old telephone message about the
canceled appointment. Was it getting hotter in here? I read the message again. It wouldn't reveal my involvement to most people, but
Addie had so much inside information on both cases. If she started
asking questions about this . . . I needed to find her quickly. If she
was suspicious, I'd know the minute she saw me. Where would she
be right now?

I glanced down at my watch and answered my own question. I
needed to get to that hearing—and Addie would be there too.

CHAPTER 40

THE HEARING WAS STILL AN HOUR AWAY, BUT, BY NOON, THE COURT-
room was filling up fast. In another five minutes, there wouldn't be
a single seat left. Cameras and recorders were banned from the room,
but reporters lined the back rows with pens and pads in hand. Eli
was sitting in the front row, immediately behind the defense table
with an empty seat beside him he'd been holding for Addie. Colleton
had finally shown up, and he and Zach were going over files together
in hushed tones. Zach had warned Eli that the judge would have a
fit if he saw or heard a cell phone in court, so Eli had sent a text to
Addie before entering the courtroom to let her know he would save
a seat for her. She texted back immediately with a thumbs-up, saying
she would be there.

Eli turned his head, surveying the room. He recognized Lee
Bowen near the back with the other unfortunate latecomers, stuck in
the standing room only section and looking around in the hopes of
finding a last empty seat. Continuing to survey the room, Eli spotted
Emma Hudson, that friend Addie had introduced on her front steps.
That was the night he'd found that damn phone in Sam's truck. He
wondered again if he'd done the right thing. Right or wrong, it was
done now. His stomach was in knots, but that was fast becoming his
new normal.

"Eli . . ."

He turned around to find Zach facing him and holding out
a file.

"What?" he asked, confused.

"Give this to Addie when she gets here."

"Sure. Will she know what you want her to do with it?"

"Don't need her to do anything. It's one of her files that got shuffled in with mine—stuff about that cold case. I don't want to get it mixed up with mine during the hearing."

Eli took the file and nodded as Zach turned back to his whispered discussion with Colleton. Eli put the file in the empty seat beside him and took a deep breath, trying to dial back the tension. Sam would be in once the hearing started, and Eli knew Sam could read him. He needed to stay strong.

He saw movement from the corner of his eye and turned to find Buford Gadsden settling into a seat behind the solicitor's table after giving Barton a brief pat on the back. Buford hurled an accusing glare at Eli before turning away. Sensing he was still being watched, Eli looked a few rows behind Buford and saw JB Beaman staring intently. Eli met his stare and held it like magnet to steel. Unlike Buford, JB didn't look away. Was that bastard actually smiling at him? It had been many years since Eli felt the kind of rage that ripped through him as he remembered the sight of the taillight shattering and the weight of Buck's still-warm body lying limp in his arms. *I know it was you, you worthless piece of shit. I know it. If it's the last thing I do, I will see you pay for it.* It was JB who finally blinked and looked away.

Eli turned back toward the door again, but still no sign of Addie. Where was she? Emma Hudson saw him this time and gave a polite nod. He returned the nod and righted himself in his seat again.

"All rise for the Honorable Judge Henry Newton," the bailiff said as the judge entered the room.

The room hummed with the sound of people rising from their seats. Standing with them, Eli glanced back once more for Addie.

He noticed Lee Bowen wasn't standing in back any longer—he must have lucked into a seat, though Eli couldn't see him from here. Still no sign of Addie, either. Stranger still, her friend Emma was gone now too. Why would she come early for the hearing only to leave before it started? Eli didn't have time to think about it now.

CHAPTER 41

Driving home from the coffee shop, Addie replayed the conversation with Logan like a never-ending loop in her mind. It made her think of those reversible images—if you stared at them long enough, they turned into a picture of something entirely different. That's what was happening here—she'd been looking at the right images but seeing the wrong picture.

"*Why?*" she'd asked Logan in the coffee shop. Why would it matter that the last meeting with Emma was on a Friday?

When Logan asked Emma about the jeans instead of her usual suit, she said she was leaving for the weekend right after our meeting.

WHY does that matter?

The answer seemed to have stunned him almost as much as it did her.

A friend had offered to let her use a beach house for the weekend.

A beach house?

Yeah—at Edisto.

Edisto! Emma had been at Edisto the night of the murder. Addie parked the Jeep and looked at the clock on the dash. She still had time before she needed to leave for Sam's 1:00 p.m. hearing, and she wanted to compare notes from some of her other files while the interview with Logan was still vivid in her mind.

She entered the house and put the file from Danny on the kitchen table with the others. The same questions kept swirling around in her head. Why hadn't Emma told her she met with Logan the day of the murders? The bigger question was why Emma hadn't mentioned she'd been at Edisto that night. Forgetting she and Logan met that day was a stretch, but forgetting she was on Edisto the night of the murders? Not possible. There would have been law enforcement and emergency vehicles crawling all over that little island. Anyone in Emma's line of work would have known what was going on. Emma had kept that from Addie on purpose. But why?

Emma had been adamant about being assigned to represent Logan. Did she have some reason to want to protect him? Could that be why he asked for her in the first place? If Emma controlled his defense, she might be able to do that. That fit with her comments about Lee Bowen—Emma complained that Bowen was too focused on Logan.

Finding that wristband on Buford's boat was too convenient, especially with the anonymous call. Logan thought he'd lost the wristband earlier that day—before the party. What if he'd dropped it while he was in Emma's office? Was Emma's connection to Logan so important to her that she would risk everything—her license to practice, her career, her reputation—to plant evidence on a boat that would clear him? Addie wondered if their *history*, as Emma referred to it, was more personal than professional. Logan was only a few years younger than Emma, and there was no denying he was attractive. Could they have had some romantic involvement? Was it possible Emma believed Logan had something to do with the murders?

She flipped the page to find the phone message—letting Emma know about a canceled appointment. But this time, she saw what she'd missed before. The appointment was for a tennis lesson: *T.G. called—can't make her tennis lesson next week—she'll reschedule.* T.G.—could that be Tara Godfrey? Addie's mind flashed back to the photo in Emma's office—the high school team Emma coached—a pretty blond was holding up a plaque. Was Addie imagining things, or was the blond in the photo in Emma's office the same girl in the photos of Tara Godfrey she'd found in Lee's old files?

She needed another look at those old photos of the victims. Addie reached for the file where she thought she'd put them. Damn—this wasn't even her file. It was Zach's, and it was full of invoices and reports George Holden had given them months ago showing Sam's work on Jessie's account—useless information once Sam admitted his affair with Jessie. Addie was closing the file when her eye landed on a printout of Jessie's clients, and she saw a name that hadn't meant anything to them at the time. It damn sure did now, though.

Grabbing a pen, she circled the dates Jessie had worked for that client.

Oh. Holy. Shit.

Zach needed to know this *now*. She grabbed her phone. *No!* The time flashed across the screen—1:06. Had she been here that long? The hearing had started, and there was no way Zach or Colleton would be able to take a call or even check a text. She would have to go to them. Judge Newton would frown on her coming in mid-hearing, but a bailiff would let her in as long as she told him she was with the defense counsel. There was no other choice, and she had to hurry.

She grabbed her pocketbook and keys and ran for the door. As she yanked it open, she found Emma standing there, her hand raised to knock. Addie's prickly little danger warnings were going wild.

"Addie—what are you doing still here?" Emma looked worried.

"I lost track of time," Addie said, trying to gauge Emma's expression and control her own. "Everyone's waiting for you at the courthouse. Come on, I'll give you a ride."

Emma had placed herself strategically between Addie and the Jeep, and the Beretta was still in the Jeep. Addie cursed herself for not bringing it in.

"Addie, stop wasting time—we have to hurry." Emma put her hand on Addie's arm as if to guide her down the steps.

"Thanks, but I'll take the Jeep and see you there." Addie tried to pull her arm back.

"Oh, I don't think so, sweetie," Emma said, tightening her grip. Addie felt a quick sting and looked down to see the needle pull away. Her head felt woozy, and everything softened and blurred. The next thing she knew, Emma had an arm around her waist, guiding her clumsily down the steps to her car.

"Don't fight it, Addie, it'll only take a minute." Emma's voice seemed far away. Then the car door closed, and everything went black.

CHAPTER 42

I GLANCED OVER THE SEAT. IF I DIDN'T KNOW BETTER, I'D THINK SHE was sleeping peacefully. Perfect. The light changed, and I drove on.

It had taken all my willpower to sit calmly in that courtroom this morning waiting for Addie to get there. I was stunned when she didn't show. I didn't know where she was, but what I did know was that, with Zach, Colleton, and Eli all in that room, she was as alone as I could ever hope to find her. I slipped out at the last second. It was lucky I tried the house first—a moment later, and I would have been too late. Now it was too late for her.

Logan's wristband falling off in my office all those years ago was nothing short of a miracle. I found it after he left and stuck it in my purse meaning to return it to him later. After what happened with Tara and Cindy, I forgot I had it—I was in survival mode.

I'd made it back to the beach house without seeing a soul other than Buford. At the time, I didn't know what he was up to and didn't care—he hadn't seen me and that's all that mattered. Inside the beach house, I closed the blinds and alternated between crying jags and frantic pacing. What to do? I could turn myself in, but what would that accomplish? Those two girls would still be dead, and I'd spend the rest of my life in jail—or worse.

I tried to convince myself what came next was praying. You know what I'm talking about, you've done it yourself: *Please, God, don't let me go to jail, and I promise I'll spend the rest of my life helping others*; shit like that. I may have been calling God's name, but it was the Devil I made a deal with that night. I spent the rest of the night destroying my clothes and cleaning myself up. I went home Sunday and to work the next day. I wore suits to work, so no one ever saw my bruises or scratches. Life went on like nothing happened. I couldn't believe how easy it was.

Then Lee Bowen arrested Logan. If it had been anyone else, I would have sat back and let it happen, but I couldn't bring myself to abandon Logan. I wasn't going to turn myself in to save him, mind you, but I looked for a way to protect us both. When Logan finally told me he was buying pot when the girls were killed, I remembered seeing Buford Gadsden in those woods, and couldn't shake the idea the two were related. I sketched out detailed timelines trying to work through it. Logan was only gone from the party about an hour, and it had taken me more than thirty minutes—pumped up on adrenaline and running like a bat out of hell—to where I'd seen Buford that night. Logan couldn't have gone there and back on foot. But if he'd taken his car, he could have made it there in about fifteen minutes—thirtyish round trip.

Trying to connect the dots, I drove back to Edisto one night, parked where my car wouldn't be seen, and followed the path where I'd seen Buford. Sure enough, I'd been right about the direction—it led down to the docks. The walk took maybe five minutes from where Buford's truck was the night I'd seen him. That was ten minutes walking there and back. Added to the thirty minutes of driving, that made forty. Throw in some time for Logan to do his business on the boat, and it lined up with the time he was missing from the party.

I remember being so pumped up when I figured it out. It didn't take me long to deflate when I realized the bigger problem. I couldn't tell anyone I knew Buford was there at the same time and general location as the party, because I wasn't supposed to be there either—at the same time and general location as the murders. Fuck.

I considered calling in an anonymous tip to search the shrimp boat, but that pot was probably long gone. Even if there was still pot on the boat, it wasn't going to place Logan there. Finally, I remembered that stupid wristband. I made one last trip down that path the following night and planted the wristband on Buford's boat. Then I called the tip hotline, and, from there, things took care of themselves. Logan's charges were dropped, Buford got his charges dropped down to a misdemeanor, and my secret stayed safe for decades.

Then that little bitch Jessie decided to play Nancy Drew. And she found exactly what she was looking for in my files. If I had let her live, she would have gone straight to her daddy with it. Those old murders happened before she was born, so Jessie wouldn't have had a clue that what she found meant I did a lot more than tattle on her father—but Buford would have. It might have taken him a while to see it, but he would have known who could help him fill in the holes—people like Logan Bennett. Even if he didn't pick up on the murders right away, he would have turned me in for planting the evidence. That alone would have cost me my license and probably given me some jail time—and had everyone looking closely at me. Eventually, those timelines Jessie found in my file would have led Buford or the cops to piece together the full picture, just like Addie had now. And when they did, my life would have been the one over—not Jessie's. I had to shut her up. That's exactly what I did that night on Cicada Road.

Thanks to Sam Jenkins mucking up the scene and implicating himself in Jessie's murder, it could have worked out. But not now. Now that Addie knew the connection between the two cases, this thing was way too big to keep hidden. I'd have to find a way to get rid of the body this time—or at least make it hard to identify. And I'd have to disappear for good. It wouldn't be easy, but at least I'd be alive, and that's more than I could say for Addie Stone.

CHAPTER 43

"DON'T GET UP," JUDGE NEWTON SAID PERFUNCTORILY AS HE stepped up to the bench, but everyone knew better and rose anyway, sitting only after he did. Henry Newton was the senior-most judge in the county, and there was no question that he ruled the roost. He generally referred to the courtroom as *my courtroom* and the bailiffs called him King Henry behind his back. Sharp-eyed with a temper to match, he was quick to communicate any displeasure he might have with either side. If Newton had ever had a sense of humor, it had escaped long ago.

As the room settled, a side door opened and a deputy escorted Sam to a seat beside Zach at the defense table. Sam looked shaky, and Eli could feel his fear from where he sat. Once Sam was seated, Judge Newton nodded toward the court reporter to begin recording and then he addressed the room.

"We are here today on the matter of the State of South Carolina versus Samuel Marcus Jenkins, case number 2017-GS-15-00987. This is Mr. Jenkins's second appearance, and our purpose here today is to hear Mr. Jenkins's plea and to determine whether the case should be set for trial. Is the State present and ready to proceed?"

"Yes, Your Honor, Jake Barton for the State," the solicitor stood and responded.

"And the defendant?"

"Yes, Your Honor," Zach said, on his feet, "Zach Stander and Colleton Burns for the defendant." Sam stood with them as Zach had instructed him to do.

"The court will hear from you now, Mr. Stander. How does your client wish to plead?"

"Your Honor, Mr. Jenkins would like to speak for himself," Zach said as they had planned.

"Very well," Judge Newton said, peering down at Sam over his glasses. "Mr. Jenkins, you are accused of the murder of Jessica Elaine Gadsden on the night of July 11, 2017. How do you wish to plead?"

The air in the courtroom hung heavy and silent. Even the muted sounds of Broad Street traffic filtering through the fortified walls seemed to fade as every eye and ear trained on Sam Jenkins.

"Not guilty, Your Honor. I did not do this, and I request a trial by a jury of my peers." Sam's voice was clear and strong now. The hush that had hung over the room gave way to a low rumble of murmured reactions, and Judge Newton delivered a single rap of his gavel. One was all it took—his reputation was widely known, and nobody wanted to be thrown out now.

"Thank you, Mr. Jenkins," Judge Newton continued, "you may be seated. The court has entered your plea into the record. Mr. Stander and Mr. Barton, this case will be placed on the general sessions jury roster."

As the court and counsel discussed scheduling details, Eli exhaled softly, allowing some of the tension to leave him. Sam had seemed unsure last night when they talked. He had until the second he opened his mouth to decide what to say, and Eli had been concerned that Sam would take the plea deal. He could not bear losing his grandson to a ruthless prison system for a crime he didn't commit.

He glanced down at the empty seat beside him. Addie not showing up after she said she was coming seemed out of character. He was starting to worry about her.

CHAPTER 44

THE COURTROOM WAS NEARLY EMPTIED, THOUGH ZACH SUSPECTED there was still a circus on the lawn.

"Any chance you know a secret passage out?" he asked Colleton.

"Not exactly a secret, but there is a back way that won't have quite the show going on. We might escape unnoticed."

"Sounds like a plan. Eli?" Zach turned. "You in?"

"Definitely," Eli answered, handing him back Addie's file. "She never showed."

"What do you mean, she never showed? She told me this morning she would be here."

"I know, and before the hearing started, I texted saying I was saving her a seat. She texted back saying she would be here soon." He looked down at the phone he had turned back on once the judge left the courtroom. "She hasn't sent anything since that last text, and no missed calls."

"That's not like her," Zach said, pulling out his own phone and calling her number.

"Maybe she had car trouble," Colleton said.

"No—she would have sent one of us a message," Zach said, listening as his call went to voice mail.

"And there's something else," Eli said. "That friend of hers—Emma Hudson? She was here in the courtroom. Got here early and sat there the longest time. But when the hearing started, she disappeared." He cocked his head. "Something feels off."

"Did Emma come back?" Zach asked, listening to the phone ring as he tried again to reach Addie. Eli shook his head no.

Zach's call went straight to voice mail again. What was it Addie told him last night? Something about Emma keeping important information from her? With all the tension between them lately, he hadn't been as tuned in to what Addie had going on, but he remembered her saying last night she thought Emma might be keeping something from her. He was starting to agree with Eli—something felt off here.

"Colleton, instead of going out to your place, do you mind if we work at mine instead? I'm sure we'll find Addie at home, or at least a note or something."

"Sure. I had to park the Tahoe out in the boonies with all the traffic, but I'll catch up with you."

"Leave it and ride with me," Eli said. "I'll bring you back to get it after the crowds go home."

Addie's Jeep was in the drive, and Zach felt the tension in his shoulders start to ease as he pulled in and ran up the steps. His alarms started going off again as soon as he saw the front door was open.

"Addie?" he called out, stepping slowly into the room. No answer. Nothing seemed out of place or missing. He stuck his head in the bedroom; it was empty. "Adds, you here?" he called again as he moved down the hall to the kitchen. Still no response. Her files were strewn across the table like she had been searching for something. He heard Colleton and Eli come in as he tried to call her phone again. It began to ring, only not on the other end. Her ringtone was coming from somewhere in the house. Following the sound back to the living room, he found Colleton and Eli staring at a pocketbook lying just inside the door. How had he missed that? He hung up the call and the pocketbook stopped ringing. Zach opened it and found Addie's phone, keys, and wallet. Where would she go without those?

"Did you find a note or anything?" Colleton asked, looking as concerned as Zach felt.

"No, but she had files and papers spread out on the table—maybe there was a note or something I missed," Zach said, turning back to the kitchen.

"I'll call Emma's office," Colleton said, following him. "Maybe they're together."

Zach picked up an open file only to find it wasn't Addie's but his own. This must be the file she had mixed up with the one he'd found at the hearing. In the background he could hear Colleton telling Eli that the receptionist at the front desk said Emma had gone to the Jenkins hearing and hadn't returned yet.

"But Emma left before the hearing started," Eli said. "That makes no sense."

Looking at his file, Zach noticed Addie had underlined some dates on one of the invoices from George Holden. It was a new client Jessie had recruited just a few months before her death: Emma Hudson. Zach's head started to spin. According to this invoice, Jessie had been scanning Emma's old records to electronic files right up until the week she was killed. Zach flashed back to Sam's story about Jessie finding a way to befriend someone she thought knew an old secret about her father. Emma Hudson had been involved in that old Edisto case, and the anonymous tip that freed her client also sent Buford Gadsden to jail. If Jessie had been scanning Emma's old files, maybe she was after the file on Logan Bennett—and maybe Emma figured that out. Suddenly everything fell together.

"Thanks, Lee," he heard Colleton saying as he looked up.

"I tried Lee Bowen," Colleton said. "I thought maybe she had gone to talk with him about the case—maybe lost track of time. Lee says he hasn't seen or talked to Addie today."

"She's not with Lee," Zach said, his heart racing. "I think Addie's with Emma, and I think she might be in danger." He handed the invoice to Colleton.

"Christ," Colleton said, understanding immediately.

"I think I know where they are," Zach said. He grabbed Addie's keys. The one thing that wasn't in the purse was her gun, and he was guessing it was in the Jeep.

"Where are we going?"

"Out to Cicada Road," Zach said, already running. "To the old church where all this started."

CHAPTER 45

ADDIE LAY ON THE GROUND WATCHING JB PACE RESTLESSLY BY THE door, a noose twisting in his hands. Sensing her stare, he stopped pacing and walked to where she lay. He knelt close like a coyote sniffing a carcass, and she jerked her head back in horror as his face morphed into the gored face of Jessie Gadsden. As it sneered down at her, a brick flew through the window, raining shards of glass around her. The crash shattered Addie's drug-induced hallucination, and she shook her head to clear her vision. The figure by the door stopped pacing and came into focus. Addie saw that it wasn't JB at all. It was Emma—and it wasn't a noose she was holding.

"Mind playing tricks on you, Addie?" Emma asked. "Relax, it's just a hallucination from the ketamine—it'll pass." She held a revolver in her hand.

Addie watched as the strange surroundings slowly became familiar. "Cicada Road," she said simply, finally recognizing the old shed. The distortion of time began to right itself. She could see the zip tie around her ankles and assumed another like it was what bound her wrists behind her.

"Welcome back to the living," Emma said. "Don't get too comfortable—you won't be staying." She pulled a five-gallon bucket from a hook, turned it over, and sat, resting the revolver in her lap.

"It was you. You murdered those two girls on Edisto," Addie said, fighting another wave of nausea.

"*Tch, tch, tch*, Addie, *murder* is such an ugly word," Emma said, crossing her arms and rubbing them with her hands as if to shed something. "I'm sure no one will believe it now, but Tara Godfrey wasn't murdered—I would never have raised a finger to harm her. Truth is, I was head over heels in love with her. Stupidly, I convinced myself the feeling was mutual."

Addie drew in a sharp breath, flashing back on the sad smile on Emma's face that day as she explained away the years she had spent without marrying.

"Did I shock you, sweetie? Did you think love could only look like yours? Sorry to burst your little bubble." Emma looked away, and when she looked back, her eyes were full of hate and resentment. "Do you have any idea how lucky you are to be with whoever you want and not have anyone think you're a freak for it? Maybe it's a little better in 2017, I don't know, but certainly not then. Can you even imagine what it was like to live in this small town and pretend?" She paused. "No. I did not murder Tara Godfrey. That was a bizarre accident."

"If it was an accident, why hide it?" Addie was twisting cautiously at the ties on her wrists as she tried to buy time.

"It was that fucking Cindy Crosby. She showed up and jumped to the wrong conclusion. I tried to explain but the little bitch wouldn't listen," Emma muttered. "She had convinced herself what she saw was intentional, and then when I chased her to try to talk her down, she got hysterical. There was no turning that around. In the end, it was take her life or lose mine, and no way was I going down." Emma leaned closer. "That doesn't bode well for you, by the way."

"That's why you were so sure Logan was innocent—and you planted that wristband and made that bogus call. But how did you guess it was Buford if Logan never gave him up?"

"Logan was a kid growing up in a shit situation, buying a harmless dime bag of pot. I knew it came from Buford because I saw

Buford out there that night as I was trying to get away without being seen."

Addie's eyes widened—she hadn't known that piece.

"Besides, it's not like Buford went to jail for something he didn't do."

"And Sam Jenkins?"

"Collateral damage." She shrugged. "If he needs to blame someone, he can blame Jessie Gadsden. This is all her fault," Emma said. "And you can spare yourself that twisting. Those are industrial zip ties—you'll just tear up your wrists."

"Your concern is touching, bitch."

Emma threw back her head and laughed. "You're ballsy, I'll give you that."

"So how is anything Jessie's fault?" Addie needed to keep her talking.

"I know Buford always suspected I had something to do with that anonymous tip—he never said it outright, but I could tell from a few comments he made and the way he acted around me. JB, too. I'm guessing Jessie heard or found something she wasn't supposed to that clued her in, and she went after me like a dog after a bone. Sent me a flyer in the mail—a piece about the convenience of going paperless. I threw it in the trash assuming it was a mass mailer. I suspect now I got the only one. She followed up with a phone call asking for an appointment—I was impressed with her persistence and agreed. What could it hurt to give a young entrepreneur a chance?

"Then she came walking in. She was gorgeous, and she knew it, wearing a blouse down to there and a skirt up to here. Perceptive, too. She picked up fast on my attraction to her and played me like a pro. It started with lots of smiles and personal conversations, pretending she was interested. She was constantly reading over my

shoulder or leaning over me to pick something up. Not quite touching, but oh, so close. Then came the hand on my arm or touching
my shoulder." Emma's eyes closed. "I believed it because I wanted to
believe it.

"The last time Jessie was in the office, I stepped out to take a call
and get us a cup of coffee. She didn't hear me come back, and I watched
from the hall as she dug through the old Edisto file. I don't know if
she'd already taken pictures, but her phone was out. And she didn't
have just those few sanitized pages I gave you—she had everything,
including my timeline showing the time I'd spotted Buford leaving
those woods. Suddenly, it was all so clear—she wasn't attracted to me,
she was using me. She orchestrated that scanning offer to get to my
files. Once she shared them with her father—and she would have—
he'd be on to my secrets. All of them. After I'd seen enough, I backed
away quietly and cleared my throat and made some noise in the hall.
She scrambled to put it all back, and I pretended not to notice.

"When she'd been trying to make me think we were close, she
told me about this old church and her little labor of love on Tuesday
nights. I knew she'd be here to clean later that night, and I made sure
I got here first."

"You hid your car here in this shed—and swept out all the tracks
before you left," Addie said, and watched as surprise raced across
Emma's face. "Now you're fucked."

"*I'm* fucked?" Emma recovered quickly. "Addie, honey, you're
the one tied up here."

"Zach knows too—he has photos of the shed floor swept clean,
and he knows from Pastor Ben it happened that night. Getting rid of
me won't save your cover." Addie raised her chin defiantly.

"Maybe not, but it will buy me time to run—and a fighting
chance," Emma said, knocking the bucket over as she hoisted to her
feet and put the revolver in her pocket. "You should have left that

old file rotting in storage, Addie. Why didn't you? Why do people insist on courting danger—like leaving this old thing lying around?" Emma stopped beside the gas can standing next to the rusty mower. She lifted the can and shook it. "Not much there, but it doesn't take much, does it? This old timber will flame up like kindling. They'll find your bones after the fire cools enough to clear, but by the time they identify you, I'll be long gone."

Listening to Emma, Addie realized that any rational part of the woman was long gone, and another wave of nausea and panic washed over her as she realized what Emma intended to do.

Emma sprinkled the gas along the side wall and put the can back by the mower—tipped over as if it had fallen. She pulled a faded ribbon from an old planter and laid it out with one end trailing in the spill. Stepping back, she pulled a lighter from a pocket and carefully lit the dry end closest to her, and the flame began to creep along the length of the ribbon. The flame reached the gasoline and quickly wicked up the wall, smoke already ballooning in the stagnant air inside the shed. As the flames climbed higher, Emma backed out of the shed, raised the revolver, and cocked the hammer with her thumb.

"So long, Addie."

CHAPTER 46

ZACH PRESSED THE CLUTCH AND LET THE CAR GLIDE SILENTLY off the road. He didn't see anyone out front, but he hadn't expected to. If they were here, they'd be back in that old shed. Colleton and Eli had taken a detour to drive by Emma's house, and Zach hadn't heard from them yet, but he didn't have time to waste waiting. He grabbed Addie's Beretta from the console and crept along the side of the church to the corner. He held his breath and strained to listen. Nothing.

Peering around, he saw a gray sedan parked near the shed. He stooped low and ran for it, stopping when he was shielded behind the car. From there he could hear muffled voices coming from inside— he recognized Addie's.

Emma backed out of the shed, raising a revolver. "So long, Addie," he heard her say.

"Emma!" he shouted as he stood and trained the Beretta's sight on her. Startled, she spun—wild-eyed and revolver still raised.

Smoke began to plume from the shed, and Addie's terrified scream ripped through the air as flames began to lick along the siding to the outside wall. The scream was enough to distract Emma and throw off her aim. Her shot hit the car. Seizing his chance, Zach fired, and Emma recoiled as the 9mm hollow point ripped a hole in her chest. She looked down, stunned, at the spreading red stain and staggered toward him before she collapsed to her knees. As she teetered back and forth, Emma raised the revolver again.

Zach fired, this time hitting her right shoulder. The revolver dropped from her hand, and Emma fell face-first to the ground with a blunt thud. Behind her, flames were gaining traction on the wall and the smoke was coming darker and heavier now.

"Zach!" Addie screamed again, and already her voice was raspy from the smoke. She was running out of time. As he barreled toward the shed, Zach scooped up Emma's revolver and threw it past the tree line. He'd seen *Fatal Attraction* and knew the dead woman wasn't always dead.

"Addie! Addie, can you hear me?" The air inside was thick with smoke, and he couldn't see past the end of his arm. The flames had reached the roof, and a board broke loose and fell, showering sparks and embers around him. He felt the sting as several seared through the back of his shirt.

"Zach—freeze—don't take another step," she screamed. Whatever she tried to say next was lost in a fit of coughing.

Frantic to find her, Zach dropped to his knees to where the air was clearer and came face-to-face with the reason for her warning. The startled cottonmouth was coiled in a defensive position, it's stark white mouth open in a display meant to intimidate foes. It was working. It also explained why Addie hadn't tried to scooch or roll toward the door.

"It crawled out from under the mower when the fire started," Addie yelled over the crackling and popping around them. He could see her now. Her face was red from the heat, and her hands and feet were bound.

Zach still had the Beretta in his hand, but any shot from this angle would hit Addie too. Pushing down the panic expanding in his throat, he scanned the space to see if he could get a clean shot. Maybe if he could ease to the right slowly enough not to provoke the snake, he could aim to the left—away from Addie. He shifted his weight to one knee preparing to move. From the corner of his eye, he could see flames engulfing the window—he was caught between moving too fast and moving too slow.

Suddenly, the window glass exploded, sending shards shooting in all directions, and Addie screamed again. The heat from the fire had overpowered the pit viper's heat-sensing pit, and, confused by the multiple hits to the ground in all directions, it uncoiled in a single fluid movement toward Zach only to slither between his legs and escape through the shed door. The burst of adrenaline was dizzying, and Zach shook his head to clear it.

The snake's lunge toward Zach had pushed Addie to her limit, and she was quiet now—too quiet—as she stared at the flames racing greedily across the roof above her.

"Addie! Look at me!" he yelled. Her eyes caught his and he held them. "That's it, just look at me—nothing else. I'm coming." Zach dropped to his belly and crawled low to escape the smoke.

"They're zip ties, you won't be able to get them off without something to cut them with," Addie said as he reached for her ankles. Her smoke-clogged voice was barely recognizable.

"It's okay, baby, I've got you." Shoving the Beretta into his waistband behind him, Zach scooped his arms under her. "I'll have to stand to carry you, and the smoke will be worse. Close your eyes and try to hold your breath until we're out if you can," he said. The noise of the fire consuming the dry wood was overwhelming, and he wasn't sure she'd heard him.

"On three. Ready?" Zach said, and she nodded.

He glanced behind him to gauge the direction of the door. He wouldn't be able to see it once he stood, but the afternoon light beyond it should still be visible.

"One . . . two . . . three!" He lifted her and turned in a single motion. The room went dark, but he could see a dim light that had to be the door, and he lunged forward. Zach's lungs were burning, and his legs threatened to give out, but the light from the door was getting brighter. Then he heard the heavy snap of the support beam in the roof giving way. With the last of his energy, he pushed against the pain and stumbled through the door and out into the open as the shed began to collapse in on itself.

Sucking in the clean air, Zach carried Addie away from the heat and smoke and lowered her to the grass. He reached back to pull the Beretta from his waistband. It wasn't there. It must have fallen as he'd run from the shed, and he turned to see where it had landed. He saw it immediately—in Emma Hudson's left hand.

She was unsteady but standing, her shirt dark with blood and her shattered right arm hanging useless. A swipe of red streaked across her face like war paint. Zach suspected her aim wouldn't be good enough to hit someone moving—especially not with her left hand—but Addie was an easier target with those restraints on.

Out of options, Zach placed his body protectively in front of Addie's and held his breath, but instead of the pop of the Beretta, Zach heard the sharp crack of a rifle. Emma's mouth gaped as a perfect round hole appeared on her forehead and she collapsed in a heap like a marionette with the strings cut.

Zach turned and saw Eli running, rifle in hand, with Colleton close behind.

"Are you hurt?" Eli asked.

"I'm not, but Addie needs a doctor," Zach answered. "And watch out for that one," he said, looking back at Emma. "She's already come back from the dead once."

Eli approached cautiously and knelt to check for a pulse. "She's gone this time," he said. He stood and looked down at her mangled body. She hadn't been the one to shoot Buck, but she was damn sure the one who'd set it in motion. Eli delivered the message he'd been saving:

"Buck says fuck you."

Zach tossed the empty water bottle into the recycling bin and left the waiting room where he'd been pacing until the doctor cleared Addie for visitors. Her burns were minor, and the effects of the ketamine they'd found in her system had worn off, but they were keeping her overnight.

Her eyes opened at the sound of the door closing behind him, and she gave him a tired smile.

"How are you feeling?" he asked, sitting on the edge of the bed and draping an arm possessively across her waist.

"Like I've been baptized by fire."

He lifted her arm, looking at the bandage on her wrist. There was a matching one on the other arm from struggling to loosen herself from the restraints. Placing her arm gently back on the bed, he looked out the window to collect his thoughts and then turned back to her.

"Adds, I've been such an idiot, letting old disappointments get in the way of our future. Just because my father didn't have what it took to be there for my mother and me doesn't mean you and I can't have the family and life we want. I can be better than that."

"You are better than that."

"I don't feel better. I feel like an idiot."

"So, what are you gonna do about that, Mr. Stander?"

"If you'll still have me, I'm ready for a wedding and a family. Will you marry me, Addie Stone?"

"I thought you'd never ask." There was that smile again. He leaned in for a soft kiss, and she wrapped her arms around his neck, holding him there.

"How long will it take you to plan this wedding shindig?" he asked, already wondering what it would be like to be part of Addie's large close-knit family.

"Depends," she answered. "How quickly are you planning to get me knocked up?"

"I'll race you."

CHAPTER 47

ZACH PUT THE FINAL BOX IN THE BACK OF THE JEEP AND CLOSED the hatch as Addie blew a kiss and pulled out of the drive for the last time, heading back to Charleston. Zach would follow later that afternoon, but he had a stop to make first.

The three weeks since the fire had been a whirlwind. Based on the evidence about Emma Hudson, the solicitor had dropped the charges against Sam. As a courtesy, Barton arranged a meeting between Zach and Buford Gadsden, and let Zach be the one to tell Buford about Sam's relationship with Jessie and why he had gone to the church that night. Buford had been visibly stunned and Zach could tell he was wrestling with old demons. In the end, though, Buford's only comment was that his daughter had been the light of his life, and if she believed Sam was special, he would like to think that he would have respected that. He stood, shook Zach's hand, and left without another word.

The sheriff's office had approved use of a private testing agency to fast-track a preliminary analysis of DNA taken from Emma Hudson, and it had matched the DNA found on Cindy Crosby in 1983. Emma's sample would be retested by SLED, the state's law enforcement division, but that was mostly a formality. Lee Bowen had taken a temporary slot back at the sheriff's office to oversee closing out the case.

Colleton was busy helping Addie plan a wedding. She wanted to take her white dress walk down his avenue of oaks and be married in the clearing beyond, followed by an oyster roast and cookout, with a local band to celebrate. Zach had been elated by this plan.

Sam had his job back—and then some. Eli had been right about George Holden wanting to retire, and George had agreed to sell the business to Sam. George would stay on for a year to help transition clients. Sam had saved for a down payment, and Eli let him take a mortgage on the farm to pay the rest. Eli also had convinced Sam to move back to the farm for a while—no sense paying rent on an apartment Sam didn't need, he'd argued. That was where Zach was headed now—to say goodbye.

Zach pulled down the long dirt drive and parked in front of the porch. Eli had seen him drive up and walked down to meet him. A wagging redbone hound—all ears and feet—tagged along.

"What's this?" Zach asked, watching the puppy tug at the laces on Eli's boot.

"Seems Buford Gadsden's favorite redbone hound had a litter, and, to hear him tell it, he couldn't find a buyer for this last one," Eli said. "Said he knew he'd never take Buck's place, but he hoped young Jeb here would fill a little of the hole he left in my heart." Eli's voice had grown husky talking about Buck.

"I see you got that shed built back," Zach said, changing the subject to spare his friend.

"Buford did that too—or he sent out a crew to do it. Put it up in a single day," Eli said. "Told me if he'd known what JB was up to, he would've put a stop to it, one way or another."

"Speaking of JB," Zach said, "I guess you heard the sheriff hauled him in and locked him up for burning your shed and shooting Buck."

"I did." Eli nodded. "Sheriff came out to tell me personally. Said they got an anonymous tip about a body shop with evidence of JB's taillight being shot out and replaced that night. Strangest thing, though, he said the anonymous caller sounded a hell of a lot like Buford Gadsden."

"I guess some people are exactly what you think they are, and others surprise you," Zach said.

Eli eased himself down to sit on the steps and Zach joined him.

"Is Sam around this afternoon? I was hoping I could see him before I left," Zach said.

"Sorry, Zach, he's at the office."

"No big deal—I'll catch up with him at the wedding in a couple of months. You'll both be there, won't you?"

"Wouldn't miss it for anything," Eli said with a grin.

"I guess this is it for a while then," Zach said.

Both men nodded.

"Something else on your mind, Zach?" Eli asked when Zach didn't move to leave.

"Eli, Sam and I have more in common than the case that brought me here." Zach stared off at the fields as he told Eli his story.

"Some people are born knowing who their families are," Zach said as he finished. "The rest of us have to find them."

Zach turned to look at his friend but couldn't find the words for what he wanted to say. Once again, the old man showed him the way, putting a hand on Zach's shoulder.

"Message received, son. Message received."

CHAPTER 48

ONE YEAR LATER

SAM CARRIED HIS COFFEE OUT TO THE PORCH AND SETTLED INTO the rocker that had become his favorite spot. Jeb, who had been enthusiastically harassing squirrels, bounded up the steps and flopped, panting, at the foot of the rocker next to Sam—Eli's chair. Jeb loved Sam, but they both understood Jeb would always be Eli's dog.

Looking over at the empty chair, Sam felt the now-familiar pang. Had Eli really been gone for six months? The doctors said it had been a heart attack when they'd found him slumped over the wheel of the still-idling tractor—one of the places he'd been happiest. This farm had been such a part of Eli that Sam still half-expected to see him coming in from the field. But that wasn't going to happen. As if sensing Sam's thoughts, Jeb gave a soft whine and put his auburn head on his paws.

It was Jeb who first heard the familiar engine slowing on the highway near the end of the drive, and he looked up expectantly at Sam.

"Sounds like the mailman," Sam said, standing and stretching. Jeb was way ahead of him, sailing down the steps and up the dirt drive barking his fool head off. Walking behind him, Sam waved at Mr. Harvey, who waved back before he put the mail in the box and pulled away. Jeb played his usual game of racing back and forth between the mailbox and Sam, tongue lolling out of his mouth, until finally Sam reached the box and pulled out the mail. It was mostly junk mail with a few inevitable bills, but at the bottom of the stack was a hand-addressed envelope. The Charleston return address was unfamiliar, but Sam instantly recognized Zach's chicken-scratch handwriting.

Sam opened the envelope and fished out a photo of Zach in hospital scrubs. He was beaming over Addie, who was cradling a scrunched red face peering up from a pale blue blanket. Below the photo, Zach had scribbled a single line:

We named him Eli.

ACKNOWLEDGMENTS

I have long dreamed of the day when I would have the opportunity to write acknowledgments for a debut novel. Now that it is here, I find myself without words adequate to express the depth of my gratitude to the many friends and mentors who brought me to this strange and wonderous place.

Thank you to my amazing agent, Marly Rusoff, of the Marly Rusoff Literary Agency, and to my fabulous editor, Claire Wachtel, at Union Square & Co. If these two talented, experienced, and brilliant women had not noticed me and taken an interest in my writing, I would still be another frustrated writer with a box of manuscripts no one has read. Both of you have my undying gratitude for your guidance, encouragement, and seemingly unshakable belief in me.

Thank you to Emily Meehan, chief creative officer and publisher, and her incredible team of professionals at Union Square & Co. who worked so hard to turn this story into a book and present it to the world: Barbara Berger, executive editor (who got stuck with most of the author hand-holding and came up with our beautiful title); Kristin Mandaglio, project editor; Elizabeth Lindy, cover designer; Kevin Ullrich, creative operations director; Lisa Forde, creative director; Sandy Norman, production manager; Jenny Lu, senior publicist; Daniel Denning, marketing manager; Chris Vaccari, director, school and library and retail marketing; and Diane João, copy editor. I appreciate so much everything that you did to help make this book the best it can be.

Thank you to Megan Beatie, publicist extraordinaire, for her advocacy and expertise in finding avenues to give this book the visibility it needs to shine.

Thank you to Hank Phillippi Ryan and to John McMahon for their generosity in giving their time and support to read my book in advance and offer blurbs for its cover. Words cannot express how much I appreciate their willingness to take a chance on an unknown author.

Thank you to the multitudes of booksellers whose labor of love it is to be the bridge that carries books to readers. Your steadfast support of writers so often goes unsung, but I assure you, it is not unappreciated.

Thank you to Ashley Pennington, former public defender, and to Burns Wetmore, former US attorney and assistant solicitor, for reading my drafts and leading me through the maze of criminal prosecution and defense. Anything I got right is thanks to them— anything I got wrong is on me. Thank you also to my many other friends in the criminal bar who patiently answered my questions. You guys are truly living in the wild west, and my hat is off to you.

Thank you to Mitch Lucas, Chief Deputy (Ret.) to former Charleston County Sheriff Al Cannon, who read my drafts and tried to keep me between the ditches with my law enforcement scenes and characters. Again, anything I got right was purely Mitch, and the rest is on me. Thank you also to my many other friends in law enforcement, not only for generously giving your time to answer my questions for this book, but also for what you do every day to keep us safe.

Thank you to Margaret Lawson, who found time between serving as a professor of law and associate dean to read my manuscript and give me her feedback. Special thanks to my dear friend, Kay Cross, who not only gave me feedback on my manuscript, but listened without complaining or even rolling her eyes as I blathered on incessantly about it for the last year.

Thank you to my husband, David, who waited patiently while I was busy playing with the imaginary friends and characters in my head. You are my rock.

Last but not least, thank *you* for taking the time to read my story. Without readers, this book would be nothing more than ink on paper. I hope you enjoyed it, and I hope we can do it again sometime! Until then, please visit me at my website: CarolineClevelandAuthor.com.

AUTHOR'S NOTE

Fiction, at its best, reflects life. Characters are most compelling when they experience the same emotions and face the same challenges that shape our lives in the real world. For me, the ways in which my characters and stories are born run the gamut. Some appear in my head all at once, demanding to be put to paper. Others materialize gradually, speaking so softly that I strain to hear. *When Cicadas Cry* is one of the latter.

I had long been toying with the premise—a young lawyer unraveling the mystery behind a present-day murder that is inextricably tied to two unsolved murders from decades earlier. That time span meant I needed a local's knowledge of the setting in both the present and the past, leading me back to the small town of Walterboro, South Carolina, where I grew up. The time span also presented a different kind of problem: how would my present-day characters tell the story of murders that happened so long ago? As the killer's voice began to whisper clues in my ear, an idea unfurled. Why couldn't the killer talk directly to the reader that same way— in tantalizing sidebars the other characters can't hear? At last, the plot unfolded. Then real-world events changed my way of looking at it.

In 2015, a local police officer, Michael Slager, shot a fifty-year-old man, Walter Scott, during a routine traffic stop. Scott was unarmed. And Black. Only two months later, as our community was grappling with the racism issues raised by that shooting, our foundation was shaken by the massacre of nine Black church parishioners. Dylann Roof, a white supremacist with extreme views, visited the historic Mother Emanuel AME church in Charleston during Bible study. The pastor gave him a Bible and offered him a chair. Twenty minutes later, Roof pulled a weapon, ruthlessly killing nine parishioners and wounding a tenth before fleeing. When the heartbreaking news broke, thousands of Charlestonians held hands and formed a line stretching two miles across the Ravenel Bridge, where they stood silent for five minutes.

The tumultuous aftermath came to a peak in December 2016, with both trials taking place in the same month. Slager's ended in a mistrial, but his retrial in 2017 ended with a conviction and prison sentence. Across the street in federal court, Roof was convicted and sentenced to death. During his trial, the victims' family members presented a powerful image as they stood, one by one, and voiced forgiveness.

It did not take long to realize the characters in my novel—set in the Lowcountry in 2017—would also feel the indelible stamp of these events. Racial tension had always been present in the story, with a white victim and Black suspect, but now those issues were front and center, and magnified by the insular nature of small-town life. I never set out to write a novel that confronts complex social issues. My only goal in writing *When Cicadas Cry* was to create a clever and twisty mystery. Somewhere along the way, the characters decided they had something more thought provoking to say.

By the time I finalized the manuscript, the high-profile Murdaugh trial had thrust Walterboro into the national spotlight. Although the Murdaughs left the solicitor's office long before 2017 and Alex Murdaugh's inglorious fall had not yet taken place, I suspect there will be those who envision that saga superimposed on my story, because we each bring to a book our own life experience. And that is okay. Like I said—fiction, at its best, reflects life.